Unexpected Surprises:
A Royal Heir

JESSICA GILMORE

AMY RUTTAN

KATE HARDY

MILLS & BOON

First Published in Great Britain 2022
By Mills & Boon, an imprint of HarperCollins*Publishers,* Ltd
1 London Bridge Street, London, SE1 9GF

www.harpercollins.co.uk

HarperCollins*Publishers*
1st Floor, Watermarque Building,
Ringsend Road, Dublin 4, Ireland

UNEXPECTED SURPRISES: A ROYAL HEIR © 2022 Harlequin Books S.A.

The Sheikh's Pregnant Bride © 2017 Jessica Gilmore
The Surgeon King's Secret Baby © 2017 Amy Ruttan
Crown Prince, Pregnant Bride © 2014 Pamela Brooks

ISBN: 978-0-263-30419-0

MIX
Paper from
responsible sources
FSC™ C007454

This book is produced from independently certified FSC™ paper to ensure responsible forest management.

For more information visit: www.harpercollins.co.uk/green

Printed and Bound in Spain using 100% Renewable electricity at CPI Black Print, Barcelona

THE SHEIKH'S
PREGNANT BRIDE

JESSICA GILMORE

To Rufus.

All these years I thought I was a cat person—turns out I'm all about the canine. Thank you for letting me talk plots through at you, for all those head-clearing walks and for keeping me company through long hours at my keyboard. Xxx

CHAPTER ONE

HE'D SAID HE'D be there in twelve hours, but in the end it was barely eight hours after he'd received the earth-shattering phone call when Idris Delacour strode into the cool, dark Council Chamber, his eyes still shielded against the harsh sun that had greeted him at the airport despite the still early hour. Grimly he stood by the empty seat at the end of the long table and, taking off his sunglasses, regarded the four sombre men who had stood at his entrance. They were all dressed in the customary long white robes and headdresses worn by traditionalists in Dalmaya and Idris's dark trousers and grey shirt looked both drab and shockingly modern by contrast.

He nodded at the men and waited until they took their seats before seating himself in the ornately carved wooden chair. He was aware of every curve, every bump in the ancient seat. A seat that should never have been his. A seat he was all too willing to relinquish. He cleared his throat. *'Salam.'*

They repeated the greeting back to him, the words barely uttered before he continued, 'There can be no mistake?'

'None, Your Highness.'

He flinched at the title but there was more pressing

business than his own unwanted and tenuous claim to the Dalmayan throne. 'They are both dead?'

'The King and Her Majesty, yes.'

'Terrorism?' Idris already knew the answers. He had asked the same question during the shock call that had shaken the entire chateau just eight hours before and had been extensively briefed and updated both whilst travelling to the airport and again once on the private jet that had awaited him there.

'We'll have to investigate further obviously,' the grey-faced man to his right answered. Idris recognised him as Sheikh Ibrahim Al Kouri, Dalmaya's Head of Security. 'But it doesn't seem so. It looks like it was simply a tragic accident.'

Simply? Such an odd way to describe the annihilation of an entire family. The better half of Idris's own family. 'And what? The car simply ran off the road?'

The General shook his head. 'The King and his wife were returning from a day's excursion and I believe His Majesty may have challenged the guards in the accompanying car to a race.' He paused. 'It would not have been the first time.'

Of course not. Fayaz loved to compete, always wanting to prove he was a winner in his own right, not just because of the privilege of his birth.

Sheikh Ibrahim continued in the same monotone voice, shock seemed to have flattened all his usual military pomp. 'The road was flat and empty and should have been quite safe but it would seem that either His Majesty or the other driver lost control of the wheel and crashed into the other car with a loss of all lives. We have experts on the scene and should have more information for you imminently.' He looked down at his notes. 'Four of my agents were in the crash.'

Idris pinched the top of his nose, the words spinning around in his head. He could see the scene so clearly: Fayaz laughing as the open-topped four-wheel drives wove in and out of each other's path on the wide, sand-covered road, encouraged by the screams of Maya, his wife and Queen. At what point had those screams become real—or had it all been over too fast for any of the party to be aware of how the game would end? He hoped so. He hoped they were laughing right until the end; it would be how he remembered them. Happy and so full of life it hurt.

'I'm sorry. Please pass on my condolences to your agents' families and take care of any outstanding pension and compensation arrangements.'

The General nodded and Idris turned to the man on his left, Minister of the Interior and his own great-uncle. 'What happens next?'

Sheikh Malik Al Osman pushed his tablet to one side. His eyes were heavy, his shoulders slumped as if he couldn't bear the burden that had fallen upon him. 'We've kept news of the accident under wraps while we made sure of no hostile involvement, but now you're here we'll brief state media and Parliament. The funerals will take place this evening and the official mourning period will commence then.'

Idris nodded. 'And then?'

Sheikh Ibrahim jumped in. 'Your Majesty. You know the terms of your grandfather's will. His Highness Sheikh Fayaz Al Osman and his line inherited the throne of Dalmaya, but if he died without issue then the kingdom passes to you and your line.'

Of course Idris *knew* this. Technically he had always been aware he was Fayaz's legal heir. He remembered the shock—a shock mingled with the warmth

of acceptance—when his grandfather's will had been made public, cementing him firmly into the family. But the prospect of actually *becoming* King had been so far away he had never considered he would actually be called to do so. Fayaz had already been married at the time of their grandfather's death and his wife was young and healthy. There was no reason to believe they wouldn't soon have many children of their own to take precedence over Idris.

Besides, despite his grandfather's decree, Idris knew how unorthodox his claim was. 'My claim to the throne is through my mother. No King has ever inherited through the maternal line before.' Not only that but his mother's name was a byword for scandal in Dalmaya and, possibly even more unconventionally, his father was French—would the people of this proud kingdom accept the son of such a pair as their ruler?

The point was moot. His vineyard, chateau and his wine export business were all the kingdom Idris needed. He was fond of Dalmaya but he had no intention of living and ruling there. He didn't belong.

'Your grandfather's will…' the General repeated, but from the corner of his eye Idris saw a speculative look pass over his great-uncle's face and turned back to him.

'What do you think, Sheikh Malik?' Hope twisted in his chest, mingling with the fatigue and grief already consuming him. He knew how hard his grandfather had worked to keep the kingdom safe, to modernise it, to introduce universal healthcare and education. He couldn't just walk away from that legacy, not if there was no other option. But the Al Osman family was extensive. Surely there must be someone qualified and near enough the ruling branch for Idris to be able to hand over the crown with a clear conscience?

His uncle looked directly at Idris. 'His Excellency is of course correct and if Fayaz died without any issue you are by law the next King. But there *is* the baby…'

Idris blinked. He'd seen Maya just a few months ago and she hadn't mentioned any pregnancy. Besides, Fayaz would have told him straight away if he had had a child. Wouldn't he? 'The baby?' The rest of the table looked as confused as he felt. 'What baby?'

Saskia stretched and stared out at the enticing view. The sky was so bright and blue it almost hurt, the colour mirrored in the infinity pool just outside the folding glass doors and in the still sea beyond that. Another beautiful day in paradise, and if she could just drag herself off the insanely comfortable sofa and brave the intense heat for the ten seconds it took to step outside the air-conditioned villa and plunge into the pool then she would definitely have a swim. After all, the pool was the only place she was truly comfortable any more, her weight buoyed by the water, her bulk less ungainly.

Her hands strayed down to the tight bump as she caressed it. Just six weeks to go. Not that she was exactly looking forward to what awaited her at the end of that six weeks despite her daily private pregnancy yoga lessons, her doula, personal midwife and the deluxe delivery suite already pre-booked and awaiting her arrival. Nothing but the best to ease the birth of the new Crown Prince or Princess of Dalmaya.

Stretching again, Saskia winced as her back twinged. Even with the best care possible, pregnancy was the most uncomfortable experience she had ever been through. *Don't be so spoiled*, she told herself firmly, heaving herself to her feet and padding towards the doors. She was safe, ultra-healthily fed, looked after

and, more importantly, so was Jack. Once the baby was safely delivered and in the loving arms of his or her parents then she and her little brother could get back to their lives. Only this time she would be able to afford to give Jack the kind of childhood he deserved. And she would finally catch a break.

Right. Saskia heaved herself off the sofa and took an unsteady step and then another, regaining her balance as she did so. *Balance.* She missed that, along with being able to see her toes and not swiping things off tables with her belly when she turned around. A swim and then she would settle down and tackle the essay she had been putting off. She might have the money to go back to university thanks to Fayaz and Maya, but if she could just get the first year completed long distance then she would have more money for a house—and for Jack.

Shucking off the loose cotton robe she wore over the frankly vast maternity swimsuit, Saskia opened the door, almost recoiling from the scalding temperature that hit her the second she stepped out. She hurried as best she could to the pool and cautiously sat herself down by the side, near the wide steps that led down into its blissfully cool depths. Sitting on the floor without needing a forklift to help her back up, that was another simple pleasure she was looking forward to.

'Sorry, little one,' she murmured, her hand slipping back to her belly. 'I do appreciate what a good baby you've been to look after for Maya but I think we're both getting a little uncomfortable here. Besides, you must be looking forward to meeting your mummy and daddy, hmm? I know they can't wait to meet you.'

That was an understatement. Fayaz and Maya were determined to be there for every step of the pregnancy. They had recorded stories for Saskia to play for the baby

daily so that their voices would be instantly familiar when it was born and Maya had been as regular a visitor as she could manage. 'Not long now,' Saskia continued as she slid her aching legs into the deliciously cool water. 'Mummy comes to live with us next week so she can spend every moment with you until she can take you home. Won't that be lovely?'

Sharing this huge, luxurious villa would be very different from the old days, gossiping in the college student kitchen, but Saskia was still looking forward to some heart-to-hearts with her old friend *and* to some adult company. Fayaz and Maya hadn't wanted anyone to know that Saskia was carrying their baby and so she had been confined to the villa since her arrival in Dalmaya nearly seven months ago. No matter how luxurious it might be, a place she wasn't allowed to leave couldn't help but feel like a prison. A self-imposed prison, sure; Saskia had known every single term and condition before she'd signed the surrogacy agreement, but a prison nonetheless.

She lowered herself into the water, a shiver of delight trembling through her as the cold enveloped her uncomfortably warm skin, and kicked off. She had been warned not to overexert herself and consciously made herself swim slow, considered lengths, concentrating on her breathing and the style of each stroke. Excited as she was to start her new life, there *were* some things about her prison she would miss. There were unlikely to be any infinity pools in her future, and in London grey skies were far more probable than this never-ending blue. Saskia turned onto her back and floated, eyes shut against the bright sun.

She didn't know how long she stayed there, an ungainly mermaid basking in the sunshine, but a prickling

at her neck and a sense of unease penetrated through her sun-induced haze. Saskia opened her eyes slowly, lowering her body until she was treading water upright, her hair slicked back. Whatever, whoever it was that disturbed her was behind her, at the head of the pool. Slowly she turned, awareness of her vulnerability rippling through her. She stopped. Shock hitting her hard.

'Idris?'

It couldn't be. Maya had promised her he was in France and swore she would never reveal to him that Saskia had carried her baby. No one outside Maya and Fayaz's immediate family was supposed to know the baby had been born to a surrogate at all.

But of course Idris *was* their family.

Her toes found the bottom of the pool and Saskia anchored herself as she stared at the tall man regarding her inscrutably. He looked exactly the same as he had done seven years ago. No, there were a few small changes. He was more put together, less earnest than the young man she had once been so besotted with. It wasn't just the well-cut, if slightly crumpled suit, the expensively tousled haircut or the dark shadow grazing his cheeks and chin. It was the confidence in the way he carried himself, a self-assuredness that, for all his pretence, the younger Idris hadn't yet achieved. The harsh lines around his mouth were new and looked to be forged by fatigue and grief and the dark brown eyes were dull—at first anyway.

Saskia stood tall, wishing she weren't in a tight swimsuit and stuck in a swimming pool looking up at him like a suppliant, as recognition dawned and Idris's gaze kindled, his eyebrows snapping together.

'Saskia? What on earth are you doing here?' She'd forgotten the impact his voice had always had on her,

low, almost gravelly, his French accent more of a hint than a full-on reminder of his heritage.

'Taking a swim.' Thank goodness her voice didn't waver. 'The question is, Idris, what you are doing here. This is private property and I don't recall inviting you in.' Petty but the words felt good. A small revenge for the way he had treated her all those years ago.

'I'm here to see the surr...' He stopped mid-sentence, his gaze dropping to her stomach, and incredulity stole over his face. 'You? *You're* the surrogate?'

Saskia raised her chin. 'I don't see how that's any of your business. I'm not supposed to be experiencing any stress so please leave and let me get on with my swim.'

He glared. 'Gladly. Only I need to speak to you. It's important.'

'Okay. Make it brief.'

'No, not out here. You need to be sat down. Dressed.' His gaze swept down her, impersonal, as if he had never seen her body before. Never touched her. Saskia's cheeks burned but she remained upright, head held high.

'You don't give the orders round here, Idris. You ask. Nicely.'

His gaze smouldered but he bit back whatever cutting retort sprang to his lips. 'Please,' he ground out. 'Saskia, this is important. Believe me, I wouldn't be here if it wasn't.'

She held his gaze, searching for answers within its darkness, fear uncoiling down her spine. Something was very, very wrong here. Why wasn't Idris in France? Where was Maya? Saskia nodded, slowly. 'Give me fifteen minutes. Everything takes a little longer right now.'

For the last couple of months Saskia had lived either in yoga pants or sheer voluminous kaftans, which made

her look as if she were about to act as a sail in an am-dram version of *The Tempest* but, crucially, were cool and comfortable. Neither seemed right just now, instinct warning her that she needed more armour than casual, comfortable clothes would provide.

Luckily Maya had provided her with a designer preg-nancy wardrobe fit for a princess. Saskia had pointed out that, confined to the villa as she was, she wouldn't have the opportunity to wear a tenth of the clothes but Maya had waved off her objections. 'You can keep them all and use them when you have your own baby, Sas,' she'd said. Saskia hadn't had the heart to tell her that having a baby of her own didn't figure anywhere in her plans, sensing Maya was buying her the wardrobe she herself wished she could have owned. So Saskia had accepted each gift with a smile and tried not to think about where on earth she would store several wardrobes full of unworn maternity clothes when she finally re-turned home.

She selected a pair of white cropped linen trousers and teamed them with a nude pink vest top, which gath-ered in a knot just below her breasts, the material flow-ing nicely over her bump. Many redheads eschewed pink, even as pale a shade as this, but Saskia loved the colour. She pulled her still-wet hair back into a loose plait and slipped her feet into a pair of flat sandals. She was ready.

Idris was here.

The enormity of what was happening hit her anew and Saskia reached out to the ornately carved bedpost for support. What on earth had brought him back to her after seven years? It was clear that he hadn't expected to see her; he'd looked just as thrown by the recogni-tion as she had been.

Her lips tightened. She was a different person now. Strong, independent. A survivor. Just because Idris's kisses used to make her forget who she was didn't mean he had any power over her now. She had this situation in hand. She had to.

Summoning a confidence that wasn't quite real, yet not entirely fake, Saskia left her suite and slowly descended the villa's majestic staircase. The stairway led to the large central hallway from which all the other ground-floor rooms were situated. All marble and dark polished wood, it was lined with two impossibly long, armless couches. Idris lounged on the right-hand couch, seemingly completely at ease as he scrolled impatiently through his tablet. He didn't even raise his gaze to watch her as she walked carefully down the marble stairs.

One of the many occasional tables that were scattered around the villa had been brought to his side and a jug of coffee sat there along with a half-full cup. The aroma floated tantalisingly towards Saskia. Coffee was one of the many prohibited food and drinks she had agreed not to touch until three months after the baby was born and her duties had ended. Many she barely touched anyway—she didn't have the budget for shellfish, brie or wine—but coffee was her lifeline and she missed it every day; mint tea just didn't have the same effect.

As the thought flitted across her mind Hamid, the houseboy, pulled up a second table and placed a cup of the herbal beverage upon it. Suppressing a longing sigh, Saskia smiled her thanks. She made no move to sit, nor did she have any intention of standing in front of Idris and waiting for him to notice her. Instead she picked up the cup and walked away into her favourite sitting area, the smallest of the living rooms with stunning views of the pool and the sea beyond. She curled

up on the couch, picked up a book and waited for Idris to come to her.

She didn't have to wait long. A smothered exclamation was followed by short sharp footsteps. '*Tiens*, there you are. Why didn't you let me know you were ready?'

Saskia hadn't taken in a word on the page but she still made a show of finishing her sentence before half closing the book and looking up with a mild smile. 'You looked busy. Take a seat, Idris, and let me know how I can help you.' There, she had established that this was her home and she was the one in charge.

To her surprise Idris didn't react with impatience or irritation. He sat down on the chair at right angles to her and leaned forwards before jumping up and striding across the room, his face set and eyes clouded. The premonition Saskia had felt in the pool returned, fear icy on her skin.

'What is it, Idris? Why are you here?'

He turned and the grief on his face clawed at her heart. 'There was an accident. Fayaz...' He stopped and swallowed.

'What kind of accident?'

'A car accident.'

'He will always drive too fast. Such a boy racer.' If she could keep chatting, keep the conversation light and inconsequential then she wouldn't have to hear the rest. Because of course there was more. Idris wouldn't have flown over from France for a minor injury. Nor would he have come here to tell her—to tell the unknown surrogate—in person.

'Saskia.' She could only sit paralysed while he walked back towards her, each deliberate, slow step echoing around her brain. He sat next to her, so familiar and yet a stranger and, to her increasing dread,

took her hand in his. Once the simple touch of his hand would leave her incoherent and unable to think about anything but him, but right now she couldn't feel anything. All she could do was wait for the words she knew were coming.

'Saskia, the accident, it was a bad one. Fayaz didn't make it. Nobody did.'

Nobody? Her free hand crept down to her belly, whether to reassure the baby or herself she didn't know. 'Maya?' Her throat was so swollen she could barely croak the word out, but she knew that he heard her when his grip on her hand intensified.

'I'm sorry, Saskia. She was with him.'

She didn't move, didn't react, couldn't react, couldn't process anything he was saying. Fayaz and Maya. Such a golden couple; beautiful, wealthy, powerful sure but also caring and loving, and they had known their share of tragedy. Years of IVF and three miscarriages had left Maya utterly bereft—which was why she had come to Saskia.

Saskia's hand stilled on her belly. She pulled her other hand out of Idris's clasp and turned to him. 'The baby? What happens to their baby?'

CHAPTER TWO

IDRIS STARED UNSEEINGLY out at the sea. He needed to get back to Jayah. The funerals would be taking place in just a few hours' time and there were a hundred and one things demanding Idris's attention, but his business at the villa wasn't done. Not nearly. Saskia's question echoed round and round his mind. What happened to the baby? Orphaned before birth. His cousin's baby and, morally, the rightful heir.

But the burning question remained unanswered: was it the legal heir? Idris had no idea; which was why he was still kicking his heels at the villa, awaiting both the lawyer who had drawn up the surrogacy agreement and his great-uncle so that he could get their advice. Advice he was praying tied in with his own plans, because *if* the baby could inherit and *if* his great-uncle was prepared to take on the Regency until it was of age then Idris could return to France as soon as the mourning period was over.

He pushed away the guilt clenching his chest. Fayaz would have understood why he couldn't stay; he knew how alone Idris always felt in Dalmaya. How out of place. Set apart by his accent, his French upbringing. Tainted by the dishonour his mother had brought on her family, not just by her elopement but by her subsequent

lifestyle. Fayaz knew how duty already ruled his life, knew how hard Idris had worked to restore the chateau, the vineyards, to make the Delacour name mean something again. He wouldn't expect Idris to put all that aside for a country that had never quite acknowledged him. Would he?

The all too familiar burden of heavy expectations descended onto his shoulders. Fayaz might not have expected Idris to put everything aside, but he would have known that it was almost impossible for Idris to turn away.

Almost…

At the back of his mind another question burned white hot. What was Saskia Harper doing here? Why on earth was she acting as Maya's surrogate? The guilt pulsed harder. He'd spent the last seven years doing his best not to think about Saskia, but occasionally he would see a flash of auburn hair, hear an imperious English accent and his heart would stutter to a stop, a tiny part of him hoping it might be her.

He hadn't expected to be so numb with grief when he did finally see her again that he had barely registered the shock of her presence.

The doctor's footsteps echoed through the hallway and Idris turned to the doorway, impatient for some answers. The midwife who worked full time at the villa had taken one look at Saskia and hustled her straight to bed, insisting that she be seen immediately by a doctor. The guilt pulsed again. Fayaz would expect him to do his best for his child *and* for its mother. 'How is she?'

The doctor took off his glasses and rubbed his eyes. 'As well as can be expected, Your Highness. A severe shock at any stage of pregnancy should be avoided if possible, but she's strong, healthy and has had the best

possible care throughout. However, as a precaution, I've suggested bed rest for the rest of today and that she take it as easy as possible for the next few days. It's out of the question for her to attend the funerals, of course. She shouldn't be travelling.'

The funerals. Idris clenched his jaw and refused to acknowledge the grief beating down on him. There was no time, not now. 'Of course.'

'I'm leaving Nurse Wilson in charge. She has my personal number if there are any concerns. I'll come out straight away but I don't foresee any problems. Try and keep Sayeda Saskia calm, and make sure she eats something.' The doctor paused. 'I'm very sorry for your loss, Your Highness. Your cousin was a good man and Queen Maya deserved the happiness this baby would have brought her. I'll be back in the morning.'

Idris spent the next couple of hours sending emergency emails. Just because it felt as if he were standing in the eye of a storm, unable to move while events whirled around him, didn't mean he could neglect his own concerns. He closed his eyes briefly, picturing the weathered grey stone, the chateau turrets, the acres of slowly ripening vines. He'd made his home, made his mark at Chateau Delacour, knew every inch of soil, every man, woman and child in its environs. Last night he'd gone to bed expecting to wake up to another spring day, making sure he put some time aside to join the workers in the field as they carefully hoed and weeded the precious vines. What was the point of living in the glorious French countryside if he spent all his life in an office? Instead he'd awoken to a panicked call and his life had come to an abrupt halt. The vineyard felt like a lifetime, not a continent away.

He knew his managers could take charge of the vine-

yard and his export business until he returned and he made sure they had all the relevant authorisation to do so, warning them that he would likely be difficult to get hold of and so they should contact him only in an emergency. He stopped as he typed a reassuring message promising them he would be back as soon as possible—he just hoped he was telling them the truth. Meanwhile a flood of panicked emails flooded in from the various ministries all needing guidance. He told each one to carry on as usual, promising an announcement on the succession imminently. He hoped he was telling them the truth as well. It was a long, testing couple of hours and he was relieved to hear the car pull up heralding the advisors he needed.

'*Assalamu alaikum*, this way, please.' Idris gestured to the stairs. On the midwife's advice he had decided to hold the meeting in Saskia's rooms—the doctor had said she was to be kept quiet but she clearly had a stake in the subject under discussion and Idris sensed it would be far more stressful for her if she was left out.

The houseboy led them up the staircase and indicated the door leading to Saskia's apartments. Idris paused, the reality of the situation hitting him anew. Fayaz was gone—and Saskia was here. Here in Dalmaya. Not quite his territory but close enough to discombobulate him with her unexpected presence.

Her bedroom was huge, the outside wall made entirely of glass, doors leading out to a large terrace filled with plants and shaded seats overlooking the sea. The room was decorated in soothing shades of blue and cream; a gigantic bed with ornately carved wooden bedposts sat on a platform at one end of the room, a seating area grouped at the other. Two doors were slightly ajar, and Idris could see they led into a dressing area

and a bathroom. Refreshments had been placed onto the coffee table and Saskia was already lying on one of the three couches arranged around it. She smiled wanly at the lawyer as he greeted her and extended her hand to Idris's great-uncle.

'Please excuse me for not getting up but I have been ordered not to move.'

'No apologies needed.' The elderly man bowed over her hand. 'Sheikh Malik Al Osman. It's an honour to meet you, Sheikha Saskia.'

Idris started at the honorary title, nodding curtly at Saskia and taking the seat farthest away from her. A quick glance showed him how pale she was under her tan, the pain in her eyes reflecting the pain he saw in the mirror. He ruthlessly pressed on; there was far more at stake here than personal feelings. 'I don't have much time,' he said, opening proceedings briskly. 'So let's get going. Can somebody explain just what is going on here and why nobody knows anything about this baby?'

The lawyer nodded, setting his briefcase on the table and taking out a sheaf of papers. 'I acted for Their Majesties in this matter so maybe I should start. You have to understand, Sheikh Idris, that legally surrogacy and adoption are still grey areas here in Dalmaya. Historically if a woman couldn't conceive she would simply raise a family member's child as her own—either a sister's or cousin's or a fellow wife's child, and that child would be considered hers. Plus any child she bears during marriage is legally her husband's regardless of actual biological fatherhood; that goes for any child she raises for someone else too.'

Idris frowned. 'So all Maya had to do was call herself the baby's mother and the baby became hers and Fayaz's without any need to adopt it legally?'

'*Traditionally* that's all that they had to do. Of course, by using a surrogate they had ensured the baby was Fayaz's biological child anyway, but because Sayeda Saskia is a British citizen, and to make sure there was no confusion in the future, they were planning to adopt the baby in the British courts as well.'

'So why the secrecy? You said it yourself, raising someone else's child is culturally acceptable and the baby is Fayaz's biologically, so there should be no quibbling over inheritance.'

'Your grandfather's reforms and his subsequent decision to take just one wife, a stance followed by his son and grandson, hasn't been popular amongst traditionalists, partly because it has greatly reduced the number of potential heirs in the Al Osman senior branch. Your grandfather had just two children and his only son died while Fayaz was still a child. If it was known that the Queen couldn't conceive there would have been great pressure on Fayaz to take a second wife.'

'Maya felt like such a failure,' Saskia said, staring down at her hands. 'She put herself through hell. IVF after IVF, three terrible miscarriages. She knew how important it was that Fayaz had an heir…she knew that you didn't want…' She came to a halt, flashing one quick glance over at him. He'd forgotten just how disconcerting her green eyes were, no hint of hazel or blue diluting them.

'How many people know about this?'

'I have known from the start. Fayaz discussed it with me before they went down the surrogacy route,' Sheikh Malik said. 'As head of the junior branch of the family he wanted to make sure I had no objections, that there would be no repercussions later on. The staff here know, any lawyers involved in the adoption and surro-

gacy agreement and certain medical staff here and in the UK. They all signed binding non-disclosure agreements, of course. The heads of the Privy Council are now aware after this morning's meeting, but they can all be relied on to keep quiet, if it's for the good of the country. But do we want to keep it quiet? If Fayaz has a son and heir then surely we need to let people know.'

'Or a daughter,' Saskia said quietly, her hands back on her stomach. Idris could hardly drag his eyes away from her slim, long fingers as they stroked the bump; the gesture seemed automatic, maybe as much comfort for mother as for child. But Saskia was only the mother until birth... Idris watched her hands in their rhythmic pattern. No child should be born motherless. Even his own beautiful, selfish, careless mother had been around sometimes for kisses and bedtime stories. Occasionally even two nights in a row.

Of course there had been the many weeks he had barely seen her at all.

'The problem is—' The lawyer's voice recalled Idris's attention back to the matter at hand. He tore his gaze away from Saskia and concentrated on the papers spread out over the coffee table. 'A baby's paternity in this country is proven only in two ways. Either the father claims the child as his, which is what Fayaz intended...'

'What about the surrogacy agreement?' Saskia asked. 'Doesn't that prove Fayaz was going to claim the baby?'

The lawyer shook his head. 'Surrogacy isn't recognised here. The only way Fayaz could posthumously be recognised as the father would be if you had been married to him.'

Idris's heart stopped for one long, painful second

as he processed the words. There was no way out. If Fayaz couldn't legally be proven as the father, if the child wasn't legitimised, then it couldn't inherit. Which meant the Kingship fell heavily onto Idris's own shoulders. A burden he had never asked for and certainly never wanted. He glanced out of the window at the relentless blue and his chest ached as he recalled the myriad colours of the French late spring: greens and lavender and red.

'In that case who does it belong to?' Saskia's voice cut into his thoughts. 'Isn't that the most important thing we need to decide? Who is going to raise this baby? Time isn't on our side.'

Idris stared at her. 'What do you mean?'

'I *mean*,' she said, emphasising every word, 'its parents have died. It's due in six weeks and it needs a family regardless of whether it can inherit the throne or not. Could another branch of the family adopt it? Would that be what Fayaz would want? Do we know? I mean, that surrogacy agreement covered everything down to what vitamins I should take pre- and post-pregnancy. I can't believe Fayaz didn't have a contingency plan if something like this should happen.'

The lawyer nodded. 'He had named a guardian for the baby.'

'Who?' Saskia and Idris spoke together.

The lawyer's gaze shifted to Idris. 'His cousin, Sheikh Idris Delacour.'

'Moi?'

'Him?' Again the two of them were in unison. Idris looked over at Saskia. He'd spent the last seven years doing his best to forget about her. How could he raise a child that was half hers? A child who would remind him of its mother every second of every day?

How could he raise a child at all? His mother said all he cared about was the vineyard, about work, and for once she had a point.

'Let me see that.' He held out his hand for the sheaf of papers and scanned them quickly. Even through the dense legalese Fayaz's intentions were clear. If anything happened to Fayaz, then Idris was to be guardian to any children until their twenty-first birthday. Idris swallowed. Fayaz was just like their grandfather, intent on making sure Idris was part of the family even if he was French by birth and name. But Fayaz couldn't have meant to make him responsible for a motherless newborn; he knew nothing about children—and by the incredulous look on Saskia's face she was thinking exactly the same thing.

He turned his concentration back to the papers, flicking through them until he reached the surrogacy contract. Saskia was right, it *was* thorough, covering everything from diet to exercise to location, stating she was to travel to Dalmaya as soon as the pregnancy was confirmed and stay until three months after the birth in order to provide nutrition for the baby. It took every bit of self-possession he had not to look up at that, not to look over at her full, ripe breasts. He took a deep breath and continued to read.

All her medical bills paid, of course, accommodation, clothes and food provided throughout the timespan of the agreement, school fees paid—school fees for who? His eyebrows flew up in unspoken query, only to lower as he read the allowance made to her every week. Bound to the villa, every need catered for, she was going to be pocketing a nice profit by the end of the contract. He turned the page and stopped, rereading

the words again before tossing the contract contemptuously onto the table as he glared at Saskia.

'You're being paid for this?' It took everything he had not to spit the words out. His cousin and his glowing wife, desperate for a baby. How hard must it have been for Maya to watch Saskia do so easily what she couldn't, knowing that the baby was just a way for the surrogate mother to make money?

Saskia flushed. 'That is none of your business.'

'I think you'll find it is very much my business,' he reminded her silkily and her colour heightened. 'I don't know why I'm surprised. You always did like to play games. But this isn't a game, Saskia. This was Fayaz and Maya's life!'

Her colour was still high but her eyes flashed as she shifted. 'Maya came to me, asked me to do this. I *didn't* play games or negotiate on payment. I took what was offered, yes, why wouldn't I? I have given this baby over a year of my life. Restricted my diet, my liberty, taken fertility drugs, undergone invasive procedure after invasive procedure to give this baby the best possible start in life. So don't throw the fact I'm to be paid in my face as if it makes me some kind of whore. Of course I was happy to help Maya, but I was in no position to give her a year of my life for love alone.'

'It's not a payment as such, that's illegal under British law and the baby was conceived in the UK,' the lawyer interjected quickly. 'It's compensation for Miss Harper's loss of income and freedom. The compensation is to be paid at the end of the contract if every condition has been adhered to and if Sayeda Saskia ensures that she prioritises the baby's well-being until it reaches the age of three months.'

Taking a deep breath to quell his anger, Idris turned

to his great-uncle. 'I know what my grandfather's will says, but surely my name, my heritage precludes me from taking the throne? Isn't there anyone more qualified in another branch of the family? Your branch?'

Sheikh Malik shook his head. 'Not without tremendous upheaval and turmoil, Idris. The kind of turmoil your grandfather spent his life trying to ensure the country would never go through again. Yes, your father is French but more importantly you're the grandson of the Great Reformer. I don't think the people will reject you. Your name doesn't matter but if it worries you it's easy enough to change it to Delacour Al Osman.' He paused, leaning forward, his gaze intent on Idris. 'I can't force you to accept the throne, but, Idris, I can and will beg you to. For your grandfather's sake, for your cousin's sake, for your country.'

A great weariness descended on Idris. His destiny was as clear as it was unwanted. He'd never appreciated his life properly before, the old chateau lovingly restored piece by piece, the vineyards, finally back in profit, and making wines he was proud to put his name to, the family coffers filling again despite his parents' best efforts. It was hard work involving long hours but it was satisfying and he was in control. Best of all it was quiet. No drama, no press, no obligations beyond those of the people who worked for him. How could he swap that for life in the spotlight, an entire country reliant on his success? For a child who wasn't his?

How could he not? His parents showed him all too well the consequences of living for nothing but self. Thanks to them he had grown up always worrying how the next bill would be paid, where they would be living next, even what they would be eating that night. Thankfully he had been able to escape to his grand-

fathers, to the two men who had never met but would have liked and respected each other, if their paths had ever crossed. The men who had taught him that duty and honour and responsibility weren't burdens but the measure of a man.

Sometimes he envied his mother, her carefree waltz through life, her refusal to be bound by convention. But such a path was selfish, had consequences for all those around.

A King's life wasn't his, he knew that all too well. His own needs, his own desires, his own likes always second to duty. And Idris saw his duty all too clearly. All of it.

His mind raced as he ruthlessly ousted all emotions from his mind, concentrating on the cold, hard facts, looking for the path ahead. First, it was clearly in the baby's best interests to have a mother's care right from birth. Second, he, Idris, was the *legal* heir, whether he liked it or not. But, third, at the same time the unborn baby was the *rightful* heir. Fourth, he was said baby's guardian. The pieces began to fall into place one by one.

What had the lawyer said? That if a man was married to the mother when a child was born then he was automatically that child's legal father regardless of actual paternity? He looked over at the other man. 'Let me get this straight. If I marry Sayeda Saskia then the baby will be my child, my heir, in both law and in the eyes of the world.'

The lawyer's words were drowned out by Saskia's indignant, 'There is no way I am marrying you, Idris Delacour, not if you were the last man alive!' But Idris saw the nod and he knew what he had to do. For Fayaz,

for the country, for the baby. He had to marry the only woman he had ever come close to loving. The woman he had walked away from. He had to marry Saskia Harper.

CHAPTER THREE

IT WAS ALL very well being told not to allow herself to become agitated but how was Saskia supposed to stay calm when Idris dropped a bombshell more explosive than she could possibly have imagined, and then calmly wrapped up the meeting and disappeared as if she had meekly fallen into line with his insane plans? Marry Idris? The man who had ripped her heart and self-esteem to shreds and then stomped on them without mercy? The man who had let her down at the lowest point in her life?

'Sorry, baby,' Saskia told it that sleepless night. 'I know it's scary now that Maya isn't here to look after you, but marrying Idris isn't the best thing for either of us. I'm not ready to be a mother yet, and you deserve more than that. He's going to be King. He can give you everything you need.'

But he couldn't give the baby a mother who would love it unconditionally—and she knew that was the only thing Maya would ask of her. Saskia's eyes filled and she hurriedly blinked back the tears, trying to focus on her indignation instead. The only positive thing to come out of this whole mess was that her anger with Idris helped her to manage the shock of losing Maya and Fayaz. She was so busy thinking of one hundred ways

to tell him that she would rather marry Jabba the Hutt than him that the grief had released some of its painful grip from her chest—although she did keep reaching for her phone ready to text Maya with a planned, clever comeback, only for the grief to descend again with all its painful intensity when she remembered she would never be able to text her again.

Not that she had had an opportunity to test even one of her scathing put-downs on Idris yet. Twenty-four hours had passed with no word from him and she had no way to contact him. Saskia stared out of the window. Of course, he had been a little busy burying his cousin and closest friend. She choked back a sob, the lump back in her throat. She wished she had had the opportunity to say goodbye too. No, that wasn't true. She wished more than anything that she could have handed her newborn baby over to Maya and seen the moment her friend fell in love with her much-wanted child.

Yes, she had agreed to be a surrogate for the money, she had never pretended her motives were anything more altruistic, but she had also wanted to be the one to make her friend's dreams come true. At least Maya had died knowing she would soon be a mother. Saskia twisted her hands together. Would Maya have wanted Saskia to raise her baby for her? She knew how much Saskia had sacrificed already raising Jack; surely she wouldn't have expected her to sacrifice more?

'His Highness Sheikh Idris Delacour Al Osman,' the houseboy announced and Saskia jumped. She hadn't even heard the car pull up, too absorbed in her thoughts. She turned, glad she had dressed ready for his return whenever it might be, in a severely cut grey linen shift dress, her hair coiled in a businesslike knot on the top of her head.

She sat upright in her chair—no more reclining, no more weakness—and folded her ankles and hands. Poised, collected and ready to do battle. But the cold words she had prepared faded as soon as Idris entered the room. He was grey with fatigue, shadows pronounced under his eyes and the grief lines cut deep. She held out her hand with no more thought than the need to comfort someone suffering as she suffered, only to drop it as he walked straight past it as if it weren't there. She leaned back and regarded him, doing her best to hide her humiliation and anger. How dared he treat her like that when he was the one who had let her down at the most vulnerable moment in her life? *She* should be the one shunning *him*.

Idris stood, back to her, staring out of the windows. Saskia regarded him for a few moments before turning to the houseboy and requesting some tea and refreshments. She sat back, displaying a composure she was a long way from feeling, and waited. Several long minutes passed before he spoke, the tea served and the houseboy dismissed, Saskia not moving or speaking, refusing to be the one to break first. Finally Idris shifted, although he still didn't face her.

'I've discussed our marriage with the heads of the Privy Council. They agree a big royal wedding is not in the country's best interests right now. We're still in the mourning period and your condition will give rise to the kind of speculation it's best to avoid. However, time is clearly not on our side so the consensus is for a quiet wedding here as soon as possible. The lawyer is drawing up the paperwork right now and we are thinking the day after tomorrow for the ceremony. In accordance with Dalmayan law it is simply the signing of a contract. Traditionally the elder of your house would

negotiate the contract for you, but my grandfather decreed that women now act for themselves. As time and secrecy are of the essence the lawyer who drew up the surrogacy will advise you and I suggest you go over the contract with him before the ceremony.'

Saskia listened to every crazy word, her mind busily coming up with—and discarding—several considered responses pointing out exactly why this was such a bad idea but in the end she settled for a simple 'No.'

Idris turned slowly. 'No?'

'No. No to the wedding. No to marriage. No to spending any more time with you than I have to.'

His mouth compressed. 'Believe me, Saskia, if there was another way...'

'You don't need me. You're the baby's guardian regardless of whether I marry you or not. Marry someone else. Someone you can bear to be in the same room with.'

'This isn't about you and me. This is about what's right.'

'Oh, don't be so sanctimonious. The last thing Fayaz or Maya would want is for *us* of all people to be trapped into marriage with each other. Not for us and not for the baby.'

'And the baby's right to inherit?'

'If you adopt it...'

'You heard the lawyer. Formal adoption is still an unknown process in Dalmaya.'

'Well, then marry someone else and adopt the baby quietly, like Maya intended to.'

'You want me to woo and marry someone in less than six weeks?'

'You're about to be King. The kingdom must be full of women desperate to fall at your feet and into your

arms.' Funny to think she was one of those women once—and she hadn't needed a title, just one of his rare smiles.

'There can be no ambiguity about the baby's heritage. No, Saskia, this is the best way. The only way.'

'Then you are in trouble because I am not going to marry you.' She clasped her hands to stop them shaking and waited, heart hammering.

There's nothing he can do, she told herself. *Dalmaya is a civilised country. He's not going to drag you to the altar by your hair.*

She stared straight at Idris, defiant but a little confused by the look on his face. He didn't look angry or upset, he looked amused, bordering on smug. Her throat dried.

'You signed a contract.'

'To have a baby.'

'*Non*, you agreed to a lot more than that. You agreed to do whatever is in the baby's best interests until he or she is three months old and, if required to *in extremis*, to come to its aid in later life.'

Saskia blinked. 'Yes, but that's because Fayaz and Maya wanted me to express milk for the baby for the first three months so I need to stay here for those three months and adhere to the right diet. That's all that the *in the best interests* part means.'

'That's not what it says,' he said softly, gaze still intent on hers. 'You did read the contract before signing it, didn't you?'

'Of course, and my lawyer took me through every clause…' She halted. That clause was written exactly the way Idris had phrased it. They didn't know what would happen, her lawyer had explained. What if the baby needed a blood transfusion and she, not Fayaz,

was the right match? Or, later on, a kidney, unlikely as that might be? Even a donor sibling? The three months post birth she was glad to agree to; it was an opportunity to recover from pregnancy and birth in comfort and peace. The statistical chance of the *in extremis* clause being invoked had been low enough for her not to be concerned—compensation would be offered commensurate with whatever was needed and, besides, of course she would want to help if it was within her power to do so. 'It doesn't mean what you're implying.'

'Oh?' He raised an eyebrow. 'The baby doesn't need a mother for its first three months? Being orphaned before birth isn't *in extremis* enough? Tell me, Saskia, what have you been doing since the last time I saw you? Apart from dropping out from university?'

Her hands curled into tight fists. How could he be so dismissive? Act as if they hadn't once been, if not in love, so very close to falling off that cliff? Maybe it had just been her, so besotted she hadn't noticed how little he felt for her. But for all his faults, for all his arrogance, she had never known Idris Delacour be deliberately cruel. Even that last time…she hadn't actually managed to tell him about her father's death when he sent her away.

Surely Maya and Fayaz had filled him in on what had happened to her, told him about her father? She'd assumed so. But if he hadn't known she was their choice of surrogate, hadn't known she was in Dalmaya, then maybe not. Thinking about it, they had always been very careful not to discuss Idris with her beyond mentioning that he had achieved his dream of renovating the chateau and the vineyards. Her pulse began to race as she took in his politely contemptuous expression. He couldn't know, not about her father's death, not about

Jack. After all, she hadn't even known of Jack's existence when they were together.

She lifted her chin. 'This and that.' If he didn't know about Jack then she wasn't going to enlighten him. The less he knew about her life, her circumstances, the better. The less ammunition he would have.

'No husband? Fiancé? Significant other? Career? I thought not. I'm offering you it all on a plate, Saskia, a family, a home, a position that comes with all the luxuries and money a girl like you needs to get by.'

She wouldn't cry. Wouldn't give him the satisfaction of even a chin wobble. 'You know nothing about a girl like me.'

'*Non?* Well, I suppose I have the rest of my life to find out.'

'The answer is still no. You can sue me, Idris. See what people think about the King of Dalmaya suing a woman into becoming his wife. I can take that kind of humiliation, can you?'

His eyes were hard and flat. That shot had gone home. He'd always been abominably proud. 'I don't need to sue you, Saskia. If you don't marry me and legitimise the baby then the lawyer agrees you have broken the *in extremis* clause and the first three months agreement. We won't owe you a red cent. You'll leave here not a penny the richer for your year and a bit's hard work.' His eyes flicked contemptuously to the side table laden with little pastries and fruits.

The world stilled and stopped. No money? No money meant no house, no university, no way of clawing herself out of the exhausting cycle she had found herself repeating over and over for the last seven years. No money meant a return to long hours and mind-numbing work, to low wages and choosing between food and heating.

To damp flats. No money meant no security for Jack…
She couldn't breathe, the lump in her throat outsized
only by the heavy stone in her chest. She couldn't do it
all again. She couldn't…

Somehow, she had no idea how, she managed to take
in a breath, only her whitened knuckles giving away her
inner turmoil. She *could* do it. She'd done it before. She
would have no choice but to pick herself up once again.

But not without a fight. 'I'll talk to my lawyer.'

'You do that,' he said affably. 'I can afford to fight
this all the way. Can you say the same, Saskia? Daddy
must be keeping you short if you've resorted to surro-
gacy and you've been off the party circuit for a while.
Will any of your boyfriends pick up the tab?'

The casual, contemptuous mention of her father was
like a physical blow but she didn't waver, keeping her
voice low and cold. 'Don't you worry about me.'

'You'll be a single mother as well. That's not the kind
of accessory men look for in their dates.'

Her gaze snapped up to meet his. There was no hu-
mour in his dark eyes, just a searing contempt. 'What
do you mean?'

He shrugged. 'The lawyer was quite clear. Under
Dalmayan law there's no way of proving that the child
is Fayaz's. I don't have any obligation to take in a child
of unknown origin.'

'The agreement. His DNA…' But she remembered
the lawyer's words as clearly as Idris did.

'Inadmissible.'

'Not in the UK.'

'Saskia, we're not in the UK.'

'You'd turn your back on your cousin's child?'

'This country is going through enough right now. I
wasn't born here or brought up here. My first language

is French, my surname is French. My mother ran away surrounded by the biggest scandal of the last century. That's the legacy I inherit. I need to be seen as committed to Dalmaya. The last thing I need is a motherless baby who isn't mine muddling up the succession. Now, I'm willing to marry you, legitimise the baby and make it my heir. But it's all or nothing, Saskia. Pick wisely.'

Go to hell.

The words were so tempting but she reined them in while she desperately searched for a way out, a way to reach him. Her earlier thought ran through her brain like a track on repeat, reminding her that the Idris she had known before wasn't cruel. Single-minded, yes. Definitely ambitious. But not cruel. Not until the last time she'd seen him.

But that man, that man who had turned his back on her, he was capable of turning his back on the baby too, she was almost sure. Almost…it was a slim word to hang her hopes on to. Could she risk it?

If he was in earnest then she wouldn't just be returning to the UK penniless, she'd be returning with a baby. A baby would make finding a job, a place to live so very, very much harder…

And of course there was Jack. She'd promised him a better life. Could she drag him back to an even more difficult childhood than the one he'd left? He'd never complained before but he'd never known another way before.

'Saskia!' A voice broke through her thoughts and she looked up. Was it that time already? She'd meant to keep Jack well away from Idris but it was too late. Her brother raced through the marble hallway, dropping his bag in the middle of the room as he kicked off his shoes. His au pair followed, picking up his discarded

belongings as she went. How quickly he'd adjusted to the heat and the space and the staff. How could she take him back to an inadequately heated one-bedroom flat?

He skidded to a halt by her chair. Ignoring Idris's raised brow, she held out her arms for the cuddle her brother still greeted her with. 'Jack, how was your day, tiger?'

'Good. I scored three goals during playtime.'

'Three goals, huh? Good to see you're learning something in that fancy school of yours. Jack, I want you to meet someone. This is Idris. I used to…' She faltered. 'We knew each other when I was younger. He is Fayaz's cousin.'

Jack turned, a little shyly, but stuck out his hand. 'Pleased to meet you.'

Idris threw her a startled glance as he shook Jack's hand. 'Pleased to meet you too, Jack. Are you over visiting Saskia?' But his keen eyes were scanning Jack and Saskia knew he had noted the school uniform, the au pair, the houseboy standing to one side with a tray filled with milk and cookies. All the signs that Jack was a permanent member of the household.

'No.' Jack sounded surprised. 'I live here.'

'You live here?' His brows had snapped together and he was looking at Jack assessingly.

'Jack is my brother and I am his guardian,' Saskia interjected smoothly. 'Jack, go and have your milk and cookies in the kitchen, okay? Then I think Husain has offered to give you a swimming lesson.'

'Really? Cool!' And he was gone in a blur of elbows and calves.

'He lives with you?'

'Yes.'

'Where's his mother?'

She shrugged. 'I'm not quite sure. She *was* in Brazil last I heard but she doesn't keep in contact.'

'Your father?'

'Dead. Look, Jack is none of your business so let's…'

If the news of her father's death surprised him he hid it well. 'If your brother lives with you then he is very much my business. When we are married…'

'You haven't listened to a word I've said, have you? I am not marrying you, Idris. Not in two days' time, not ever.' But although her words and tone were defiant despair flowed through her. There was no happy ending here. Her dreams of returning to England in just a few months ready to restart her degree and with enough money to buy a small house somewhere within commuting distance of London had turned into a nightmare. Either she returned back to the same hardship Maya had rescued her from—only this time with a baby in tow—or she stayed and married Idris. There would be no money worries if she chose the latter. But there would be no hope of escape either.

Idris reached into his pocket and pulled out a small card, which he handed to her. Numbly she took it, barely glancing at the plain black type on the crisp white background. 'My number. If you change your mind call me tomorrow. If not then I will organise a plane to take you and your brother back to London as soon as possible. The choice is yours.'

And then he was gone. Saskia put the card down, her hands trembling so much she wasn't sure she would ever be able to make them stop. She wasn't going to give in. Never.

Tucking Jack in wasn't easy; she couldn't bend over the bed any more. Instead Saskia had to perch on the side

of the bed while she read to him. Saskia could forget her worries for a short while as she read the story of a boy wizard and his adventures out loud, doing all the voices as instructed.

'At least I never had to sleep under the stairs,' Jack said as she closed the book and laid it on the bedside table.

'Not up to now,' Saskia agreed.

'When we go home, will you have a bedroom too?' Jack had always thought it most unfair that he had had a room of his own while Saskia had slept on a sofa bed in the flat's all-purpose living and dining room. But it had been an impossible conundrum. The temping agency she had worked for supplied offices around London's West End. The wages were very good for a temp job but to get into work for just before nine, to pay as little as possible on transport and to ensure she could fit in with the childminder's hours, Saskia had had to live as close to central London as she could afford. Which had meant compromising on space. The exorbitantly expensive, tiny new-build flat would have been bijou for one person; for a family of two, one of whom was an active growing boy, it was oppressively small. It had, however, been home but she had given up her rental agreement when she'd left England. Who knew where the two of them would end up?

The three of them…unless Idris was bluffing. But the coldness in his eyes had given her no hope of that.

Thank goodness Maya had insisted that she be paid an allowance—and thank goodness there had never been anything to spend it on. With some careful budgeting—and she was an expert at that—she could keep herself, Jack and the baby for six months. *Where* she was going to keep them was a whole other matter. London was out

of the question financially. But London was all she knew, except for nine months spent in Oxford a lifetime ago.

'A bedroom of my own? I hope so.'

'And will we have a garden? With a footie goal and a basketball hoop and space for me to ride a bike?' He was drowsy now. This was the way he always fell asleep, talking about all the things they would have once their stay in Dalmaya was over. He wasn't greedy, he didn't want video games and gadgets, just space to run around and play. Saskia brushed the hair back from his forehead, her heart aching. He deserved to be able to play.

'That's the plan.'

'I wish we could have a pool like we have here. Dan's dad said he would teach us to ride and to sail, but I won't be here much longer.' Dan was his best friend and Jack had spent a lot of time at his house, although due to the secrecy surrounding the surrogacy he had never invited any of his friends to the villa. Another thing she had promised him: a home open to anyone he wanted. 'Can I learn to ride horses and to sail when we get home?'

'I'm not sure about that. It depends where we end up.'

'I'll miss the sun. And the sea. And the sand. I like it here. I wish we could stay…' And he was gone. Saskia didn't move, continuing to stroke his hair, watching his face, mobile even in sleep.

Funny to remember how resentful she'd been when she'd realised there was no one else to care for him, that along with the shame and the debts and the mess her father had bequeathed her, there was a toddler who needed clothing and feeding and taking care of. If she hadn't taken him in her life would have taken a very different turn; she would probably have taken her degree, got a job. She wouldn't have lived the gilded life she had enjoyed before her father's suicide; those circles

had closed to her as soon as his embezzlement had been discovered. But she would have found something approximating her original plans of a career in the media, a shared flat in Notting Hill, parties at the weekend, skiing in winter and beaches in summer.

Instead she had spent her days filing, answering phones, typing up reports, eating her packed lunch on a bench in a city square, shopping in sales and charity shops. No holidays anywhere, weekends spent exploring London's abundance of free museums and city parks. She knew every exhibit in the Natural History Museum, every room, every sign.

She couldn't remember when resentment had turned to acceptance and then to love. Couldn't remember the day she'd looked at Jack and seen not a burden, but a gift. The day she had started to be grateful for what she had, not what she had lost.

Hauling herself to her feet, Saskia adjusted Jack's covers. He looked so well; no longer pale and over the winter he'd escaped the hacking cough he usually caught in the damp London cold. The dry desert air agreed with him; he'd grown inches, filled out a little, and he loved the international school he now attended. He was going to find it hard to adjust going back, especially when the promised new home didn't materialise and she was preoccupied with a newborn baby.

Saskia went straight to her room, opening the sliding doors and stepping out onto her terrace. The moon was bright and round, its reflection on the sea offering her a path to who knew where. If only she could get into one of the boats moored on the wooden pier and follow its enticing, silvery road. She leant on the balcony and breathed in, enjoying the faint sea breeze that cooled the warm, desert night.

She had agreed to become a surrogate to give Jack a better life. But, damn him, Idris was right. As soon as the baby had been implanted in her womb she had taken on an obligation to put him or her first as long as they were dependent on her. She had worked so hard not to get too attached to the baby, to remember she wasn't its mother, merely its caretaker, but of course she loved it. It was half her. She felt it move, hiccup, knew when it was sleeping and when it was restless.

Didn't the baby deserve a better life too? The life it was supposed to have? It was supposed to be the Prince or Princess of Dalmaya. To grow up surrounded by the sea and the desert, to be loved and cosseted and so very much wanted. And that life was still within her power to bequeath.

Jack could learn to sail and ride, stay at the school he liked so much, keep growing stronger and healthier.

And she? She could endure…

Slowly Saskia reached into her pocket and pulled out the white card with Idris's name and number on it. She stared at it, her mouth dry and her hands numb. Married to Idris. No university, no home of her own, instead a life with a man who despised her. Who she despised.

A life that would provide for the two children in her care.

She had told herself that she had a choice but, really, she had no choice at all. Fumbling, she reached for her phone and, blinking back the tears, dialled.

CHAPTER FOUR

THE YEAR SASKIA turned eight she was a bridesmaid for her friend's elder sister. The wedding was held in the village church and afterwards the whole congregation had walked in a joyful procession along the narrow lane to Saskia's house, where her father had allowed a marquee to be erected in the old manor house's extensive gardens. It was a perfect wedding and small Saskia, starry eyed, vowed that one day she would have one just like it. Of course the manor house had been sold to pay off her father's creditors and she had given up on romantic dreams a long time ago. Still, she had never imagined that she would get married while heavily pregnant to a man who disliked her and although she had no desire for white lace or ivory organza the calf-length, long-sleeved black dress screamed funeral rather than wedding—which seemed fitting enough.

The lawyer had spent the afternoon with her, once more taking her through a contract clause by clause, although as this one was written in Arabic Saskia knew she was putting a lot of trust in him; she could be setting her name to anything. The contract went on and on, detailing expected duties, allowances, long lists she could barely take in. One thing stood out: the marriage contract pragmatically contained provisions for a di-

vorce with generous allowances for both herself and any children resulting from the marriage. An escape clause. It didn't quite lift the suffocation from her lungs or the heaviness from her heart but at least she would be dry eyed when she signed her marriage contract.

'Sayeda Saskia, they are waiting for you.' Leena, her maid, stood at her bedroom door, her eyes bright with excitement. The staff seemed to view the whole secret wedding as wildly romantic and she didn't like to disabuse them.

'*Shokran*, Leena, I'll be down shortly.' She paused. 'Actually, could you please ask Sheikh Idris to step up here for a moment?'

'You want to see him alone? In your bedroom? Before the wedding?' Her maid's eyes widened in shock.

It was a little too late to worry about incurring bad luck or risking her reputation—after all, she was already heavily pregnant. What else could happen? 'You can leave the door open and wait in the corridor.' That should be sufficient chaperonage. She sank back onto the sofa and awaited the arrival of her soon-to-be husband.

She didn't have to wait long. The sound of his decisive tread reached her within two minutes of sending Leena for him and within seconds he stood at the door of her room, unfairly devastating in a traditional high collared cream tunic embroidered with gold thread and matching loose trousers. Saskia's heart thumped and despite herself she felt the old sweet tug of attraction low in her belly.

How could this still happen? She knew exactly who Idris Delacour was: a man who had no compunction about blackmailing a vulnerable woman, hijacking her life with no care for the consequences. But somehow her

body was out of step with her mind. She noted his every detail without trying: the cut of his cheekbones, the stubble grazing his jaw, the quizzical slant of his brow, the coiled strength in his stance. His body had filled out since university, no longer a boy's rangy torso but a man's body. One used to hard work. Strong, capable.

'You didn't need to make such an effort,' she said, her mouth dry.

He cast her plain dress a contemptuous glance. 'One of us had to.'

Ignoring his cutting tone took every ounce of self-control she had. Summoning a smile from goodness knew where, she waved a hand at the chair opposite her. 'Will you sit?'

Idris didn't take the offered chair; instead he stayed leaning against the door, his arms folded. 'What can I do for you? Or have you decided you don't want to go through with it after all?' He wasn't sure whether he would be more furious or more delighted if she changed her mind about the wedding.

'Do you want me to change my mind?'

He didn't dignify her with a response. 'Saskia, my uncle, his wife and the lawyer are downstairs waiting for you. If you have cold feet...'

'I need to know what this marriage entails,' she cut in. 'What it is you expect of me. And I need to know what I can expect from you.'

'You read the contract?'

'No, it was a little tricky seeing as it is written in Arabic, but it has been read to me. Idris, I don't want to know about clauses and agreements. I want to know about you and me. About our marriage and your expectations.'

'My expectations?' He drawled the word out, allowing a cold smile to curve his mouth. 'You don't have to worry, Saskia. We may be married but I have no intention of consummating our marriage at any point. Your *honour…*' he put a faint stress on the last word and watched the flush spread across her pale cheeks '…is quite safe with me. I have no interest in rekindling our past relationship.'

Liar, his conscience whispered. Saskia Harper had been a pretty girl but she had grown into a beautiful woman. The strawberry blonde hair had darkened to a bright auburn, a colour that reminded him of the grapevines back home in France as autumn fell. She was slightly tanned, a few more freckles sprinkled across her nose, her cheeks, and her body matured and ripened. But she had changed more than physically; Saskia had always been marked by her utter confidence. No nervous freshman, she had arrived in Oxford looking as if she fully expected the world and everything in it to fall at her feet—and they had. Idris had instantly placed her in the category of privileged girls who treated Oxford not as an education but as a launch into society, a place to meet influential people and date—and marry—influential men. Her instant friendship with Maya had made it hard for him to avoid her, but, despite the naturally flirtatious way she had treated everyone, he had been immune to her enchantment.

Or so he'd thought. Looking back, he'd been a little too smug about his immunity, a little too aware of her conquests, a little too surprised to find her in the library that Saturday afternoon, struggling with her essay on Marlowe, frustrated because she'd desperately wanted to impress a notoriously difficult tutor. After he had

talked it through with her, Marlowe's immortal words had made sense in a way they never had before.

O, thou art fairer than the evening air
Clad in the beauty of a thousand stars

A woman like Saskia could launch one thousand ships, her beauty and intelligence and the depths he spied under that confident exterior utterly beguiling. Utterly dangerous. But in the end, just like Faustus's creation, the woman he'd thought he'd seen was just an illusion.

This new, older Saskia was no pushover either, but she didn't look as if she expected life to roll over at her feet any more. There was a hardness in the green eyes that hinted at past hurts.

'No, Idris. I'm not even remotely concerned with your sleeping arrangements.' That voice though! Still clear and cold, each word spoken with precision in her most English of accents, like a lady dowager in a breeches and bonnets film. 'I want to know how this works day to day.'

'How this works? You're going to be the Queen, Saskia.' And he the King. The words still sounded absurd, the whole situation unreal. He, Idris Delacour, a King, with all the pomp and circumstance and responsibility and lack of privacy it entailed. His chest tightened. He wasn't ready. He didn't think he would ever be ready.

Idris glanced at Saskia, noting the tension in her shoulders and tell-tale shimmer in her eyes and a bolt of sympathy shot through him. He instantly clamped down on it. Like him she was a victim of circumstance.

Like him she had no choice but to see this through. Pity wouldn't help either of them.

'Queen, yes. But, what does that entail? Can I drive Jack to school, go shopping in the bazaar, have some kind of job?' Idris understood the subtext all too well—she wanted to know if she'd have any freedom. The sooner she understood—the sooner he accepted—that freedom as they knew it was over for both of them, the easier the rest of their lives would be.

'Saskia, you are about to become a very privileged woman. A woman with a driver, an expense account, a bodyguard. There's a gym and spa in the rooms at the palace being prepared for you, the palace stables are world renowned, you'll want for nothing. Sure, take your brother to school, shop to your heart's content but always have at least two guards and your driver with you. Try the bazaar every now and then by all means, it will make good PR, but there are some very exclusive malls, some with Dalmayan designers, who would love your patronage.'

Her lips tightened, frustration clear on her face. 'Malls. Right. That's one day a month at the most sorted. Working out, an hour a day or so. What about the rest of the time? Maya was on the Council, wasn't she? And Patron of several projects. Will I do that?'

'Maya had a degree in economics from Oxford. You dropped out of your English degree before you even took your first-year exams,' he reminded her.

'And I've been working ever since,' she retorted. 'I'm used to being busy.'

'You'll be busy,' he said silkily. 'Schools to open, dinners to attend, dignitaries to entertain, that kind of thing. You are going to need more than a day a month at the mall because you will be photographed and judged

and God help you if you are found lacking. You will need to research every guest, every function, dress appropriately and make the right kind of small talk. And you will need to look like you want to be there and like you want to be with me. That's your role. That's what I expect from you as a wife. What Dalmaya needs from you as Queen. A hostess. A well-paid, professional hostess. Is that within your capabilities?'

If he hadn't been studying her so intently he would have missed the wobble of her chin, the flash of hurt in her eyes. 'A hostess. Thank you for clarifying. That's what I needed to know. If you will give me five minutes I will meet you downstairs.'

Returning to the downstairs study, Idris tried to pull his mind back to the documents in front of him, but all he could see was the look on Saskia's face as he had spoken. She had tried to look impassive, he could tell, her hands twisted and her chin tilted high. But those green eyes were as impressive as ever and they had been burning with emotion; with anger, with humiliation.

'Dammit,' he swore. He had promised himself he would never let Saskia Harper get under his skin again but in one conversation she had brought out the very worst in him, just as she had all those years ago.

She was about to become his wife and he owed her his loyalty and courtesy at the very least. If he continued to forget himself around her then this marriage was going to be a long, bleak affair. He had to do better. For the baby's sake if not his own.

The ceremony took so little time Saskia couldn't believe she was actually married. Sheikh Malik, Idris's uncle, made a speech in Arabic and then she and Idris signed the documents. That was all. Usually, Sheikh

Malik informed her, this was just the precursor to the marriage celebration, but in their case there was to be no party, no celebration. No family and friends gathered round to mark the occasion. That was fine. She didn't feel much like celebrating anyway. A speech she didn't understand, a contract she couldn't read and no ring. The stuff of daydreams. It was a good thing she didn't believe in romance.

Short as the ceremony was her head throbbed by the end of it, her feet aching in the unaccustomed heels. All Saskia wanted was to be left alone by everyone including—especially—her new husband and go straight to bed. The beaming smiles on her staff's faces and the delicious smells emanating from the kitchen suggested she was unlikely to get her way. She glanced over at Idris. The last thing she could cope with was a cosy evening *à deux* and she had sent Jack to his friend's house for the night, not wanting him to witness the short, loveless ceremony. Her mind raced with possible excuses, reasons to put the meal off and then inspiration struck; she turned to Sheikh Malik and his sweet-faced wife with her most welcoming smile.

'I know we are all still in mourning.' The words were a guilty jolt at her conscience. So few days since her friends had died, but she was so caught up in her own tragedy the bigger tragedy seemed distant somehow. 'But my kitchen staff wanted to mark the wedding and have been cooking up such a feast there is no way Idris and I will be able to manage it all. Would you join us for dinner? And you are very welcome as well,' she added to the lawyer. Idris's narrowed eyes made it clear that he understood exactly why she had extended the invitation. But he didn't gainsay her; he probably looked forward to a romantic meal as little as she did.

A white-covered table and chairs had been set up on the terrace, overlooking the sea. Jewel-coloured lanterns were strewn through the trees and plants creating a magical effect straight out of *The Arabian Nights*. Saskia stepped out onto the mosaic-tiled floor, her throat swelling as she took every carefully constructed detail in: the candles on the tables, the cushions scattered over the benches, the beautiful table decorations, the soft music floating out of hidden speakers. Her staff had gone to such an effort and if this really were her wedding night, if she had married someone she loved, then this would be the most charming, romantic dinner possible. Blinking back sudden, hot tears, she stepped over to the terrace rail and looked out at the floodlit beach below, the sea a dark shadow beyond.

'The city is that way.' She jumped as Idris spoke, unaware he had followed her. 'The mouth of the river is just there, you see? Where those lights are, that's the ships heading up to the port. Ships have been sailing up the river Kizaj for thousands of years to unload their cargoes at the harbour here and to take spices and silks back to Europe and further afield.'

Saskia turned and shivered when she realised just how close he was standing, almost within touching distance. The lanterns cast a soft jewelled glow on him, his face a mosaic of reds and greens and blues. The light made him seem younger, like the boy she had once known. The young man she had been so desperately in love with. Her heart ached, the locked-away memories flooding back as she looked into his dark eyes.

She had been so young, just eighteen. New to university, new to Oxford, she hadn't taken long to fall in with a crowd as self-assured, as gilded as she had been then; it hadn't taken long to realise she and Maya were

kindred spirits. Young, beautiful, rich, indulged, confident. Looking back, she barely recognised that Saskia Harper. Did she envy her that innocence? Maybe.

Maya had already been engaged to Fayaz. Saskia, fresh from school and ripe for adventure, had been shocked that the poised girl with laughing eyes was ready to make such a commitment, but as soon as she had seen her with Fayaz she had understood; they had fitted together in a way she had never imagined fitting with anyone, fitted in a way she found herself envying. The revelation that Fayaz was Crown Prince she had taken in her stride; her exclusive boarding school had been full of royal offspring, many without a throne, the children of oligarchs and old aristocratic families.

But she hadn't been able to take Idris in her stride. He had already graduated from the Sorbonne and was doing a postgraduate year at Oxford. Older, serious, disapproving; she hadn't understood why she was so attracted to him then, naive for all her sophistication, but somehow he had got under her skin, into her very blood, with that first unsmiling nod. It hadn't been his looks—he was handsome but she had known many good-looking boys—nor his conversation—he barely spoke to her—but she had craved his approval more than anything she had ever known.

And when she had finally got it, when he had finally looked at her, into her, as if he knew her very soul, she had fallen. Hard.

It hadn't been easy. He had been so disciplined, so focussed on his future, and she had known he thought she was too flighty, too flirty, too frivolous. She had been all of the above, unapologetically so, refusing to

change for anyone, wanting Idris to love her despite her flaws. She'd thought he did love her.

She'd been wrong.

It would be so easy to fall into that trap again. To believe that she could win him round. To think that behind that cool, sardonic mask there was a boy who needed saving. A boy only she could save. But if the last seven years had taught her anything it was that there were no happy endings and, in the end, the only person she could rely on was herself.

And yet she didn't step back. His eyes were so dark, like the bitterest chocolate, his skin a warm olive, his profile proud and aloof. She knew every millimetre of his face by heart. It was imprinted on hers. Trembling, Saskia raised her gaze to meet his, preparing herself to meet the old disdain, only for a fiery jolt to blaze through her whole body when, instead, she saw the old flicker of desire, a hunger she hadn't seen or felt for such a long time.

'Idris,' she whispered, raising her hand to his cheek, the rasp of his roughened skin setting every nerve in her fingertips on fire, a flame that licked its way right down to her toes with an almost painful intensity. He had always been able to ignite her with just one touch. Slowly his hand travelled up to cover hers and she closed her eyes, all her senses concentrating on his touch, only for them to fly open as his hand dropped hers and he stepped back, beyond her reach, shutters slamming down over his gaze, the desire extinguished as if it had never been.

'Sheikh Malik, Sheikha Salma,' he said, walking past her as if she weren't there, hands open, a smile on his face as he greeted his aunt and uncle as they stepped onto the terrace. Saskia took a deep trembling breath

and turned, her own smile firmly in place. She could do this. What other choice did she have?

It was like being in a play, remembering her lines and her cues, ensuring she had the correct expression at all times and that her audience believed her confidence and interest to be real, even when her thoughts strayed to those brief seconds she and Idris had stood looking out over the sea. Luckily Idris's uncle and aunt were all too aware of the reasons for the hurried ceremony and worked hard to put Saskia at her ease. Sheikha Salma was a charming woman in her mid-fifties and she spent much of the meal asking Saskia about her pregnancy and plans for the baby and suggesting shops and places to visit that Saskia might like.

The conversation moved naturally on to the Sheikha's own children, all now grown up and living away from home. 'They are all so independent, not like when I was young,' she confided in Saskia. 'Adil is right here, in the army, but Aida works for a bank in London. Very clever girl. But clever won't bring me grandchildren.' She cast a longing look at Saskia's stomach. 'Farah is a teacher in Jayah but she lives in an apartment with other girls. In my day such a thing would have been completely scandalous but she just laughs and tells me I am old-fashioned.' She shook her head. 'There we are with our big house, room for sons- and daughters-in-law, for grandchildren, and it is just us rattling around.' She laughed but there was a sadness behind the laughter. 'Progress is not always such a wonderful thing.'

'I've looked after my brother, Jack, since he was two. The hardest thing to adjust to was the lack of privacy or time to myself—he wanted to talk to me even when I was in the shower! But now I can't imagine life with-

out him. The thought of him growing up and moving on is unbearable. I hope you get some grandchildren soon but, please, you must visit the baby whenever you like.' As if on cue the baby kicked and Saskia automatically ran her hand over her bump, offering unspoken reassurance, an unspoken promise. The decisions she had made were hers alone; she would never burden the baby with guilt, never let it know that raising it, loving it were thrust upon her.

'And what about you, Sheikha Saskia? What did you do when you lived in London?'

'I was a temp,' she said. Idris and his uncle were both listening in and she forced a smile. 'Not the most high-powered career but it had variety.'

Sheikh Malik smiled back at her in response. 'There is always a need for good temps in the world.'

'That's true. I always had work.'

His wife patted Saskia's hand. 'But now motherhood will keep you busy. For the next few years at least.'

Saskia stilled. She needed to prove that she was more than just a brood mare. Prove to herself—and to Idris—that she had worth beyond that which her body gave her. 'I'm sure that's true and I know the first few months will be hard, but I would like to work as well. I have just completed the first year of a law degree, long distance, and, even though I know I won't be able to practise, I would still like to finish it and maybe find a way to use it.'

Sheikh Malik raised his eyebrows. 'You were planning to be a lawyer? You should have drawn up the contract today. Is that what you always wanted to do?'

'Not for a long time. Originally I assumed I would head into PR or something. I did a lot of temping for law firms, mainly big city firms, and it was fascinat-

ing. I would take minutes, or type up letters and think, well, I could do this.'

'I see, you wanted to work for one of the big city firms. That shows a lot of ambition.'

'They certainly pay well.' Idris leaned back in his chair, his eyes full of scorn. 'Money's a great motivator, isn't it, Saskia?'

'No. Not corporate law, although obviously that has its place, it isn't completely full of big business types thinking about a big wage packet.' Her fingers tightened on her glass as she met Idris's gaze as evenly as she possibly could. She knew full well that he had rebuilt his family fortunes back in France, restored the vineyards to produce wine that sold for more than her weekly rent. He didn't live on some kind of moral high ground—every shirt he possessed was handmade. 'I wanted to do family law. Advocate for those who can't speak for themselves. I'd still like to do that in some capacity. One day.' She raised her water glass to Idris, allowing the defiance to gleam in her eyes. She would achieve her dreams, Queen or not. She would just have to redefine what those dreams were and not let anyone, no matter how igniting his touch, stand in her way.

CHAPTER FIVE

'Saskia? A moment, please.' It was couched as a request but Idris knew that she was fully aware of what he really meant.

It was a command.

Saskia stilled, half turned away, her full body angling towards the door leading back into the villa, poised for flight. 'It's late and I am very tired. It's been a long day.' His uncle and aunt had only just left after what had been a curiously lighthearted evening in the end.

'This won't take more than a few minutes.'

She hesitated for another long moment and he tensed, relaxing as she let out a small, indignant huff. 'If it really can't wait.'

Idris nodded at the servants, still clearing the table, and at his signal they melted away, leaving the two of them alone. 'Please sit.'

'I'd rather stand.'

He gave her stomach a pointed look, but he didn't press the matter. If she chose to be uncomfortable who was he to stop her? '*Bien*. Stand.' He picked up his brandy glass and studied the liquid just covering the bottom before setting it down and transferring the same keen study to his new wife. 'Is it true what you said just now? You're studying law?'

'Yes.' Her eyes flashed as she tilted her chin defiantly. 'I'm not in the habit of lying, Idris. I just completed the first year online—and passed with honours, with the intention of transferring to a bricks and mortar university for the next two years and for my qualifying year. But plans change.'

'Yes.' He knew that all too well. It was common ground between them; enough of a common ground to build a marriage on? It was a start. 'That's why you agreed to become Maya's surrogate? To pay for your degree?'

Her face reddened. 'And to buy a house. Jack needed a proper home. *We* needed a proper home.'

It still made no sense. 'But what about your father's money?'

Saskia stared at him, incredulity sharpening her gaze. 'Come on, Idris, you know what happened to my father. Don't tell me there's not a nice little dossier on your desk right now.'

He nodded his head in acknowledgement. Of course the Dalmayan Secret Service had torn her life inside out the second the marriage had been agreed and he had spent last night reading the slender file, disbelief increasing with every word. Where was the trust fund? The parties, the boyfriends, the socialite existence? Instead all they could find on Saskia was a tiny rented flat in Wood Green, temping jobs, menial at first, better paid once she had taken some courses to improve her administrative skills. The only scandal was seven years old and lay at her father's door.

He hadn't been able to sleep last night, trying to reconcile the entitled girl he had known, the girl he had tried not to fall in love with, with this backstreet Cin-

derella, toiling her twenties away. 'I'm sorry to hear about your father. I know how much you loved him.'

'Sorry? Because he was a thief? Because he committed suicide? Because in the end I adored a liar and a sham. Save it. I don't need your pity, Idris.' The words and tone were dismissive but she leaned against the chair as if for support, her knuckles whitening as she clutched the chair back.

Idris's lips tightened. The coward had shot himself the second he was discovered, leaving Saskia to deal with the mess. 'He was a clever man. He *must* have left you something. I understand you have to be careful not to flaunt it but surely there's enough money for you to live...' He couldn't believe a man like Ted Harper hadn't hidden money away in offshore accounts ready for this kind of eventuality. That he would have abandoned his beloved only daughter to poverty.

But Saskia shook her head vehemently. 'He left me nothing. Nothing except shame and debts.'

'Your mother couldn't help you?'

'She was never really part of my life. They divorced when I was small. Idris, why are you dredging this up? You knew about my mother back then. Why would anything have changed?'

'I know you weren't close but surely she didn't just abandon you?'

Saskia put her hand in the small of her back and straightened, her face contorted with effort. Idris glared pointedly at her unused chair but she ignored him, leaning against the table instead. He almost admired her stubbornness. Almost. 'She didn't want any publicity that might connect her with my father. She had remarried and her celebrity yoga business relies on good press and good karma, which I apparently was very short of.'

She blew a frustrated breath. 'I mean, I don't know if I had turned up that she would actually have sent me from her gates but there was Jack…'

Yes. There was Jack. For some reason the boy was Saskia's responsibility—which now made him Idris's. Three days ago he'd had no responsibilities beyond the vineyard and his business apart from his mother's occasional dramas and bailing out his father on occasion. Now he had a kingdom, a wife, a dependent child and another on the way. It was as if he had pressed fast forward on the game of life and been catapulted five years on with no real idea how he got there.

'Where is his mother?'

'I don't know and I don't care. That woman. God, Idris, she didn't want to be a mother at all. She was my father's mistress, I didn't even know of her existence—or of Jack's—until a week after my father…a week after he died. I was still at the house then, gradually realising just what a mess he had bequeathed me, and she turned up at the door demanding her maintenance. Apparently she had only agreed to keep Jack in return for a lavish allowance. No allowance, no Jack. She just walked away and left this tiny boy behind in the hallway, as if he was an unwanted cat…'

Idris pictured the bright-faced boy running into the villa, disgust twisting his stomach at the thought of someone just abandoning their child. 'There was no one else who could help?'

'No. It was all down to me,' she snapped. 'I was—I am—the only person I can rely on. I found that out the night my father died…'

Idris stilled, an unwelcome realisation creeping over him as he added two and two together and came up with a sickeningly certain four. Her father had died seven

years ago. She'd dropped out of Oxford seven years ago. He had ended their relationship seven years ago…

Ended it because she was a distraction, because he knew all too well where following your heart not your head led. The final straw had been the evening she'd shown up drunk and hysterical. He'd turned her away—and that was the last he had seen of Saskia Harper until three days ago.

But looking back he recognised that neither drunk or hysterical were typical of her. She was carefree, sure. Insouciant. Thought rules were for other people, but she wasn't the dramatic type. He swallowed, casting his mind back to the press cuttings, trying to recall the date of her father's suicide. 'The night your father died?'

Saskia whirled around, her aches evidently forgotten as she faced him, tall and defiant. 'It's such a cliché, isn't it? The worst day of your life? And you know, until that day, every day had been pretty damn good. Since then?' She shrugged, an angry, brittle movement. 'There was the day I was fired when I didn't let my boss feel me up in the photocopier room, the day I literally couldn't afford baked beans. The day I realised Jack had been going to school with holes in his shoes. The day I dragged myself to work with flu because there's no sick pay if you're a temp. The day Maya died. Yeah, there's been some competition for the worst day of my life but the day my father died still holds the crown.'

Every word dropped heavily straight into his heart. How had he not known? Not known that her gilded life had tarnished, not known that she had willingly accepted a burden far too heavy for her? Guilt flooded through him, guilt edged with anger. Anger at every person who had let her down, himself possibly included in that tally. Idris curled his hands into fists as he vowed

to hunt down that particular boss and make him regret he had ever set foot in the photocopier room.

'That day,' she continued, her eyes harder than the emeralds they resembled, 'the police turned up at college to take me home. They told me that the man I idolised had shot himself. That they suspected fraud. That there was a possibility that everything I had, everything he'd lavished on me, had been bought with stolen money. I identified the body, answered questions until I couldn't speak, saw enough papers to realise that their accusations had merit and all I wanted was you to help me make sense of it all. Somehow I got myself back to Oxford, I don't remember how. But you weren't there, not at your flat, at your college, nowhere. You weren't answering your phone or texts. I bumped into Tatiana and, although her all-day party-girl shtick usually bored me, that day her offer of a drink seemed like a good one, and so did the next and the next and the one after that because I needed to somehow be numb. I got to numb, stupidly I kept drinking past numb, and somewhere along the way I hit hysterical. That's when it seemed like a good idea to try and find you again. To find comfort.' She held his gaze, proud and true like the Queen she would so shortly become. 'And you sent me away.'

There it was. Two and two did make four, after all. He held a degree in maths and business—how could he doubt it? He'd ended their relationship on the day she had lost her father, lost her entire life. Ignorance did not seem much of an excuse. If he had known why she had turned up so late, so drunk, so incoherent, then of course he would have acted differently. Been gentler. But he hadn't asked, hadn't given her the chance to tell him. She had just had her world destroyed and he had

put in the final boot, stomping down on what was left of her. Shame twisted in his gut, hot and fierce.

But the truth was he would still probably have finished their relationship, not that night but soon after. She had been the ultimate distraction and his work had started to pay the price. Idris had known his path—it was straight and clear and sensible and there had been no room on it for a red-headed siren no matter how seductive her song.

He knew all too well what happened when people threw duty away for love: it tore families apart. Duty came first, always.

For once the certainty didn't feel quite as comforting as it usually did. It didn't matter; the undeniable truth was that Idris had made a success of his life thanks to his one hundred per cent dedication and commitment. He'd restored the vineyards, restored the chateau, built up a business. The Delacour name was no longer a fading star, relegated to gossip pages, but a force to be reckoned with. He had inherited the crown as a worthy heir. As a man who achieved. A man who built and restored. It was enough. It had to be enough. It was what he had.

'Why did you?' She no longer sounded angry, she sounded exhausted, and Idris glanced over at her, concerned. The baby wasn't due for six weeks and so far he'd done a terrible job of helping her to keep her stress levels down. 'I thought you loved me. You never said it, but I could have sworn I used to see it in your eyes, in your smile. Feel it in the way you touched me.'

The air around them grew thick with memories, the scent of the night-blooming jasmine permeating the terrace. Idris's grip tightened on his glass as her words sank in, as he remembered the softness of her skin, the feel of her hand in his, the way she'd shivered when

he'd traced a finger along her cheek, along the curve of her waist, the swell of her breast. 'Maybe I did,' he said hoarsely. 'Maybe I was close, at least as much as I was—as I am—capable of loving anyone.'

Her eyelids fluttered at his words. 'I'm glad it wasn't all in my head.'

'Sit down, Saskia. Please,' he added and, after a quick glance at him, she slid carefully into the chair, accepting the glass of iced water he pushed over to her with a wan smile. 'You know that Fayaz was my cousin?'

If she was surprised at the change in topic she didn't show it, nodding slowly. 'Of course, your mother was his aunt.' She looked up. 'Shouldn't your mother be Queen then, instead? Or is that not allowed here?'

'It's not been done, nor has any King inherited through his mother as I am doing, but my grandfather, the Great Reformer, didn't allow little things like thousands of years of tradition to stop him.' He stopped, visions of the proud, straight-backed man flooding his thoughts. Would he be proud of the man Idris had become? Of the sacrifices he had made? 'If things had been different maybe my mother would be in Dalmaya preparing to take the throne right now, but she hasn't set foot in the country since she was nineteen. She's not welcome here.'

'She's been exiled? In this day and age?'

'Not officially, but as good as.'

'What on earth did she do?'

What hadn't she done? His mouth twisted. 'She ran away with her ski instructor when she was nineteen.'

'Okay. That doesn't sound too awful.'

She didn't understand; how could she? 'Saskia, in this country arranged marriages are still common, and

education for girls over eleven still relatively new. My mother was a royal princess, a role model, and she not only lived with a man she wasn't married to but she was pictured—extensively—smoking, drinking, flirting. She modelled, did some acting. There were nude shots. She left the ski instructor for a racing driver and then, after some public scenes, she left him for my father. My father is a well-known *provocateur*, an artist, and there's no controversy he hasn't courted…their parties, their affairs, their arguments have been photographed and written about for the entirety of their marriage.' Neither cared. His father thought even noticing such things beneath him; his mother just laughed.

'Compared to an embezzling fraud they don't sound too bad to me, but I'm the first to admit my standards are pretty low. An actual parent would be nice to have.'

He barely heard her, trying to find the right words to explain. 'That night. That night you came to me, my mother had called me. My job, Saskia, my role, was to be the sensible one, to be the grown-up. It still is. There was no room for three juveniles in my family and neither of my parents had any intention of growing up.'

'What did your mother want, that night?'

He cast his mind back to that day. His mother hadn't been able to speak at first; it had taken hours to calm her down. 'There was some transgression of my father's. It wasn't uncommon, for her to call and cry at me, but this was worse than usual. It took three hours to calm her—she was hysterical, threatening to leave him, to kill herself. To do something crazy. She is quite capable of anything when she is in that mood. I couldn't ignore her, no matter how much I wanted to.'

He poured himself a little more brandy, trying to re-

member the emotions of that night. It was all so long ago; he had been a different person then, still a boy in so many ways. 'For the first time, academically, things were slipping. I wasn't in control and that scared me. My essay was late, my tutor concerned, my final proposal flawed, work in general not up to scratch and I knew it was because I was spending too much time with you. *Non*,' he said as she looked ready to retort. 'The fault was all mine, but I knew I had to remedy it. My future, the family expectations demanded it.

'And then you turned up and it was like watching my parents' marriage mirrored in our still fledgling relationship, seeing our possible future in their present. My mother crying, my father frustrated because he couldn't work, I could smell the alcohol on you, you made no sense…'

'I see.'

'I couldn't allow myself to be dragged into any more drama. I couldn't allow my feelings for you to develop any further, to distract me any more. I didn't know how serious things were for you, and I am truly sorry I didn't find out and help…'

'I didn't need your help. I just wanted your support.'

He couldn't, didn't answer. What was there to say? He couldn't lie and tell her that of course he would have supported her, shouldered her troubles, carried her needs and expectations along with all the others that had been thrust upon him. They'd only been dating for a few months. His mother might throw caution to the wind for the very idea of love but Idris had spent his life living with the consequences.

'I know,' he said finally. 'But it wasn't the first time, Saskia. Not the first time you turned up and demanded

attention no matter what I had planned, no matter what I was doing. No, you had never been drunk before, never hysterical—but you were impulsive and wanted me to be impulsive too.' Spontaneous, she had called it when she cajoled him to miss a tutorial, take the weekend off, jump on a train and head off who knew where. He hated spontaneity, had grown up with it. What was wrong with order and a planned existence?

Saskia twisted her water glass around and around. 'Did you ever wonder where I was? Why I dropped out? Did you ever ask Maya about me?'

The honest truth was he'd been relieved. Relieved she wasn't there to distract him any more. Relieved he would no longer be tempted and could bury himself in his work. Relieved that, in the end, he hadn't allowed emotion to weaken him. 'Saskia, you knew so many people, had so many invitations—to parties, to ski resorts, to country houses. There were so many men waiting in line for you to notice them. You talked of studying abroad, of travelling. It didn't seem like you needed Oxford the way others did. I just assumed you'd flitted on to another university, another place. Maya didn't mention you to me once. I didn't ask.'

His assumptions had strengthened his resolve. If she could drop out that easily then at heart she was the party girl he had first met, not the scholar agonising over her Marlowe essay. If she could just flit away from one life then she was a butterfly like his mother, never settling. His assumptions had made it clear he had done the right thing. His assumptions had been wrong.

'She didn't know where I was. I bumped into her on Bond Street a couple of years ago but that was the first time I had seen her since I left Oxford. I didn't mean to

cut ties so completely. I went home to try and salvage what I could with every intention of returning, but one week later there was Jack. And, honestly, I couldn't face people's pity—your pity—I couldn't bear the shame, for people to know how far I had fallen. From then on it was a battle. A battle to keep Jack fed and clothed and warm. Oxford was a lifetime ago.'

'You were never tempted to walk away from him?'

'We're all allowed to be weak for a moment, Idris. We're all allowed to be tempted. It's how we proceed from there that counts. But yes, there were times.' Her voice dropped and she stared into her water glass as if it held the answers. 'Times when we were hungry, times when Jack was ill. Times when it was all so bleak and so hard that I didn't know how I was going to get up the next day and start again when I wished for someone to rescue me.' Had she hoped that he would find her and make it all better—or did she know he was no knight in shining armour for all his inherited military titles?

'So when Maya found you and asked you to have the baby you said yes.' He'd judged her with such contempt when he'd seen the contract, but in the end what choice had she had? None, just as he had given her no choice over this marriage.

'Not at first. Her terms were very, very generous but they drove a hard bargain. Three months of a special diet and exercise to make sure I was healthy. Fertility drugs, which are not pleasant, believe me. Then as soon as it was confirmed I was pregnant I was flown here, to live in seclusion. Yes, it's beautiful here and I have everything I could need but I wasn't allowed to leave. No deviating from the prescribed exercise or diet. No seeing Jack's school or meeting his friends. No sight-

seeing. And you know the rest. I was locked in for life. If the baby needed anything I could give then I would be legally bound to. I would never be truly free of my responsibilities. I had to weigh all that up against the benefits.'

'And it was worth it?'

She turned her hand, staring at her glossily painted nails. 'I thought so then. I can't wish the baby away but I can wish we could turn the clock back three days and avert that accident.' She sighed. 'I didn't just jump at the money. I thought about it long and hard. But Jack and I needed a real home. And he deserved to have things other kids his age had, to be able to go to clubs and swimming and on holiday. To have the adult in his life around before school and in the evenings, not spend his time in a jigsaw of breakfast clubs and childminders' and friends' houses until I got back from work. And I deserved the chance to take my degree. To try and be something more than a glossy smile and a bright manner. But it wasn't an easy choice. And if I'd known the outcome...' Her voice trailed off but he understood.

She would have chosen to remain in poverty rather than be trapped into marrying him. He couldn't blame her.

'Would you really have done it?'

He looked over at her. 'Done what?'

'Turned your back on Fayaz's baby?'

He paused, lifting up his brandy glass and examining the amber depths. 'I told myself yes, but in reality?' He shrugged. 'I hoped I would not have to make a decision either way.' He glanced at her curiously. 'How about you? What if I'd simply cancelled the contract and told you that you could leave the baby here, take Jack and go home?' Would the woman who had given

up her whole life for her small brother have turned her back on her baby?

She was silent for a long time. 'I don't know either. My pride wants me to say that of course I would have gone, head held high. But in reality?' She shrugged. 'Maybe I would still be here. Probably I would still be here.' Her hand stole to her stomach. 'He or she is my responsibility. Not because a contract says so but because it's half me. I've nurtured it and loved it and looked after it. I could have handed it over to Maya gladly because I knew she wanted it so much. But how could I have walked away and left it with you when you had so much else thrust upon you?'

Idris pushed his chair back and hauled himself to his feet, suddenly exhausted mind, body and soul. He held a hand out to Saskia. She stared at it for a long moment before laying her cool hand on his, allowing him to help her up. She made to pull away once she was on her feet but he kept her hand imprisoned in his. 'Truce?'

'Truce? In what way?'

'You're right. We are married now. We have a child to raise. Two children,' he amended and her eyebrows shot up in surprise. 'Neither of us chose this but here we are. We both have things to regret from back then, but that shouldn't stop us from doing the best we can now with the cards we've been dealt. Let's make a pact.'

'A pact?'

'To respect each other. Honesty.' Idris closed his eyes and thought of his parents' marriage. About the profligacy, the constant drama. Of the extravagance. Respect and honesty seemed a good antidote to that. So it was best not to dwell on how soft her hand was under his. Or to remember the way she was back then. Fearless and so full of passion it shone out of her. Better not to

remember the way she'd made him feel. Because down that path lay a madness he had no intention of ever returning to.

Respect and honesty. They were worthy goals. They were all they could possibly ever have.

CHAPTER SIX

THE MOURNING PERIOD was over at last—officially at least. Idris wasn't sure when he'd actually stop grieving although, with a sharp stab of guilt, he knew he was grieving for his lost life as much as for his lost cousin.

With the end of the mourning period came a lightening of mood throughout both the palace and the country and Idris's advisors were beginning to discuss an official Coronation date. He'd attended Fayaz's Coronation and knew what the day entailed: ceremonies, speeches, inspections of the guard, feasts; an interminably long, unbearably hot day under scrutiny for every single second. Thankfully Saskia would need to be by his side for the whole time, which meant an imminent date was impossible.

She had elected not to return to the royal palace with him after their wedding, preferring the cooler sea air to the stultifying city heat—and the truth was adjusting to his new life, to his new role was easier for him without her. The distance gave them both the opportunity to ease into this marriage, into this truce, slowly. Time to adjust to the truths unearthed on their wedding night.

Idris headed over to the villa twice a week, but there were no more confidences, no more heart-to-hearts. No moments when memories swirled around them thick

with regrets, with remembered intimacies. It was best that way. Nothing had really changed; he still had a path to follow, a duty to fulfil. It was best he walked that path alone. Besides, he was still coming to terms with the knowledge that he had wronged her all those years ago. He had been so sure of himself back then. But he had lacked compassion. Lacked honour. The truth burned into him. No wonder she could barely meet his eye, ensured they were never alone.

His PR department had waited until the wedding ceremony was completed before sending out a brief press release introducing His Highness Sheikh Idris Delacour to the world as the prospective King Idris Delacour Al Osman. The press release had dwelled on his loving relationship with his grandfather and Fayaz, and his successful business empire before briefly mentioning that he was recently married and his first child would be born imminently. It wasn't a lie even if the intention was to mislead the public into thinking the marriage of greater duration than it really was.

Luckily the docile and reverential Dalmayan press didn't look for any more details. As expected the European—and especially the British, frothing with excitement at the new Queen's nationality—press were a lot more interested in the newly royal couple and had published several exposés of their student affair, digging up Saskia's father's suicide and subsequent disgrace in gleeful detail and reliving every one of his mother's scandals. But they didn't seem to suspect that the baby wasn't Idris's nor that the marriage wasn't real. As long as it stayed that way let them dig.

He pushed his laptop to one side and swivelled his chair to look out of the office window. The palace gardens were internationally renowned, an oasis in the des-

ert interior of his coastal country. Long terraces, each planted to a different theme, led down to the extensive lawns, palms fluttering overhead, and the garden was famous for its many fountains providing a cool comfort for those who worked inside the palace walls. Further out, beyond the lawns and just out of view, were the stables, home to over one hundred thoroughbreds, many past or present racing champions. The stables had been one of his favourite places to visit during his long holidays in Dalmaya. A place where Idris and his grandfather had bonded, where he had felt as if he belonged. He hadn't had time to visit once in the month he had been back in the country.

Saskia used to ride, he remembered. She'd said all the horses were sold after her father's death and she hadn't ridden since. Maybe he should give her a horse, as a wedding gift. It would make for some nice PR photos after all...

A buzz from his personal mobile phone interrupted his thoughts and he turned back to the paperwork-laden desk to look for it, apprehension hammering through him. Not many people had that number. His chest tightened when he saw the name on the screen. Saskia. Usually she preferred to contact him through their assistants, just as he contacted her in the same distant way.

He pressed answer. 'Yes?'

'Idris?' She sounded breathless. Frightened. He pushed his chair back, jumping to his feet.

'What's happened?'

'The baby. Idris. I think it's on its way. Come quickly. I can't do this alone. Please, please come now.'

Idris didn't think he had ever moved so fast, not even thirty-two days ago when he had received the phone

call from Dalmaya telling him of his cousin's death. He wasn't sure what compelled him most—the fear in Saskia's voice or the knowledge she had called him, begged him to help. Of course, there *was* no one else. First Maya and Fayaz, then Idris himself had made sure of that. Saskia had no friends, no family. She was as alone as he was. More so. He still had his parents, little though he saw them.

It usually took an hour to drive from Jayah, the capital city, to the villa but today Idris made the journey in less than forty-five minutes, his security detail barely able to keep up with his bike. He knew that his guards disliked his motorcycle, thinking it a risk, hard to guard and dangerous to ride. Idris had given up too much when he took on the throne. There was no way he was relinquishing his beloved, carefully restored vintage Triumph as well.

He got to the villa to see Saskia, her midwife and the doula, a woman trained to be her birth partner, walking towards a waiting car. He pulled the bike up to a stop and swung off it, removing his helmet as he intercepted the small group. Saskia was pale, her freckles standing out in stark relief, leaning on the two women as they escorted her to the car. Idris tucked his helmet under his arm as he reached her side. 'Are you all right?'

She nodded. 'Yes. Only when people said it hurts I didn't realise it hurts this much. Oh, no…here we go again,' and Idris could only stand there helpless while she gripped the hands holding her up, her face contorted with pain as she was reminded to '*Breathe*, Saskia, breathe.'

'Her contractions are quicker and longer than I would expect at this stage,' the midwife told him as Saskia sagged against her. 'It's imperative we get her to hos-

pital as quickly as possible. Are you coming with us? Are you planning to attend the birth?'

Idris froze. Maya had intended to be with Saskia, he knew. Now, although she had two paid personal attendants with her and a whole team waiting for her at the hospital, she didn't have anyone on her side, anyone who chose to be there, for whom it wasn't a job. They had called a truce. Had many years of marriage ahead. But did that mean he should attend the birth? It would be one thing if Saskia and he had married for love and if the baby were really his; this felt as if he would be intruding into a world he was not meant to see.

'No,' Saskia gasped. 'Jack. He's scared. He needs…' She bit her lip as another tremor ran through her body and the midwife and doula exchanged concerned glances.

Idris jumped at the opportunity to be helpful in a way that didn't involve witnessing childbirth. '*D'accord.* Don't worry, you just get yourself to hospital. Jack and I will be absolutely fine.'

They were brave words, but as Idris watched the car pull out of the gates he realised he had barely exchanged a word with his small brother-in-law beyond asking how school was. He didn't know any children, didn't know how to interact with them. That was going to have to change with not one but two children in the royal nurseries.

There was no sign of Jack as he entered the villa. The whole house was unusually quiet and still; the airy villa had a family air, all the staff on first-name terms with Saskia and her brother. It was usually a welcome release from the formality of the palace; today it just felt empty.

Idris wandered fruitlessly through room after room before thinking to check the terrace, where he found

Jack slumped on a lounge chair, a huge umbrella providing shade from the late-morning sun. A handheld games console lay on his knee but it was switched off and his thin face had the kind of determined set to it Idris recognised as a way to hold back threatened tears. Idris perched on the lounge chair next to him. 'Hey.'

Jack barely looked over. 'Hello.'

'How's it going?'

A shrug.

Idris blew out a breath. Was there a book he could buy—*How To Communicate with Pre-teens for Dummies* maybe? He'd met Jack maybe eight times now but struggled to think what to say to the boy—especially as it was clear Jack was confused by Idris's new status in his life and more than a little wary of him. 'Saskia is on her way to the hospital now. I'm sure we'll hear as soon as there is any news.' He wasn't sure who he was trying to comfort most: Jack or himself.

'Will she die?'

Idris stared over at the small boy. 'What?'

'Saskia. Will she die? She sounded like she might. She was crying and saying it hurt.'

'That's how it is, Jack. Having a baby hurts and there's nothing you and I can do but wait. But *non*,' he said, hoping fervently that he wasn't lying to the tense child. 'She isn't going to die. She has the best doctors and midwives in the country helping her.'

'Maya died.'

'Yes, yes, she did. But that was an accident, not because she had a baby.'

'She was *supposed* to have the baby. Saskia was growing the baby for Maya. That's a secret and no one but you, me and Saskia must ever know.'

It was a big secret for the boy to keep. 'No. Do you know why it's so important?'

'Because you are the King and the baby will be the next King if it's a boy.'

'That's right. I know it seems odd but if you have any questions or worries then just come to me, any time.'

Jack nodded. 'Saskia says we are staying in Dalmaya, that we won't be going back to London.'

'Once the baby is born you'll be living in the palace at Jayah. But you'll go to the same school you're at now. Does that sound okay?'

'Will my friends be able to visit? Will there be room for me to ride my bike?'

Idris suppressed a smile as he thought of the hundreds of rooms and hundreds of acres in the palace grounds. 'Plenty of room for friends and bikes.'

'That's good. I didn't have a bike in London and the flat was too small for friends to come over. And will…?' He hesitated. 'Saskia said once the baby was born and we went home we would have our own bedrooms.'

Idris blinked. 'You didn't before?'

Jack shook his head. 'Saskia slept on the sofa only it turned into a bed and we had to share the wardrobe and things.'

For the last seven years Idris had been the only occupant of a chateau with enough bedrooms for him to choose a new one every night of the week if he chose while Saskia bunked down in the living room. His chest tightened. 'You'll definitely have your own room with plenty of space for all your things. No sharing required.'

'And will Saskia stop crying?'

Idris stilled. 'What do you mean?'

'In London she used to cry when she thought I was asleep. When things broke or there was a school trip

or when my shoes got holes. When we moved here she stopped crying until Maya died. Now she cries every night. She thinks I don't hear her but I do. I don't want her to cry any more.'

'Nor do I,' Idris said softly, the weight of his responsibilities bearing down on him. It had been too easy to forget about Jack, but the boy wasn't just Saskia's charge, he was Idris's too. And, like his big sister, he had been carrying burdens that were far too heavy for him. Idris knew what it was like to be young and helpless and yet feel that the weight of the whole family rested on your shoulders. He could at least relieve Jack of his load. 'Let me worry about Saskia, okay? You worry about school and homework. Deal?'

Jack didn't move but some of the tension left his body. 'Then I guess I don't mind staying. Dan's dad is going to teach us to ride and to sail and that will be cool.'

Idris made a mental note to get Dan and his family checked out. 'We have horses and boats at the palace.'

'You do?'

'*We* do,' he corrected the boy. 'I married Saskia and that makes us family.'

'The baby too? Saskia has to be its mum now Maya isn't here to take care of it.' The big brown eyes turned their disconcertingly direct gaze on Idris. 'And you are going to be its dad.'

A *dad*. Idris stared back at the small boy as the word echoed round and round in his head. He'd known he would be the baby's father and that was fine; father was a more formal word, a more formal role. It called to mind school reports and admonishments. Guiding and helping. But a dad? A dad was a whole other being. A dad loved and played. A dad stood on the sidelines

at a match and cheered. A dad held hands during first footsteps and carried small people on broad shoulders. A dad read stories and checked under the bed for monsters. He could be a father but could he be a dad? A good dad?

He was aware that Jack was waiting for a response and tried a smile. 'I suppose I am.'

'Saskia says it makes no difference, that I'm still her boy. She says that's the amazing thing about love, that it just keeps expanding to fit all the people you need it to fit. She says I'll love the baby too but I don't know. My friend Dan has a baby sister and he says she does nothing but cry and get messy and he can't play with her. I don't think that sounds like a lot of fun.'

'Babies aren't that much fun at first,' Idris agreed. 'But I think they grow on you. I don't have much experience of them myself.' He suppressed the urge to look at his phone. He'd hear if there was a call and he didn't want to worry Jack any further. 'What do you want to do? We could sit around here and worry or we could do something.'

'Like what?'

'What do you like to do?'

'Well,' Jack confided. 'In London we mostly went to museums and parks because they're free but it's a bit hot for parks and I don't know where the museums are.'

Idris's mind flew to the stables. To how he and his grandfather seemed to strengthen their bond every time they went there. 'Come on,' he said. 'Let's go to the palace and you can check out your rooms—and then we can see about your first riding lesson.'

'Saskia!'

All she wanted to do was sink into the firm, cool

pillows and float away, but Saskia forced herself to sit up and smile as Jack ran into the room. 'Hey there, my boy. Are you okay?'

'I've been to the palace and I have not one, not two, but three rooms all to myself. And a bathroom! And there's a staircase which takes me to your courtyard so I'm not far away. And Idris gave me a riding lesson and says I have a very good seat.'

Saskia blinked at the torrent of words. 'Goodness. Sounds like you've been busy.'

'Idris says I can have a horse all of my own when I show I'm ready to take care of him, if you say it's okay. It is okay, isn't it?'

She looked over Jack's head and met Idris's eyes. He was lounging against the far wall of her hospital room— a room much more luxurious than many five-star hotels could boast. He didn't look bored or strained; he looked amused. A quiver of hope ran through her. Jack needed a father figure; she was well aware of that. If Idris took a liking to him it would make such a difference to the boy's life. He'd never complained about not having the time and money to do the things his school friends took for granted but she knew their straitened, cramped existence wasn't much fun for a growing and active boy. At least money and space were no longer issues, although myriad other problems had cropped up in their place like some kind of hydra; she sorted one obstacle only to find another three in its place.

'I'm sure it is. A horse is a big responsibility though so make sure it's what you really want. Now, are you ready to meet…?' She paused. 'Well, technically he's your nephew. Do you want to be Uncle Jack or shall we go with brothers? Up to you.'

'I'm the oldest either way but I don't feel ready to

be an uncle yet,' her brother confided and Saskia suppressed a smile at the solemn note in his voice.

'How about you, Idris?' She swallowed. The marriage was about to begin in earnest; there would be no going back once Idris acknowledged the baby as his. 'Do you want to meet your son?'

He nodded, those dark eyes still fixed on her, and Saskia smiled an instruction at the nurse. 'They put him in another room so I could get some sleep,' she said. It had physically hurt her when they took him away, even though she knew he was warm and safe and looked after. She could have sat and looked at him for an eternity and never got bored. For the first time she wondered what she would have done if Maya had still been alive. Was this instant rush of utter love because she knew he was hers to love and care for or would she have felt like this anyway? Would giving him up have torn her in two? She would never have to find out but, for the first time, Saskia was easier about the choices she had made and the life that lay ahead. It might not be what she had dreamed of but her brother and son would be with her and safe. She wasn't trapped, she was lucky.

She straightened as the nurse brought the baby, bundled up in a white blanket, into the room, shaking her head when the nurse made to hand him to her, even though every fibre in her wanted to reach out and take him and never let him go. 'It's time he meets his father,' she said, her gaze fixed on Idris.

Uncertainty played over Idris's face but he pushed off the wall and allowed the nurse to settle the baby in his arms. He pushed the cloth off the baby's head and stared down at the small, wrinkled face. Saskia held her breath.

Please let him love him.

He looked up, finally, his eyes suspiciously wet. 'He looks like an Al Osman,' he said gruffly and she knew exactly what he was trying to say: *The baby looks like Fayaz*. He did; from the silky black hair to the dark eyes, the coffee-coloured skin such a contrast to her own, he was Fayaz's son through and through. She swallowed, fighting back her own tears, grief rising once again for the young parents who would never meet their perfect son. 'Yes,' she said.

'There's a look of you too.'

She almost snorted. 'Me? There's nothing of me in there, which after all I went through feels a little wrong.'

'Oh, there is, a certain expression, a tilt of the chin. He might not have inherited your red hair but I am pretty sure he's inherited your stubbornness.' He looked across, his expression soft. 'Was it very bad?'

She shot a quick glance at Jack but he didn't seem to be listening, standing close to Idris and engrossed in pulling faces at the baby. 'I've never been torn apart by wild horses but I imagine it was close.'

He grimaced. 'Lovely.'

'No. It wasn't. Maya was keen I try and do it all naturally although, believe me, nothing about that felt natural, but in the end I had no choice. It all happened very quickly, too quickly they said. I couldn't have had drugs if I had wanted.' She blew a breath out, trying to wipe away the memories of those shocking, agonising hours; she'd felt so alone despite the team of doctors, despite her personal midwife and doula. She'd needed a friend, someone she trusted to tell her it was all going to be okay. She had even wished that she hadn't sent Idris to Jack, had asked him to come with her. He might not be friendly but he was familiar. 'So, what shall we call him?'

He glanced up, surprised. 'I get a say?'

'You *are* the dad.'

Surprise and something she couldn't read flared in the dark eyes. He didn't answer for a while; when he did his voice was hoarse. 'Something that works for all of us. Something Dalmayan, French and English for a baby with all those cultures in him.'

Saskia's heart clenched at his words. By including France in there Idris had claimed the baby as his in the most natural way possible. 'That makes it easy. It's going to narrow down the choices anyway! What do you think, Jack? Any favourite names?'

Her brother frowned. 'Harry after Harry Potter?'

She nodded. That would work. 'Maybe. Idris? What do you think?'

He was looking deep into the baby's eyes. A private communion. At her words he glanced up. 'Did Maya and Fayaz have any preferences, do you know?'

'I think they mentioned Sami. It means...'

'It means *exalted*,' Idris said softly, staring down at the baby. 'A big meaning for a little person. Do you like it?'

'Yes. I really do. Do you?'

'Yes. Come along, Prince Sami Harper Delacour Al Osman, I think your mother wants you.' Carefully holding the baby, he walked slowly across the room, bending as he handed Saskia her son. Their hands met and for the first time in weeks Saskia didn't flinch away, holding his gaze, answering his smile with one of hers. He had claimed her son, accepted her brother and by doing so he had bound her to him irrevocably. For the first time that didn't feel quite so much like a prison sentence. For the first time Saskia hoped they could really be a family.

CHAPTER SEVEN

'THAT WILL BE ALL, thank you.' Saskia smiled at her assistant, breathing a sigh of relief when the diminutive brunette left the courtyard Saskia tended to use as a living-room-cum-office. It wasn't that Saskia didn't want to be busy, to be useful, but she was hoping for something more interesting than learning how to address an ambassador and the exact depth of curtsey needed when she met another Queen.

She had come to the palace straight from the hospital. A huge, sprawling, ancient monument in marble, the Al Osman seat of power felt more like some kind of gigantic temple combined with a government building than a home. High walls kept the city at bay but the palace complex was as busy as any thriving metropolis: armed guards, civil servants, advisors, gardeners, drivers, maids and cooks working and in many cases living inside the gates.

Saskia and the boys were housed at one end of the building, their rooms at the back away from the hustle and bustle of the formal governing offices and chambers. Saskia's own suite was on the first floor: a bedroom, sitting room, small but well equipped gym, study, bathroom and dressing room arranged around an internal courtyard. Her rooms were traditionally decorated

with jewel-coloured mosaics and cool, marble floors, bright throws, rugs and cushions softening the effect. The bedroom and sitting room both had doors leading onto the terrace, which boasted a small infinity pool as well as shaded hammocks and seats overlooking the vast, lush gardens. Not that she could reach the gardens, not without travelling through what felt like acres of corridors and down staircases, flanked at all times by her guards and maids. It was easier to stay on her terrace and look out.

Sami had his own suite next to hers: a bedroom, nursery, bathroom and en suite accommodation for his three attendants, and Jack's rooms were on the floor above, a secret staircase connecting his playroom directly to Saskia's courtyard. She didn't know where Idris's rooms were; she hadn't been invited to see them.

Living in the palace was like being a guest in a sumptuous hotel: lovely at first but cloying after a while. For the first six weeks, still adjusting to the demands of a tiny baby and healing from the birth, it had been wonderful to have no demands made on her at all. No laundry, no meals to even plan let alone cook, no need to lift a finger or use her brain in any way. It had been the same at the villa but there the staff had been much, much smaller, the villa her domain. If she wanted to cook or bake the kitchen was hers to use or not. Here she had no idea where the kitchens were. She relayed her instructions to one of her maids, or phoned or even ordered online. Just like a hotel.

Odd how appealing her old staple of beans on toast seemed now, eaten at the kitchen counter, book in one hand, cup of tea right by the other.

'What's so funny?'

Startled, Saskia looked up. She hadn't even heard

Idris come in—but then her rooms were about as private as Piccadilly Circus, an ever-rotating crew of cleaners, florists, stylists, masseuses and aides wandering in and out seemingly at will. 'Funny?'

'You were smiling.'

Were her smiles that rare? She realised with a shock they probably were, especially when he was around. Grateful as she was for the way he seemed to have taken to the boys—and they to him—the past was still too present, too raw, especially after its exhumation on the night of the wedding. She wanted to find a way to be friends, partners, but she couldn't help being wary. She had to protect her bruised heart somehow.

'I was just thinking that only a year ago I would have been happy never to eat beans on toast ever again—and now it sounds like the most delicious meal imaginable.'

'Order it, then. There are plenty of British supermarkets around if the kitchens don't have any in stock. Which they probably don't have,' he added with a superior sneer, which was all French.

'I can't order it, Idris. That's not the point of beans on toast.'

He didn't reply, just raised a sardonic eyebrow and she shut her mouth with a snap, achingly aware of how entitled she sounded before trying again. 'It's not the beans exactly.'

'It's not? That's a relief. The palace chef has earned Michelin stars at three different establishments. If he knew you were yearning for baked beans he would walk out on me.'

'The truth is…' Saskia looked around her, at the gorgeous courtyard in which she sat. Trees shaded the shallow long pool filled with fish, plants growing with an abandon not allowed in the extensively manicured gar-

dens, at the carved wooden benches laden with cushions, the coloured lights that came on with a tap of an app. There was even a large TV screen hidden behind a mosaic if she wanted her own secret cinema experience. 'I'm bored.'

That eyebrow again. One day she would shave it off. That would teach him. 'Bored? You've just had a baby. I thought being a new mother was meant to be tiring and hard. I didn't know there was time to be bored.'

Stay calm, Saskia.

'Most new parents don't have night nannies, day nannies and nursery maids,' she pointed out. 'They are trying to fit in never-ending piles of laundry, buying nappies and snatching sleep. My laundry is done for me, the nursery is equipped with everything Sami needs before I know he needs it, I get more sleep than I ever have before.' She blew out a frustrated breath. 'Listen to me. It's not that I'm not grateful. I got six weeks to rest up and recover and thanks to all the amazing people who have been helping me and taking care of me I actually feel fitter than before I got pregnant. I know how incredibly privileged I am.' She paused, trying to find the right words to express her frustrations.

'For the last seven years I've worked and taken care of Jack and started studying for my degree but now I'm not needed to take Jack to school or make his snack or supervise his homework or make sure he has everything he needs. And I know that I should be relieved to be freed of some of that work but I'm not made to do nothing. I can't even get on with my degree; I didn't register to study online this year because I expected to be back in London by now. And part of me wonders what the point of studying even is if I'm never going to be able to practise anyway.'

Now she had started venting she realised she couldn't stem the words if she wanted to. 'I spend my days working out, letting the stylist tell me what to order and learning about etiquette. The highlight of my day is when Jack gets back from school and I'm not alone any more. Truth is I thought I was hemmed in in that tiny flat of ours but at least I was free to walk out the door whenever I wanted…'

'You're free here.'

'If I take my maid and the guards.'

He didn't deny it. 'It's safer that way.'

'In the palace? In my home? These apartments are gorgeous but I have barely set foot outside them in three months. I need a purpose, Idris.'

'There's time.' To her surprise he walked purposefully across the room and sat on the bench by her side. It was a long, wide bench, made for reclining, it should have been plenty big enough for two, but his proximity made the bench shrink or maybe she, like Alice, had grown bigger. He was dressed in Western clothes, light linen trousers and a short white shirt. Saskia stared at his forearms, at the light smattering of dark hair on olive skin, trying not to remember how it felt when she used to slide her hands along his arms, the strength in every muscle, the way his hands would capture hers. 'We haven't even planned the Coronation yet.'

'The Coronation?' Her stomach contracted at the thought of the pomp and circumstance surrounding such a huge event. At the thought of the publicity. She'd had a tiny taste of notoriety after her father's death; there was nothing like a former society girl brought low to get the paparazzi salivating, and she had no desire to ever be in the spotlight again.

'Normally they hold the official Coronation for the

new monarch directly after the mourning period has finished for the old; it's meant to be a sign of hope after the darkness of grief, but, for several reasons, it was decided to wait for six months this time.'

'What reasons?'

'To give you time to recover from the birth. To give me time to get my business affairs in order. To give Dalmaya time to adjust to me and for me to adjust to living as a King. So if I decided to step aside and let one of my cousins take over—or if they wished to ask me to step aside—then it could be done with as little scandal as possible.'

Of course, this was as big an adjustment for him as it was for her. She forgot that sometimes. Not that he showed it in any way. 'I didn't know you were considering not staying on as King.'

She looked up at him but his gaze was hooded, his eyes giving nothing away. It was frustrating how hard he was to read. 'I hadn't intended to. I always loved being here, thanks to Grandfather, but Dalmaya isn't my home. I'm too Western, too French. He held up his hand, turning it from palm to back as he stared at it. She followed his gaze, her own lingering on the strong, well-shaped hand, the long, elegant fingers, her pulse speeding up. 'Of course in France I was always too dark, too Eastern. Growing up I didn't really fit in anywhere. But I made myself as French as I could be. I restored the chateau, restored the vineyards. Made myself a success. Now I have to start again. Remake myself again.'

'So why don't you go back?' She wanted to add, *Why force me into this marriage?* but managed to stop the words escaping. She didn't want him to revert behind the polite screen again.

'If it was just me then maybe. But Fayaz trusted me to do what was right for his son...'

Despite herself, despite every promise she'd made to herself not to allow herself to feel anything but mild amiability towards Idris, Saskia's heart ached at the desolate tone in his voice.

'So the Coronation is in two months? What does it entail?'

'A day of ceremonies, parades, photos and feasts. I would like you to be involved in helping plan it, especially where the children are concerned. I would like them both, Jack too, to wear traditional dress. After all, he is your family and that makes him mine.'

'Jack? Why does he have to be involved?' Panic rose in her, inexhaustible and painful.

Idris's brow crinkled in puzzlement. 'I thought he would like to be included.'

'But it's public, right? The ceremony. He'll be the focus of attention. People will want to know who he is and why he's there.' Saskia jumped to her feet and began to pace, agitation twisting inside. 'His mother left him because she was no longer being paid to care for him, Idris. And every day for a month, two months, many weeks after that day, I prayed that she would be sorry and she would return for him. And then every day since I've prayed she wouldn't. Because she just *left* him with me, Idris. I have no actual legal guardianship. It didn't occur to me at first that I might need to, and then I couldn't afford it.' She swallowed. 'And I was afraid that if I tried to make him mine, if the authorities realised, then they might think a one-bedroom flat and a sister who worked forty hours a week wasn't a fit environment and take him away from me. But if his mother sees me on TV or in a magazine and realises

Jack is still with me and I have money, or access to it, then she'll be back, I know it.'

'You love him?'

'Of course I love him! I've raised him. He's mine.'

She was a lioness, fierce in her defence of her cub, and Idris couldn't help being a little envious of Jack, that the boy had someone who would always fight for him, always put him first.

He pulled out his phone and punched in a quick message then sat back and watched her pace. Saskia hadn't lied when she said she was in great shape; she might have railed against her recent seclusion but her skin glowed, her hair shone and she looked fit and toned with new, enticing curves. Curves he couldn't drag his eyes away from despite himself. 'It's usual for the King to take a tour of the country after the Coronation, an opportunity to meet all the different types of people who live here from the fishermen to the nomads, and for them to meet him,' he said as if she weren't still stalking up and down, despair flaring in her green eyes.

She halted and swivelled. 'What?'

'A grand tour. I know, it sounds a little medieval and obsolete when even the nomads have smartphones but it's the custom. Only we're going to go on our tour before the Coronation. The Council think it will help ease any fears about my dual nationality—and to be honest I barely know Dalmaya at all, only this palace and the city and the coastline where you were staying. My grandfather always vacationed there. It's important I understand the land a little more before I am formally crowned. We leave on the first leg in a week. My aide has sent yours a list of what you'll need. Your stylist is

already working on your wardrobe and your assistant will make sure you're fully briefed.'

'You want me to embark on a grand tour? Are you insane?'

'Not that I know of. I thought,' he added silkily, 'that you were bored. You needed a purpose. Here's your chance. Time to practise being a Queen, Sheikha Saskia.'

'But…but…the boys need me. The last couple of months have been a huge adjustment for Jack and Sami can't even sit up yet. How can I just take off for weeks at a time?'

'No taking off needed. At least not much,' he amended. 'Unlike my ancestors we have access to cars and planes and helicopters. We may need to be away for a night or two here and there but mostly we can fit each visit in in a day. It will mean early starts and late nights but you said yourself you're well rested and raring to go.'

'A few nights? Will we have our own rooms during those nights?'

He stilled. Nobody at the palace thought it odd that Saskia was housed so far away from his own quarters. Fayaz and Maya had shared a suite but his grandfather had always had separate rooms from his grandmother and *his* father had had several wives, each with their own distinct quarters.

On the tour Saskia and he would be visiting and staying in places far more humble than the palace and in this day, this age, people would expect their French King-to-be and his English wife to sleep in the same room.

His throat tightened. He had told her that her honour was safe with him and the implication had been clear—

separate rooms, separate beds. He hadn't fully realised the implications for either of them.

The thought of housing a discreet mistress somewhere chilled him. As for Saskia, did he really expect her to opt for a life of chastity? As Queen, the standards expected of her rightly or wrongly were higher, harder, the judgements harsher. The people would turn a blind eye to any extracurricular activity Idris might choose to indulge in. Saskia would be disgraced for ever.

A sudden pain in his palms surprised him and he glanced at his hands; he hadn't realised that his hands had curled into fists until his fingernails dug into his palms. He didn't want her turning elsewhere, to somebody else. 'I don't know any of the details yet.'

'But…' She paused, lips compressed, as his aide bustled in, two folders in his arms. He passed them to Idris with a bow, then bowed towards Saskia before backing away. Saskia eyed the folders. 'What're they?'

'Answers. To some of your questions at least.' He put the blue folder down on the bench beside him and held out the green one. 'Here.'

Cautiously she took it, flicking it open. 'What's this? I don't understand.'

'The palace needs to be aware of any possible problems, Saskia. They've been monitoring my mother from the day she eloped. They've probably monitored me as well, although no one will give me a straight answer about that. And now you bring a new family into the mix and it's a complicated one. Your father left a trail of headlines. Well, we can counter that with the fact you've spent the last seven years living quietly and working hard. But your mother? Jack's mother? Jack's existence? They're more problematic.'

'So you tracked them down? I could have told you

where my mother was.' She dropped the green folder contemptuously onto his knee but her eyes flickered to the blue folder and he knew she wanted—needed—to see the contents. 'She runs a yoga retreat in New Mexico, along with her third husband. She says she has achieved inner peace. That was why she didn't want me to come over when it all happened. Too much negative energy surrounded me apparently.' She was going for scathing, pretending she didn't care, but the hurt in her eyes was unmistakable.

'She's no worry to us at all. Your stepfather...'

'I've never met him. He's no father to me in any way.'

Idris paused. 'Her husband,' he amended, 'has some wild ideas. He's written several books about UFO sightings and aliens amongst us but seems harmless. We won't be inviting them to the Coronation.' He looked at Saskia to see how she would take the news but she didn't as much as nod.

'Of course not. She walked out of my life when I was three and never walked back in again. She doesn't even send me a birthday card most years.'

'This is what we compiled on Jack's mother.'

Her composure crumpled, her hand shaking as she took the folder from him. 'I used to wonder what kind of woman had a child for money. Until I became that woman.'

His own words echoed back at him. He knew better now. 'The situations don't compare. Besides, you didn't raise Jack for money.'

'No,' she said hollowly. 'You know, Rosa was with my father for four years yet I didn't even know she existed. He bought her a house, made her an allowance but she didn't accompany him to functions or meet his friends. What kind of person is happy in that kind of

second-rate relationship? She said she didn't mean to get pregnant but Daddy was delighted when she did. Persuaded her to have the baby, promised her he would look after her if she did. But he still didn't marry her. Didn't live with Jack, help raise him, not properly. Just visited. I didn't even know I had a brother until after my father died. I think that hurt more than anything else.'

He nodded at the file. 'Go on. Open it.'

Her hands shook as she flipped the folder open and then she hissed a long breath. He knew what she saw. The portrait. A family portrait. Rosa with her much older husband, a baby in her arms, a toddler by her side. 'She has more children?'

'She married well. Very well. That's Chuck Weissberger, multimillionaire retail King. They live in Connecticut in a riverside mansion.'

'She got her rich husband after all,' Saskia said tonelessly, still staring at the contents of the folder.

'She did. And he has no idea about Jack. He's very family orientated. If he knew she had abandoned a child that marriage would be over quicker than she could beg for forgiveness. She's not coming anywhere near Jack, Saskia. He's safe. My lawyers are petitioning for us to legally adopt him right now. Rosa signed the papers last week. I was going to get you a horse as a wedding present but I thought you might appreciate this more.'

The folder fell out of her hands, the contents spilling onto the mosaic floor. 'I...you...what did you say?'

'The adoption proceedings are going through. It does mean I will legally be Jack's father. As we are married it would have been too complicated to apply in just your name.' From a single, child-free businessman and winemaker to a married father of two and King in one step. From simple Monsieur Delacour to Sheikh Idris Dela-

cour Al Osman, ruler of all he surveyed. The thought wasn't as terrifying as it had been several months ago.

'But how? I don't understand.'

'Rosa has signed a deposition to say you had been Jack's primary caregiver for seven years and giving up her parental rights and we have statements from Jack's old school in London, his childminder and your neighbours. The lawyers don't anticipate any problems. They obviously need to interview you—and me as well. We'll all fly back to the UK in a month for the final interviews.'

It had all seemed so simple when he'd put this in motion. The first day he had spent with Jack, the day of Sami's birth, it had been painfully apparent that mixed in with the boy's worry about Saskia, excitement about the baby and the thrill of discovering the palace and his first riding lesson, Jack had also been harbouring deep fears that a baby of her own might alter his own special relationship with the only mother he had ever really known. For seven years it had been just the two of them—now Jack found himself in a family of four. And something in the boy had struck a chord. Idris knew what it was like to be a child and unsure of your place in the world, in your family, that fear that everything and everyone could just disappear.

If there was anything Idris excelled in it was solving problems and the solution here seemed so simple. They were already a made-up family. All they needed to do was cement Jack's place. But now, looking at Saskia's white face, he couldn't help but wonder if he had overstepped. He wasn't really Saskia's husband, Jack wasn't his brother and they weren't a family. They were a glossy PR exercise.

'I thought,' he said carefully, 'that this was the right

thing to do.' Legitimising Jack's presence in her life made things easier for him, for the crown, but it was also his way of making amends for forcing her into a life she had never asked for.

Her face crumpled. 'I... Oh, Idris, thank you.' She threw her arms around his neck, his shirt clinging damply as her tears began to flow. All he could do was put his arms around her and hold her while she wept. Hold her and try not to notice how good she smelt, like night-flowering jasmine, how her body melded into his as if it belonged there, the silkiness of her hair on his cheek. Try not to remember that this was the closest he had physically been to another human being for longer than he cared to remember. Tried not to remember how she used to feel in his arms, how he had once made her gasp. How she had made him feel invincible, an intoxication he had fought and lost against over and over. All he had to do was hold on.

CHAPTER EIGHT

TEARS WERE A PRIVATE, shameful indulgence. They had been ever since her father's death, since the moment she left Idris's apartment with nowhere else to turn.

But now she'd allowed that first tear to fall. Now someone else was holding her up. Now arms were around her, a strong shoulder supporting her. Now for the first time in many, many years someone else had taken part of her burden and it undid her.

Saskia shuddered as great, racking sobs forced their way out: grief for Maya and Fayaz, wistfulness for the life she had planned and would never now live, guilt at how much, how very much she loved Sami, a love she knew Maya would be grateful for and yet that some-how felt like a betrayal.

Fear for the long years ahead, Queen of a country she didn't know. Worry at being married to a man she barely knew and yet knew all too well. And now grati-tude. This man she'd thought didn't know her at all had realised the dearest wish of all. Jack was hers, always. Rosa didn't want him, wouldn't take him away. And the rest of his childhood would be safe and happy and filled with security.

She was barely aware of Idris's hand on her back, moving in slow, comforting circles, of his mouth

pressed into her hair telling her softly that it was okay, that it was all going to be okay. She was barely aware of the solid strength of him, of the way she fitted right into him, of his subtle sandalwood scent. Barely aware until, with a gulp, the sobs began to subside and then, then she was all too aware. Each circular caress burning hotter and hotter, the touch of his mouth branding her, every nerve firing up at the feel of his fingers. She tensed, regretting it immediately as his hand stopped its torturous caress, as he lifted his head away from hers, stepped away. The absence of his touch a physical ache.

'Feeling better?' His voice was low, hoarse. Had he felt it too? That connection? Or was he just being kind, desperate to grab his folders and escape his hysterical wife?

'No.' She wasn't sure what she was doing—although she was aware she was probably making a terrible mistake. But she also knew that she was desperately lonely. Had been for a long, long time and here in this palace, surrounded by people, in almost unimaginable luxury, with two beautiful, healthy children, she was lonelier than she had ever been before. She knew that she felt safer than she had for a long time while in his embrace. She knew that she craved human contact. Touch. Idris's touch.

She'd sworn she would never be vulnerable again. Not in front of Idris, not in front of any other human. Sworn she would never let him reject her again. But looking at the suppressed need in his dark eyes, she was certain that he wouldn't reject her. Certain that he craved her touch as much as she craved his.

'No? I'll call your maid. Maybe a massage and a nap will help.' He took a step away but Saskia caught his

hand as he turned, her fingers sliding into his so easily it was as if they were meant to be there.

'I don't want a massage. Or at least,' she amended, 'not from my maid.'

'You don't…' With primal satisfaction she noted his eyes flare as he took in her meaning. 'What *do* you want, then?'

'We're married, Idris. We have two children. You want me to accompany you on this grand tour, stand beside you at your Coronation.'

'Our Coronation,' he said huskily, his eyes fixed on hers.

She moved a little closer. 'Yes.'

'You didn't answer, Saskia. What do you want?'

'I want to remember what it's like being me. Who Saskia is. Not a mother, not a consort. I want to feel like a woman again.' She lifted her gaze to his, emboldened by the passion smouldering in his dark gaze. 'It's been a long time, Idris. Help me remember.'

He didn't answer straight away and Saskia held her breath. If he rejected her again…she kept her eyes fixed on his and saw the moment the flames burst into life, a bare second before his fingers tightened around hers. 'Are you sure?'

'Stop asking me stupid questions and kiss me already,' she retorted with a smile, but he didn't return the smile, just stared at her consideringly, an intense look in which she felt as if the clothes had already been stripped from her body and that she were laid bare before him.

'*Non*, not yet.'

Rejection slammed into her, hard and painful and all-consuming, but before she could turn away he had pulled her in close. 'I thought you wanted a massage.'

She froze, need pulling at her. Devouring from the inside out. 'I...'

Now he smiled, slow and triumphant. 'I asked you if you wanted a massage, Saskia, and you said—correct me if I get the words wrong—you said *not from my maid*. From which I deduce that you do want a massage. Am I right?'

Her mouth was so dry she could barely speak, her insides a quivering mass of want. She summoned every vestige of sass remaining. 'Are you offering?'

'Think you can handle it?'

'I'm sure I can handle a massage, Idris.' The gauntlet was well and truly thrown down and she quivered with anticipation as Idris drew a finger slowly down her cheek.

'Are you sure about that?' But he didn't give her time to answer; still holding her hand, he turned, leading her out of the courtyard and into her pretty bedroom, not hurrying, every step utterly precise. Saskia caught her breath as she caught sight of her bed, huge, perfectly made and suddenly looming larger than life. But Idris ignored the bed, leading her into her dressing room, a space bigger than the kitchen/diner/living space in her old apartment. Half the room was taken up with her dressing table and walk-in wardrobes, the other with a professional hairdresser's sink and chair—and the massage couch. She swallowed as she looked at the innocuous-looking platform, half covered with a white sheet.

Idris took one of the fresh, folded towels from the pile next to the table and carelessly laid it out over the sheet before turning back to her. 'Okay,' he said. 'Strip.'

Saskia folded her arms. 'Turn your back.'

His eyes gleamed. 'I don't think so.'

She hoped he didn't see her hands shaking as she

raised them to the first button on her dress. Slowly she undid it then stilled as she reached the second. She couldn't do this, couldn't undress in front of him, not while he stood waiting, watching.

'Changed your mind?' he asked softly.

Tilting her chin, she undid the second button. 'No.' Then the third, then the fourth. She wore a yellow silk maxi dress, which buttoned up the front from the waist to her throat, and as she reached the fifth button and the fabric fell away to reveal the silk of her bra, the flesh spilling out over the cups, desire washed over his face, Idris's eyes flaring. And then she understood, then she knew. She had all the control here. She kept her gaze on his as she slowly, deliberately unfastened the last buttons then shrugged the straps off her shoulders and let the dress crumple, falling in folds at her feet.

She stepped out of it, reaching behind her, not allowing her gaze to falter as she unhooked her bra and, clad only in her bikini pants, strolled slowly over to the table. She knew his gaze was fastened on her, knew his breath was coming faster as she straddled the table, slowly lowering onto it, her head cushioned on her arms, her back and legs bare to him, just the wisp of peach silk barely covering the curve of her bottom.

She had no idea how she managed to lie so still, so nonchalant, eyes closed. She heard footsteps as he crossed over to the shelf where her oils were kept, then the fragrance of her favourite jasmine, bergamot and rose blend wafted through the room. She swallowed, her insides quivering as his steps slowly but surely neared the table, the silence as he reached her side almost too much to bear. She waited for four or five excruciating, timeless seconds before he touched her, a light line drawn from her neck to the base of her spine and, de-

spite her best endeavours to stay cool, she shivered at his touch, His laugh was low and triumphant as she reacted. Another line tracing back along the first before his hands moved to her shoulders and he began to knead.

A massage was supposed to relax and unknot, but every inch he touched tensed up with need, her skin burning under his clever fingers. Saskia buried her head deeper in her arm to try and stifle the moans his touch elicited. He touched nowhere her masseuse wouldn't touch, his movements precise and measured; all her senses were concentrated on his every move until she knew she couldn't play this game any longer. She turned and sat up, winding her arms around his neck, pulling him in, pulling him close, hungry for his kiss, hungry for his touch, hungry for him. And with a guttural moan he obliged, picking her up, his mouth on hers and carrying her through to the bedroom. Saskia knew there were one hundred reasons why this was a bad idea, one hundred reasons why she needed to safeguard her heart; recklessly she pushed them all to one side because right here, right now, this was all that mattered. She needed to feel, she needed to not be alone, she needed to be wanted, to be noticed, and under his mouth and hands she finally came alive.

Idris disembarked from the helicopter, scanning the desert until he saw Saskia standing under a canvas shelter on one side of the palm-tree-fringed, sandy landing strip. It was as if they were in the middle of nowhere.

It was noticeably hotter out here. Although Jayah was twenty miles inland it was built on either side of the wide tidal River Kizaj and so, although it didn't benefit from the sea breezes that kept much of the coast

at a bearable temperature, it was usually manageable except during the very height of summer. The heat in the desert was more oppressive, a visible shimmering wall, and Idris was glad he had opted for the coolness of traditional robes, a headdress protecting his head and eyes from the sun's glare. Saskia was also traditionally dressed in long, loose gold trousers in a light fabric, over which she wore a long-sleeved cream and gold tunic, a matching scarf wrapped around her head. Her maid stood by, a bag filled with water, moist towels and suncream at her feet. While preparing for the trip there had been some concern over Saskia's fitness to cope in the desert, her red hair and pale skin designed for the cold, sun-starved, northern European climate, not the relentless sun. But she would have to endure if she was to be accepted.

She didn't ask for this, his conscience whispered, but he pushed it to one side. Neither of them had asked for it but here they were. They had to deal as best they could.

He moved to her side and their guards and attendants fell in behind them as, on cue, a group of people on horseback emerged from behind the trees and dismounted. A middle-aged man in bright robes strode towards them and bowed his head. The nomads were a proud people who traditionally recognised neither borders nor rulers, although pragmatically accepted the Dalmaya's sovereign rule. Idris and Saskia nodded in response, a polite acceptance of his role as leader of his tribe.

'*Mahajan*, Your Highness Sheikh Idris Delacour Al Osman, Princess Saskia,' he said.

Idris knew the tribal leader had studied in France and England and spoke both languages perfectly. '*Salam*,

Badr Al Bedi. Thank you and your people for offering us your hospitality,' he replied.

'Come, we have horses for you. Let us ride and talk as we go. We have much to discuss.'

'It is an honour to be asked to ride your fine horses. The mounts of the Al Bedis are coveted across the world,' Saskia said, and by the beaming smile she received in response Idris knew she couldn't have said anything better.

Two hours later he was even more impressed. Saskia had obviously read all the briefing documents and managed to keep up in the general conversation. Old topics such as grazing rights, territorial disputes and minority rights were touched on and Saskia showed that she was aware of the history and disputes, with a knack of acknowledging the issues and then deftly turning the conversation to something less contentious. She would have made a good lawyer.

The Al Bedi weren't continuously on the move, often making camp for weeks or even months at a time while smaller trading parties journeyed to the bigger cities and coasts, especially during the hotter summer months. Badr Al Bedi explained that they would spend the first day riding to the large summer camp, where his own family had sheltered during the summer. Now they had reached the last days of September the camp would soon be dispersing, the feast tonight the last in that particular spot.

Tomorrow Idris and Saskia would accompany a trading party who were taking a group of horses to the nearest town. The town was two days' ride away from the camp and Idris, Saskia and their entourage would be picked up from there. The first stage of their Royal Tour would be completed.

'It's a good thing,' Idris said quietly to Saskia, 'that you're not vegetarian. We're being honoured with lamb tonight. It's a dish always served to honoured guests.'

They were just arriving at an oasis for a rest stop and water. Saskia and Idris were slightly ahead of the group, their host falling behind to check on some detail, their entourage and most of their personal guard trailing behind, although Idris knew several guards had ridden ahead and to the side of the main group. He might not be able to see them but they would have a very clear idea of where he was while keeping an eye out for any possible threat.

Saskia laughed at his words. 'Actually I did eat a mainly vegetarian diet for most of the last few years, though that was mainly for financial reasons, but that very thorough surrogate agreement was very clear that I needed to be a carnivore until Sami was weaned. I don't miss meat when I don't eat it, but I'm not going to turn down a feast cooked in my honour either.'

'I hope you feel the same way when they present you with the yogurt. It's very much an acquired taste. Of course, you can sweeten it with honey but a true warrior takes his—or her—yogurt straight.'

'I'm sure I can…oh!' Saskia broke off in alarm as her horse danced backwards. Luckily her grip hadn't been too loose on the reins and she managed, somehow, to keep her seat as the beast neighed and then reared, its front legs kicking out. 'Whoa, come on, boy.'

But Idris's own horse had also taken a step backwards and he could see quite clearly what had spooked Saskia's mount. A viper of some type must have been dozing in the shadow of the tree and been disturbed by the horse's footsteps. It was half coiled, half upright, swaying from side to side, fangs clearly exposed. Idris

couldn't tell who was more scared, the snake or the horse—or who was likely to do most damage.

'Whoa!' The horse reared again and Saskia fought to stay on. Idris's heart thumped, adrenaline running through his veins as he assessed the risks. If the viper bit the horse Saskia might fall; if she managed to dismount safely then she would be directly in front of the angry snake. Could he manoeuvre his horse over and take the reins safely or would he just spook his own horse and make matters worse? He looked behind. They were further ahead than he had realised and although several horses were galloping towards them there was a real possibility they wouldn't reach the group in time.

Saskia was still hanging on, her lips white and her face pale but determined as she battled the terrified horse, the snake hissing louder, pulling itself up further, weaving closer and closer. Idris pulled his own pistol from its holster; the pistol he had baulked at wearing when it had been issued to him, and pointed it at the snake, his hand steady despite his thundering pulse. If he missed the even more terrified snake would strike. If he killed the snake then possibly both his mount and Saskia's would bolt. He checked again. It would be at least thirty seconds before the head horseman reached them and the snake was swaying in...

'Idris. Do it. I have this.' Her voice was low and tense, her grip hardening on the already panicked horse's reins.

He inhaled, concentrated—and shot. Time slowed down to an unbearable lassitude, the sound of the pistol reverberating around and around and all he could do was take his own mount in a firm hand and wait and hope and pray... The snake buckled then collapsed and

Saskia's horse, maddened beyond any control, took off, Saskia clinging grimly on.

He swore and dug his heels in, urging his own horse after her, Badr Al Bedi and several of the palace guards close behind him as they chased the terrified mount across the sands. Saskia was hunkered down low, obviously concentrating on staying on rather than trying to check her horse. 'Just hold on,' Idris muttered as he urged his horse on. 'Hold tight.'

What if something happened to her? How would he tell Jack? How would he raise Sami, made motherless twice before he was even able to speak? How would he be able to raise two boys and govern this harsh, beautiful country on his own? He might not have chosen Saskia but she was his partner now—in every way—and he didn't want to take this journey alone.

His blood thundered as her horse increased his pace. She'd only just come back into his life. He wasn't ready to lose her again. Not yet.

She was close, so close, any moment now he might be able to grab the reins and help slow her horse. But at that moment her horse tripped, twisted and, with a sickening yell that froze his blood, Saskia fell, rolled and lay crumpled in the sand.

CHAPTER NINE

'I FEEL LIKE a prize idiot.' Saskia stared down at her strapped ankle and winced. If pride came before a fall then humility was the result of one—humility along with a sprained ankle and many bruises. 'And I've ruined the whole visit. Badr is embarrassed and I can't go to the feast and...'

Idris held up a hand and Saskia stuttered to a stop, both surprised by his high-handed manner and more than a little indignant.

'You have ruined nothing. In fact, right now, several ballads are being composed about the flame-haired Queen who rides like a warrior...'

'...and who falls like a fool.' Now the adrenaline had faded away the realisation of how close she had been to something much worse than a sprained ankle and bruises shivered at the edge of her consciousness. Much better to concentrate on embarrassment than near death.

Luckily she hadn't been unconscious for long. She'd come to blearily to find herself cradled in a pair of strong arms. Cradled by Idris. Had blinked to see the fear on his face, fear that had quickly drained away, replaced by the same calm, shuttered look he habitually wore—unless he was with the boys. Or unless they were in bed.

'I didn't think self-pity was one of the signs of con-cussion.' Idris held up his phone so she could see the medical website he was referring to. 'But if it is we need a helicopter out here immediately. You are obviously in a bad way. I think we should get one anyway,' he said for the tenth time in the last hour.

'I'm fine. Honestly. My shoulder and leg got most of the impact. Thank goodness I remembered all my pony club training and insisted on wearing a riding hat. I know you thought I was in more danger of heat stroke than I was of falling off but this way I got to suf-fer two in one.' The hat had been almost suffocating and only pride—and a childhood in which the impor-tance of wearing a riding helmet had been drilled into her—had kept it on her head. Thank goodness she had; although there was a definite tender spot on her scalp she was sure that she had got away without any serious injury. 'Idris. It's bad enough I had to ride to the camp behind you on your horse like a child. Bad enough that I've been told to eat soup and have an early night and miss everything that was organised in our honour. If I get helicoptered out of here, two days early, then people are going to think I can't hack the desert life here. That I'm not fit for this role.'

'No one who saw you handle that horse would ever say you weren't fit. The Al Badi would love to claim you as one of them. The first thing we need to do when we get back is get you a mount of your own. You are far too good a horsewoman to go without.'

Well, they did always say to get right back on a horse. As a girl she'd been fearless, the higher the jump, the wider the ditch, the better, never thinking anything of heading straight into the stable no matter the horse's temperament. Today she realised just how mortal she

really was. The thought of getting back into the saddle—
of allowing Jack to have another riding lesson—made
her chest swell with panic and her stomach drop, fear
breaking out like perspiration. But horse racing and
horse breeding were national passions—and a signifi-
cant part of the Dalmayan economy—and if she was to
have a role and a life here then one fall couldn't stop her.

She stretched out and winced again. Idris and she
had been housed in a beautiful white canvas tent, held
up by two poles, the inside draped in gorgeous orange
and red silk matched by the intricately woven rugs that
covered the floor and the cushions heaped on the low
couches and the wide bed. Intricately carved tables
housed lanterns; jugs of chilled water and bowls of fruit
were dotted around the interior. It was all very invit-
ing and usually she would have been utterly charmed.
As they had ridden in she had noticed that the tents
all ringed a large central square, covered over with a
huge canopy, a fire pit prepared in the middle and sur-
rounded by seats. All set up for the feast and festivi-
ties. The spicy smells emanating from the cooking tents
made her mouth water and her stomach rumble and the
thought of bland soup failed to lift her spirits.

'Idris, I don't need you here keeping an eye on me.
Go out and enjoy the lamb and the songs and the fire.
It's not like I'm far away. It seems a shame that they
went to such an effort and for one of us not to attend.
And you said yourself that things have been tense be-
tween the crown and the Al Bedi for many years, since
your grandfather's reforms. This is a good chance for
you to start off in a more positive way. I'll be fine. I have
soup coming, after all.' She tried to smile and, after a
searching look at her, Idris nodded.

'You're right. I know Badr takes this whole accident

personally. It would be good to show him that we are
not holding him to blame.'

'It's not like he planted the snake there.' She managed
not to shudder when she said the word. Saskia hadn't
ever had any phobias before but she was pretty sure she
was going to see that particular snake in her nightmares.

'No, but the horse should have been better trained.'
Idris sounded grim and she looked up.

'That was pure instinct, Idris. He was a perfect gent
up to that part. In fact…' She swallowed. Along with
snakes she would be quite happy never to see that par-
ticular grey stallion again. But this wasn't about her. It
was about diplomacy, about a proud man, about a coun-
try. 'I would like him. As my own.'

Idris stared at her incredulously. 'Are you insane?'

Possibly. 'He was on his way to market so let's buy
him. Just think how proud Badr, how proud the whole
tribe will be if they see him on TV or in a magazine.
Knowing he's in the royal stables. My first real contact
with Dalmaya.'

'They'll never let you buy him. They'll insist he's
a present.'

'If they do, then we'll accept.'

Idris stood, obviously torn between accepting that
she made sense and an understandable desire not to
allow any of the family near the horse again before
agreeing with a curt nod. 'I'll talk to Badr. But tomor-
row you ride pillion behind me again. No arguing or I
will definitely call a helicopter.' And with that he was
gone.

The evening passed slowly. Saskia's head throbbed,
her ankle ached and every bruise was making its pres-
ence felt in its own unique way. The soup had been de-
licious although she really hadn't been hungry at all

once she started to eat but, under the solicitous gaze of the local healer, she managed to finish the bowl and eat some of the flatbread as well. The sounds of laughter and music drifted into the tent and, lulled by the sound, she drifted into sleep.

The sound of the tent unfastening woke her and she looked up to see Idris undressing by the light of the lantern. The shadows played on his back, highlighting his slim muscles, the dips and hollows in his back, and she swallowed. He was so ridiculously attractive. How could she keep her heart safe when his nearness made her tremble, her name on his lips made her ache? When just the sight of him half naked and unaware made her forget every bruise?

She shifted and he turned, his eyes black pools in the darkness. '*Pardon*, Saskia. I didn't mean to wake you.'

'You didn't. I wake every time I turn over.'

'I think it's best that I sleep over here.' He gestured to one of the low couches and Saskia felt that old ache of rejection spread out from her chest, chilling her bones. He was willing to have sex with her but sleeping together was an intimacy too far. In the palace it kind of made sense for him to return to his own room. Maybe. But out here?

'It's very narrow,' she pointed out, trying to sound non-committal, as if she really didn't care one way or the other. Of course she shouldn't care... 'If you fall off and hurt yourself we'll both be riding pillion. It's not going to be very kingly when you show up at the trading post tucked up behind Badr, is it?'

He scowled. 'I don't want to hurt you.'

'Idris, this bed is big enough for four. But we can put a pillow down the middle if you would feel safer,' she added sweetly, and the scowl intensified as he stalked

towards the bed and climbed in. Saskia held her breath. She often shared a bed with Jack, at least she had done before getting pregnant, but she hadn't slept beside another adult—beside a man—since Idris all those years ago. Here they were again.

'You're sure I'm not hurting you?'

'There's at least a metre of space between us,' she said. 'You may be overestimating your masculine powers.'

To her surprise he chuckled, low and deep. 'It's a good thing you're injured or I'd make you regret that.'

Could it be her husband was actually flirting with her? Flirting knowing that there was no way they would be having sex as a result? *Probably* no way they would be having sex. She flexed her ankle and only just managed not to yelp as a jolt of agony ran through her. No, make that definitely no way. 'Promises, promises.'

Saskia turned on her side and faced away from Idris but the drowsiness had ebbed. She was all too achingly aware of him despite the space between them; the slope in the mattress, the sound of his even breath, the scent of him. She swallowed, want racing through her hot and sudden, the throbbing of her bruises replaced by the steady thrum of her heart, the ache in her breasts, the pull deep at the base of her stomach. It was just good old lust, a biological imperative, she knew that. She'd been without a mate too long and now she had started sleeping with Idris her body was urging her on. Evolutionary science at its most basic. But thinking scientific thoughts wasn't calming her hormones; they were continuing to jump around like excited cheerleaders urging her to cuddle in closer, urging her to 'go on, reach out and touch him…' She turned over, lifting a hand then

dropping it. It was late. She was supposed to be staying quiet and getting some rest.

With a huff she turned back over, wincing as she landed on a bruise, and grabbed the thin pillow, punching it to try and get some more support.

'Trouble sleeping?' Idris drawled, sounding like a man who had never suffered a restless night in his life.

'No,' she lied. 'I'm fine. It's just…' She paused. She didn't want to sound like a whiny girl and admit every bruise was making itself felt and her ankle was tight and seemed to be three times its usual size. 'I'm a soft European who needs something more than a thin bolster for a pillow,' she said instead. 'It's hard to get comfortable.'

There was a long pause and all she could hear was the frantic thump of her heart until: 'Come here, then,' and she heard the unmistakable sounds of Idris shifting across to the middle of the bed. She scooted back a few inches until she collided with the solid wall of his body, heat instantly enveloping her, a heady mixture of body warmth and those pesky hormones brightening even more at the realisation he was bare-chested. A strong, bare arm slipped around her neck, another across her stomach. 'Better?'

'Uh-huh,' she said unconvincingly even to herself.

That laugh again, low and rumbling right through her until every atom quivered. 'Still not comfortable?'

'Well…' But whatever she was about to say was lost as Idris swept aside the fall of her hair and pressed one kiss to the back of her neck.

'Does this help?'

'Maybe a little…'

'Then maybe this…' another kiss, just below her ear '…will help a little more.'

'Mmm, just a little bit.'

'And here?' This time the hollow between her neck and shoulder. She shivered and felt his amusement reverberating through her. Amusement tinged with something more dangerous. 'Of course, you are an invalid. Tell me if it gets too much.'

'I think I can cope with a little more.' Saskia arched against him as his mouth found the delicate skin behind her ear, his breath sweet and warm and, oh, so tantalising. 'In fact this is definitely making me feel better...'

'In that case...' his hand slid up her waist to graze the tender swell of her breast '...I think it's best that I carry on, don't you?'

Saskia was awake again and, judging by the jerkiness of her movements, in some discomfort. Should he have overridden her wishes and called a helicopter to whisk her back to Jayah? The moment Idris had seen her crumpled and still in the sand, that damn horse racing away from her... His pulse escalated at the too-recent memory, at the fear that had taken over as he had raced towards her. Understandable fear: he had just lost his cousin; he was responsible for Saskia's presence in the desert, for her safety; she had two children dependent on her...but there had been something else behind that mad dash, a thought he hadn't been able to banish.

I've just found you again.

Which was ridiculous. He had never lost her in the first place; he had chosen to exclude her from his life.

He sighed. It didn't matter how much he justified his actions back then. It didn't matter that he had made the right decision at the wrong time and in the wrong way, he was still shamed whenever he thought about that last night in Oxford. It said a lot, a hell of a lot, about Saskia that she didn't hold it against him, that she was willing

to be not just a trophy wife in a loveless marriage but a partner, that she didn't want to spend her life shopping and living a privileged expat dream but wanted to find a role that stretched her and gave back to the country she now lived in.

She shifted again, this time letting out a small, hastily smothered cry and Idris was out of the bed in one stride, heading over to the water jug to bring a glass over to her. He moved back to the bed, sitting by her side, helping her sit up. The tent was dim in the pre-dawn grey but he could see that her sweat-soaked hair was pressed to her scalp, that her eyes were huge and fatigued with pain.

'Here.' He passed her the glass and she accepted it with a wan smile of thanks. Idris touched a hand to her cheek and was relieved to find it cool. At least she had no fever.

'I really think...'

'No, no helicopter.' She drank again and passed the glass back to him, lowering herself against the thin bolster with a grunt. 'I just don't want to slow the caravan down too much.'

'Don't worry about that. Can I get you anything else?'

'That glass, next to the fruit bowl. It's got some kind of natural painkiller in.'

He reached out and scooped it up, nose wrinkling as he sniffed the cloudy liquid. 'Are you sure this is safe?'

'Alya, the healer here, is a qualified nurse as well as a traditional healer. It's fine. Disgusting but works miracles. Not that I enquired too closely what was in it.' She downed the contents of the glass and pulled a face. 'Ugh. Anything that tastes that nasty has to be good for me, surely.'

He half smiled, watching her as she drank. 'As predicted Badr insists on gifting you the horse, although I want it put through its paces by the best trainers at the stables before you go anywhere near it again. We can't run the risk of it throwing you again.'

'There's always a risk, Idris. Horses, cars—we know that more than anyone.' She was silent for a moment and he thought she was falling back asleep but then she turned to face him, eyes still too wide, too shadowed but her face more relaxed, the drawn expression of pain softened. 'You know, the nearest clinic is a day's ride away. Alya works between there, here and another clinic three days' ride in the other direction.'

'Hmm?'

'That's where the schools are too. She says the children do a lot of learning remotely when they're between schools and she diagnoses a lot through video calling. It's odd, isn't it? No cars and living in tents but everyone has a smartphone.'

'It's the way of the world.' Where was she going with this? It didn't sound like idle conversation. There was a spark in Saskia's eyes he hadn't seen for a long time.

'She's the only qualified midwife as well. She says most of the women give birth in special tents, attended by traditionally taught women. Mortality rates are higher than in the cities because there's no way to get them to hospital when things go wrong. Alya lost her own baby just a year ago, a miscarriage that might have been prevented if she'd got to a hospital in time...'

'It's a tragedy, I admit, but this is a nomadic tribe. Clinging onto tradition means tragedies happen. It's the price they choose to pay. Dalmaya is a big country and there are huge swathes where there is very little approaching civilisation—or at least the trappings of it.'

'That was pretty much Alya's answer. That these things happen. But if I had concussion or had broken my leg then we wouldn't have left that to fate, would we? You wanted to call a helicopter in for a sprained ankle and a few bruises!'

'I still want to call a helicopter to make sure that's all that it is.'

'If there's a helicopter for me then why not for Alya and her patients? To get people to clinic in minutes, not days, to hospital if the clinic can't manage, to transport her and the one other nurse out to patients?'

Idris couldn't answer. Money? Dalmaya was a rich country. 'Tradition, I suppose.'

'Tradition stated that girls stayed at home and didn't go to school, let alone university—and your grandfather's edicts may have worked in the cities but not out here in the desert. Luckily Alya's father indulged her and allowed her to study and now, thanks to the Internet, all Al Bedi girls are educated and any that wish to study further have the freedom to go on to college. True, most prefer to stay at home but at least they have that choice. Technology helps girls get to school. Why can't it help with medical emergencies? Beyond a video-call diagnosis, I mean. The Al Bedis contribute a lot to Dalmayan culture—the horses, the tourist camps. We should give something back. Something of value. Lifesaving medical help shouldn't be restricted to princesses by marriage.'

Slowly Idris got to his feet, looking around at the tent, now illuminated in the pinks and reds of a desert sunrise. It all looked so traditional but the bed easily pulled apart for transportation. The glasses were made in China and bought from a Swedish furniture store. The Al Bedi might seem unchanging but they knew

how to incorporate what they needed from the modern world to keep their traditional life viable. Allow their girls to study and bring their expertise back to the tribe, welcome tourists and by doing so safeguard their freedoms and their lands.

His grandfather, educated at Oxford and the Sorbonne, had been full of reformist zeal. He had taken the oil money and invested it, not into a lavish lifestyle for a few, but into a new Dalmaya. Invested it into schools and hospitals and opportunities for all who wanted to take advantage of it. But like all reformists he had been iron-willed and impatient of those who didn't see his vision—and the Al Bedi had not been the only ones who had rejected his Western influences to modernise at a slower pace. Fayaz had been King for too short a time to break the coldness between the throne and the nomads. Could this idea, a flying medical service, be the thing to bring them properly onside? Badr too was new to leadership and far more conciliatory than his father had been…

And Saskia had complained of being bored. This idea of hers could solve two problems before they were even formally crowned.

He turned and looked at her, still obviously sore but lit up with enthusiasm. 'How do you know all this? About the healer…'

'Alya.'

'She was with you for what, an hour? Working for most of that. And yet you seem to know her life history!' It would usually take Idris months if not years to work up to that level of personal detail. 'And it isn't just Alya. You were incredibly well prepared when you were introduced to Badr, not just about the right way

to be introduced, but you asked all the right questions, had him charmed within an hour.'

'I read the briefing documents,' she said then smiled. 'Look, I admit that when you knew me before I may have come across as a little self-absorbed.' He raised an eyebrow and she coloured but carried on. 'Of course I was. I was an only child, doted upon by a dad who gave me everything I wanted before I knew I wanted it, raised to think I was the most fascinating, desirable, interesting person in the world.'

It should have made her unbearable, yet that confidence, that utter sureness in herself had been self-fulfilling. Everyone had wanted to know her, the girls had wanted to be her friend, the boys had all wanted to sleep with her.

'It was a shock when I started temping. No one cares about a temp. They want you to be up to speed straight away and to blend in. That's it. I blundered around my first few jobs acting—thinking—like photocopying was below me—even though I had no idea how to use the machine—that I was too good to make coffee and people should be falling over themselves to help me. A few bruising encounters showed me how wrong I was. And I soon realised that to get the good jobs, I had to be the best. Be prepared, do my homework, cause as few problems as possible and solve as many as possible. Be so indispensable they want you back.'

'So that's what you did.' It wasn't a question.

'It wasn't easy but yes, I learned what the most important things were: security codes, how to work the printer, where the kettle was, how the switchboard worked. How to retain that information. How to ask the right questions. How to fit in. Turns out temp skills are very transferrable for being Crown Princess, for being

Queen.' She laughed a little self-consciously but she was right. She'd walked into this hostile tribe a stranger and a foreigner and would ride out a valued friend and ally because she'd taken the time to ask the right questions, and, more importantly, to care about the answer. Something he should have learned in all his business dealing. Maybe he had where stock and figures were concerned but not with people.

'But you wanted to change careers?'

'Well, yes. Temping was fun but turns out it was temporary.' Her smile made it clear the pun was purposeful. 'I wanted a new challenge, to be able to put down some roots. But I liked problem solving, helping. I thought I could do that as a lawyer.'

'You can do that here,' he said, aware how brusque he sounded. 'Look into an air ambulance. Look into costings and potential problems as well as benefits and write me a report—or commission one. Then we'll talk and, if it adds up the way you want it to, then I'll talk to the Council. Or you can...'

The somewhat self-deprecating smile broadened until it shone from her eyes. 'Really? I can do that? Thank you. That's amazing. Thank you, Idris.' She made to rise but fell back with an 'Oof!' as her ankle hit the floor and he stepped back, shy of her thanks.

'I'll get your maid.' He grabbed his robe and hastily threw it on, backing out of the tent before she could say another word. He didn't want or need her gratitude, not for merely giving her a purpose and not when his plan suited him just as well as it suited her. Nor did he want to dwell on how it had felt to sleep with her nestled in close, her hair soft on his chin, her body warm and yielding against his. And he definitely didn't want to think about the day ahead, Saskia sitting before him

on a horse all day long, every jolt pushing their bodies together. It was going to be a very long, very hot journey and he was going to need every bit of self-control he could muster.

CHAPTER TEN

'HAPPY BIRTHDAY!'

Saskia blearily opened one eye to see a card and present practically touching her nose and, right behind the garishly wrapped gift, Jack beaming down at her.

'Morning, tiger,' she croaked, a quick glance at her watch confirming that, yes, it wasn't yet six a.m. 'Is that for me?'

'Let Saskia have her coffee first,' Idris interjected. Saskia refocussed to see him standing behind Jack, Sami in his arms. She smiled a weary thanks at him; she had only started drinking coffee again a few weeks ago but was already as addicted to her favourite wake-me-up as she had ever been.

As she struggled to a sitting position her maid put a tray on the bedside table; figs and freshly cut oranges, little cinnamon-dusted pastries and a pot of steaming coffee making an aromatic and visually appealing feast. Saskia took a fresh-smelling Sami from Idris as he poured her coffee, adding exactly the right amount of milk to it. He was already dressed, but this was the first time she had seen him upon awakening since their night in the desert. Even on the occasions when they shared a room on one of their tours he awoke, dressed and left before she stirred and although he now came

to her most nights in the palace he was gone before she awoke.

She understood it, his need to separate the intimacy of sex from the intimacy of sharing a bed, but her heart still ached when she woke in an empty bed—or when she tried to fall asleep, all too aware of the empty space beside her, his scent still permeating the pillows.

'Open it, open it.' Jack thrust his present at her and, laughing at his eager face, she accepted it.

'Okay, okay.' Slowly, more to tease Jack than out of patience, she slid her finger underneath the sticky tape, her mouth opening as the paper unfolded to reveal a slim A4 book, the front cover a posed portrait of Jack and Sami. She took a deep breath as she opened it, discovering pages full of photos of both boys, some posed, many candid shots—including plenty of Jack as a toddler and small boy, several of her posing for selfies with him. 'What? How did you get these?' She glanced at Idris in shock. Most of the photos existed only on her laptop or on her email account.

'Jack knows your password. We only looked for the albums with him in there,' Idris added hurriedly.

'There are no other albums.' She mock glared at Jack. 'A hacker eh? I need to change my password. But this is lovely, so thoughtful. Thank you.' She swallowed, aware of the lump in her throat, the burning at the backs of her eyes as she flicked through page after page, memories unfurling as she looked back at the last seven years of the life she had shared with her brother. She glanced towards Idris, trying to convey her thanks. He must have thought of this gesture, noticed she only had one framed picture of Jack on her bedside table and that was years old.

'This is from Sami.' Jack held another gift towards her. 'I helped him choose it.'

'It looks intriguing.' Saskia took the bulky, heavy present with raised eyebrows, squealing as she opened it to see her favourite chocolates, wrapped cheese, oatcakes, a packet of scones with a pot of jam and her usual brand of tea. The food in Dalmaya was fantastic but occasionally she yearned for a Wensleydale and pickle sandwich, a chocolate bar or a cup of Earl Grey tea. 'Amazing. What a clever baby.' She kissed Sami and then Jack. 'And isn't he lucky to have such a helpful big brother?'

She reached a hand out towards Idris, who had awkwardly curled his tall frame into the small nursing chair next to her bed. He had to have organised these presents, had heard her occasional wish for a 'plain cup of English tea' or her laughing promise to Jack that when they next visited London she was going to eat scones until she burst. Their eyes connected and Saskia ached with wishing that this was real, that they really were a family bound by love and the bonds of affection, not by duty and an attraction born from nostalgia.

Her eyes roamed over the familiar face, pausing at the hollows in the lean cheeks, the early-morning stubble grazing his chin, the curve of his proud mouth, the fall of the dark hair, her mouth drying out as she drank him in. Her commitment to Jack had made it near impossible to date but the truth was that although, thanks to her temping jobs, she had met plenty of men, had had plenty of invitations, she had never been tempted to accept. Idris was nothing but temptation and like Eve she fell, night after night.

'This is from me.' His voice was gruff as he handed

over a small box and Saskia's eyebrows rose in surprise as she took it.

'You didn't have to.'

'I believe…' a teasing note entered his voice '…that the correct response is thank you.'

'Thank you.' She repeated it as she bent her head to examine the small box, her heart thumping harder than ever. Her fingers felt too big, refusing to work as she carefully opened the present, folding the paper neatly and putting it to one side, aware she was delaying opening the box.

It was probably a duty gift. She had been given plenty of jewellery over the last few months, Dalmayan custom dictating that a woman's worth, a family's wealth should be reflected in the jewels she wore. Glittering ropes of emeralds and sapphires and amethysts, jingling bangles of gem-studded platinum and rose gold, elaborate headdresses and tiaras, heavy rings—she wore them on formal occasions, for feasts and celebrations and some meetings. They helped transform her from plain Saskia Harper, hard-working temp, to Sheikha Saskia DelacourAl Osman, soon to be crowned Queen of Dalmaya. She fumbled with the catch, finally opening the box. 'Oh!' A slender charm bracelet sat inside, two tiny charms already attached. Jack leaned over, pointing to one. 'That's my hand print, all shrunken down and made into gold, and that's Sami's. Do you like it?'

'Like it? I love it.' She could hardly get the words out for the lump in her throat. A year and a bit ago she would never have believed this possible. That she could be lying in such luxurious surroundings, a warm, contented baby in her arms, a healthy thriving Jack by her side and married to a man who surely must care about

her even if he didn't love her. She should be happy. It was greedy to wish for more.

Saskia lifted out the bracelet and studied each tiny charm, knowledge racing through her. She didn't just wish for more, she craved it, just as she had long ago. She had craved Idris Delacour's love then and she craved it now, and, despite everything, part of her had never stopped loving him.

'Jack tells me you have a long-standing birthday tradition.' Idris's elegantly French-accented rumble broke into her thoughts and she started, sure her wishes must be written all over her face.

'Tradition? Yes.' She smiled at her small brother. 'We always spend the morning at the V&A because it's my favourite museum and then we have a picnic in Kensington Gardens, right by the fountain.'

'With bought food not a pack up,' Jack added. 'And lots of cake.'

For the first couple of years after she took Jack in Saskia hadn't celebrated her birthday. It was too much of a reminder of what she had lost. Before every birthday had been an event, a celebration orchestrated by her father. But as Jack got older he insisted they do something special and so the tradition had been born. Her favourite museum and then a little celebratory autumn picnic.

Later, as they put down tiny roots in their neighbourhood, there had been other celebrations, a glass of wine with their neighbours, dinner at Jack's friend's house, but the birthday picnic remained a staple and Saskia loved it, never wishing that she could replace it with the lavish parties her father had always thrown for her.

'I can't manage the V&A but how do you fancy a night at the villa and a picnic on the beach instead?'

Idris suggested and Saskia almost sagged against her pillows with relief at the idea. The autumn was a particularly hot one this year and even the well-ventilated marble halls of the palace felt oppressive at times. The very thought of being back by the sea, in a place where the staff were more like friends, where she felt at home, not like a pampered guest, was the most perfect gift of all.

'Don't we have a Council meeting today?'

'I'm sure you can be excused under the circumstances. I'll make your apologies.'

'Oh. Right, thank you.' Disappointment flooded through her at his calm, almost dismissive words. Of course she didn't need to be at the meeting; of course he didn't want to come to the picnic. He was making all the right gestures but that was all they were, right? And she was a fool for wanting more, for hoping for more.

'You're not coming?' Jack looked up, the disappointment on his face a mirror to that which Saskia was trying so hard not to show. 'But, Idris, you promised me a horse-riding lesson on the beach. And you said we'd play cricket. Please come, it won't be the same without you.'

The sun had begun to redden when the nanny retrieved the two tired, sandy boys to take them back to the villa for baths and bed, Jack well and truly exhausted by a day of horse riding, cricket and swimming. Saskia turned and watched the small group climb the steps to the villa, her face soft with love. 'What a fantastic day he's had. Thank you, Idris.'

'You don't need to thank me. Besides, it's your birthday. Have you had a good day?' Idris hadn't intended to accompany the family to the villa. He had so much

work to do, so many meetings to attend, a day and a night off seemed unachievable. Turned out he couldn't say no to a pair of beseeching brown eyes and a small boy's flattery—nor had he escaped the flitting wistfulness on Saskia's face when he said he'd stay behind. They didn't want anything more from him than his company. It was a refreshing change in a world where his grace and favour was sought at every turn.

'A lovely day, thanks. I would have liked to have ridden but my ankle is still a little weak. Blissful to swim in the sea though. I stuck to the safety of the pool when I was pregnant but there's nothing like the wildness of salt water.' Saskia looked a little like a wild water creature herself, the red hair still damp, pinned back off her face, a turquoise sarong knotted around her waist.

'As good as the V&A?'

'Well, I do hate to miss out on my annual pretend-I'm-in-a-costume-drama trip. I only just made it last year—we moved out here just a couple of weeks later. I was a few weeks pregnant at the time, already feeling tired and queasy, so the picnic wasn't quite the treat it usually was and even the regency costumes couldn't distract me!'

Idris led her over to the picnic area, just below the villa. A gazebo had been erected to protect Saskia and Sami from the sun, colourful woven blankets and cushions laid out on the fine white sand and several of the villa's loungers brought down to the beach. Now the light was beginning to fade torches were lit and the fairy lights strewn around the gazebo's edge sprang into life. The housekeeper and houseboy were busy setting dishes out on the long low wooden table and aromatic aromas filled the evening air.

'*Shokran.*' Idris nodded at the beaming pair. 'We'll serve ourselves.'

'I didn't expect you to stay for dinner.' Saskia seated herself on a lounger, peering over as Idris lifted the heavy silver lids to reveal a slow-cooked lamb stew, couscous, bursting with vegetables and plump raisins and spices, flatbreads, round falafel and a platter filled with figs, peaches, grapes and melon. 'Goodness, the kitchen have done us proud. I hope they don't expect us to eat it all. I've only just digested lunch! Do you have time to help eat enough so the cook isn't offended before you head back?'

'I thought I might spend the evening here. It doesn't seem worth going back to the palace when I promised Jack more cricket tomorrow.'

Saskia stilled, her eyes fixed on him. Idris didn't meet her steady gaze, busying himself with filling her plate. She knew as well as he did that it would take him only an hour to return to the palace, that he could be back before Jack had even noticed his absence.

Idris had never stayed at the villa before. It was Saskia's territory. He had no rooms here, nowhere to run, nowhere to hide. His pulse began to beat hard and fast as he handed her the plate and poured a glass of the rich red wine, imported from his own estates. 'If that's okay,' he added, setting the wine down beside her.

'Of course, we're married, you don't need to ask my permission.' She picked up the wine, lying back against the padded back of her lounger with a contented sigh. 'When I first came here I couldn't believe it, that this view, this beauty, was to be mine for a whole year. I'm glad you kept it on. The palace is beautiful, but it doesn't feel like home, not like this place does.'

Idris poured himself a glass. 'I'm glad that you have a place in Dalmaya where you feel like home.'

'Do you have somewhere too?' Her gaze was far too penetrating. 'In the shock of all these changes it's easy to forget that this life is almost as new to you as it is for me. Do you feel at home?'

'Sometimes.' He paused, weighing his words carefully. 'Not in a place, not yet. When I take Jack riding or sailing or Sami for a walk. When we're in Council and the leaders stop bickering and listen to my suggestions. When I see the solution to a problem.' When he was holding Saskia, his mouth on hers, her body wound round his. Then he felt at home—and yet also like a trespasser, on ground he had no right to occupy.

'You miss France?'

'Not so much France as the vineyard, the chateau.' He stopped, trying to find the right words. 'I knew what was expected of me there, who I was. I'm still working that out here. My grandfather, my Dalmayan grandfather, would tell me that his blood ran in my veins, that I was an Al Osman in all but name, but I knew that to everyone else I was the French son of an immoral woman. I had to be better behaved than Fayaz, stronger, cleverer, nicer. It made no difference. They all loved him anyway. Everyone loved him. He had that gift.'

'Did you come here a lot when you were a boy?'

Idris shifted, uncomfortable with the personal turn the conversation had taken—and yet relieved to share. Now he was living in Dalmaya full time, the memories and what-might-have-beens haunted him around every corner. '*Non.* My mother, she and my grandfather didn't speak at all. But when I was eight he invited me over. Acknowledged me as one of the family. Usually I spent all the summer holidays with my *grandpère* at the

chateau so I began to spend the winter and spring holidays here. Just four weeks a year.' Weeks he had both loved and loathed. Loved for the bond with the proud old man—and because this desert kingdom was in his blood, just as his grandfather claimed.

Loathed because he was always an outsider, always other. 'There was some resistance when Grandfather named me as his second heir. This is why we must always be above reproach, you and I. There is no room for error, for scandal, for gossip. I must be my grandfather's heir, not my mother's son, and you have to be the perfect Queen. It won't be easy but it's the only way.'

Saskia nodded, her face pensive. 'Does your mother miss Dalmaya? I know when the Manor was sold, it felt like part of me had been ripped away. I was raised in that house, and suddenly I was homeless. To lose a whole country must be worse.'

'She knew what she was doing,' he said, his mouth compressing into a thin line. 'Knew that if she crossed that line she could never go back and yet she jumped right across it with no thought for how it would affect me or her father.'

Saskia put her glass down. 'I am angry with my father every day. Angry because every moment of my childhood was a lie, because he abandoned me, abandoned Jack. I don't see any reason, any excuse for what he did. But, Idris, your mother is still here, still in your life. That has to count for something.'

'Oh, I know she loves me. I know she's proud of me. She is very free, very open with her affection—everyone she meets adores her.' His mouth softened as he thought about his beautiful, whimsical mother.

'It's just in her way she's as much a child as Jack and because *mon père* thinks of nothing but his art, if

he decided we needed to be in Switzerland then off we went to Switzerland, no matter that we had nowhere to live, I had no school to go to. It would work out, my mother always said, details were for other people— for me—to worry about. As I grew up I realised other children didn't spend some months with money to burn and other months without a centime, that they didn't flit from town to town, country to country. That they didn't worry about paying the rent because their mother had bought a new dress or get home from school and cook dinner not knowing where their parents were. My time with my two grandfathers, here in Dalmaya, at the chateau, they were the times when time slowed, when I knew who I was.'

'They must have been two exceptional men.'

'Yes, they were.' He paused again, recoiling from the disloyalty of his thoughts. 'Yes, but they always expected so much from me. They never met but they were similar in many ways, both needing me to right the wrongs of the past, to be everything my parents weren't, to be the legacy they needed. They made sure I knew where my duty lay and how to achieve it.'

He hadn't noticed her leave her lounger, noticed her walk around to sit by his side until a cool hand covered his. 'No wonder you got so irritated when I suggested you skip a lecture to jump on a train and see where we ended up!'

Memories flooded back. 'But somehow you persuaded me and we found ourselves up in that little town, with all the thatched roofs and the castle.'

'The sun was out, so even though it was freezing we sat in the pub beer garden and shivered as we had our pints.'

'Then we walked along the road and quarrelled over

which house we would buy. You wanted all the tiny, impractical cottages…'

'And you wanted all the boring, sensible houses with no character.'

'You would love the chateau,' he told her, sliding his fingers through her hair. 'It has all the balconies and turrets and hidden rooms you could desire. My grandfather lived in a suite on the ground floor while the house crumbled. Restoring it has taken me five years—and now it's done I won't get the opportunity to enjoy it.'

'You could.' She placed a hand on his cheek, turning his face to hers. 'You chose not to. You chose to take on Dalmaya and Sami and me even though we were the last things you wanted.'

Had it been a choice? It had felt like an inescapable destiny. 'I didn't…'

'You did have a choice. No one would have blamed you for walking away. No one but you. You don't choose the easy path, Idris Delacour, and you don't make it easy for those of us who are journeying with you, but you choose the right path.'

'Even back then?' Her breath was soft on his cheek, her eyes full of a compassion that struck him to his core.

'Not the way it happened, but you're right. I didn't respect your need for privacy or your boundaries. I just jumped straight in wanting everything my own way. It's funny.' A soft, nostalgic smile curved her mouth. 'I don't recognise that Saskia but I do envy her. Her utter self-belief and confidence in her right to be heard and loved and her knowledge that she mattered. She was a little selfish and a little foolish but she wasn't all bad.'

'She took in a small child while she was reeling from her father's death. That doesn't make her selfish and foolish. That makes her someone with a huge heart.'

Saskia's eyelids fluttered shut, red staining her cheeks. 'You make it sound far more heroic than it was. I did what I had to do.'

'Maybe we're more alike than we realise.' Idris slid his hand to the back of her neck, her still-damp hair heavy on his skin. 'Maybe it's a good thing we ended up here together.'

'Maybe.' The word was a breath as she leaned in towards him. Idris lowered his head to capture her mouth with his. They had mutual goals, they had compatibility and they had this chemistry. Was it enough? Once he had thought he might be on the verge of falling in love with her and had recoiled from the idea, recoiled from the extra sacrifices love demanded. Now she was here, their lives irretrievably intertwined. And right now, right here, he wouldn't have it any other way.

CHAPTER ELEVEN

'GOOD, YOU'RE READY.' Idris strode by Saskia and paused at the door, clearly impatient to be off. 'Is there a problem? There's time to run through the briefing notes in the car.'

Tapping one expensively shod foot, Saskia remained standing by the first of five pillars that ran the length of the aptly named Gold Salon. 'No problem, but when it's taken over an hour of three people's time to get me ready I would appreciate a comment to let me know I pass muster.'

Despite the secular nature of the country many Dalmayans were still deeply religious and old traditions ran deep. Most women still covered their legs and arms as a matter of course, and in rural areas it was common to cover hair as well, although the veil was rarely seen. Saskia had adopted these traditions out of respect for her new country. It made sense to fit in with her compatriots when she was working and mixing with Dalmayans. However, tonight's reception was at the British Embassy and she knew her outfit would be under intense scrutiny. Her decision to wear silk trousers with a matching, long, close-fitting tunic instead of an evening dress would mark her as different, apart from her

own compatriots, and she wasn't sure she was ready for that, to give up her old identity so completely.

At least she wasn't expected to cover her hair in the city. Her maid had styled it into a loose, gleaming chignon, the bright red locks set off by the green and gold silk of her *salwar kameez*. But the long diamond drops in her ears, the emerald and diamond headband holding her hair off her face, the matching collar covering her throat in tiny glittering gems and the heavy emerald and gold spheres ringing her wrists and fingers went far beyond any Western tastes in jewellery. Saskia wasn't sure she would ever feel comfortable wearing the value of a house in Mayfair on her body.

'Is it too much?'

Idris's eyes gleamed as he looked her over, head to toe, her body tingling in response to his deliberate scrutiny. 'You look stunning—and I am looking forward to unwrapping every inch of you later.'

Her stomach clenched at his words and the wolfish smile that accompanied them. 'Promises, promises,' she said, walking forward and taking the arm he proffered, allowing him to lead her out of the palace and to the waiting car.

He came to her every night now and although he still usually slipped away to sleep in his own rooms, occasionally, worn out by the demands of the day, he would fall asleep in her bed. Saskia loved those nights, loved curling up next to him. She had to keep reminding herself not to be too happy. Not to take any of his affection for granted. Not to consider their intimacy as anything more than two people thrust together and making the most out of a difficult situation. As anything more than lust. To remind herself that they were getting close to a real friendship and that was more than she had ever

thought possible four months ago. Remind herself that there could be nothing more.

Idris had warned her, back on their wedding night. Told her that he didn't know if he was capable of love, confirmed that he had walked away from what they had shared then without a backwards glance. Only a fool would be ensnared twice.

But no matter how much she reminded herself she still would find herself sneaking looks at him during formal occasions, find herself shivering at the touch of his hand, find herself basking in his approval when he bestowed one of his rare smiles on her, find herself needing him every night.

She told herself that this was perfectly normal— after all, he was still her only confidant in the whole country, the adult she spent most of her time with—but deep down inside, she knew. She was falling in love with him again. Not with all the fire and drama of first love: a crush mixed with lust mixed with the hedonistic optimism of youth. But with a deeper, steadier, more realistic love. This wasn't just passion or a need to be liked. It wasn't about winning, about craving, about impressing. She was falling in love with the way he made time to listen to everyone at Council meetings even when they seemed interminable. She was falling in love with the man who had a framed picture of his vineyards and chateau on his desk but had walked away from his beloved business to do the right thing. She was falling in love with a shrewd negotiator and a patient diplomat. She was falling in love with the man teaching her brother to ride. The man who spent an entire hour playing peekaboo with Sami. The man who had safeguarded Jack's future. The man who made her feel

that she had something to offer. The man who made her feel that she was worthwhile.

Dangerous, forbidden feelings. But try as she might she couldn't push them aside.

Idris seemed preoccupied as their car drove smoothly along the great driveway leading from the palace to the gates, barely speaking for the first few minutes. Saskia smoothed her tunic, trying to calm her nerves with deep breaths. She had been to several formal receptions over the last few weeks, she had done her research on to-night's hosts and guests but still her stomach tumbled with nerves.

'Thank you for wearing traditional dress,' Idris said abruptly and Saskia turned from her perusal of the narrow city streets.

'Of course. I probably would have even if you hadn't requested it. It seems appropriate somehow.'

'There is still an inordinate amount of interest in us, especially in the UK press. They print stories every day, all inaccurate, print photos every time we're in public...'

The air swirled and stilled. Whenever she closed her eyes it was easy to conjure up those claustrophobic few weeks after her father's death, cameras everywhere, her face on the front pages as every detail of her extravagantly funded life was laid out for people to moralise over. 'They photograph us?'

He waved an impatient hand. 'That's to be expected but what wasn't expected is the amount of interest after several months, several quiet months at that. They report that we argue about your spending, that my mother hates you and wants to be crowned Queen...'

'I've never met your mother!'

'It doesn't matter.' His eyes were weary. 'My parents were tabloid staples in their day. Your father dominated

the headlines. You're the spoiled socialite brought down to earth, I'm the wine king. To them we're a match made in heaven and truth has no place in the fictions they spin. Tonight, we will be on British soil for the first time since we married. This is a good chance to make the right impression. There will be members of the press there, influential people. Let's start putting these lies and rumours to bed. I don't want Jack or Sami reading about us the way I grew up reading about my parents. I want this intrusiveness to stop. Show them you have changed, Saskia, that you are the dignified, compassionate Queen Dalmaya needs.'

Saskia's hands began to tremble and she folded them together so Idris wouldn't notice. How had she not known that these stories were circulating—and why hadn't Idris warned her before? 'I'll do my best.'

'Do better. These parties aren't fun, not for you and I, they're work. You mustn't let your guard down just because every accent is English and the people seem like friends. They're not.'

He leaned back, every inch the unapproachable King. Saskia swallowed, trying to quell the nausea swelling inside at the thought of the ordeal that awaited her. Usually she felt a little as if she was playing a part, the traditional dress and elaborate jewellery her costume, her briefing document, her lines, and it was getting easier to step into each situation and perform. Idris was right—tonight would be different. Everyone there would be watching her, scrutinising her, would think they knew all about her and suddenly she felt more like a child playing dress up than a Queen.

The British Embassy was housed in a walled palace in the old town. Armed guards manned the outer walls but the royal car was waved straight through to

the inner courtyard. The building was an odd contrast of traditional Dalmayan architecture, all mosaics, courtyards and pillars, and bureaucratic efficiency. As Saskia was escorted through the courtyard and double-height hallway, with its domed ceiling and pillars standing to attention on either side of the walkway, she caught glimpses of glass-walled offices, of laptops and printers and all the other accoutrements of modern-day work life. The hallway opened into a huge receiving room, which was all luxurious charm from the fountain in the middle to the sparkling chandeliers hanging from the high ceiling, each ray of light rebounding off the diamonds she was so liberally bedecked in so she felt as if she were in a spotlight as she moved into the room.

It was already full. Men and women in evening dress stood in intimidatingly glamorous and confident groups, every single eye turned to her, assessing her. Wait staff circulated with canapés and drinks and, with a jolt, Saskia realised that nearly everyone was drinking champagne. Dalmaya wasn't a dry country but most Dalmayans didn't touch alcohol and the export duties on wine and spirits were so high that even those that did rarely partook. Idris drank wine most evenings—his own brought straight to the palace from the Delacour vineyard's cellars—but not one of the dinners she had been to had served it.

The tray was presented to her and she hesitated, glancing at Idris for guidance, but he was talking to the British Ambassador and didn't notice her dilemma. Then he reached out and took a glass without breaking off the conversation. Saskia exhaled. *In that case...* With a smile of thanks she took a glass and took a sip. The champagne was tart and refreshing, as unlike the cheap cava she had occasionally treated herself to as

the diamonds on her wrists and at her throat were unlike her mass-produced high-street jewellery.

'Welcome, Your Highness, it's an honour to have you here. It's been quite a few months, motherhood, a new country and such a prominent role,' the Ambassador's wife said as she escorted Saskia away from the group. 'It must be a lot to adjust to.'

Some of Saskia's tension ebbed away at the friendly tone. It was nice to be able to speak her own language without feeling like an ignorant foreigner. She had been so busy letting Dalmaya adjust to her, get used to her, that she hadn't put any thought into her own life here. She had her boys and, now, work of sorts, looking out for communities and people who needed help and finding ways to alleviate that need, but she still had no friends. Maybe Idris was being pessimistic; this could be her chance to meet some women she clicked with. Potential friends.

She smiled. 'It is. I have a lot of help, of course, so I haven't had to do any of it on my own.'

'And His Highness Sheikh Idris must be of great help as well. After all, he's had to straddle two cultures for many years. Have you known him long?' The Ambassador's wife's eyes were bright with curiosity and, with a sinking heart, Saskia knew she would need to tread carefully. Everything she said would be remembered and repeated.

'Many years,' she answered with a polite smile. 'We met at university. I was at Oxford with his cousin's then fiancée.' They had discussed whether to keep her friendship with Maya quiet, another layer of protection for their secret, but although Saskia's stay at Oxford had been cut short she'd been well known there and there must be many pictures of Maya and her floating around.

As they toured the room Saskia's optimism ebbed even further as she conceded that Idris's caution hadn't been misplaced. Everyone wanted to meet her, but all they seemed to be interested in was finding out any gossip about her marriage or trying to get a contact at the palace. In the first, long, hot hour she didn't meet one person she could imagine having a relaxed coffee with, let alone an actual friendship, and the lonely reality of her new life hit her anew. Her feet ached, her head ached, the jewels weighing her down as she smiled and made small talk feeling more like a robot fulfilling a role than a real person.

'Rob, can I introduce you to Her Highness Princess Saskia Delacour Al Osman. Your Highness, Robert McBride runs a well-known adventure travel company specialising in Middle Eastern excursions.'

Saskia held out her hand, an automatic greeting on her lips when she caught the twinkling blue eyes of the man she was being introduced to and stopped, her first real smile of the night curving her mouth. 'Robbie? What are you doing here? I thought you were destined for accountancy! It's so good to see you. Robbie and I were at the same college at Oxford,' she explained to her hostess. 'It feels like a million years ago since we were karaoke duet champions in the union bar!'

'Saskia Harper! I mean...' he took her hand and executed a perfect sweeping bow over it '...Your Highness—or as I always remembered you, the Sandy to my Danny. I was always hopelessly devoted to you but you only had eyes for one man—and...' his gaze cut across to where Idris stood in a sea of suits '...I see you still have. You look beautiful as always, like a vision from *The Thousand and One Nights*. So what have you been up to since disappearing from Oxford? If Royal

Highnesses are allowed to make small talk with lowly subjects like myself?'

'I think I can make an exception.' Saskia took the champagne he handed to her and allowed him to usher her to a place near the spectacular fountain. 'Never mind me. I want to hear all about you and why you are organising desert adventures not spreadsheets. What on earth are you doing here?'

These events were always the same. A lot of hot air and people trying to get his approval ahead of more formal meetings. Not that Idris could blame them. He had once been on the other side, the exporter looking for good deals and favourable tariffs, the producer knowing if potential customers would just try it then they would instantly be converted to his wine, his brandy, his brand.

It would be nice though not to have to spend an entire evening never committing himself, on guard at all times. Fayaz had known what was in store for him and, from an early age, had built a small but trusted circle of friends including Maya so he could have time away from responsibilities, commitments and those attempting to take advantage of his position. Idris had always been slower to make friends and to trust people and now he had no one. Nobody except Saskia.

Had they ever really talked during those long ago lust-fuelled nights? He didn't remember much conversation. But now they talked. Now he listened to her thoughts and ideas, ran his ideas past her, trusted her advice. It was as if they had been set adrift from the rest of humanity and they might never have chosen to spend their lives cooped up in a small boat together but somehow they had made peace with their situation, realised that by cooperating they would somehow make it even

if that destination was unknown and not where either of them had set out to go. Or something, his mouth twisted wryly. Overblown metaphors had never been his style.

The noise was almost overpowering. Although most people were speaking in English there were enough other languages audible enough to make the room resemble a flatter Tower of Babel. Idris himself had conducted conversations in Arabic, French and his faltering Italian as well as English. The most relaxed group seemed to be by the fountain; a younger, more fashionable group had congregated there and judging by the peals of laughter they weren't discussing trade tariffs. For one self-indulgent second he wished he were free to head over and see what was so amusing—but the truth was he had never been one of the cool crowd. Always working, always aloof. What had Saskia seen in him all those years ago? What did she see in him now? Or was she just making the best of a bad deal? She was pragmatic, especially where providing for the boys was concerned.

The laughter intensified and he looked back over at the lively group, freezing as he saw the sea-green silk, the red hair, the flashing of precious jewels identifying his wife. She stood in the middle of the group, a half-empty glass of champagne in her hand, smiling up at a tall, fair man. Recognition flared as the man turned—hadn't he been one of Saskia's acolytes in Oxford? Richard? No, Rob. Robert McBride. They used to sing together, he remembered, perform elaborate karaoke duets, which always brought the bar to a standstill, arms wrapped around each other, exchanging kisses as if they were compliments. Jealousy shot through him, cold and sharp as a shard of ice. His eyes narrowed. How much had she had to drink? Did she

know everyone was watching her, judging her? Or did she simply not care? She had always loved being the centre of attention...

As he watched Rob put a hand on her arm—*on his wife's arm*, jealousy whispered—and leant in to whisper something in her ear. Idris watched her eyes widen before she blushed and laughed. Another sip of champagne.

People were watching her—of course they were. Even without the title, the jewels, the traditional dress, she lit up the room. But the soon-to-be Queen of Dalmaya shouldn't be the centre of attention in this way, shouldn't shine so brightly or so freely. It wasn't decorous.

She put her hand back on Robert McBride's arm, laughing, and Idris's chest tightened. A soon-to-be Queen certainly shouldn't be flirting, especially not in public. Had she lost her mind? His gaze dropped to her glass of champagne. How many had she had? Was she tipsy? Her eyes glittered too brightly, her smile was too wide.

A remark was addressed to him and Idris nodded and smiled, adding automatic replies when it seemed appropriate, but he couldn't drag his focus from the group. He tried to catch her eye but she didn't look in his direction once. And then Rob handed her his glass, Idris wasn't sure why, but he was rolling up his sleeves and the group was widening around him, giving him space. Saskia stepped back too, both glasses high as she backed up and then time seemed to slow down to a trickle as she seemed to trip, turning that weak ankle, and she fell backwards, still laughing, still holding those damn champagne glasses, as the liquid cascaded down her front, turning the delicate silk translucent,

the dampness moulding the material to her breasts as she fell into one of the giant urns serving as plant pots. The room came to a standstill everyone turning to look, phones pulled out in a flash as one of the bracelets fell from Saskia's wrist and fell to the floor scattering precious stones like confetti.

CHAPTER TWELVE

'PLEASE COME WITH US, just for a little while.' Jack's eyes pleaded for her to say yes and Saskia's heart ached as she shook her head with as big a smile as she could muster.

'Best not. You'll enjoy the park more if there are no cameras around, you know that. Be a good boy, listen to Faye and look after Sami.' She kissed him on his unresponsive cheek, hating the disappointment on his face, then kissed the baby, deliciously wrapped up in a padded all-in-one. 'Are you sure you're okay with them both, Faye?' Lucy, the day nanny, had the day off but the nursery nurse, Faye, had been trained at one of the UK's most exclusive childcare colleges and Saskia knew the two boys would be in safe hands. Besides, two body-guards would be trailing them at a discreet distance the whole time. 'Say hi to Peter Pan for me, Jack, okay?'

He nodded, the sullen look receding from his face. The two of them had made many trips to see the famous statue over the years and he was thrilled that they were staying within walking distance of Kensington Park.

Saskia turned to the window, uneasy until she saw them turn into the park free of any press interest. London was a cold contrast to Dalmaya, the autumn the grey, windy, drizzly variant. Grey like her mood. It was

her fault she couldn't take the boys out herself, her fault they had to exit the embassy by a side door, on a constant lookout for the press. She had messed up.

It didn't matter that the fall had been an accident, that despite appearances to the contrary she hadn't been drunk. No matter that the clasp had been weak on her bracelet. What mattered was the photo. The photo that was on every gossip website and in most papers. A drunk-looking princess, laughing as she sat in a giant, priceless plant pot, a glass of champagne held aloft in both hands, their contents dripping down her so her outfit was see-through, her breasts, her underwear clearly visible, diamonds and emeralds showering from her wrists. She looked as if she were participating in some kind of drunken orgy, not tripping over her own shoes. And to Idris, appearances seemed to be everything.

Not that she had realised that at first. He had appeared at her side like a superhero, helping her get up, shrugging his jacket off so that she could slip it on, joking that it was a good idea he had worn Western clothes, taking the glasses out of her hands and putting them on a tray and then escorting her from the room, all before she had really grasped what had happened. But when she had turned to thank him in the car he had frozen her out. 'We'll talk about this later,' he had said, as if she were an errant teen, not his wife. But there had been no later. He hadn't come to her and she hadn't been invited to any Council meetings. Instead she had been left alone in her rooms—to think about what she had done?—until it was time to travel to London. She had assumed Idris would be accompanying them but he wasn't in the car nor on the private jet and there was no sight of him here in the embassy nor any indication that he was planning to join her there.

He had warned her, it was true. She had to be dignified, make sure there were no errors, and she had ignored his advice, giddy at seeing a friendly face. But the punishment outweighed the crime. Was this how it would be? Would she spend her entire marriage fitting in, treading carefully, alone? Idris had walked away before—and by his own admission he hadn't looked back even once.

She wouldn't, couldn't live like that. Couldn't set that kind of example to her boys. Couldn't undo those painful seven years of self-discovery and growth.

But Idris and she were married and tomorrow she would be talking to a social worker, proving that she was the right person to look after Jack, that Idris was the right person to father him. And he wasn't here. Even if he turned up would they be able to put on a united front? Could she spend the rest of her life pretending?

Even worse the paparazzi were everywhere. The social worker would have to be escorted through them, which was going to be an excellent start to the interview. The photo had stirred the already feverish press into a feeding frenzy and her father's suicide, Idris's mother's elopement, their own affair at Oxford were dissected, written about and discussed as if they held the answer to world peace, climate change and space travel in their sordid details. She hadn't been able to take Jack to the theatre or the museums or anything she had promised him; instead she had been stuck inside the Georgian town house that housed the embassy, just as she had been stuck inside the palace, inside the villa.

Saskia curled her hands into fists, blinking fiercely. No more tears. She was done with them. She was an adult now, not a teen forced to grow up too soon. She had two boys to care for and she needed to decide how

she wanted to live the rest of her life. Was she any happier now for all her designer clothes and the diamond watch on her wrist?

If she wasn't prepared to live like this, then what were her options? She swallowed. Divorce, she supposed. Divorce wouldn't affect Sami's chance to inherit the throne. He was legitimate now, after all. And if the adoption was finalised first then Jack would be safe. And for all Idris's threats nearly six months ago she knew now he wouldn't leave the children penniless. Nor did she think he would try and take them from her.

She looked around her at the warm colours and comfortable, elegant furniture. Once she had walked the streets of Kensington, playing the *Where would I like to live?* game. She had always chosen either a mews house or a town house, complete with basement and attic like the houses in the old-fashioned children's stories she loved so much. Nothing ostentatious. No basement cinemas. Instead she had yearned for a large kitchen diner, for cosy furniture you could sit on, warm furnishings, not acres of marble covered in spindly chairs. No gilt.

Here she was in exactly that house, in a large Georgian terrace with black iron railings in the front and a garden out back. The royal apartments were situated on the first and second floors and the décor was testament to Maya's good taste, showcasing the best of Dalmayan décor while still accommodating itself to the vagaries of British weather with stoves, throws and huge rugs giving the large rooms a much-needed cosy feel. Saskia had made it, was living in her dream home. And yet her victory was completely hollow.

Despite the warmth Saskia shivered. It was time to take control of her life, not allow circumstances to buffet her from disaster to makeshift solution. Taking care

of Jack, getting pregnant, marrying Idris, these had all been thrust upon her and just because two out of the three were the best things that could have happened didn't make her lack of agency any less real.

As for that third...marrying Idris had brought her security, true, financially and personally. The clothes she wore cost more than her previous entire wardrobe had, the watch on her wrist would have paid for a year's rent. Sami was hers in every way and soon Jack would be. Hopefully. But she couldn't spend her life with someone who didn't like her. The knowledge she was in love with him just made her isolation worse.

Accidents happened and there was every chance Saskia would mess up again unless she spent her life hidden in the confines of the palace walls. If Idris couldn't understand that then what chance did she have? Maya had often spoken about the future pressures awaiting her as Fayaz's wife and Queen. Society held women to a higher, more unachievable standard, she had said one night, and it was doubly, triply true in Middle Eastern countries, even ones as theoretically progressive as Dalmaya. She loved Fayaz, but she knew marrying him meant surrendering many of the freedoms she took for granted. That she would be watched, judged every moment. But, she said, with Fayaz by her side, supporting her, needing her, it would be worth it.

A dull ache pulsed in Saskia's chest, in her heart. That, right there, was the crux of the matter. Maya didn't just love Fayaz, she had known that she could depend on him too, no matter what. Could Saskia say the same of Idris? If he truly supported her, needed her, then they could laugh off any subsequent embarrassments. But if he was just going to freeze her out...

She deserved better. She was no longer a spoiled

teenager. She was a hard-working mother of two with so much love to give and if that wasn't enough for Idris...

Staring blindly out of the window at the Georgian square, at the private garden in the middle of the square, at the photographers still loitering with intent, Saskia acknowledged the truth: she couldn't live this way, loving Idris, destined to disappoint him. She couldn't raise the boys with that kind of marriage as a role model. She turned and picked up her phone, finding Idris's details, and fired off a quick text.

We need to talk. In person.

Idris's phone buzzed and he glanced at the screen to see Saskia's name flash up followed by a short text. Just four words but they shot straight to his heart. The words *We need to talk* never boded well but, he conceded, he didn't deserve anything more. He had left Saskia to travel to England alone, left her to face the fallout from the photo alone. If he had stayed next to her, laughed the picture off, then the story would have died by now but his absence was raising speculative headlines.

He got stiffly to his feet and headed over to the window, looking out over the old courtyard, at the stone barns and the grey walls. He should have followed Saskia to London; instead he had come home, to Chateau Delacour. Oh, he still needed to sign some papers, to delegate some more of the responsibilities, but he knew he could have done that from the palace or the London Embassy. The vineyard was running smoothly in his absence thanks to his more than capable manager but the chateau was his home in a way the palace could never be. Generations of Delacours had lived here and

tended the fields just as generations of Al Osmans had lived in the palace and tended Dalmaya.

Maybe he could step down when Sami was old enough and return here, to vineyards and fields. To the old grey chateau, weathered and crumbling in parts. To the deep green of the French countryside and the peace and tranquillity. To a life where a mistake meant ruining a year's vintage, not ruining a country, a life, a marriage. To a place that used to feel like home.

He should have gone to London. He just didn't know how to speak to Saskia, what to say. Where to begin. He'd spent his life avoiding drama in every permutation. He didn't have the weapons to deal with it now. Or the armour.

He needed a walk, wanted to examine the bare vines. The grapes had all been picked in his absence, a few trodden in the traditional way at the harvest festival, the rest pressed. He'd missed both. Hadn't tasted the grapes, hadn't stood in the traditional wooden tub, barefooted, the grapes squelching under his cleansed feet. Despite a childhood being dragged around France, around Europe, despite the darker skin and name that marked him out as foreign in a countryside that still regarded outsiders with suspicion, he had always felt at home here. Here and in the stables at the palace. These were the places his two grandfathers, proud men who had never met, had passed down their wisdom and their traditions and their family pride. He didn't think either would be proud of him just now.

Nor should they be.

He reached the front door as a car drew up, a sleek silver convertible he didn't recognise. His chest tightened as a chic, petite figure sprang from the driver's side, her dark hair barely touched with grey swept up

in a loose bun, huge sunglasses obscuring half her famously beautiful face.

'*Yaa bunaaya,*' she said, hands outstretched towards him.

'*Maman.*' It took a second for him to recover from the shock of her arrival and step forward to take her hands and kiss her on both cheeks. 'This is a surprise.'

'But a welcome one, I hope?' She reverted to the English they usually spoke at home. His father had no Arabic and, despite living most of her adult life in France, Princess Zara still spoke barely passable tourist French.

'Of course. Come on in. Would you like coffee?'

'But you were just leaving.'

'Only for a walk.'

'Then I shall accompany you and we shall dine together later. You are sure I am not interrupting you, Idris? You aren't on your way to London perhaps?'

'Tomorrow.' He couldn't miss the social worker's visit and Saskia was right. They did need to talk. 'You seem very well informed about my whereabouts.'

'A mother has her ways, even a mother who missed her son's wedding and has yet to meet her grandson?' She raised an eyebrow and shame shot through him. Shame mingled with uncertainty. Lying about Sami's heritage seemed like the right thing to do in the abstract but lying to his own parents was another thing completely. And would they tell Sami the truth one day? After all, Jack knew some version of it. The marriage, the deception had all made such sense in those first grief-laden days but now nothing seemed to make any sense at all.

He took her arm and, after shooting an incredulous glance at her delicately heeled suede boots, which

seemed totally unsuited for walking through the vine-
yards, set off away from the house. He let her chatter
on for some minutes; about his father's latest project,
their plan to move to the Alps for the winter, some gos-
sip about mutual friends before he said jerkily: 'Sami
is your great-nephew, not your grandson, although I
consider him my son and I hope you will think of him
as a grandchild.'

'I see.' She didn't, he noted, sound surprised.

'Maya had trouble conceiving and so she asked
Saskia, my wife…' if his mother noticed him stumble
over the words she made no sign '…to have a child for
her. As a surrogate. Fayaz was the biological father
and Saskia the mother. But they died before the baby
was born and before they could acknowledge him as
theirs. So I…'

'So you married the mother, told the world the baby
is yours so he can inherit. Of course you did. It is ex-
actly what I would expect you to do.' Her voice was
oddly neutral, neither approving or disapproving.

'What else could I do?'

His mother patted his hand. 'You could have walked
away, Idris. No one would have blamed you. But you
were always one to shoulder all the responsibility
whether it was yours to shoulder or not. So, I have a
daughter-in-law and a grandson. When will I meet them
and why are you not with them?'

Her words reverberated around his head. She made it
sound as if he had choices. As if he could just walk away
from his duties and responsibilities—as she and his fa-
ther had. Didn't she realise that someone had to pick
up behind them? 'You've seen the photo, I expect. The
headlines. The speculation. Is that why you're here?'

Her hand tightened on his arm. 'I need a reason to

see my son? It's not easy when you have made it clear you don't want me in Dalmaya, never mind that it was my home once. But yes, I saw the photo. Not that it matters. Photos are never the whole story, not even half the story. The press are never kind to the young and the privileged once they transgress and she, I think, is being punished more for her father's sins, for my supposed sins, than for one moment's lapse in concentration. Is she managing?'

'As far as I am aware.'

'As far as you...' Her lips compressed and she didn't speak for a long moment. They reached the edge of the vineyards, stretching out over undulating low hills, the sky a clear blue, the air crisp with the hint of an autumnal chill. The Princess tugged him towards a bench, set in the side of the vineyard, placed there for the tourists who came to watch the grapes grow, the wine made, to sample and to buy, and, after gingerly inspecting it for dirt, sat down and looked at her son.

'I blame myself, Idris. Your father, he likes me full of *joie-de-vivre* and so I am. Not thinking about tomorrow or worrying about what-ifs. He didn't want to be weighed down by responsibility, by all this...' She waved her hand, encompassing the vineyards and the chateau. 'By his name and expectations. That was a breath of fresh air to me, as someone for whom family expectations had been so all demanding.'

'So you both just turned your backs on everything and everyone.' Leaving him to fulfil both families' expectations.

'No, no. I was already disgraced, remember? Your grandfather. He had plans and we all had our place in those plans. Me? I was to be the example of perfect modern womanhood: educated and career-minded,

chaste and sensible. I was to study and then come back to Dalmaya and spearhead women's education. Marry wisely and raise my children to carry on his dreams. I hated to study, Idris, and knowing I had years and years ahead of me… Running off with Pierre wasn't a moment of madness, it was calculated. A Dalmayan Princess who eloped with her ski instructor? Worse, who left him within a year? I knew I would be free. I didn't realise…' here her voice faltered '…that my freedom would be so absolute. That your grandfather, your uncle would cut me off so completely. But if I had known I would still have done exactly the same.'

Idris sat and stared over the fields as his mother's words sank in. He had always thought of her as impulsive and thoughtless. Not someone weighed down by expectations who sought her own path to freedom.

'I met your father soon afterwards. He was so talented and his ideas, his rejection of his birthright and all that went along with it called to me. It's not easy being married to a genius, especially one who thinks commercial is a dirty word. Neither he nor I were brought up to budget and I know it wasn't easy living from boom to bust over and over. Travelling around all the time. And I know that we are both so volatile, it wasn't the most peaceful of childhoods. Too much smashed crockery. That's why I made sure you spent so much time here, or in Dalmaya. I was happy that my father wanted *you* there, if not me. But maybe those two old men put too much on you. Wanted you to make up for the sins of your parents. I was so angry when my father went against convention and named you in the succession, when your *grandpère* left you this place with its debts and obligations. But you like responsibility. You

have made the vineyard a success. I know you will be a great King, my son.'

'Thank you.' It was hard to get the words out.

'But you can be...' she hesitated, choosing her words carefully, it seemed '...rigid. You make your mind up and that's that. I am feckless and court scandal. Well.' She shrugged. 'I see why you think that. I don't always think first and the papers will never allow me to forget my transgressions. But I love you—I always have. I love your father. I would never do anything to endanger our family. Even when your father had that infatuation with that model of his, you remember?'

'I remember.' His mother had phoned him, hysterical. That was the day Saskia had come to him for help and, angry at already losing his day to one woman's drama, he had turned her away, turned his back on her for good. Shame lay, heavy and painful on his heart.

'I was so angry. So humiliated, Idris. I could have walked away. But he is my husband and you are my son and so I swallowed my pride and I stayed—although he knows there must be no more *affaires*. He may be French and an artist but I cannot abide anything as boring as a cliché. I know you don't see it, think it, but I love you, *yaa bunaaya*. I am so proud of you. But I just want you to be happy.'

'You don't think I am happy?'

'I know you're not. I think you're scared to be, Idris. I think you see your worth in work and solving problems and taking on the world. You were embarrassed by me, I know that. And I think that photo has embarrassed you too. Love is about forgiving, Idris. About looking beyond the obvious to what is real and true. About never being too proud to say sorry. And true happiness is loving and being loved, no matter how inconvenient, and I

think you are too scared. And that must be on me. And I am so sorry.' Her large eyes shimmered with tears. Idris sat rigid and then sighed, leaning against her for the first time in a long, long time as her words sank in, each one painful in its truth.

'Thank you, *Maman*. I need to get back to London. Do you want to come with me and meet your grandson and your daughter-in-law? If she still wants to stay married to me, that is.'

CHAPTER THIRTEEN

NEITHER IDRIS NOR his mother spoke much on the walk back to the chateau, his mother's words spinning round and round in his head. She had never been the kind of mother to dish out advice or talk about feelings; he loved her, but, he acknowledged, maybe he'd allowed his view of her to be shaped by his disapproving grandparents, by the persona she adopted. He'd never wondered what it must be like being exiled from your home, cut off from your family, married to someone whose work always came before anyone and everything.

Shame flushed through him, scalding in its intensity. His mother had been badly hurt by his father's affair, so hurt she had turned to her only son for advice and help—and all Idris had wanted was to end the phone call and get back to work. Just as he had wanted to put Saskia in a taxi and close the door on her. He had thought his work, his peace more important than two people who had so desperately needed him. What kind of man did that make him?

And here he was doing the same again. Saskia had worked incredibly hard to fit in at the palace, to be the Queen Dalmaya needed her to be. She sat up late revising customs and history and language. She knew the names of the wives and children of everyone they met,

when to speak and when to stand back. She had a gift of summing up a situation with one glance and defusing it or working out a solution, whether it was an air ambulance for the Al Bedi or a new community centre in the poverty-stricken town they had visited last. The only thing she complained about was not having enough to do.

How had he thanked her? By treating one mishap as a catastrophe. By freezing her out. Just as he'd frozen out his own mother. His fear of drama and confrontation when it came to anything personal meant he would rather walk away than sort out a difficult situation. Rather leave Saskia to face the press alone.

He loved both his grandfathers and was grateful for everything they had given him, but from them he had inherited a sense of shame. Shame every time his mother was on the front page of a gossip magazine, shame when his father's latest, controversial exhibition hit the headlines, shame when their relationship was the subject of speculation. From them he had learned the value of hard work, a good lesson it was true, but not of compassion. Of pride but not of humility.

Saskia knew all about humility and hard work. She was filled with more compassion than anyone he had ever known. She was straight and true, always putting her own needs last—which was why she needed him. Needed him to put her first. But he had let her down again.

There would be no third time. That he swore.

'I've messed everything up, *Maman*.' Idris felt her falter as he said the words, then she slipped an arm through his and squeezed it.

'Idris, you of all people know that there is nothing that can't be fixed. Just look at this place. Your grand-

father left a tumbling-down building, cellars full of antique equipment and a work ethos steeped in traditions that were out of date before he was even born. In just a few years you have restored the chateau and made Delacour wine one of the most sought-after brands.'

'Places and things and figures I can fix, but neither Oxford nor the Sorbonne offered me a course in human emotions,' he said. 'Even if they had I probably wouldn't have taken it.'

'Do you love her? This Saskia?'

He winced at the directness in his mother's gaze. 'That's a complicated question.'

'No, no, *yaa bunaaya*. It's the easiest question of all. If the answer is no then you must decide whether you can live with a lifetime of duty with no chance of love. If the answer is yes then you must win her back.' She patted his arm. 'Don't worry. I'll help you.'

Idris touched his mother's hand in thanks while her question repeated over and over in his mind, in his heart. Did he love Saskia? He'd told her once that he'd been as close to loving her as a man like him could ever be. Was that true or was it a way of hiding from anything as messy and real as love?

He desired her, that was true enough. He respected her intelligence and compassion. He liked the soft expression that stole over her face when she was rocking Sami, as if he was the most precious thing in the world. He admired the way she had raised Jack, the comradeship between them, her determination to give him the best childhood she could. She frustrated him, her obstinacy out in the desert when she wouldn't allow him to call the helicopter—but it had paid off. The Al Bedi had been impressed by her courage and her insistence on owning the horse that had thrown her.

She was beautiful, that went without saying. But hers was a beauty that went beyond the physical, a sweetness in her soul that hadn't been soured by the hardships she'd endured.

And he desired her. No matter he had already listed it. It was important enough to list twice. He couldn't imagine holding another woman, kissing another woman. Loving another woman…

His hands curled into fists. Of course he loved her. How could he not? Deserve her? That was a different matter. He had to prove he deserved her, prove he was worthy, show her how much he loved her—everything that she was. He stepped up his pace, heading towards the chateau.

How did a man prove his love? Especially a man who had screwed up so royally. His brain began to tick, pulling in ideas and thoughts and images, discarding others. He'd always been a good problem solver, now was the time to prove it. 'Don't worry, *Maman*, I have a plan.' He fished his phone out of his pocket and searched for a number. 'Faye? Is Jack there? Great, pass him to me. I need to check something with him.' For his plan to work he needed to enlist some help and Jack was his go-to guy.

Saskia didn't know whether she was more grateful that Idris made it to London in the nick of time or furious that he had waited until barely a half hour before the social worker was due before sauntering in, a glamorous, petite woman at his side. It took her one glance to identify the woman as Zara Al Osman Delacour, the famous Runaway Princess herself. She didn't look scandalous in her neat little black suit, her coiled dark hair

only lightly streaked with grey and an emotional smile on her face; she looked happy.

'Saskia, I am so excited to meet you at last. And you, Jack. I am to be your *grandmère*, I understand.' She pronounced the French word with a distinctly Anglo-Dalmayan accent. 'I have many, many plans for the two of us. I do hope you like trips out to exciting places. And this? This must be Sami.' Her face softened.

Saskia glanced over at Idris, uncomfortable with misleading his mother about Sami's parentage, but his expression was inscrutable and she couldn't catch his eye.

'Ah, he does look like Fayaz. That makes me so happy. A fragment of happiness from such a tragedy. Yes, Idris told me,' she said quietly as Saskia looked at her in surprise. 'You are a very brave young woman.'

'Thank you.' Saskia swallowed, the lump in her throat almost more than she could bear as Sami's great-aunt kissed him, sadness mingling with love on her vivid face.

'Fayaz came to visit me when he started Oxford,' Princess Zara said. 'He and Maya, he wanted to meet the fun side of his family, he told me. He was a lovely boy. I cherished my friendship with them. Thank you for giving them this hope, Saskia. And thank you for doing what needed to be done. It can't have been easy.'

'Nothing worth doing usually is,' Saskia replied, taking her son back, conscious of the older woman's scrutiny as she did so. She caught Idris's eye and for a moment she thought he was going to say something to her, but at that moment the social worker was announced and everything around her, every other emotion and problem, disappeared, her entire focus and will centred on convincing this stranger that she was a fit mother for the small boy.

Thankfully a scandal involving two reality-show stars, a fight and an arrest had lured the press away late last night so they could welcome the adoption official through the front door of the Embassy. She didn't mention the photo at all; the only hint that Saskia and Idris weren't like any normal couple looking to adopt came in a few questions about living with security and how Jack was adjusting to palace life. Luckily Jack was so enthusiastic about his life in Dalmaya the subject was quickly dropped.

'That's a lovely wee boy you have there,' the social worker said with a smile as Saskia saw her out at the end of the two-hour session. 'You've done a good job, Your Highness.'

'I've been very lucky,' Saskia answered, more than a little choked. 'What happens next?'

'Next?' The social worker looked surprised at the question. 'We'll notify your lawyers of the court date. I don't think you will be waiting long, not in a case as straightforward as this.'

Saskia waited until she had left before sagging against the wall. Straightforward? That had to be good, right? She glanced up the stairs to where the family were waiting for her. Idris had been wonderful throughout the interview, calm and measured, even when the questioning had felt intrusive, no hint of the coldness that had characterised the last week. And he had brought his mother to the Embassy—officially Dalmayan soil. The first time the Princess had been anywhere near her home country in over thirty years. Saskia didn't know what to think. All she knew was that it was time she and Idris had a good, long talk and this time she was going to be the one calling the shots.

Intentions were all very well, but try as she might

Saskia didn't manage to get Idris alone at any point for the rest of the morning. He disappeared several times for long periods, once or twice with Jack. If the idea didn't seem ridiculous, she would have said he was avoiding her on purpose. He didn't seem cold or angry—at times his expression rested on her with a heat that made her quiver. But every time she made a move to draw him away he slipped away so seamlessly she couldn't see how he had managed it.

'We need to talk,' she managed to quietly say as they finished a celebratory lunch in honour of Jack's interview and Idris paused, his gaze serious.

'I know. Later. I promise.'

Frustrated, she made to turn away and he caught her arm gently, pulling her around to face his scrutiny. 'You look tired.'

'I've not been sleeping, worrying about this interview I suppose. My head is pounding,' she admitted, softened by his concern.

'Why don't you lie down for a couple of hours? I'm sure two nannies, one man and one doting grandmother can take care of two boys for an afternoon.'

Excuses sprang to her lips. She didn't want to show weakness to anyone, especially not Idris, but the words wouldn't come. Truth was she was exhausted, physically and emotionally, and although an afternoon nap wouldn't cure either it could only help. 'Okay. I will. Thank you.'

The short sleep refreshed her more than she thought possible; a quick shower and a change of clothes and she felt like a new woman, ready to talk to Idris, ready to make sure her feelings were not just heard but that some

kind of consensus about the future would be made. She put a hand to her stomach, trying to press away the nerves, the fear she might get this wrong. The boys deserved a loving family, that wasn't in doubt, she just needed to ensure there was a place for her in Idris's life. A place where she would be happy and respected if not loved.

The spacious living area seemed strangely quiet. Saskia wandered through the snug, the living room and the less formal sitting room used primarily by the boys, but there was no sign of anyone. She sat by the window and looked out at Kensington Gardens, feeling a little ridiculous at how forlorn she was. Of course there was a reasonable explanation for their absence; they were probably in the park. She was overtired and a little overwrought, that was all.

She blinked back a tear. 'I don't even know why I'm crying,' she said aloud. Maybe it was the relief that the adoption seemed to be going well. Maybe the anticlimax that after gearing herself up to tell Idris how she felt, she hadn't managed to say more than a few words to him. He couldn't just waltz in here and expect everything to be okay...

She should head out to the park and see if she could find them. Now the press had gone she'd be able to walk out of the front door and straight over the road like any normal tourist. Mind made up, Saskia headed back to the pretty master bedroom she had chosen to occupy, only to come to an abrupt halt. A small bag she had never seen before sat on her bed, a note on the top. Her heart sped up to a panicked thrum. That hadn't been there a few minutes ago. Who had put it there? Was Idris sending her away? She stared at the note for a long

moment then slowly walked towards it, picking it up gingerly as if it might come to life under her fingertips.

> *There's a car downstairs.*
> *You're expected at the London Palatial Hotel spa.*
> *There may be scones.*
> *Enjoy.*
> *I*

Saskia read the note through and then through again, her heart slowing as she took in the words. An afternoon to herself in a spa was an unusually thoughtful gesture—or not that unusual, she thought, fingering the charm bracelet she rarely took off. She took a deep, steadying breath. Maybe it would be a good thing to have some time out before she tackled Idris.

The famous spa was as imposingly luxurious as Saskia had heard, although as Princess Saskia of Dalmaya she was accorded the kind of reverential welcome plain Saskia Harper with her maxed-out credit card and second-hand clothes would never have enjoyed. She pushed that thought away, determined to wring the most out of the hot stone massage, facial and manicure that had been booked for her.

By the time she was escorted to the personal hot tub with rose petals sprinkled in the water and candles lit on every conceivable surface she felt like a new woman and ready for the difficult conversation that lay ahead. It wasn't that she didn't appreciate this thoughtful gesture, but she recognised that through her entire childhood she'd been bought off with lavish gifts. Her questions had never been answered. She had never found out why she didn't meet her father's dates, why her mother had

left her, where her father's money had come from. Not until it all came crashing down.

She needed knowledge and agency, not just gestures.

Before she knew it her time was up and a smiling assistant helped her into one of the luxurious silk robes, guiding her to a small dressing room. Saskia stopped at the threshold and stared. A beautiful, full-length dress in her favourite pale pink hung on the wall, its cap sleeves embellished with a silver thread, the same thread accenting the waist and the hem, tiny delicate crystals shimmering in the chiffon overskirt. Silver sandals and a matching clutch bag were carefully placed on a stool and a make-up artist stood by the dressing table, the tools of her trade spread out in front of her. 'Please take a seat, Your Highness,' she said. 'Would you like your hair up or down?'

'I…' Saskia looked over at the dress again. 'I don't actually know where I'm going.' What on earth was going on? Her pulse sped up; surely she wasn't heading straight to an official event? Not when she was still living down the last one?

'Half and half, I think, if we're going to use this tiara.' The stylist held up a delicate silver chain punctuated with crystals in every twist.

'Fine. Thanks.' Every item in this room was perfect, exactly what she would have picked for herself, from the rose-pink bra and knickers draped over the chair behind her to the tiara dangling from the stylist's fingers. Only she had no idea who had chosen them for her and where she would be going in them.

Saskia took a deep breath, willing her panicked pulse to calm. She'd spent the last seven years micromanaging every second. It was the only way she had managed to survive. She didn't know what Idris expected from

this gesture but as far as she was concerned their talk
had just moved from important to urgent, and once they
had had that talk she'd know whether she could stay
with him, or if the marriage he offered was too pain-
ful for her to bear.

CHAPTER FOURTEEN

IDRIS PACED UP and down the famous domed foyer, re-flecting that with all the marble and archways it was a little like being back in his own palace. He should feel at home, but, despite the coolness of the autumn evening, his suit felt too warm, too constricted. He pulled at his bow tie, wishing he'd opted for Dalmayan formal dress rather than the restrictions of a tuxedo. He glanced at his watch. Saskia should be here by now. Had he done the right thing, springing this on her? What if she hated it? What if he had got it all wrong? Relying on the judgement of a nine-year-old boy and of his impulsive mother could be the biggest mistake of all.

No, not the biggest mistake. That had happened seven years ago. It was time to atone.

His heart thumped as the great doors finally swung open. Saskia stood poised at the entrance, eyes wide as she looked in at the well-lit hall. 'What on earth are we doing at the V&A?' She stepped inside but made no move to come any closer to him.

'It's your favourite place.'

'Yes. But…' She shook her head, the soft waves of her hair rippling as she did so. 'I don't understand.'

'I wanted you to know that I notice things, that I'm not quite as cold, as unfeeling as I appear. I wanted you

to know that I know your favourite colour is pink even though fashion tells you not to wear it.'

She tilted her chin at that, one hand touching the ends of her vibrant hair. 'It's a stupid rule.'

'You look beautiful in pink,' he said softly. His mother had picked out her dress with her unerring eye for style. Saskia was like a goddess of light, the silk and chiffon draping every curve and falling in folds to the floor. Marlowe's immortal words came back to him, just as they had that day at the library all those years before. She could launch one thousand ships, ten thousand and he would be at the very lead, doing whatever it took to win his wife back.

'I know afternoon tea is your favourite meal. How were the scones at the spa, by the way?'

'Delicious.' Her face was still suspicious. 'Everyone else was on watercress soup. I thought I might be lynched, especially when I spread the butter on extra thick.'

'I know that you prefer white gold to rose gold and your jewellery less ostentatious than Dalmayan fashion.' The delicate tiara flashed, wound through her fiery hair, and the charm bracelet glinted on her wrist. 'And I know I owe you an explanation.'

She held up one elegant hand. 'Idris, why did you put those clauses in the wedding contract?'

He stilled. This wasn't what he had expected her to say. 'Clauses?'

'Yes. I asked one of the embassy staff to translate it for me. There were clauses in there that weren't in the version my lawyer read to me. Handwritten clauses, which were evidently added after I'd approved the draft.' She watched him carefully. 'In the version I read I was to have appropriate alimony for the boys if we

divorced. Generous alimony, life-changing alimony but appropriate. In the version I read this week I have been given the villa outright, I am allowed to divorce you at any time with no contest, keep full custody of the boys, as long as I bring Sami to Dalmaya every summer, and I'm entitled to the kind of alimony people tear each other apart in divorce courts for. That's not just generous, Idris.' She swallowed. 'That's an invitation. An invitation to divorce.'

He had added those clauses the night after they slept together, knowing they had crossed a line they might not be able to retreat back to. Idris held her gaze. 'I forced you into marrying me. I wanted to make sure you had options, a genuine choice.'

'I didn't go into this marriage intending to end it as soon as it got hard. I'm not saying I thought we'd grow old together but neither was I planning to cash my chips in and waltz out as quickly as I entered. My word means something, Idris.'

'I know.'

'Was it about giving me a choice or about giving me a push? I know I embarrassed you, embarrassed the palace…'

'No, Saskia. You didn't.' Here it was. The moment he had been both anxious for and dreading. The moment he told her who he was and what he was and allowed her to judge him. To walk away if he was unworthy. The moment Idris Delacour stopped hiding from life, from love, from the agony of feeling. 'The truth was I was jealous.'

'Jealous?'

'Jealous. You were having so much fun, and not with me. That's understandable.' He huffed out a laugh. 'I sent you into that room with a list of strictures and rules

and didn't think for a moment that a woman in her twenties, a woman who's done nothing but be responsible for the last seven years, might need to unwind sometimes. Just because I never allow myself to unwind. When you fell I could have, should have laughed it off. It was nothing, but all I could see was headlines, judgements.'

He paused, searching for the right words to confess. 'The truth is I was still reeling from seeing how happy you had looked just before you fell, how happy you were away from the palace and the responsibilities I had forced on you. Those aren't escape clauses, Saskia, they are a promise that you can walk away any time. That I was wrong to bully you into this world. God knows, it's hard enough for me, and I at least had some training, some awareness of what it entails.'

Saskia's eyes were fixed on him, her gaze almost painful in its intensity. 'It was just so nice to see Robbie I forgot why I was there. What I should have done was arrange to see him later, at the palace, when you were there and we could have caught up away from prying eyes and cameras. I know that now. I was just so tired of everyone watching me, of being on display all the time, I relaxed too much. The fall was an accident but it wouldn't have happened if I'd been more careful.'

She took a deep breath. 'The thing is I can't guarantee I won't mess up again, Idris. In fact I can guarantee I will. I'm not trained for this, any of it, and I'm not naturally dignified like you and Maya. And that would be okay, if I thought you were on my side. But if you are going to freeze me out every time I mess up...' She shook her head. 'I don't need obscene alimony or want it. But if you're not on my side then I can't stay with you. Not even for the boys because they shouldn't have to grow up seeing that...'

His heart swelling, Idris walked over to his wife, to the woman he knew he loved so much he would let her walk away if that was what she needed—the woman he would then spend every moment winning back, proving he could love her the way she needed to be loved, valued for everything she was. He took her hands. 'Look at me, Saskia.'

She raised her eyes to his, the vulnerability in their depths striking him harder than anger or hatred ever could have.

'I am on your side,' he said. 'Always. It took me a while to realise that, but I am. I let you down, back when we were younger, and I let you down last week. I let you down because I put my pride first, because I didn't want to admit I was jealous. Because I didn't want to admit I loved you.'

The words echoed round and round the great hallway. 'You...you what?' Saskia was trembling, with hope, with the first glimmers of happiness, with fear that this was all a dream.

Idris's grip tightened on hers and she returned the pressure, holding on as if he were all that was holding her up. 'I love you, Saskia Harper. You have grown into an extraordinary, intelligent, compassionate woman and Dalmaya is lucky to have you as its Queen. Saskia, I am so proud to be able to call you my wife and I'm so sorry that I haven't made that clear, that, rather than show the world how much I love you, our wedding was behind closed doors.' He looked down at her, the dark eyes simmering. 'I said I wanted to give you choices, Saskia, and I am. Here, today.' His mouth quirked into a half-smile. 'If that's what you want, that is.'

'Choices?' All she could do was parrot the words back to him.

'Choices. And this time the choice is genuinely yours. Either we stay as we are, a marriage of convenience. Joint monarchs, parents, hopefully friends. I know it won't be easy, not after the events of the last few weeks, but I promise to work harder, to make it easier.'

Saskia could feel the beat of her heart, each one just that little bit faster than the one before, the rush of her blood around her shaking body. Could she go back to the marriage of convenience she had agreed to? Knowing that she loved him and that he loved her?

'Or,' he continued, 'you take advantage of the clauses in that contract and walk away, no hard feelings.'

Just like that she could have her life back. The house, the degree, the career. They didn't hold the allure they once had. She was beginning to love Dalmaya, the people and the desert and the all-encompassing heat. She could see a role there, a way to make her mark on the evolving country. 'They're my choices?' The hope had fizzled out, flat like left-out lemonade. He'd said he loved her but there was no love in this sterile pair of choices. She tried to tug her hands away but he still held them firmly in his grasp.

'No. There's one more.' The tenderness in his eyes was new and as Saskia stared into their dark depths she knew she had no defences against it. All she could do was stand there, holding onto him. 'Through there, in one of the galleries and the gardens, are your friends. Work colleagues who miss you, fellow students who can't wait to discuss essays with you, neighbours hoping you're coming back. Some of our old Oxford friends— including Rob—who mourn Maya and Fayaz as much as we do. Jack's old school friends and their parents.

You told me you had no one, Saskia, but when my mother, Faye, Lucy and I rang around the names Jack gave us I realised you made an impact on every person you knew. The mother whose sons you took to the park with Jack when her baby was colicky. The neighbour you made stews for when she was ill. The students you coached online. The other temps you supported through job after job. They all love you and they are all here.'

The litany of names was a revelation. Saskia felt the truth of Idris's words as each one sank in, warming her from within. She'd been too scared to let anyone in, to confide in them, to admit how hard it was but she hadn't been a lone wolf, not all the time.

'They're here?'

'Officially they've been invited to celebrate our new family, a party for Sami and Jack. But there's an official standing by ready to marry us, if that's what you want. If you want more than signing a contract in a language you don't understand. If you want to make vows, a commitment. Because that's what I want, Saskia, to tell the world how much I love and cherish you. To make you my wife in more than name, to make you the wife of my heart.'

It took several moments for his words to register. To realise just what he was saying. 'I...I...' She pulled her hands away and placed them on her hips. 'You call that a proposal, Your Highness Sheikh Idris Delacour Al Osman?'

The anxiety vanished from his eyes as Idris's mouth tilted into his rare and, oh, so sweet smile. 'Sheikha Saskia Harper, Princess, mother, wife, Queen. Will you do me the very great honour of becoming my wife in reality as well as in name?' He reached into his pocket and pulled out a box, opening it up as he sank onto one

knee before her. 'Rubies, Saskia. Red like your hair, like the desert sunset, like the fire in my soul. A fire I didn't even know existed until I met you.'

At his words her heart swelled, all the love she had been keeping banked up, hidden away, finally rushing free, filling every nerve, every atom, every cell with the knowledge she was his as he was hers. Saskia stared at the antique ring, her heart swelling, then back at Idris, allowing herself to soak in the tenderness, the hope and passion in his eyes.

'Yes. Of course I will. I thought I loved you when I was nineteen, and in some ways I did, but I was just a child. I didn't really understand what love was. But I do love you now, with all my heart, and I want to marry you, properly, with vows and meaning and love. Yes, I do.'

Idris slid the delicate ring carefully onto her finger before getting up, joy writ all over his usually impassive face. 'You won't regret it,' he vowed as he held her close. 'I love you, Saskia.'

Looking up at him, she saw the truth of it and knew that although their road would never be an easy one if they could walk it together they could face anything.

* * * * *

THE SURGEON
KING'S SECRET BABY

AMY RUTTAN

This book is dedicated to all the mothers waiting next to their child's hospital bed. Waiting for a miracle.

And this book is also dedicated to all those doctors out there who perform those miracles on tiny humans.

Thank you.

PROLOGUE

Isla Hermosa—war-torn country

"I NEED A unit of packed cells—stat!" Reagan shouted over her shoulder. But no sooner had the words left her mouth than another explosion rocked the mobile hospital unit.

She had a wounded man open on her table, and instinctively she threw her body over her patient's to try and prevent dust and debris from entering into the exposed body cavity.

After working in this war-torn place for over a year, throwing herself over a patient came as second nature. It shouldn't have to, but such was the nature of war.

Isla Hermosa had been a beautiful, peaceful country once. A paradise in the Atlantic for vacation-goers. A country founded by Spanish and Greek settlers over seven hundred years ago, full of pristine beaches and tall palm trees.

Now the beach they were on just held the charred remains of its tall palms, and the blue sky was blackened with plumes of smoke rising from the capital. Dust filled the hot air, making it hard to breathe. There was no relief.

It was not ideal to be operating out in the open like this, but it was stiflingly hot on the beach, and being closed up in a tent in this humidity would not make matters any better. What they needed was a hospital, but that was impos-

sible. Most of Isla Hermosa had been taken over by the rebellion, and Canadian peacekeepers, along with those on Isla Hermosa who remained loyal to the dysfunctional Hermosian King Aleksander, had been pushed out of the city and back to the Atlantic Ocean.

The mortar fire stopped and Reagan went back to work on saving this Hermosian soldier's life. As a trauma surgeon for the Canadian Armed Forces she had seen her share of war-torn countries. As soon as she'd had her medical training she'd joined up for active duty. She wanted to serve her country. To prove to herself.

To whom?

She shook that thought away and continued her work. It wouldn't matter soon. Her agreed-upon tour of duty was ending and she had to return to the attending position that was waiting for her in Toronto.

She didn't know quite what she was going to do with herself back there, besides work. During patients there was down time, card games and a camaraderie. She didn't really have any one in Toronto. The people she served with were like a family. Not like *her* family, though. Not really, because her real family was cold and barely in her life.

The people she served with were her family.

In Toronto she'd be all alone. Again.

Toronto was her home town in the sense that she had been born there, and knew it well. She had a job waiting for her, but it wasn't really home. Her parents weren't there anymore.

Her parents had retired and moved to warmer climes while she'd served. They hadn't even told her that they sold her childhood home until a letter she'd sent them came back marked "Return to Sender."

Only the Canadian Army had ever wanted her, but she had to return to Toronto. She'd served the time she'd signed

up for and her leave of absence from the Toronto hospital was ending.

The friends she'd made here would forget her soon enough. No relationship ever lasted and that was fine. She was used to that. She didn't want to rely on anyone.

Her parents had taught her well. They'd always told her to make a life for herself. Not to rely on them. So she didn't.

I wish I had someone.

She was annoyed that she'd let that little thought sneak in.

Get a grip on yourself, Reagan.

Now was not the time to get maudlin.

"The packed cells you were looking for," a rich, deep voice said, and her body instantly reacted.

Dr. Kainan Laskaris, the foremost trauma surgeon in all of Isla Hermosa, stood beside her. Kainan always unnerved her. He made her feel exposed, vulnerable, as if he knew the pain she was hiding. Knew all her insecurities.

He was the first man in a long time to unnerve her in a *good* way.

"Thanks," she said, barely glancing at him.

When she'd first arrived there she'd tried to keep him at a distance, but it had never worked. He'd wiggled his way in and, though they didn't really talk much about personal stuff, she enjoyed his company. And he was a damn fine surgeon.

He hung the unit of packed cells, calmly drowning out the chaos of the war that was going on in the background.

His presence made her very aware of how very close the quarters were in this tent, but he helped her focus. He distracted her from all that was going on outside.

"How do you keep such a calm demeanor?" she'd asked, the first time they'd worked together on the wounded during mortar fire.

"I drown it out. I ignore it. I think of it as thunder, or

something else, and focus on the person in front of me. I try to picture my patient's life and on my duty to return this patient to those who love him or her. Clear your mind and picture the life you're saving."

It had worked. The tactic had worked and helped her focus.

She was going to miss working with him.

"Do you need help, Dr. Cote?" Kainan asked, but he was already pulling on a pair of surgical gloves.

If he had been any other surgeon she would have barked orders to him, as she outranked most in her unit, but there was something about Kainan that commanded respect.

She could never turn him down, and she didn't want to. He knew what she needed in surgery without asking. He was like a second set of hands for her.

"Thank you," she said. "Are there no others?"

"No, the fighting is ending. The rebels are being driven back—that's the last report that I heard."

Kainan went straight to work, helping her repair the damage to the soldier.

He shook his head and *tsked* in disgust. "This situation should never have happened."

"I agree," she responded.

She didn't know much about what had caused the once peaceful island kingdom of Isla Hermosa to erupt into revolution, but she knew it had something to do with King Aleksander, after he'd been crowned after his father's death.

The former King, Mateo, had been instrumental in aligning his kingdom with Canada, and had had a good relationship with the country and good trade agreements.

King Mateo had been a great king for more than fifty years, but his eldest son, Aleksander, was not proving to be so great.

Isla Hermosa had severed its ties with Spain five hundred years ago, so when the revolution had broken out

Canada had promised to help. Isla Hermosa had called to Canada and Canada had responded.

Which was why she was there.

"I hope this is over soon," she said as she finished her repair of the spleen. "My orders came in last night and I'm shipping out tomorrow."

"So soon?"

There was a hint of disappointment in Kainan's voice, which made her heart skip a beat.

Don't get hung up. It's probably nothing. You're a good surgeon and he can see that.

The mortar fire had become distant and the unit of soldiers that had been lying in wait to protect the hospital began to move. Tanks were soon going by, kicking up dust.

Reagan cursed under her breath and covered her patient again.

Kainan helped her. She was very aware of his body close to hers as they protected their patient.

"I thought you would stay until the end," he said, after the roar of the tanks had died down.

They went back to work as the dust settled.

"No, a new unit has come in to relieve us. They'll stay until Isla Hermosa is back on its feet."

"That could be some time," Kainan muttered darkly. "I wonder if Isla Hermosa will ever recover from this."

"Hopefully it will. Your country has seen enough bloodshed."

"Yes." There was sadness in his voice.

She wondered if he'd lost loved ones. They worked well together, and he was a brilliant surgeon, but they didn't delve much into personal issues beyond the sphere of this surgical unit.

Which was fine with her.

Even though she knew little about Kainan, there was still camaraderie between them. They'd experienced the

war together here, patching up soldiers and civilians. They were friends and she'd miss him.

Even though it would be good to put some distance between them. She didn't want to do something she'd regret.

Live a little.

"I've grown accustomed to working with you," he said, and those dark eyes held her captive.

It thrilled her, unnerved her, this effect he had on her.

Reagan smiled behind her surgical mask. "I like working with you too, but it looks like this is the end."

Kainan nodded. "I guess so."

Reagan finished her repair and began to close up. Her patient would be taken to Spain which was the closest hospital they could get to, where he would be monitored in a military hospital. At least now he would survive the journey.

They didn't say anything as they prepared the soldier for transport, loading him onto the waiting helicopter that would carry him to an American aircraft carrier. A medical plane would take the soldier on to Spain.

When Reagan pulled off her surgical mask and gloves she let out a sigh of exhaustion. She had been working straight for almost twenty-four hours, since the peacekeepers had been pushed back to the beach. It was late afternoon, and though the sun was no longer beating down on them it was still sweltering, and she had the urge to run into the ocean and cool herself off.

Except for the fact that the beach was littered with boats belonging to the allied forces coming ashore.

Kainan was staring back toward the hill where the tall, ancient city gates were. There was smoke rising from the city and he was frowning.

"I'm sorry," she whispered.

She wanted to tell him she knew how he felt, but really she didn't. She didn't know what it was like to lose

the country of your birth. To have it mangled and everything destroyed.

She couldn't even imagine what he was going through.

"You okay?" Kainan asked.

Reagan closed her eyes and shook her head. "You don't need to worry about me. I'm just exhausted."

He cocked his head to one side, those dark brown eyes penetrating her to her very core, and she fought back the urge to run her hands through his thick chestnut curls.

"I think there is more. Sadness has come over you."

"I was just thinking of leaving here. I was thinking..." She trailed off, getting choked up.

She didn't want to tell him that she was sad she was leaving the people she considered friends, the people who were like her family, in order to return to a lonely life in Toronto.

It had never bothered her until now.

"I hate leaving a job undone. There is so much work here, but my tour is over."

He sighed and dragged his hand through his hair. "Yes, there will be many pieces to pick up once the dust settles, but Isla Hermosa will rise again. There have been other wars, other strife that has hit our shores, and we have stood the test of time."

Reagan smiled and they walked in silence back to the tent. There were no more critical patients. Just those with minor wounds that were being made ready for transport off the island.

"Captain Cote, you're officially off duty," said Major Smart as she came to the hospital tent. "You've done a wonderful job, but we're getting ready to pull out. The next rotation is here and you need your rest."

"When does my transport leave, Major?" Reagan asked.

"Zero one hundred. I suggest you get some rest—and that's an order."

Reagan saluted Major Smart and stood there for a few

moments. She had been relieved of duty and at one in the morning she'd leave Isla Hermosa and head back to Petawawa, before being formally and honorably discharged from the Canadian Armed Forces.

"You hungry?" Kainan asked. "You look like you need food and rest."

"I do—but don't you have to move to the front with the Hermosian Army?"

Kainan shook his head, a strange expression crossing his face. "Not yet. I have time. Why do you think I came here to help with the wounded when our mobile medical unit is further up the line?"

Reagan smiled. "I've just got used to seeing you hanging around these last few months. Usually getting in my way."

Kainan grinned that mischievous grin which always caused her pulse to race. If they weren't here in the middle of a war... But they were, and Kainan was off-limits. She was leaving in a matter of hours and she wasn't even sure that she'd ever see him again.

"You have a beautiful smile, Reagan."

A blush crept up her cheeks. "What?"

"You never smile for me. You're always so serious."

"This is war. I don't feel much like smiling."

Kainan stopped and took her hand, those intense dark eyes focused on her. She wasn't used to that. She wasn't used to the attention.

"You look tired, Reagan. You need sleep and food."

"I'm fine."

"Come."

It wasn't a request, it was an order, and technically he outranked her. Kainan placed his hand on the small of her back and led her toward the mess tent.

She was so exhausted that she let him get food and a Thermos of coffee, but he didn't let her sit down at a table. Instead he led her outside.

"Where are we going?" Reagan asked tiredly. "The beach is full of armed personnel."

"We're not going to the beach. We're going to my tent. It's in a shady spot and we won't be in any danger."

"There was mortar fire not that long ago," she said, falling into step beside him.

Kainan sighed. "The rebels have surrendered and there's a cease-fire. We should be at peace for a while."

Kainan's tent was on the edge of the Hermosian camp that bordered the Canadian forces' camp. And it *was* in a shady spot, with camouflage netting. They took a seat down in the sand under the awning, and felt the breeze blow in off the Atlantic.

Reagan closed her eyes and let the cool air wash over her.

"Here, drink this." Kainan passed her some coffee.

"I'm supposed to be resting."

She took a drink of the dark, sweet Hermosian coffee. She couldn't remember the last time she'd been able to savor a cup of coffee. Usually she downed it quickly, burning her tongue in the process, as she tried to patch together the wounded soldiers and the unfortunate civilians who'd got in the line of fire.

"If you go to bed now you will be even more tired by the time your transport comes because you won't sleep when you're so stressed. Unwind and relax."

"This is nice," she admitted.

"I will miss you," he said out of the blue, and he smiled sadly at her. "You have been a great friend and you're an amazing surgeon. I've enjoyed working with you."

Reagan was shocked, but pleased, and she squeezed his hand. "Ditto."

"Really?" he asked, surprised.

"Of course."

"You could've fooled me. You're so closed-off around me sometimes."

"Then why will you miss me?"

Kainan grinned. "Because you're brave, compassionate…"

"You just called me closed-off," she teased.

"Compassionate with your patients. You have a kind heart."

She blushed again. "Thank you."

"You're also beautiful."

He ran his thumb across her knuckles. His hands were rough from the dry heat and the tough conditions, but they were strong, surgical hands. And the simple touch was both calming and exciting at the same time.

"You're the most beautiful soldier I have ever seen."

His eyes twinkled and he smiled, causing a dimple to pucker in his cheek under his stubble.

Blood heated her cheeks at the compliment. No one ever paid her compliments. She wasn't sure how to take it.

"Why do you need my approval all the time, Reagan? For goodness' sakes, leave me alone. You don't need validation for something that is so ordinary."

Her mother's harsh words rang in her ears.

She began to tremble, thinking about her mother and the lack of parental compassion she'd had growing up.

"You're trembling." Kainan pulled her close and whispered, "Why?"

"Tired. That's all." She was lying, but she didn't want to think of her mother now.

Kainan held her. She buried her head in his chest, drinking in the scent of him, and the human connection she hadn't realized she'd been craving calmed her.

"Where are you going after we pull out?" she asked, still clinging to him.

"To the front lines," he said tersely. "Tonight."

Her heart skipped a beat. The front lines were dangerous. Even if there was a cease-fire, the capital city of Heli-

cia had become a tangled mess of debris, mines and IEDs. The thought of him getting hurt scared her.

"You're shivering again," he whispered as he rubbed her back.

"I'm just worried about you advancing tonight." She looked up at him. "It'll be dangerous."

He grinned at her. "I will be okay. I will worry about you too, you know."

"I'll be on military transport, headed back to Canada."

"Things happen—and Canada is a long way away. A whole ocean divides us."

He reached out and stroked her cheek, wiping the tears from her face, and before she knew what was happening he was kissing her. Tenderly at first, and then possessively, but it felt so good and she kissed him back, gripping the collar of his tattered linen shirt as if his life and hers depended on it.

"I'm sorry," he whispered breathlessly against her mouth. "I don't know what came over me. I've gotten so used to being around you, seeing you every day, just the thought of not seeing you…"

She should put an end to it, the kissing, but she just wanted to *feel*. She wanted to give in to the attraction she felt for him. The white-hot lust.

It would be once.

Just one time.

It had been so long since she'd been with someone, since she had any kind of intimacy.

"No apologies—and don't stop." She kissed him again, running her hands through his hair.

"Reagan, we need to stop."

"Why?"

"I'm advancing and you're leaving. What future do we have?"

"Right now, none. But I'm not asking for a future, Kai-

nan. I just want to *feel* tonight. I just want a connection with you. I've been fighting it since I met you."

He nodded, his gaze holding hers. "Me as well."

"So don't stop," she whispered, pulling him into another kiss which seared her very soul.

He stood to his feet, helping her up. "Come."

Reagan thought that he was going to take her back to her camp, but instead he led her inside his tent, taking her in his arms.

"I want you so much, Reagan. I wanted you the first moment I saw you. But I don't want to make you a promise I may not be able to keep," he whispered against her ear.

"I care for you too. And you don't need to promise me anything. I just want this."

"As you wish," he said, before kissing her again, making her melt into his arms completely.

It was dark outside and she could hear movement. People on the move to the front lines. She rolled over in the narrow cot that she and Kainan were sharing and glanced at her watch. It was midnight. In an hour her transport would be leaving. She had to pack up what little gear she had and get to the rendezvous point.

Kainan was already up and dressed in his uniform, which she'd rarely seen him wear at the mobile hospital. It was a bit surreal, and thinking about him in danger made her stomach knot with unease.

"I was just about to wake you," he said gently.

"Sorry I slept so long here."

"No, it's okay." He leaned over and kissed her. "I have to go with the next transport to the front lines. There is fighting going on in the city. More wounded. I'm needed there."

"I thought there was a cease-fire?" she said, dressing quickly in her wrinkled clothes.

"There was, but some insurgents have been found hiding in the city. It will be taken care of."

He said that with a finality which sent a shiver down her spine.

She finished dressing.

He took her in his arms and held her close.

"Please be safe," she whispered, drinking in the scent of him. She wanted to remember every moment of this time with him, and she sent up a silent prayer that he would be safe.

"You too, Reagan. My beautiful Reagan. I shall never forget you." Kainan kissed her. "Come, we'd better go."

They walked out of his tent and saw the Hermosian camp was a flurry of activity. He walked her as far as he could, to where the Canadian forces were packing up what they could, ready to join the Hermosian Army.

"I'll never forget you," she said, and she wouldn't.

How could she forget him? A man who had seemed to see past her façade. A dangerous and yet gentle man, and one heck of a surgeon.

A man she'd been proud to serve with.

"Ditto."

He kissed her hand one last time and then headed toward a large transporter that was waiting for him. He climbed up into the back of the armored vehicle and waved at her as the truck rumbled away into the darkness toward the front lines.

Please keep him safe.

Reagan headed back to the tent she shared with another surgeon. She packed up her kit bag and then waited for her transport.

It was past 1:00 a.m. when the radio in the mess hall crackled to life.

"Explosion. Hermosian medical transport attacked. All personnel dead."

The words hit her like a rock and her stomach knotted. She closed her eyes and bit her lip as the words hit her.

Maybe it wasn't Kainan's transport?

She wanted to stay and find out if his name was on the list, but her transport came then.

She was airlifted to the waiting Canadian vessel which would take her back home. She was assigned her berth, but as soon as she'd set her bag down she found the nearest commanding officer from her unit.

"General Travis, do you have a list of casualties from that Hermosian medical transport?"

General Travis shook his head. "No, not a full list, but I know who you're asking about and I'm sorry, Captain Cote. I know that you worked with Dr. Laskaris, but his name *is* on the list of those who perished. His dog tags were found and not much else. An IED near the palace went off."

Reagan's stomach twisted and she ran to the side of the boat, losing what little food she'd managed to eat since leaving Kainan and arriving on the transport, over the side of the ship.

General Travis patted her back. "I'm sorry, Captain."

She nodded, and managed to keep the tears at bay.

This was why she kept people at distance, why she never let anyone in. Because in an instant they could be taken from you. They left. They died.

Kainan had wormed his way in past her defenses and now he was gone.

She was alone.

Completely alone.

She should have known better. She was *meant* to be alone.

It was easier that way.

CHAPTER ONE

A year later, Toronto

REAGAN WALKED THROUGH the halls of the hospital in a daze. There wasn't enough coffee in the world to wake her up. It had been a long shift at the hospital and then her infant son had a bad night. The cot in her son's hospital room in the pediatric critical care unit wasn't exactly comfortable, and she could use a break to go home and have a shower.

The problem was there was no one to give her a break.

It was just her and Peter in the world.

A year ago she'd spent an unforgettable night in Kainan's arms. A night that she would cherish forever. Then he'd gone to the front lines and died for his country.

She'd come back to her life in Toronto, empty and alone.

Although it had turned out she was not completely alone, because her one night with Kainan had resulted in pregnancy.

It was the best gift.

A piece of Kainan.

A child.

Someone to love.

And she wasn't going to make Peter feel like a mistake, the way her parents had made *her* feel.

Nothing she'd ever done had pleased them.

Her father had never wanted kids. When her mother had got pregnant with Reagan he'd stuck around, but he had always been distant. Over time, her mother had come to resent her for causing such distance in her marriage.

There had been times when she'd got shreds of love and affection from her mother, but it they had been few and far between.

She'd thought maybe being grandparents would soften her parents' hearts.

She'd been wrong.

When she'd told her mother about the situation—about the baby and the father dying—her mother's response had been heartless. Painful.

"Get rid of the problem, Reagan. You can't raise a baby on your own."

"I'm not getting rid of the baby, Mother."

"Then what do you want from me, Reagan?"

Honestly, she didn't know. Some part of her had hoped her mother would change, but she should have known better.

Reagan had always been a burden to them. And her getting pregnant overseas on a mission was just another disappointment for her parents. They were even more disappointed that she'd kept the baby.

As soon as Reagan had found out she was pregnant she'd vowed that she'd protect Peter. She'd give him the love she had never had, the compassion she had to learn by herself.

No one would hurt Peter. *Ever.*

Her parents had never cared about her. They'd only taken care of her because they were legally obligated to do so.

"I've never run from my mistakes, Reagan. That's why I took care of you. At the time, abortion wasn't an option."

Reagan was a mistake. It hurt to hear it time and time again.

She focused on the lukewarm coffee she was drinking.

A baby had never been in her plan, but she was responsible for her actions. There were plenty of single parents out there, going it alone. And she would do the same. She would *never* let Peter feel as if he was an obligation or a mistake.

But what should have been one of the most joyous days of her life, when Peter was born, had quickly turned into her worst nightmare.

In all her years as an intern and then a resident in hospital, and then her time in the field with the Canadian military, serving as a trauma surgeon during natural disasters and being tossed into the fray of war zones, she'd seen many sick children. Critically ill children. It had always been a deep-rooted fear of hers that one day, if she ever had a child, something might happen to that child.

She had never been able to handle the thought of it.

And then it had happened.

She'd had Peter.

"Let me see him!" she'd cried, relieved that the birth was over.

Only none of the doctors had answered her. Marisa, her OB/GYN, hadn't looked at her. It was in that moment that Reagan had realized the baby wasn't crying. There wasn't a sound coming from him at all.

"What's wrong?" Reagan had asked.

She'd craned her neck as Marisa had turned back to her, watching the pediatrician on call with her baby in his hands, blue-grey and barely moving.

It had only been a couple of hours later when she'd learned that her baby had cardiomyopathy and would be staying in the hospital indefinitely. The only reminder of her and Kainan's time together was placed on the list for UNOS and would be staying there while he waited for a new heart.

The nursery she had so painstakingly started to prepare in her small apartment before his birth was still unused,

and she hadn't been able to look at it the few fleeting times she'd managed to get home.

Don't think about it—and don't think about Kainan.

Even a year since his death often Kainan crept into her thoughts because Peter looked like him so much. And she couldn't help but wonder what it would have been like had Kainan lived.

Reagan had had a couple of relationships before Kainan, but they'd failed because of *her*—because she couldn't trust. At the back of her mind she was terrified she'd disappoint, that she'd never be good enough and her heart would be broken. Again.

It was better this way.

She was better off alone.

"Reagan, you look like you didn't get a wink of sleep!"

Reagan rubbed her tired, sore eyes and saw the Chief of Surgery leaning over the central desk, where he'd been studying a chart.

Michael McNeil had been so understanding. He'd trained her as a resident, and encouraged her into the Canadian Armed Forces to expand her skills, and since she'd announced her pregnancy and Peter's birth he'd been accommodating, knowing she needed to work. Right now he was looking at her with pity. Like most people. She hated pity.

"We need better cots on the NICU floor," she mumbled, stifling a yawn.

"Are you going to be able to work with this new doctor?" he asked.

Reagan nodded. She needed this job. It was more pay, and not so much time spent doing surgical rounds. Right now she couldn't do a lot of surgery. A call about a heart might come in at any time, and she needed to be near Peter.

Peter was all she had.

She really needed sleep, but right now she needed work

more. It kept her sane. And she was looking forward to this new job. It was more flexible.

"Yeah, I'm good." She walked to the other side of the central desk and poured herself another cup of coffee into a plastic cup and capped it.

"Good. I know things have been hard—"

She held up her hand to cut the chief off. "Michael, I'm okay. I need the work. I *love* the work. And Peter is not that far away. Besides, I'm the only staff member available who knows American Sign Language."

"And you worked in Isla Hermosa as well," Michael said, setting down his chart.

Reagan's heart skipped a beat—which was silly. "The new specialist is from Isla Hermosa?"

Michael nodded. "The Canadian government is giving him asylum. His work is important. That's all I know. And he's a brilliant teacher. I think he will be an asset to our medical students."

"I wonder if I worked with him?" Reagan said, taking another sip of the bitter coffee. The caffeine was doing its job. There had been many other Hermosian physicians out in the field whom she'd worked alongside, but none had been like Kainan.

No one will ever be like Kainan.

She couldn't think about him now.

"I don't know, but the Canadian government was very adamant that he should be given asylum here, and after chatting with him over email I'm very excited to have him on board."

"I'm looking forward to meeting him," said Reagan. "To become a surgical consultant when you can't speak— that's impressive."

She couldn't recall any nonverbal surgeons out in the field on Isla Hermosa. Of course it had been a war zone. Everything was a bit blurry about her experience. Except...

"Well, he could speak before. He was injured at the front and a badly placed endotracheal tube damaged his vocal cords. I'm told he can speak a bit—but not much, and not for long periods of time. He will be getting corrective surgery here before the New Year, but for now you'll help him."

"Of course," she agreed. She would be happy to. "Does he know about my son and my need for flexibility?"

"No," Michael said. "I told him you needed a flexible schedule, but I thought it best if you tell him about Peter if you want to."

She breathed a sigh of relief. "Thanks."

It was exhausting, constantly explaining Peter's condition to people. It drained her. The new surgeon didn't need to know about Peter, he just needed to know she needed flexibility—which Michael had taken care of.

Reagan fell into step beside Michael as they walked toward his office, where she would meet this Hermosian doctor and they could get to work.

"So, my job consists of interpreting American Sign Language to the students so he doesn't overtax his voice?"

Michael nodded. "You can use my office to draw up your plans. The first medical students will be coming at one—after the lunch rotation."

Reagan nodded. "Sounds good, Chief."

Michael smiled, and then said softly, "You know we're all here for you, Reagan. If there's anything more we can do…"

Reagan gave Michael a quick nod. She appreciated it, but she didn't want pity or help. Too many people pitied her, and she was tired of it. She was still a surgeon. She was still Reagan Cote, even if it sometimes didn't feel that way.

"I'm good."

"Are you sure?" Michael asked, and there again was that expression of pity that she loathed, directed toward her.

She couldn't push Michael away like she did so many.

He had been her mentor when she was resident. He'd taught her compassion and patient care. Things she hadn't been able to learn from her parents. When she'd started her bedside manner had been atrocious, but Michael had guided her, and he had been the one who welcomed her back with open arms when she'd finished her tour of duty.

"I appreciate it so much, Michael. You know that, but I'm fine. Let me work—it keeps me busy."

Michael gave her a quick kiss on the top of her head and whispered, "He'll pull through."

She nodded, blinking back the tears that always threatened to fall when someone started talking about Peter and his condition. Tears that she had learned to swallow because she had to be strong for Peter.

And for herself.

She had to be tough. There was no time for weeping or sorrow. If she gave in to the grief that she was actually feeling she would collapse and be useless.

This new assignment had come at the perfect time. Even though it would take her off her precious surgical rotation, it would keep her at the hospital.

It would keep her busy and close to Peter.

And that was the most important thing.

"You okay?" Michael asked.

"Perfectly."

Reagan plastered on the fake smile she was used to wearing. The one she'd perfected when she was a small girl, because her father had liked her just a bit better when she'd smiled, and had been nicer to her mother when Reagan had smiled and behaved.

Michael nodded and then opened the door.

Reagan stepped in, seeing the Hermosian doctor had his back to her. Something tugged at the corner of her mind, but she couldn't sift through the fog—or maybe she was hav-

ing a hard time seeing. Maybe she was so sleep-deprived that this was just a dream.

She began to tremble.

"Dr. Kainan Laskaris—I would like to introduce you to Dr. Reagan Cote, who will be working with you here at the hospital."

The ghost turned around, those dark, expressive eyes of his hollow and wide with shock. The beautifully chiseled face was marred with scars, and on his throat she could see where they had put the botched endotracheal tube. It was almost as if his throat had been slit, the scar was so bad. The dark brown curls were tamed, and streaked with silver. He'd aged. The war had aged him. But he was still devastatingly handsome.

He opened his mouth, as if to say something, but then snapped it shut. And his lips pressed together firmly, as if he was angry.

Her coffee shook in the cup she was gripping so tightly. Her world was spinning and her tight rein on those emotions she'd become so darn good at locking away had gone slack.

She was losing control.

"Never lose control, Reagan. Don't show your weakness to anyone or they'll take advantage of you."

Her mother's voice was screaming in her head.

"Kainan?" her voice finally squeaked out in disbelief.

"You two know each other?" Michael asked.

She waited for that deep, rich voice to answer, *Si.* That affirmation had always made her go a bit weak in the knees.

But of course it couldn't.

His voice had been taken from him.

Instead he just nodded quickly and looked away. As if he was annoyed she was there.

"We worked together on Isla Hermosa during my last tour of duty," Reagan answered, steadying her hand so

Michael wouldn't see her tremble. "And we worked well together."

Michael looked visibly relieved. "I'm glad to hear it! Well, I'll leave you two to it. I'm sure you have a lot of catching up to do."

Reagan didn't even see Michael leave. She just heard the door shut, her gaze focused on Kainan. The man she'd thought was dead.

He stared back at her, but he didn't smile at her the way he'd used to. There was no twinkle in his eyes. Just darkness. It was cold. It didn't faze her, didn't hurt her. She was used to people looking at her that way. It did sting a little, and it gave her confirmation that Kainan was like all the other men she'd met. Like her father. Cold and distant.

"You're alive." It wasn't so much a question as it was a statement of fact, because she'd thought he'd died.

Clearly, he signed in American Sign Language, barely looking at her.

"They told me you had died."

His expression softened briefly. *I'm sorry. There was a lot of confusion at first. I was reported dead for days...*

"Your medical transport was attacked and they found your dog tags in the rubble."

Again, there was a lot of confusion.

It was obvious that he wasn't going to give any further information about it.

Reagan sat down on one of the chairs at the table in Michael's office. There was a stack of materials there. New orientation information for Kainan. She needed to keep busy and not think about why he never reached out to her.

"Has anyone explained all this stuff to you?" she asked as she quickly scanned the binder full of information. If she kept busy she could ignore the racing of her pulse, her trembling hands, the urge to hug him and cry because he was alive.

He shook his head and took a seat across from her. Then he cleared his throat. "Best…come…from…you."

His voice was broken, harsh and guttural. And color bloomed in his cheeks. It was either embarrassment or anger, and knowing Kainan it was most likely anger.

She knew how much he liked to be in control of every situation. He'd commanded all those around him during surgery, and those working with him had followed him blindly.

When he lost control he got angry, but that would drive him to work harder to solve the problem and regain control.

He was an amazing surgeon.

And this loss of control…

She could only imagine what he was going through. She liked control in *her* life, but she'd learned a humble lesson when Peter was born. Control was just an illusion.

Reagan had to admit that she was angry too. That he was alive and hadn't let her know. He'd known where she was going. He'd known so much about her. Why hadn't he reached out?

Only she couldn't think about that right now. She'd swallow the anger she had and do her job. Keep moving forward as she had always done. If she stopped for a second everything would fall apart.

"Okay," she said, setting her half-empty coffee cup down and opening up the materials. "We can do this together."

Is there anyone else? he signed.

The words were like a slap. He didn't want her here. She realized his body language was more than just embarrassment or anger over his situation. He was annoyed that she was here, helping him.

Her spine stiffened.

She should have known his attention to her back then had just been seduction. He didn't want to see her again. He'd just been using her.

You wanted it too.

Well, she wasn't going to let him shove her aside. She had a job to do, and anyway she'd got the best part of him. She had Peter, and she didn't regret that for anything.

"No, there is no one else. I am the only doctor here who can interpret American Sign Language and who's free to support you." Now she was really annoyed with him. She wasn't going to let him ruin this job for her.

Fine, he signed. He crossed his arms and leaned back in the chair. His gaze was fixed on her, but instead of anger or annoyance, like before, there was bit of humor. Some smugness.

She wanted to wipe that off his face. "What?" she snapped.

I forgot how prickly you get. How fast your walls go up.

The twinkle she knew so well returned to his eyes. It was meant to lighten the mood, but she wasn't in the mood for that.

"I get prickly when people are acting like jerks."

"Sorry." He spoke, his voice now barely a whisper.

Reagan shut the binder and, though she knew she was going to regret it, she had to ask. "Why don't you want to work with me?"

The question caught him off guard. Of course this whole situation had caught him off guard. He'd known that Reagan was Canadian, but hadn't realized that she worked at *this* hospital, in *this* city. Canada was a large country. He'd chosen this hospital simply because Dr. Shaw, his otolaryngologist was here.

He hadn't known that Reagan was here. And he hadn't known that she knew American Sign Language or that she would be working in the education part of the hospital. He'd have thought she would be on the surgical floor,

wherever she worked, which was where *he* wanted to be, but couldn't be any longer.

How could a man with no voice convey what he needed to his surgical staff during an emergency situation? He couldn't, so his surgical career was over.

Of course that wasn't the only reason his career was over.

His throat tightened at the thought of why it was over. It always tightened when his stress levels rose, and he was certainly stressed now.

Seeing Reagan again was a shock.

And he'd had to hold himself back, because his first reaction when he'd seen her had been to run to her and take her in his arms and kiss her. But this wasn't the time or place.

Nowhere was the time or place.

Still, seeing her again had brought back so many memories. Even though they'd served during a war—a brutal war which had torn his country apart—working alongside her had been some of the happiest moments of his life.

He loved his country, but being called back to serve had been painful. Since his mother had died Isla Hermosa had reminded him only of loneliness and pain.

Reagan had brought back joy into his life.

One of the hardest things he'd had to do in his life was to leave her behind, knowing that she was going back home to her country and that he was going to the front lines. That he might never see her again.

It had nearly broken him, but it had been for the best that she'd left when all was said and done. Now circumstances had changed and they could never be together. He'd never trap her the way his mother had been trapped in her marriage to his father.

Still, he wanted Reagan—even though he shouldn't.

Their year apart had done nothing to extinguish the flames of passion that he felt for her.

He still wanted her.

That long, silky brown hair that was so neatly tied back. The long, graceful neck that he'd once run his hands over. And those lips he'd kissed and wanted to taste again.

Only he couldn't now. Not because he'd lost his voice, but because he would never, *ever* put her inside the dangerous situation he now found himself in.

He was a displaced king, of a country that was precarious and about to sink into oblivion, and he couldn't bring her into that situation.

There were people who wanted to assassinate him. And he would gladly take a bullet for his country, because *he* felt responsible for Isla Hermosa's downfall.

He hadn't been able to control his late brother. Kainan had tried, but his brother had ruined the country in six months after their father had ruled gracefully for fifty years.

Now Kainan was King of a broken, bleeding country. And instead of being there he was here in Canada. First in Ottawa, to recuperate from all the injuries that he'd sustained when the palace had been attacked, and now here at this hospital in Toronto, working and waiting for surgery that might or might not return his voice to him. Surgery he might not survive due to the damage in his throat.

Still, he needed a voice to rule. As King, he had a duty to his country—a tradition to uphold and a service which had so depressed his mother and made her feel trapped.

His father had been a great king, but cold, and protocol had come first. Kainan had watched his mother take second place to Isla Hermosa.

So, no, he couldn't drag Reagan into that. The crown would die out with him. And maybe it was better that way.

What's first? he signed.

"Have you got your hospital identification yet?" she asked, leafing through all the papers from Human Resources that Kainan had just skimmed.

No. I haven't got that yet.

"Okay, we'll fill out this paperwork and—"

Kainan touched her arm and got her attention. *Why aren't you practicing surgery?*

"I told you. I'm the only one fluent in American Sign Language here who has room in her schedule to assist you."

So this is a punishment for you?

"What?"

Surgery was your life.

She frowned, and continued to leaf through the binder. "It still is, but I was asked to do this and—" She was interrupted by a knock at the door. "Yes?"

A nurse stuck her head round the door. "I'm sorry to interrupt, Dr. Cote, but it's Peter."

Reagan's expression changed. She frowned, looking worried as she slammed the binder shut. "I'll be right up."

The nurse nodded and shut the door.

"I'm sorry, Kainan. I'll try to be as fast as I can but…it could take a while."

Is it a patient? he asked.

Reagan sighed sadly. Her expression was tired, broken, and Kainan couldn't help but wonder who Peter was. Was Peter her husband?

That brief, fleeting thought of her with another man enraged him. It made him jealous to think of another man loving her.

Not that he deserved to feel *any* sense of jealousy when it came to Reagan. He'd given up those rights when he'd let her go in Isla Hermosa.

"No, it's not a patient." Then she sighed again and looked almost as if she was going to be sick. "Kainan, I'm… He's my son. Peter is my son."

She stood up to leave, her body tense.

Kainan was shocked, and sat back as reality sank in. He hoarsely asked, "Your son?"

And then it dawned on him—because he knew that she hadn't had a child when she was serving alongside him in Isla Hermosa.

A cold tendril of dread unfurled in his belly. He jumped up and stood in front of her, blocking her escape and he cleared his throat. "How. Old?"

"He's three months now. He's your son, Kainan."

Reagan didn't offer any other explanation.

"Never trust women, Kainan. Never. Your mother tried to hide you from me when she wanted to divorce me, but you were a prince of Isla Hermosa. She had no right to do that. But she did try. Women are fickle. They are not devoted, they only think of themselves. Never trust them. Close your heart to them or you'll be hurt!"

Kainan didn't want to hear his late father's voice in his head. He'd been a fine king, but a terrible husband and father.

Still, Reagan hadn't told him he had a son.

"I have to go and check on him. Kainan, please move."

Numb, he stepped to the side so she could open the door.

Of course Kainan was going to let her go, but he needed more answers. His *son*? It couldn't be. Why was his son at the hospital? Why was a nurse taking care of him?

He dashed after Reagan, cursing himself inwardly because he couldn't call out to her to stop, but he caught up with her quickly and grabbed her arm, holding on to her.

She tried to shrug out of his grip until she saw it was him and relaxed.

My son? he signed.

"Yes."

Why didn't you tell me I had a son? Were you trying to

hide him from me? He instantly regretted the words. They were so much like something his father would have said.

Her eyes narrowed. "I thought you were dead. They told me you were dead. I wouldn't hide him from you—you know that."

He wanted to believe that, but his own mother had tried to hide him from his father when she was pregnant.

"I never wanted you locked away in the palace, Kainan. I didn't want you locked away like me. I tried to leave, but I couldn't hide you from him either," his mother had said on her death bed. *"I just wanted us to be happy. To be free. I didn't want you to grow up with him as a father."*

"Why?" He'd felt as if his life was a prison sentence. He was guarded and watched all the time, and though surrounded by people he'd always felt alone. *"Why did you tell him?"*

"I had to. I loved him." His mother had sighed. *"I am sorry I am leaving you. You will never be free. Even as the spare. You will never be your own man. I wanted more for you, Kainan. I'm sorry."*

His mother had died then, and his father had told him woman weren't to be trusted.

"Never trust a woman, Kainan. Never."

Kainan rubbed his temple, where a pounding headache was brewing.

Reagan didn't hide your son from you. She thought you were dead.

That was little consolation to him at this moment.

"I have to go see him," Reagan whispered.

What is wrong with him? he asked as they waited for the elevator.

"Cardiomyopathy." There was a glitter of moisture in her eyes as she cleared her throat. "He was born that way. He was born with a failing heart."

Oh, God.

His heart sank. It was too much. He'd learned he was a father and that his son was dying all in the same day.

He was no fool. He knew the severity of cardiomyopathy in a child.

Run. Turn and leave.

But he couldn't do that either. He was not the cold, unfeeling man his father had been.

The elevator dinged as the doors opened, and they stood to the side as people got off, before getting in.

Kainan didn't say anything as they rode in silence. Everything was still sinking in.

He had a son.

And his son was the Crown Prince of Isla Hermosa.

He felt bad for inflicting that burden on him. And his son was ill. Cardiomyopathy in an infant was horrific, and Kainan could only assume that he was on the UNOS wait list for a new heart, because that was his only chance at life.

Reagan led him to the NICU, giving him a disposable gown and mask. He didn't really hear anything that anyone was saying as he was led into the room.

In the far corner stood an incubator that was covered with a blue blanket.

His heart was hammering.

He had never wanted a child. He didn't want to sentence any child to a life where he couldn't live, where he was under constant scrutiny. He'd never wanted a family. Relationships didn't work. His father and late brother had shown him that. He didn't want to trap a woman the way his mother had been trapped.

Reagan raised the blue blanket and Kainan gasped as he saw a baby with dark hair. A baby who looked like him and Reagan.

A baby hooked up to a machine.

His heart ached to hold him. It was instant love. It surprised him.

This child was the future of his country. But how could a voiceless king and a broken-hearted crown prince rule a country that was already broken and bleeding?

His heart shattered and guilt washed over him. Reagan had done this on her own. He hadn't been there. He'd failed her. He'd failed them both.

All Kainan could do was turn and leave.

His heart was breaking along with his son's.

CHAPTER TWO

THERE WAS SUCH a flurry of activity that Reagan forgot Kainan had followed her in. When Peter was stable again, and she'd spoken to the doctors, she turned to introduce Kainan to Peter's team. But Kainan had slipped out.

Where did he go?

That was her first thought, and then she was disappointed that he'd left. He hadn't even come over to the incubator. She'd lifted the blanket and he'd looked once, before she'd turned her attention to the nurse. Then she'd drowned out everything else. Her main focus had been her son.

With every day that she stepped through those doors, rinsing her hands, a deep, dark part of her told her over and over again that any future with her son became darker and darker.

The other part of her—the part that had sustained her since she'd found out she was carrying Kainan's child—told her not to give up hope.

To keep going.

To be strong.

To drown out everything else and pour all that she had into her son.

And that was what she did. Day after day since he was born.

She had no other choice.

So she hadn't noticed when Kainan had left because he'd never been there before. She was used to being on her own.

Reagan turned back to Sophie, Peter's nurse in the PCCU. "I'm only a text away."

Sophie nodded. "Sorry for dragging you away from your work. I know your first priority is to work with the new Hermosian doctor."

"My first priority is Peter. *Always*."

Reagan smiled and gave Sophie's arm a squeeze. She wanted to tell Sophie that Kainan was Peter's father, but she couldn't really form the words. Like Sophie, everyone in the hospital had been told that Peter's father was dead.

And that was not the case.

Kainan was alive. He'd have rights over Peter. She would no longer be in complete control. Kainan would have a say, and that made her nervous. Kainan might return to Isla Hermosa. What if he wanted to take Peter with him?

Don't think about it now.

She didn't want to make herself sick with worry.

"You okay, Reagan?" Sophie asked.

"Yes. I'm fine. I'll swing by later, Sophie, if I don't hear from you before then."

"Okay, Reagan."

Sophie turned back to the incubator and Reagan sent a mental kiss to her boy, since at the moment she couldn't actually kiss him. She'd only kissed him once, before he was intubated.

Her heart ached at the thought that maybe she'd never be able to really kiss him, see his eyes open and look at her in wonder.

Focus. Find Kainan.

Once she was out of the PCCU she peeled off the disposable gown and mask, tossing them in the nearest receptacle. She was contemplating how she was going to page Kainan

when she saw that he was pacing at the end of a dead-end hall near the PCCU.

All the annoyance and anger she'd briefly had for him walking out on their son melted away. She put herself in Kainan's shoes. He'd just learned he had a son and that same son was gravely ill.

She remembered how she'd felt when she'd found out that Peter was so ill. When they'd whisked him away from her. When she hadn't heard any wail when he was born and she'd been left alone.

Still, he had left.

"You left?" she said gently.

Kainan's dark eyes were a bit wild, and he ran his hand through his thick, dark curls. He nodded and signed, *Sorry.*

"It was a lot to take in. I'm sorry I didn't prepare you better."

Hard to prepare for that. Hard to prepare for learning about a son you never knew you had. He closed his eyes.

"Are you okay?"

I will be fine. The question is, are you? Are you okay?

The question took her aback, because she *wasn't* fine. How *could* she be fine? Her son was ill, Kainan was alive, and she needed sleep. No, she wasn't fine.

"I'm okay." *Liar.* "I should've told you sooner."

You didn't even know I was alive until earlier today.

"True."

They both smiled then, and a bit of the tension melted away.

What's wrong with him? Kainan signed finally. *You said before, but...*

"Cardiomyopathy." The word stuck in her throat. She rarely said it out loud, because if she said it out loud it became real. And she didn't want it to be real.

She was deluding herself. It was *very* real—and scary.

At least she didn't have to explain what cardiomyopathy was to Kainan. He understood the gravity of the situation.

Is he on the transplant list?

"Yes. We're waiting."

How terrible for you. How do you do it?

A spark of anger flared up in her. It was an innocent enough remark, but it had cut her to the quick.

How do you do it?

How could she *not*? There was really no choice in the matter. Just one foot in front of the other.

"There's no choice," she said wearily.

No. I suppose not. Kainan scrubbed a hand over his face. He didn't sign anything else.

Reagan was waiting for him to sign *I'm sorry I wasn't there for you.* Or *Let me help*, but he didn't offer any of these things.

Instead he signed, *Is he stable now? Can we get back to work?*

It was a slap to the face—but then again a lot of stuff had happened to Kainan in a very short span of time. Still, he hadn't even asked their son's name.

Don't take it personally. It's a lot to process.

She'd been disappointed before. Countless times, when her parents had been too busy for her.

"I need help, Mom. Please. I'm tired and Peter is sick..."

"It was your choice to have the baby, Reagan. I told you to get rid of it."

Her mother's callous words still haunted her.

What's wrong? Kainan signed.

"Nothing."

Your expression says otherwise.

"He's stable," she said, answering Kainan and yet ignoring his questioning.

Good.

There was a hint of relief on his face, but only a brief

hint. Reagan hoped it was in regard to their son, but again she'd been disappointed before.

"Let's get back to Michael's office and we'll go through everything," she offered.

Kainan nodded and fell into step beside her. There was silence between them, which was good, because right now she was having a hard time to keeping it all together.

Kainan listened to Reagan go over protocols and some other things that he couldn't seem to focus on. All he could think about was taking care of Reagan and Peter. Doing his duty to them.

Even though it would kill him to trap them both in royal protocol.

If his brother had still been alive there wouldn't be this guilt about forcing Reagan into this life Kainan never wanted. He was the "spare," so he's pursued medicine in order to escape Isla Hermosa. He'd gone to medical school in Switzerland and worked there. He'd been happy.

He hadn't ever planned on returning to Isla Hermosa after his brother became King, but then war had broke out and his brother had been killed.

Kainan's freedom had evaporated then. It had been obliterated.

Inside he was screaming and raging, but if he tried to let it all out there would be no sound, and that made him rage all the more at his own stupidity. Yet he still wanted Reagan, and now his son. She'd been alone. She shouldn't have been alone.

I should never have let Reagan go.

If he'd have been with her... He didn't finish that thought, because it wouldn't have changed the outcome at all.

Their son would have been born with cardiomyopathy anyway. That was if he'd survived being born in a war-torn

country. The thought made his stomach clench. He tried not to think about it.

"Alek, you have to surrender. It's done. Too many lives have been lost!"

"I will not surrender! Father never would've backed down."

"He would if innocent blood was being spilled. What you're doing is folly!"

"You just want the crown for yourself, Kainan. I know you."

"You don't know me. You're completely absurd. I never wanted this. Never."

"Then why are you here?"

"To save your life. You're my brother, Alek..."

"I'm your half brother."

"Half, then—but still I'm here to save you."

"Why?"

"Because Father loved you. I'm doing this for Father."

Alek had sneered and shaken his head.

"Always trying to please Father. But he's dead and I am King. I will always be King."

Kainan shook those thoughts away. They were treading on dangerous ground. They were threatening his control. He'd tried to save his half brother's life before Alek had been overthrown. He'd been trying to drag Alek out of the palace to safety just before the IED had gone off in the throne room.

Kainan had survived the blast, but had lost his voice for his brother...his King.

In the end his brother hadn't survived after the explosion. So it had all been for naught.

Which now made *him* King and his critically ill son his heir.

His son who was dying.

"Kainan, are you okay?"

He turned and saw Reagan was looking up from the piles of paperwork.

"Overwhelmed?" she asked gently.

He smiled. "Under..." Only he couldn't finish the word because his throat closed up, He felt humiliated by it.

Her expression softened. "Statement? Understatement?" Then she smiled. That warm and friendly open smile which had won him over. She'd always tried to act so strong, but when he'd seen her smile at wounded soldiers, offering them compassion, he'd been won over time and time again. Reagan had reminded him of his mother—not in looks, but in strength and fortitude.

His mother Ariana had been compassionate, strong, independent. She'd loved his father, even though his father hadn't seemed able to love her back in the same way.

When his mother had died he'd been so lonely. There had been no love in the palace. His father had stood on formality. As had his elder half brother Alek. Only his mother had given him affection.

Reagan hadn't known he was a prince. She'd been so honest. So warm. He'd craved that warmth. Needed it like air. She'd treated him like everyone else on the unit and with her he'd been himself. There had been no formality. No protocol. It had been nice to be himself for a change, instead of Prince Kainan.

If there hadn't been a war... If he was still the spare...

He didn't want to drag her into the tumultuous situation that was still happening in his country. Still, she'd borne his child and she would be in danger if word got out. If he married her he could protect her. He had to do right by her, even though that would mean her life wouldn't be her own anymore. Even though he would be condemning her.

Yes. That. He rubbed his temples, felt his throat tightening again.

"I'm sorry there's so much. I swear we're almost done with the orientation."

Can we take a break? he signed.

She cocked an eyebrow. "A break?"

Coffee?

He had to get out of this room. He felt as if he was suffocating again. Like when he'd woken up after the blast and not been able to breathe, with a tube in his throat, burns on his body.

"Okay…"

She seemed unsure. Confused.

He was confused too—about this whole situation.

When he'd felt this way in the past, surgery and practicing medicine—his work—had helped him get through so much. Saving lives made sense to him. It made sense of this mixed-up world.

And he couldn't do that anymore. He couldn't be a proper surgeon because he couldn't speak, and couldn't sign when his hands were busy. He couldn't lead his broken country for the same reason. He was trapped in limbo.

They walked in silence to the coffee cart.

Even though there were Hermosian guards all through this hospital, and he was being monitored by the Canadian government, no one besides those watching him for his own protection knew he was King.

He was free here.

Kainan could breathe—although he hated hiding here until the surgery was done. He wanted to be on the front lines, saving lives.

Even though he didn't have a voice.

He would soon enough.

That was if it was successful. Sometimes Kainan was positive that he wasn't going to survive the surgery.

Reagan ordered him a coffee, just as he liked it. Hot,

dark and rich. No sweetener. She was so thoughtful and he was a monster.

You remembered, he signed.

"You drank it every day religiously, Kainan." She wrinkled her nose. "I can't stand black coffee. I don't know how you do that."

Kainan took a sip. It didn't taste as good as the Hermosian coffee he was used to, but it would do.

Hermosian coffee is much better. It is naturally sweet.

Reagan snorted. "I remember what it tasted like. Black coffee is black coffee."

No, it is not. This is nothing compared to what my country grows.

"That we can agree on. Hermosian coffee *is* better," Reagan said as she dumped sugar in hers.

He shuddered and she made a face at him, making him smile.

They wandered over to a table in the hospital atrium. Snow was falling gently. He was still not used to snow, but it had a nice calming effect.

"What do you think of snow?" she asked.

Cold. He took a sip of his coffee.

"Yes. It must be a culture shock for you."

A bit. He nervously began to flick at the plastic spout on his coffee cup. *Our son...*

"Peter," Reagan whispered softly, a bloom of pink on her high round cheeks.

An interesting name.

"I always liked it—and Peter Pan was the boy who never grew up." Her voice trembled, but only for a moment. "It suits him."

Peter Pan lived forever by not growing up, yes?

"Well, I suppose so. He never aged as long as he stayed in Neverland."

There you go.

Peter. His son was named Peter. Though Kainan hadn't put Peter Pan and his son's name together at first. When she'd said his name was Peter all he'd been able to think of was St. Peter, the patron saint of fisherman.

Isla Hermosa had a thriving fishing industry, so the thought of St. Peter made him happy, but it frightened him all the same. Peter was a prince.

"You're frowning again," Reagan said.

He smiled. *I frown a lot lately.*

"Why?"

I've been through a lot. Then he sighed. *I suppose we both have.*

"Our time in Isla Hermosa feels like a lifetime ago." Pink tinged her cheeks again. "I am glad you're alive. I didn't tell you that."

Kainan's heart melted. *I'm glad to see you again too.*

"So, Michael told me you're awaiting surgery for your voice?"

He clenched his coffee cup. *Yes. I hope it works.*

Kainan didn't tell her the risks he was taking. The chances that he wouldn't live through it. She didn't need to know.

Reagan nodded. "I'm sure it will, although I'm sure scar tissue is an issue in your case?"

Kainan's stomach turned. It was indeed adhesions and scar tissue that were impeding his throat. Choking him from the inside out.

I don't want to discuss it.

"Fair enough," she said.

He felt bad, but he didn't want to think about the surgery. He needed his voice by the New Year, because on January first he was supposed to be on a plane to Isla Hermosa to attend his own coronation.

Without his voice he was trapped. He was blessed that he knew American Sign Language, but without his voice

he couldn't properly rule and nor could he practice medicine. And without the surgery he might die.

So he was trapped. There was no choice over his surgery. It had to be done.

A ring tone sounded and Reagan glanced down at the phone in her hand, frowning.

Peter? Kainan signed, his heart sinking.

"No, incoming trauma. I'm needed," she said. "It must be a lot of trauma coming here or I wouldn't have been called in to help."

Go, Kainan signed. *I can find my way around.*

"Not everyone knows ASL."

Kainan pulled out his phone and typed in the word *Go*. His phone repeated it back. She smiled at him.

"I'll be back as soon as I can."

He nodded and watched Reagan disappear, a pang of jealousy coursing through him. How he wished he could be in the fray with her. Like old times.

He tossed the coffee cup in the garbage and wandered through the hospital.

He wanted to be free. And even though he wasn't in a palace, he was alone and shackled here.

You're not alone. You have Reagan.

Only he didn't have Reagan. She wasn't his. Not yet.

His stomach turned with guilt at the life he was going to impose on her.

And he hated himself for it.

CHAPTER THREE

THE INCOMING TRAUMA took longer than Reagan had expected. A multi-vehicle crash with multiple traumatic injuries kept her in surgery for hours, and by the time she got out it was evening. She was exhausted, and wondering what had happened to Kainan.

He wasn't answering his pager at all, and she couldn't help but wonder if he had gone home.

She couldn't really think about it right now. She hadn't heard from Sophie, Peter's nurse, since she'd gone to see Peter earlier. Which was good. Of course it was protocol not to disturb a surgeon when operating. Still, no one had come to find her afterward. So Peter had to be okay.

It had been the longest stretch in a while since she'd got an update and she was worried.

She'd worry about Kainan later. Right now she had to see Peter and make sure that he was all right.

As Reagan approached the pediatric critical care unit she met Sophie coming off her shift.

"Sorry, Sophie. I was in surgery. If you paged me and I didn't answer…"

"It's okay, Reagan. Nothing to mention. Peter is stable, but there *is* something you didn't tell me."

"Oh?"

"You didn't tell me that Peter's father is Dr. Laskaris."

Reagan's eyes widened. "I... What? How did you find that out?"

"He's in there now. At first I wasn't going to let him in to see Peter, per your restrictions, but he said he was his father."

"And you believed him?" Reagan's voice rose an octave.

Sophie blushed. "He offered to take a genetic test. It's still in process. We let him in the unit, but he's not in Peter's pod and he's not allowed to touch him. He's just sitting there, in the room you sleep in, watching him."

Reagan felt terrible for snapping at Sophie.

"I'm sorry, Sophie. You did absolutely the right thing. Dr. Laskaris *is* Peter's father."

"Well, I really grilled him. But you told me Peter's father died on Isla Hermosa and Dr. Laskaris is Hermosian. Also, you brought him in here earlier, even though he doesn't have privileges yet."

Reagan smiled. "I meant to tell you earlier, but I was in complete and utter shock. I thought he was dead."

Sophie grinned. "I'm sure you were. I know I would be too, in your situation."

Reagan laughed nervously. "You can let Dr. Laskaris in to see Peter whenever he wants."

"I'll make a note on his chart tomorrow."

"Thanks, Sophie. Have a great night."

Sophie waved goodbye as she walked away. And for one moment Reagan envied her because she had freedom.

When Reagan had found out she was pregnant she'd known her life would change, but she'd been expecting diapers, daycare and a messy apartment.

Not this.

Never this.

She buzzed in to the pediatric critical care unit after putting on the gown and gloves that were mandatory. The

new shift on the unit had started, and she greeted the people she knew all too well.

Kainan was standing in the little room next to Peter's, watching their son intently through the glass partition. Reagan couldn't read his expression but it didn't matter right now. All that mattered was that Kainan was there.

He was with Peter.

Her father had never been there for her. He'd barely acknowledged her. So to see Kainan with Peter softened her heart.

Maybe he did care about Peter. Maybe she had it all wrong.

"I'm sorry I'm so late," she said, coming up beside him. "I tried paging you, but you didn't answer."

My phone died, he signed. He held it up. *Forgot the charger. It's back at my place.*

"Oh." She cleared her throat. "I'm glad you're here."

He nodded and smiled at her, those dark eyes twinkling. *Me too.*

Her heart skipped a beat. "I told Sophie you're his father. A genetic test isn't needed."

It's okay. Actually, I don't mind. I would like it done all the same.

Heat bloomed in her cheeks. "Of course. You need verification. Facts. You are a doctor."

What are you talking about? He looked confused.

"You'll need scientific proof that he's your son."

He frowned. Looked concerned. *No, not at all.*

"Really?" she asked in disbelief.

Really. He turned and looked back at Peter. *In him I see me.*

Her heart skipped another beat, because she'd had that thought so many times when she'd looked at Peter.

She saw Kainan.

"Then why did you agree to the test? Why do you want it?"

Blood types. I'm curious about whether he's a universal donor, like me. It runs in my family.

"He does have a universal blood type."

Kainan smiled. *Good.*

"The cardiomyopathy is genetic, but it doesn't run on my side."

I don't have it either.

"You're sure?"

The royal family of Isla Hermosa has been recorded for a long time, he signed. Then he tensed.

"Uh…what does the royal family of Isla Hermosa have to do with anything?" she asked, confused.

Nothing. I was thinking of something else.

"Okay." Reagan couldn't help but wonder why he was getting so defensive about this. "Still, it's not on my side."

It's not on mine either, he signed. *Stop implying it's my fault.*

"I'm not."

Fine. Good, Kainan signed sharply.

Something was bothering him. "Sorry."

No, I am sorry. Family is a touchy subject for me. The war was hard for so many.

"Yes," she said sadly. "I remember that."

Peter is all I have left.

That made her pause. It made her nervous, thinking he'd take Peter away.

Kainan had rights, but she couldn't lose Peter.

Tears were threatening to escape, and she didn't want to cry in front of Kainan or in front of Peter—even though Peter wouldn't even know it if she did.

In the pediatric critical care unit she had to be strong. She was a warrior. A fighter for her son. There couldn't be an inch of give. And she didn't want to appear weak in front of Kainan or anyone.

If she did her weakness might be used against her.

Great. Now I'm being paranoid and sounding like my mother.

She had to get a grip. She was stressed, tired and stressed—in that order.

Kainan stepped closer, and before she could stop him he drew her into his arms. Her body reacted instantly to his touch. She closed her eyes, drinking in his scent, her body trembling because she'd never thought she'd experience this again.

She'd thought he was dead.

He was supposed to be dead.

And it had been so long since someone had held her. Her parents never openly showed affection and neither did she. Being in Kainan's arms brought her carefully constructed walls down a little. It was overwhelming to be held by him. Actually to be comforted. Just like it had been the night Peter had been conceived.

"Come," he said, his voice rasping, and she knew that it was a strain for him to speak. But with her head buried in his neck as she drank in the sensation of being held she couldn't see him when he signed anyway.

Reagan let Kainan lead her out of the pediatric critical care unit.

She was in a daze.

She was exhausted.

Kainan took the gown off her and disposed of it. Then he removed the gown he was wearing.

Reagan shook herself out of the daze she was in. "Peter. I can't leave him."

You can leave him for one night.

"He has no one else."

There's a team of medical professionals in there to take care of him, Reagan. You need sleep and a decent meal.

"I have to stay here," she said firmly.

Reagan, he's stable. If he's not they will page one of us.

Come back to my place and I'll get my charger. There you can shower and have a meal. Let's get your things from your locker.

A hot shower and food that wasn't from the cafeteria sounded heavenly, but she was terrified of leaving the hospital.

The nurses and doctors on the pediatric critical care unit had tried to get her to take a night off every once in a while, but she couldn't do it.

"I can't," she whispered.

My place is right next door.

She cocked an eyebrow. "You're staying at the Royal York?"

He nodded. *Yes.*

"That's pricey."

He shrugged. *I have money, and none of that matters right now. Come, let me take care of you. You shall sleep and I will be on call for Peter tonight. Let me take some of the burden off your shoulders.*

"I would like that…" She cleared her throat as emotion threatened to overtake her, but she controlled it.

Those dark eyes softened as he stepped forward and cupped her face briefly, and the simple touch eased her.

No feeling guilty. To take care of Peter you have to take care of yourself. Let's go.

She nodded and he put his hand on the small of her back, as he'd done when they had gone to his tent in Isla Hermosa. It was nice.

After they'd gathered the small suitcase that she always kept at the hospital and put on their winter coats—because it was December, and the wind chill off the lake was brutal—they walked out of the hospital together and dashed across York Street. It was quiet, as there were no commuters out and about. However, there were a few hockey fans coming and going.

Kainan raised an eyebrow in question at the hockey-go-ers, with their blue-painted faces and shouting.

"Leafs. It's hockey."

He nodded, but didn't sign anything, just squeezed her hand as they scurried up Front Street to the entrance of the Royal York hotel.

Through the revolving door Reagan stepped—into another world. She had only been in the Royal York once, and knew it was opulent with its art deco interiors from a golden age of Toronto.

"This way," he whispered, and pulled out a gold card, which meant that Kainan had a suite.

He took her to the private elevator that was used by the elite guests at the Royal York.

He swiped his card and the elevator doors opened. They got on and took the elevator to the top floor. Then he led her down a hallway to the very end, and swiped the card to open the door to a luxurious suite.

She dropped her bag and stared at the main room with its plush furnishings, and then wandered in to see a king-size bed in another room, a kitchenette. As she approached the window she could see that there was a view of the waterfront over Union Station.

"Wow…" she whispered. "I've never been in one of these rooms before."

He smiled and jammed his hands in his pockets. *Food first, shower or nap?*

"Shower first, if I can. Then food and maybe a nap. But I'm not entirely sure that I'm going to stay here, Kainan. I might have to sneak out and head back to the hospital."

He chuckled and then plugged his phone into the charger on the desk. *You go have a shower and I will order you some food.*

"You don't know what I like," she teased.

I think I remember bits and pieces. Go shower, and then after you eat we'll discuss whether you or I should go back.

"Deal."

She found the bathroom and flicked on the light. There was a plush white robe and thick, soft towels. Much better than the staff change room. She pulled out her toiletries bag, digging for soap and shampoo.

It didn't take her long to find everything she needed and soon she was turning on the shower. It was nice to have this moment to herself. And she didn't feel rushed here, like she did in the hospital staff room.

This was one of the first times she'd been out of the hospital in months. Paying her rent and utilities was done with a simple app on her phone or over the internet. She had no pets. No plants. Her life was in the hospital.

As she stepped under the shower and let the water wash away her stress she realized that in the hospital she carried the weight of the world on her shoulders. She carried the weight of her son and the life that he might not get a chance to experience. It was only in the safety of the rushing water washing over her that she let it go for the first time in a long while.

She turned off the shower and grabbed a towel to dry her hair and face.

There was a knock on the door. She wrapped herself in a robe and opened the door. Kainan was standing there.

Are you okay?

"I'm fine."

He pursed his lips together. *You were in there a long time. I was worried you'd fallen asleep in there.*

Warmth flooded in her cheeks. "How long have I been in here?"

An hour. He grinned.

"An hour?" She looked down at her hands, which were

wrinkled like prunes from so much water. She must have zoned out.

Come, there's food. You can stay in the robe.

She nodded and followed him out of the en-suite bathroom into the living room area, where there were salads, cheese, fruit and a big bowl of pasta. Her favorite kind too. Fettuccine Alfredo.

He'd remembered.

"Don't think me ungrateful, but how did you order all this?"

Through the computer. The hotel and I have an understanding.

"It smells delicious. I can't remember the last time I had real food instead of cafeteria food."

Then let's eat, instead of standing around here and talking about it.

He motioned for her to sit on the couch and remained standing until she sat.

Always the gentleman.

Even in a war zone. It had always been ladies first. And once, when a particularly crass soldier had got a little handsy with a nurse, Kainan had been there to jump into the fray and put that soldier in his place.

Of course since it hadn't been a Hermosian soldier there had been some international logistics to work out, and eventually both commanding officers had had Kainan and the other soldier duke it out in a boxing ring in the middle of the mobile army hospital.

You're smiling, Kainan signed. *What are you smiling about?*

"I was thinking about that time you boxed that soldier. Totally laid him flat on his back even though he was twice your size."

He made a funny face. *He wasn't twice my size.*

"The man was trained in special ops and he was broad."

Broad is one thing, but "broad" is often confused with muscle and mental agility.

Kainan winked and Reagan chuckled.

What made you think of that? he signed.

"I was just thinking about how you're very much a gentleman."

He raised an eyebrow. *Boxing made you think of me as a gentleman?*

"Isn't boxing the sport of kings?"

No, that's horse racing. There was a twinkle in his eyes. *I believe that boxing is the sport of manly self-defense. I believe many fine gentlemen were pugilists a long time ago.*

"Ah, see—there you go. It *is* a gentlemanly sort of sport."

Not anymore. Women box.

"Right, but still…"

Fine, I concede. So, you were thinking of me boxing and you came to the conclusion I was a gentleman?

"No, I was thinking about how you stood until I sat down, and that led me to remember your boxing."

A smile quirked his finely shaped mouth, making her recall for a brief moment the way he kissed.

Now you are blushing.

Reagan saw him sign it, but she remembered the sound of his voice and the way he would softly exhale on her neck. It had been a long time since she'd desired anyone, because the last person she'd felt that rush for was Kainan. Since Peter had been born she hadn't had any feelings like that. She had been just numb and existing.

She felt guilty for allowing those feelings to creep back in. So she picked up the bowl of pasta. "I'm glad you remembered my favorite."

Kainan sat back. The spell that had been woven over them was broken and that was a good thing. Reagan didn't have time to start anything up, even if Kainan *was* the father of her baby. Her life revolved around her son and

making sure that he survived long enough to have experiences like this.

She had to protect Peter from hurt because there was always an expiration date. Kainan would go back to Isla Hermosa. Kainan would probably leave them again. Her heart could take it—Peter's couldn't.

The conversation had taken an interesting turn before they'd started eating, and Kainan was trying to remain a gentleman but it was so hard when it came to Reagan. He'd forgotten how much he liked being with her. She brought out a side in him he'd thought he'd buried long ago.

He'd forgotten about laying that officer out in the boxing ring after he'd laid into him publicly outside of the ring when he'd started bothering that Canadian nurse.

Men like that annoyed him.

You could still be a strong, alpha male and respect women.

If only his brother had learned that.

Or his father.

"Mama, why are you crying?"

His mother had wiped away her tears with the back of her hand and then wrapped him up in her arms, holding him.

"Are you sad, Mama?"

"Never, Kainan. Never when you're here."

Kainan had glanced over her shoulder to his mother's bed and seen newspaper. There had been a picture of his father, with his arm around a woman who was not his mother.

His father had been a beloved king, but his affairs had been notorious.

Kainan had vowed he'd never be like that. Even if he became King he would never be like that. Of course he'd

never thought that he *would* be King. That was something he'd never wanted.

Never.

All he'd wanted to be was a surgeon.

Being King would be a huge responsibility. His life would not be his own anymore. His life would belong to his kingdom and the world. There would be no more privacy. It would be a life of sacrifice and stress.

Could he really do that to Reagan? To Peter?

There was no choice. He had to do what was right and make Peter legitimate.

He glanced up after they'd finished eating and saw that Reagan had fallen asleep. She was curled up on the couch, her head resting on the overstuffed armrest.

She looked so peaceful.

He hated dragging her into this, but it was the perfect solution. He would marry her and they would be a family. Then they would return to Isla Hermosa, and maybe he would be able to heal what was broken in his country.

There was a knock at the door. He got up and peeked through the peephole to see his head of security, Andreas, in the hallway.

Kainan opened it.

"I'm sorry for intruding, Your Majesty."

Kainan held his fingers to his lips to silence his security guard and motioned behind him.

Andreas peeked over his shoulder and nodded. "I'm sorry…"

"What's wrong?" Kainan asked hoarsely, rubbing his throat.

"Word has gotten out that the missing Hermosian King is hiding somewhere in Toronto."

Blast. "How?"

"The papers here are running it. Though your picture is not in the papers. Just the story. Someone has leaked it."

Kainan's stomach clenched, and all he could see was his father's face instead of his as he thought of that newspaper on his mother's bed, stained with tears.

Dammit.

Kainan wished that he could let out a few more strings of expletives, but that would wake Reagan, so perhaps it was best that he currently didn't have the ability to do that.

Please keep me informed, Andreas, he signed. *Let me know if the press come anywhere near the hotel or the hospital.*

"We've been keeping a low profile, Your Majesty. The only people on this floor are your security detail and you. Much to our chagrin, we're letting you go to the hospital alone and trying not to be too obvious."

Kainan smiled briefly. *I know that it's hard for you, but it's for the best.*

"What's for the best is for you to remain hidden and safe until you can return to Isla Hermosa."

I am safe.

"Your son is unprotected at the hospital," Andreas said.

A cold rush of dread crept down Kainan's spine. *How do you know about him?*

"I *am* head of security, Your Majesty."

We're done talking about this, Andreas. Keep me posted about the leak.

Andreas pursed his lips together and bowed. "Yes, Your Majesty."

Kainan shut the door and scrubbed a hand over his face. The idea that news about him was getting too close for comfort made him think of his helpless son, clinging to life in a hospital bed. He didn't want the press to find out about Peter. He had to protect him.

Kainan flung open the door and ran after Andreas.

Andreas turned around, confused. "Your Majesty?"

Don't be obvious about it, but protect my son, he signed.

I don't want people coming to the hospital. He needs to protected at all costs.

Andreas smiled. "Of course, Your Majesty."

Work your magic with administration, but please just keep Peter safe.

"I will, Your Majesty. Right away."

Kainan nodded and turned back to his room. He shut the door gently, so as not to wake Reagan. She was still sound asleep, curled up on the couch.

He approached her and gently scooped her into his arms. She didn't even wake, and he couldn't blame her for being so exhausted. He felt guilty for not being there when Peter was born. For not knowing and being able to help her.

Kainan carried her to bed and set her down, covering her up. She sighed, but didn't wake. So he stood over her, staring at her face and fighting the urge to touch her, to run his fingers over that graceful neck and through her soft, dark silken hair.

To cup her face and kiss her.

Yet, as much as he cared for her, in this moment his duty was clear.

He cared for her and Peter too much, and in caring for them he would have to burden Reagan. Even as vulnerable as she was, there was no choice.

He needed to make Reagan his Queen.

CHAPTER FOUR

COMFORTABLE. THAT WAS her first thought. But she shouldn't be this comfortable.

Reagan woke with a start and couldn't figure out where she was at first. She was definitely not sleeping on the cot in the pediatric critical care unit, because it was too quiet in here and the bed was too soft.

She sat up and then remembered that she was in Kainan's hotel room at the Royal York.

She heard a sigh and looked over to see that Kainan was sleeping next to her, still in his street clothes. He wore a dress shirt, but the tie that he'd been wearing was gone, and the shirt was unbuttoned. He was lying on top of the covers, his ankles crossed and his hands across his chest.

He looked so peaceful. She wondered how long she'd been sleeping, and when she glanced at the clock on the bedside she saw that it was nine in the morning.

Oh, my God. Peter!

She'd slept through the night. Away from Peter and the pediatric critical care unit.

How could she have been so foolish? What if something had happened to him?

She got out of bed quietly, so as not to wake Kainan. She found her things and quickly dressed, brushing her hair,

which had dried naturally and now had a horrible kink in it. That was solved by tying it up in a bun.

She cursed under her breath. Angry at herself for leaving Peter's side. She had been weak when Kainan had convinced her to leave the hospital. She had to be stronger. She couldn't let Kainan sway her so easily.

Who are you kidding?

Even after all this time Kainan was the only one who got through her barriers, and she was angry at herself for letting him through.

Once she was dressed she snuck out of the hotel room, quietly shutting the door behind her. When she turned around, though, she jumped back in surprise to see several men in dark clothes loitering about the hallway.

They'd been talking, but stopped when she shut the door. They watched her with a sense of reverence, almost awe. Whatever it was, it was super-creepy.

"I'm sorry, miss," one man said, stepping forward.

He had a slight accent similar to Kainan's, and she wondered if they were Hermosian refugees as well.

"Did we wake you? These walls are very thin."

"No, it's okay."

"We're sorry if we startled you. Congregating in the hall before we all head to a…a workshop is not proper."

"It's okay," she repeated.

The man nodded and the other men smiled, stepping back as she scurried down the hallway toward the elevator. She pressed the button and the elevator appeared instantly.

If she didn't know better then she would almost swear those men were security guards.

That's ridiculous. Who are they guarding?

She shook that thought away as she pulled on her winter jacket in the elevator. She pushed through the crowds of people in the lobby of the hotel and then went downstairs

to the concourse level and took the Avenue from the hotel to the hospital.

That way she wouldn't have to go out in the cold.

Reagan weaved her way in and out of the morning rush of commuters who were walking the concourse in underground Toronto from Union Station to all the tall office buildings that connected to the PATH system. When the trains came in the concourse level was flooded with people.

It was a great system, but so crowded during certain times of the day. Like now. But Reagan was a pro at fighting her way through crowds.

At the hospital level, she punched in her access code and took the elevator up to where the staff change room was located. She stashed her coat and the bag of clothes and changed into a fresh pair of scrubs and a lab jacket.

First she would check on Peter, and then she would do her rounds.

You're not doing rounds anymore, remember? You're supposed to be working with Kainan and you left him in the hotel.

Reagan groaned inwardly.

Well, she'd just stay with Peter until Kainan came to start his shift at ten. That was when they would head down and work with the medical students who were coming in.

When she got to the pediatric critical care unit the morning shift had started and Sophie was back at the PCCU's desk.

"I'm so sorry, Sophie—" Reagan started.

Sophie looked confused. "For what?"

"I fell asleep…at my apartment."

It was a lie, but she didn't want to divulge the fact that she'd spent the night with Kainan, even though Sophie knew that Kainan was Peter's father.

"I went there to take care of some business and just crashed."

"Don't worry about it, Reagan. Nothing happened. Peter's stable." Sophie opened up his file on the computer. "I don't see any notes that you were paged."

"I wasn't paged." Reagan bit her lip and sighed. "Actually, I didn't even check to see if I *was* paged. I just woke up and raced over here. I was feeling incredibly guilty for not being here."

Sophie smiled and gave her shoulder a sympathetic squeeze. "You have the right to sleep. We all know you're always here and always reachable. Hovering won't heal him."

She knew that, but she didn't want Peter to be alone. Like she had been when she was seven and had had her tonsils out. She'd been alone. Her parents had never come to visit her.

They'd been working.

She'd got a lot of pity then from the nurses.

Even though Peter was too young even to know she was there, she didn't want him to be alone as she had been.

"I have to be here," Reagan said firmly.

It was her duty to be here for Peter. Her parents might be standoffish, but Reagan had sworn she'd never be like that. She *had* to be there, even if she could use a break, but thoughts still ate away at her. Made her feel like a terrible mother.

"I know. I've been a pediatric nurse for a while now, and I know that you need to be here. Peter knows that you're here, but you need to take care of yourself too. When he gets his new heart and gets out of here you're going to have to contend with a baby, and then a toddler. He's not going to know that he has to take it easy, and you'll need your strength for that phase. Usually my sickest little ones are the ones who are the most mischievous when they get out of here."

Reagan laughed and tried to picture it, though it was

hard to see because of her uncertainty. "I'm looking forward to that."

"It's not easy to see it, but it *will* happen. I have faith that it will."

Sophie picked up her charts and started to do her rounds of the patients she was in charge of. Reagan let out an exhausted sigh and headed over to Peter's incubator.

She lifted the blanket that covered him and a smile crept across her face. There was a brief sense of relief to see him stable.

But she didn't know what to do.

Not that she could do much when he was at this critical point in his life.

He was stable. Sophie wasn't hovering currently. Sophie was doing her rounds and Peter was just lying there. All she wanted to do was hold him, but she didn't want to stress him by picking him up.

So she just stood there, watching him, feeling absolutely useless and helpless at the same time. She'd felt this way before, but usually when he was ill and she wasn't sure he was going to make it, when she didn't have time to ponder these thoughts. To let them really sink in.

Now she did, and Reagan didn't like it very much. But she couldn't think that way or she'd go mad.

There was a tap on her shoulder and it was Kainan.

You left, he signed.

"I'm sorry. I didn't realize that I had..." she lowered her voice to a whisper, heat blooming in her cheeks "...spent the night."

Why are you whispering? Everyone knows that we've once spent the night together before. The evidence is right in front of us.

There was a mischievous twinkle in his eye and he grinned.

Reagan chuckled. "Sorry."

Don't apologize. You didn't leave a note or anything and I was worried.

"You were worried?" she asked, shocked.

Of course. I went to sleep with you there beside me and I woke up and you were gone.

"Sorry, I should've left a note."

Yes, he signed gently, and then his gaze drifted down to Peter and she could see hesitation in his eyes.

It stung.

She'd thought he cared for Peter. His hesitation now worried her. She didn't want Peter to be rejected by his father the way she'd been rejected by hers. That rejection had caused loathing in her mother, and Reagan knew her mother blamed her for her husband's distance.

"How did you know where I was?"

Andreas told me.

Then he frowned and pursed his lips together, as if he hadn't meant to sign that. As if it were a slip-up.

"Who is Andreas?" Reagan asked, confused.

The man in the next suite. He saw you this morning when you snuck out.

"Oh." For some reason she didn't quite believe Kainan. There was something he wasn't saying.

Once he said you'd snuck out I put two and two together and knew where you'd be.

"Of course." She sighed.

Kainan frowned. *What's wrong?*

"Nothing." She couldn't look at him right now. He wasn't telling her the truth and she was having a hard time trusting him. "What time is it?"

Almost ten. Are you ready to meet the medical students?

"No, but I suppose we must. We put them off yesterday when I was called into surgery." She smiled the fake smile she'd mastered. "Are you ready?"

Of course. He grinned.

There was a confident air about him. One she envied.

"Well, let's go, then."

Reagan waved at Sophie on her way out and Sophie nodded in response. Reagan would be in the hospital. There was no way she was going to leave Peter for another night.

"So this Andreas..." she started.

What about him? Kainan asked.

"He sounded Hermosian to me."

Kainan frowned. *What makes you say that?*

"I spent over a year in Isla Hermosa. He reminded me of someone, but I can't remember..."

Déjà vu, that's all. It's being around me. You think anyone with that type of accent is Hermosian, he signed, cutting her off.

He was annoyed.

"Why are you getting so angry?"

I'm not angry.

"You're being very touchy about it."

I don't know where Andreas is from. He arrived at the hotel with some coworkers around the same time I did and we've met in the hall a few times. Can we just drop it?

"Sure."

And she should. She didn't want to get involved with him. Peter was her priority. The only problem with that was that Kainan was Peter's father.

She couldn't lock Kainan out. For the sake of Peter she had to care, had to be involved and let Kainan in.

Plus you cared for him once.

Yes, she had, but that felt like a lifetime ago. They'd both been very different people back then.

"Good." He said the word out loud and then cleared his throat, interrupting her thoughts.

It was apparent that he was still annoyed about the course their conversation had taken, and for some reason

Reagan couldn't help but wonder if he was hiding something about Andreas. And, if he was, why?

It's not your concern.

But Reagan knew when people were lying, and she had the gut feeling that Kainan was lying to her.

The question was why.

Who cares?

And that thought made her force those doubts from her mind. She really didn't have time for this. What Kainan did was his own business. She didn't have time to form a relationship with Kainan outside the bond of their son and their professional relationship. All she had time for was her son.

That was all that mattered.

Kainan opened the door to the lecture hall that was inside the hospital and gestured for her to take the lead.

Right now she had to focus on translating the American Sign Language for the medical students in this room. This was her new assignment. She was here to work with Kainan and that was it. Her feelings with respect to Kainan couldn't be allowed to come into play.

She had to keep reminding herself of that fact.

When Kainan had been able to speak, and before civil war had torn his country to shreds, he'd been at the forefront of surgery. He'd been on a fast track to win a Nobel Prize in medicine for his surgical advances.

Of course then his father had died and his brother had taken over. He hadn't even lasted a year and then everything had gone to heck.

One of the perks of working here in this hospital in Toronto, while waiting for surgery to correct his voice, was being able to continue with his medical research. He was looking forward to that.

That was, of course, if he could train his medical students in triage in time to work on his research. It had been

a long time since he'd taught. And he wasn't sure he had the patience for it.

Of course with Reagan by his side it would be a snap. Not only because she would be able to help him communicate with these eager medical students, but because when they had worked together in the field, in the mobile military hospital, everything had just seemed to flow.

And as he worked with her now, guiding his students through triage in a mock active war zone, he was happy to be with her again.

He'd forgotten how well they worked together. Two surgeons from two different countries, different backgrounds, but they came together seamlessly to create perfection.

Just like Peter.

His heart swelled with pride for a brief moment as he thought of the beautiful boy who was clinging to life in the pediatric critical care unit.

Everything was right when he was with Reagan. It thrilled him, but terrified him just the same.

If his brother were still King, then he would be jumping into the fray with her, begging her to stay with him. But now that *he* was King he didn't have his own life, and he hated the thought of ruining her life too. As much as he loved his country, he hated being King. He hated the shackles, the restrictions it entailed.

It was tearing him up inside. Just as it had destroyed his mother. And although Reagan was strong, she was vulnerable, and he didn't want to hurt her or overtax her.

"Mother, why are you so sad?" he'd asked once, when his mother had barely looked at him.

She'd put her arm around his shoulders as she'd sighed, looking out at the sea.

"I want to be free, Kainan."

"You are free. You are the Queen."

"I know."

Kainan turned his focus back on the students. This was his task now. He couldn't let memories distract him.

"Good," he said, to a student who was performing a very complicated stitch with makeshift tools.

"Thank you, Dr. Laskaris." The student was beaming.

Kainan nodded and moved on.

As he walked the room, watching Reagan showing a couple of medical students a technique for draping with plastic, he saw Andreas out of the corner of his eye, standing outside the window of the lecture hall where they were with the medical students.

Kainan's stomach dropped to the soles of his feet.

There was a determined look about Andreas. Kainan had known Andreas for some time, and he knew when his head of security was stressed. And Andreas was stressed now.

Kainan darted out of the room. Reagan called after him, but he ignored her as he caught up to Andreas.

"The press know," Andreas said, not mincing his words. "I do not know who leaked it, Your Majesty. The press are outside the hotel and in the avenue below us…"

Are they here in the hospital?

Andreas pursed his lips together and nodded.

Dammit.

Kainan raked his hand through his hair. He was enraged that he'd been discovered, and if he found out who had sold him out he was going to ignore his Hippocratic Oath and do horrible things to that individual.

"Kainan, what's…?" Reagan trailed off as she looked at Andreas closely, and she wasn't just recognizing him from this morning either.

Kainan's heart skipped a beat, because Andreas had been a soldier as well as a bodyguard during the Hermosian civil war. Andreas had been injured and Reagan had been the one to aid him.

And, by the way Reagan looked at Andreas now, she

was picturing him with his head shaved, instead of with the long dark hair that Andreas now sported.

"I know you," she whispered.

"Of course—we met this morning," Andreas said, trying to bluff it out.

Reagan shook her head. "No, you were a soldier. I treated you. I remember you with shorter hair and you...you are Hermosian."

Andreas looked worried and sent Kainan a look, which Reagan caught.

"What's going on?" she asked, her voice rising. "And don't get annoyed with me, Kainan. I *know* something is going on. There's something you're not telling me."

Let me explain, Reagan, Kainan signed, and scrubbed his hand over his face.

He saw that Michael McNeil, the Chief of Surgery, was rushing toward them.

"Dr. Laskaris—a word!"

Reagan frowned. "Michael? Are you okay?"

"No," Michael said hurriedly, and then he crossed his arms, looking directly at Kainan. "I have press surrounding my hospital."

"Press?" Reagan asked.

"Yes, and they're blocking the ambulance bay. I have all my security guards trying to keep them out, but how do you keep people out of a hospital?" Michael looked annoyed. "Dr. Laskaris, they're looking for *you*!"

Kainan's stomach knotted. He was angry, but he felt defeated, because there was no sense in hiding now.

He'd been found. Even though he'd been trying to keep a low profile until after his surgery, when he hoped he'd have a voice again.

Reagan looked confused. "Kainan, what's going on?"

Andreas cleared his throat and Michael stood behind

Reagan, his hands on his hips, looking just as confused as she was.

Kainan took a deep breath and mustered all his strength to whisper breathlessly, "I am the lost King of Isla Hermosa."

CHAPTER FIVE

"YOU'RE...WHAT?" REAGAN ASKED, not sure that she'd heard Kainan correctly. "You're a king? The Hermosian King? I thought he died?"

Kainan sighed and turned to look away.

"Dr. Laskaris?" Michael asked.

Andreas stepped forward. "He became King when his brother King Aleksander the Seventh died after an explosion in the palace. As you're all aware, King Aleksander's rule was tenuous, at best..."

Kainan spun back round, and there was a fire in his dark eyes that scared her.

I am King. My brother is dead and I am the missing King, he signed.

Reagan frowned. "The name Laskaris isn't associated with the Hermosian crown, and you told me when we first met that your family was from Greece."

Kainan sighed. *My mother was born in Greece. Isla Hermosa was founded by the Spanish and the Greeks. The name Laskaris is tied to the Hermosian crown, but it is kept for the "spares." Like me. I didn't want to change it when I became King. I am still Dr. Laskaris.*

There was a sadness to his expression which softened her a bit. It was apparent that he wasn't happy with his new position in his country.

"You *were* injured in an IED blast?" Reagan asked. "At the front?"

Yes. I was injured trying to save my brother, but that was for nothing. He died after the explosion. I am the last of my line, so the Canadian government thought it prudent to take me away from my country. They brought me here, where I recuperated, and now I wait for surgery. I cannot sit idly by and do nothing. But it is not safe for me to go back yet.

Reagan nodded, but it was hard to take it all in.

Why hadn't he told her that he was a prince when they were working together? She'd thought he was just a surgeon.

But had they ever really talked about personal stuff?

No, they hadn't. Not ever.

It explained why Kainan had that air of command about him. Why other people in the Hermosian Army and the wounded civilians had been in such awe of him. He'd been a prince and she'd been too blind or naive to see it.

Another scary thought sank into her mind. If Kainan was King that meant Peter was a prince.

Peter might not be able to stay with her if it came to a custody fight. Even at his tender age Peter had a duty to the country of his father's birth. He belonged to Isla Hermosa.

Not to her.

As if sensing her apprehension, Kainan signed, *This changes nothing. Peter is your son. I will not take him from you.*

She wanted to believe him, but she was having a hard time processing all this.

"I'm surprised that your brother allowed you to serve as a doctor in a field hospital," she said, because she didn't know what else to say. She didn't know of many surgeon kings.

My late brother didn't care much for me. I was only the

spare. Kainan turned to Andreas. *Please help Dr. McNeil deal with this security situation.*

Andreas bowed deeply. "Yes, Your Majesty."

Michael and Andreas walked away. Kainan turned to her, pain etched across his face.

I am sorry, Reagan. I could tell no one. Not until I'd had the surgery. Canada needs to protect me until my coronation.

"When is that? When is your coronation?"

New Year's Day.

"And your surgery?"

The twenty-sixth of this month. It's risky.

"How risky?"

With the severe amount of scar tissue...

He frowned and her heart sank. She knew.

"It's bad, then?"

Yes.

She nodded, but still the reality of it all was not sinking in. "That day at the palace..."

I tried to save Alek, but Alek wouldn't leave. The fool thought I wanted to be King.

"Why would he think that?" she asked.

My brother was a fool. The IED went off as I was trying to get him out of the palace and he didn't survive his injuries. So here I stand. King of Isla Hermosa. A voiceless king.

"I don't know what..." She trailed off as she thought about Peter upstairs. The sense of dread was threatening to drown her. The thought of the press pushing their way into Peter's room was too horrible to think about. "Do the press know about Peter?"

Kainan shook his head. *No, they do not. They do not know about you or Peter, and I plan to keep it that way to protect you both.*

She nodded, but she wasn't sure that he would be able

to. She wasn't sure about anything, and she didn't even really know him anymore.

Reagan had thought that Kainan was just a simple Hermosian surgeon. Nobody famous, just a person who tried to save lives, like her. But instead he'd been living this whole double life when they were on the island.

He was a king. Kainan might have called himself the "spare," but he was still royalty. It was a little too much to take in at the moment.

No wonder there was so much security surrounding Kainan at the Royal York. No wonder the Canadian government had insisted that Kainan come here, Dr. Shaw was one of the best otolaryngologists in the country. It also explained why he was being put up in such an opulent hotel.

Kainan was being protected.

"Dr. Laskaris, Dr. Cote...what should we do now?" asked a medical student.

Reagan and Kainan both spun round to see a few of the medical students in the doorway. A couple of them were staring at Kainan with wide-eyed awe.

These students must have heard about the civil war that had ripped the island nation of Isla Hermosa apart. How the late King Aleksander had been a tyrant and driven the country's resources into the ground. As well as cutting off a lot of trade and manufacturing, King Alek had been an ill-informed, misguided playboy who had cost a lot of lives.

And they probably all knew about the missing King too.

The missing King who was standing in front of her. Who was the father of her baby.

At least the press doesn't know about Peter, and we have to keep it that way.

"Why don't you head back to the university? Class is dismissed for today," Reagan said, making an executive decision.

The students turned back into the room to gather up

their stuff and Reagan started to walk away, because she needed to let all this sink in.

Kainan caught up with her as she headed down a quiet hallway that was rarely used. The beds on that wing were closed, and she needed the peace of the closed ward to regain her composure. But she had a feeling that was not going to happen, because Kainan had followed her and insisted on signing.

I meant what I said. This changes nothing, Reagan. My being King changes nothing about this situation. We're in Canada. We're not in Isla Hermosa.

She wanted to believe him, but she couldn't.

It's Kainan, a little voice said, but that didn't matter anymore. She didn't know him. Not really. The man she'd thought she knew didn't really exist. He was a stranger.

Nothing changes, he reiterated.

"Oh, really?"

"I am still me," he whispered breathlessly.

"I don't know who that is." She stopped to face him. "I never really knew you. We spent all that time together, working side by side, but we were strangers."

Kainan scrubbed a hand over his face. *I couldn't tell you I was spare to the heir. Do you know how many women found out who I was and immediately changed. They just wanted my wealth. They wanted status. With you I could just be me.*

"You *knew* I wasn't like that."

In the end, yes, I did. But you can understand my hesitation. At the beginning I knew nothing about you either.

Reagan thought about this, then nodded. "How many women are we talking about?" she asked, trying to ease the tension a little.

Kainan smiled. *Okay, not that many. When women found out who I was they pursued me. I wasn't the playboy my brother was.*

"I just wish you had told me."

What would telling the truth have done? Nothing. We were at war. I don't think of myself as a leader. I wasn't trained to step into my father's shoes. All I ever wanted to be was a surgeon, and it was refreshing to be just that when we were working together.

"What does this mean for our son?"

Nothing at the moment. He is illegitimate.

Her eyes widened at his words. *Nothing at the moment.* What did he mean by that?

Despite what he'd said about nothing changing, did he mean to legitimize Peter and take him away? And then she recalled what legitimizing meant to a royal. It meant marriage. And if it meant what she thought it meant, she would need more than a moment. She would need a lifetime.

There was no way she was going to marry Kainan just because they had a son together—just because they'd once had feelings for each other and had had a great night of sex.

That was not something to base a marriage on. Her parents had married for that, and her mother had resented her for pushing her father away. First of all because he'd wanted a son and then because he'd thought Reagan was a burden, cramping his lifestyle.

Reagan didn't want a marriage like that.

She never wanted to get married.

"At the moment?" she asked, trying not stumble over the words.

If we marry...

Reagan began to laugh at the absurdity of it all. "No, I don't think so."

Kainan's dark eyes narrowed. *I didn't ask you.*

"I'm saving you the trouble. There's no way."

Reagan, he's my son too.

"I am very aware of that, *Your Majesty.* But just because he's your son it doesn't mean that I'm going to marry you.

Just because you're King it doesn't mean that I want to marry you."

Kainan rolled his eyes. *This is exactly why I didn't tell you. You've changed.*

"I thought that was why you liked me—because I wasn't after your title or your money. I'm still not, by the way. I haven't changed."

You're more cynical.

"I have every right to be!"

Why? he asked.

She couldn't tell him. She didn't want to share with him or anyone her painful past. To do that would be letting him in, leaving her exposed.

Reagan softened. "I'm sorry. I can't marry you. I don't ever want to get married."

Kainan nodded and then took a step closer to her. *Are you saying you never cared for me in that way?*

"I cared for you, Kainan. It just feels like a lifetime ago, and you are not the man I thought you were either."

And you would've turned me down back then?

He reached out and touched her cheek briefly, before signing again.

You would've turned down a proposal of marriage from me then? When I was the man you thought I was?

Yes. I would.

Only she didn't say it out loud. That was for her only.

"We were friends. Did you really want to propose to me back then?" she asked, but her pulse was racing.

His simple touch still affected her and she recalled the moment when he'd finally taken her in his arms and kissed her.

She remembered it with vivid clarity. The sweltering heat, the sound of the waves crashing against the shore and all the chaos that had seemed to still around them in that moment.

"If things had been different…" Kainan whispered, then stroked her cheek again.

His arm slipped around her as he tipped up her chin and captured her lips in a kiss. She closed her eyes and drank it in. This stolen moment that took her right back to that time.

And even though she didn't want to feel this way about him, because she didn't have an inch of her heart to give him, she couldn't help but be swept away.

It was like a dream.

All those months when she'd thought he was dead, and right now he was a reality.

He was here.

Alive and kissing her.

He was affecting her, bringing down her walls.

She couldn't let him in.

She pushed him away. "Kainan, it doesn't change anything. I never want to marry. Royalty or not, it doesn't change how I feel about marriage."

Reagan, I can take care of you and Peter.

"How?" she asked. "You can't give him a new heart by making him a prince."

He looked crestfallen. *I can protect you both.*

"From what?"

Those who wish to end the monarchy of Isla Hermosa.

She frowned. "But you said it yourself—he's not legitimate so he's not a threat. If I marry you so you can protect us, I'm actually endangering us further."

Kainan's shoulders slumped. *You'd still be a target if people found out. I am sorry. I just… I want to protect you both. I haven't done much for you, but I can do that. Let me do this. It's the right thing to do.*

She reached out and grabbed his hand. "Being here now is enough, but we need to protect Peter. His last name is Cote, not Laskaris. The only people who know that you're

his father are the pediatric critical care unit staff and Michael. They won't say a word."

My security team knows.

Reagan's stomach knotted. "You'll have to keep them away from him. They'll attract attention."

He pursed his lips together, annoyed. *I will not call them off. I don't even think that I can anyway. They're protecting the monarchy of Isla Hermosa.*

"Then the press will find out."

Security will keep them out of the hospital.

Reagan rolled her eyes. "Don't underestimate the press."

Fine. They will keep their distance. But the moment something happens to you or Peter I am bringing about the security detachment in force.

"Deal." She held out her hand to shake his.

Kainan didn't take it. *I'm going to check in with Andreas and make sure that everything is good.*

"Okay. I'm going to check on Peter and then see if they need any help in the emergency department, since we sent the medical students home early."

I want you to have dinner with me tonight.

"How is that keeping your distance, Kainan? Won't the press see me having dinner with you?"

Not if you come to my hotel room. No one will notice you and my guards can provide a distraction.

Reagan crossed her arms. "Why do you want me to have dinner with you?"

Kainan pinched the bridge of his nose. *Why must you question everything?*

"I'm not leaving the hospital tonight, Kainan. I shouldn't have left yesterday. I'm needed here."

To do what? Peter is stable.

"I'm not leaving. So, no, I'm not having dinner with you tonight."

Fine, but I'm not giving up on this.

Kainan walked away and Reagan shook her head. She knew he was stubborn enough that he would persist until she agreed, but she wasn't going to leave the hospital tonight.

She was going to stay right by Peter.

With this threat of the press, and people who would do harm to Kainan, she was going to make sure that no one got to Peter.

Kainan waited outside the pediatric critical care unit. He didn't want to go in on the off-chance that someone from the press had snuck inside. It was killing him not to see Peter, but this was for the best.

Until he could make Reagan his wife and legitimize Peter he had to keep his distance from his son. Only he didn't want to. He didn't want to be like his father, a distant, remote figure.

If the press found out about Peter then all hell would break loose. Yet Kainan had to legitimize him. He had to marry Reagan and provide for them both. It was the right thing to do.

He saw Reagan walking toward the pediatric critical care unit, her head down and rubbing her neck. She looked tired and he didn't blame her. He needed to do more. Reagan needed help, even if she didn't trust him.

He had heard from Sophie that Reagan had spent every night since Peter was born watching him. Except for last night. She hadn't even had a chance to recover much from the birth. She was always there, beside Peter.

One night of sleep would not make up for all the nights she'd lost. All the time she hadn't taken to heal. All the weight she had on her shoulders.

Kainan wanted to help her because the guilt of not being there for her was eating away at him like so many things

did, but this was more real. This was a weight that he would gladly bear, that he *wanted* to bear for her.

"Reagan." He said her name uncertainly, because he wasn't sure his voice would be able to say it in a way for her to hear him.

She stopped and looked up. "Kainan—I thought you had returned to the hotel. Your security detachment isn't here."

Not that you can see. They're always around.

Reagan gave him a halfhearted smile. "What're you still doing here? I told you I didn't want to have dinner."

I know, but you do have to eat sometime.

"I'm not leaving the hospital, Kainan. I told you that."

I know, and that is why I have arranged for dinner in the classroom.

"What?" she asked, raising a finely arched brow.

It's cafeteria food, and I know that you said yesterday that you were tired of cafeteria food, but seeing how you won't leave the hospital, and I don't want to draw attention, I didn't really have a choice.

She crossed her arms, a smile spread across her face. "You *are* persistent."

I may be King now, but I haven't changed that much.

"Is a king supposed to change?" she teased.

I don't know.

They both laughed at that.

Come on, he's stable. He's fine right now. Eat first, and then you can man your post by his bedside, or I can man the post and you can sleep in a proper bed.

"You want to take a shift by Peter's bedside?" she asked, surprised. As if she didn't quite believe him or the help he was offering.

Yes.

"You? Shouldn't you be resting before your surgery?"

That's not for a few days yet. Let me take a shift. I want to do it.

"I don't know…"

She looked over her shoulder at the door of the pediatric critical care unit and he knew the pull she was feeling. He was feeling it too.

It was hard not to when your child was lying there sick. *You are no good to him weakened. You need to eat, Reagan. Come.*

Reagan tore her glance away and nodded. "You're right."

Of course I am. I am King, after all.

It was a tease, and Reagan rolled her eyes, but she laughed all the same.

"Lead the way, my liege."

I'm not your liege, Reagan. You are not Hermosian. He held out his arm. *However, I am a gentleman, so if you'll do me the honor and let me escort you?*

Reagan took his arm and they walked away from the pediatric critical care unit to the classroom that was at the far end of the hall, on the other side of the hospital.

They didn't say anything. It was night, and the hospital was quiet. All the regular appointments and coming and goings that happened during the day, making the hospital a busy place, were gone. There were a few staff members walking past, because the emergency room never stopped running, but for the most part the hospital was deserted.

The lighting was low and it was very calm. The cafeteria was only serving coffee and sandwiches. The gift shop was closed and through the atrium window he could see snow falling softly.

In a couple of days it would be Christmas, then his surgery, and then New Year's, which would be his coronation. *If* he survived the surgery and *if* the surgery was successful.

Kainan couldn't remember the last time he'd celebrated Christmas. He'd always made excuses to his father in order

to avoid the holiday since his mother had died. So for years, he hadn't celebrated it. He'd worked and he'd enjoyed that.

And then war had broken out.

He'd spent last Christmas with Reagan, in the mobile military hospital. She had sung Christmas carols to the soldiers. Just thinking about that made him smile.

"What're you smiling about?" she asked.

I was thinking about last Christmas with you.

She smiled. "I remember that night."

You brought a lot of hope to those wounded soldiers.

"It was Christmas—it's all about hope. Although I wouldn't really know..."

Did you not celebrate Christmas as a child?

"No. Well, sort of. My parents never really liked to spend time with me. I had a grandmother until I was about seven, who made the holiday special, but after she died my parents were very cold to me. They didn't want me and they made it clear."

He frowned. *I'm sorry, and I can understand that.*

"You understand? I thought your father was a great king?"

Yes—a great king, but a very cold, detached father. I was the spare, so he didn't spend a lot of time with me. Besides, Christmas was all pomp and circumstance. It was all for show.

"Sounds like we both had it rough," she whispered. "Still, Christmas is a time for hope."

Do you feel hopeful about this Christmas?

The wistful smile disappeared, to be replaced with sigh. "I'm trying, but it's hard. This is Peter's first Christmas and he's spending it here."

Kainan understood. He wished it was different.

At least he's still alive.

She smiled at him, her eyes glistening. "Yes. He is."

Kainan opened the door to the classroom, where he'd set

up a small dining area. He'd borrowed plates and cutlery from the cafeteria, with Andreas's help. He only wished there were candles or something, so he could set some mood lighting, but candles weren't allowed in the hospital. He wanted to make it special to her.

He pulled out a seat and beckoned for her to sit. Once she'd sat down he pushed her chair in and then took the seat next to her. The table was too long, and he didn't want her to have to shout across the room. This way, if he wanted to speak to her then he wouldn't have to shout.

He longed to speak to her as he'd used to be able to do. With his voice he could offer to hold her hand, touch her and comfort her.

At least she could understand him, though. Not many people knew how to use American Sign Language. He had learned it in medical school, because he'd wanted to converse with hearing impaired or nonverbal patients in his medical practice. He'd had no idea that it would become a part of his life.

"What's for dinner?" she asked.

Kainan lifted the lids on the salads he'd ordered before the cafeteria had shut down. *I believe it is called Cobb Salad.*

"It looks good. Actually, the cafeteria makes a great Cobb salad."

Well, this is just the starter. The main course is macaroni and cheese. I can't say that I've had the pleasure of trying macaroni and cheese.

"You're pulling my leg," Reagan said.

No, it's true. It's not really a staple on Isla Hermosa, and I grew up in a palace with a team of cooks. Macaroni and cheese wasn't in their repertoire.

"Then you missed out, my friend," she teased.

He chuckled. *I took a peek at it. I highly doubt that.*

Reagan smiled brightly, her dark eyes twinkling under the fluorescent lighting.

You have beautiful smile, Reagan.

Pink crept up her neck into her cheeks. "You've told me that before."

It's the truth.

"Why are you doing this?" she asked.

Doing what?

"This dinner. Why?"

I'm doing this because I wasn't there for you when Peter was born. I see the burden you carry and I want to help. Don't be on the defensive so much. You can trust me.

She looked away. "It's dangerous for you to help right now."

I know, but at least I can do this. I may not be able to directly help him, but I can help make things easier for you.

Her spine stiffened a bit. "I don't need help. I got myself into this situation and I can handle it."

I believe I was part of this "situation", as you call it. Unless Peter was another immaculate conception, I had a hand in helping you.

Reagan sighed and relaxed. "Okay, thank you for dinner. I appreciate it."

Kainan nodded. *Eat. You need to eat to keep your strength up. You're no good to our son if you get sick or collapse from exhaustion.*

Reagan nodded and they ate in silence, but it wasn't awkward. It felt right, and it was nice just to sit there with her and enjoy the peace and quiet, alone in this section of the hospital.

When they'd finished, Reagan leaned back in her chair. "That was good. What did you think of the macaroni and cheese?"

It was...interesting.

He made a face and she laughed, then she picked up her phone and frowned.

What's wrong? Kainan asked when she looked up again.

"It's Peter. His stats are a bit low." She bit her lip and then got up. "I have to be with him."

Kainan nodded. *Go and keep me posted. Please.*

Her expression softened. "I will. Thank you for dinner. I really appreciate it."

He nodded and she left the room.

Kainan sank back in the office chair he was been sitting in, spinning a bit as he tried not to think about what was happening to his son, or the fact that he was helpless. It was too much to bear.

He had to marry Reagan to protect her, to protect them both—especially if he didn't survive the surgery. Although he was very aware that he would be ruining her life *and* Peter's by staying and subjecting them to royal protocol.

He should just walk away. Only he couldn't. And the fact that he couldn't scared him.

CHAPTER SIX

IT HAD BEEN a couple days since their impromptu dinner that night in the classroom. It was the nicest thing that anyone had ever done for her in a long time. Actually, Reagan couldn't remember the last time someone had done something so nice for her.

Maybe there was still a piece of the man she'd thought she knew in there. Kainan had promised her nothing would change with respect to Peter. He wouldn't try and take him away.

Could she believe him?

She sighed, hating the doubt that still crept in.

He had been trying really hard, but since that dinner he had kept his distance both from her and Peter. It broke her heart to see him keeping Peter at arm's length, especially when Peter wasn't doing particularly well at the moment.

You asked him to stay away, remember?

And she had. He was doing what she'd asked.

It had been to keep Peter safe. Now she wasn't so sure that it had been the right decision.

Peter needed both his parents, and Kainan was alive. It was a miracle, and she shouldn't keep Kainan away from Peter or vice versa, but there was danger attached to Kainan and that made her fear for her son. She feared Peter might be hurt when Kainan returned to Isla Hermosa.

It was across the Atlantic. If Kainan had meant what he'd said about not trying to take her son away from her, Peter wouldn't see Kainan much. As King, Kainan's duties would take over—and what would happen when he married?

A king needed a queen.

You could be that queen.

No, she couldn't. Her life was here.

What life?

Still, she was protecting Peter's heart. She didn't want him to feel abandonment as she had. It was the right decision that he stayed away, so the press wouldn't discover Peter. News of Kainan's presence in Toronto was in all the papers. Not that she'd had a lot of time to read in between her duties at the hospital and being with Peter.

All she'd had time for was the headlines.

The world was waiting for Kainan to say something. Anything. Yet he couldn't. Not until after his surgery.

Reagan knew that Michael was overwhelmed in keeping the press out of the hospital so that they didn't pry into Kainan's life. Or hers.

At least there had been no mention of her. Which meant they didn't know about Peter.

That was good, but who knew how long that would last? It was something she didn't want to think about it.

She watched Kainan now, from a distance. He was sitting in the empty classroom, writing. When they'd served in Isla Hermosa he had told her that he was at the forefront of a new surgical technique that would save lives, but the war had put an end to that.

He was researching again now, while the medical students were on a break for the upcoming Christmas holidays. That meant Kainan didn't really need Reagan unless he was out and about in the hospital. Although she couldn't help but wonder how he would be able to develop a surgical technique when he couldn't speak.

To develop a surgical technique he had to be able to perform surgery, and without his voice that was something he couldn't do at the moment.

She was impressed by him. He was so strong. That was what had drawn her in last time. She smiled to herself, still watching Kainan. How did he get to her? Especially when no one else did.

It was thrilling, but unnerving. Those walls of hers had protected her for so long, and yet Kainan could get through to her.

"You do remember me, don't you, Dr. Cote?"

Reagan spun around to see a security guard—the one who had spoken to her in the hallway at the Royal York. The one she remembered working on in the field. Kainan's security guard—Andreas.

"I do. It took me some time. I wasn't used to seeing you with hair."

The security guard smiled. "I prefer this length over the required shaved head for military service. His Majesty does not care if I keep my hair long, as long as it doesn't interfere in my duties."

"I'm sorry I didn't recognize you right away, sir," she said sheepishly.

He smiled gently. "It's Andreas—and do not worry. I suspect you have a lot on your mind, especially in regard to your son being so ill."

Reagan nodded. "I appreciate the fact you're keeping an eye on him. He's not Hermosian…"

"He may not have been born there, but he is still half-Hermosian. He is heir to the throne—that's if he is legitimized." There was hope in his eyes as he looked her.

She chuckled nervously. "Right…"

That wasn't going to happen, but Andreas didn't need to know that.

"I thank you for saving my life that night and for sing-

ing me those Christmas songs. I have never forgotten that moment."

Reagan smiled. "I was just doing my duty—as were you. There is no need to thank me."

Andreas dipped his head. "Ah, but you sang so sweetly. It gave me such hope. You *still* give me hope."

Warmth flooded her cheeks and she discovered she didn't like the attention he was lavishing on her. "How do you mean?"

Andreas opened his mouth to say something further, and then looked over her shoulder and froze. "My apologies. I must get back to my duties."

Reagan turned to see that Kainan was standing in the doorway. His hands were in his pockets and he was glaring at Andreas. It was an expression that meant business. It caused a shiver to go down her spine.

Andreas skulked away and Kainan's gaze never left his retreating form. He looked like a true king—or at least like the ones she'd seen depicted in movies.

"That was rude," Reagan snapped. King or not, she didn't like it when people treated others badly.

He was treading where he should not, Kainan signed, and mouthed a curse word.

"What're you talking about?"

There are affairs of my kingdom that do not concern you. You do not need to know about them.

"Okay…"

And he does not need to know our personal business.

"I agree," she said, relieved.

Kainan's expression softened. *How are you? I have not seen you these last couple of days.*

"I've been busy. Actually, I'm on my way to see Peter's pediatrician in his office. I came to see if you wanted to come."

Kainan frowned. *What's wrong?*

Reagan sighed. "Peter hasn't been doing so well and the doctor wants to touch base."

His brow furrowed and she could tell that something was bothering him.

Does this doctor know who I am?

"That you're his father and the King of Isla Hermosa? Yes, he knows, and he's signed the confidentiality agreement that Michael has forced upon all those dealing with our special situation."

Kainan let out a sigh, relief on his face. *Then I would like to go and hear for myself.*

"Okay."

Kainan hesitated. *That's if you want me to go?*

"I wouldn't have offered if I didn't."

I have been staying away, like you asked.

Her stomach flip-flopped with guilt. "I know, but perhaps I was wrong."

He cocked an eyebrow.

"Yes, I was wrong. Don't stay away."

She was afraid Kainan that would leave, and that would hurt Peter, but Peter not knowing his father at all and growing up to learn that Reagan had kept Kainan away would be worse.

Peter needed Kainan.

Kainan smiled, those dark eyes twinkling as his gaze held her captive. *Then I won't.*

"Good."

Kainan locked up the classroom and they headed toward the pediatric wing of the hospital, where Dr. Braccio worked.

Reagan sighed. "You know, I sometimes wonder if I would have been better off without my parents."

Why is that? Kainan signed.

"They never wanted me. Their resentment was horrible. I wouldn't wish that on anyone."

You had no love?

"Did you? You said your father wasn't the best."

Yes, but my mother loved me. He smiled wistfully. *So I was lucky.*

"I'm glad you're here, Kainan. Peter needs you. He needs both of us. I didn't have my parents when I really needed them and…it was miserable. You're here, alive, and Peter should have every opportunity to get to know you."

Kainan nodded. *Thank you. I want to get to know him too…before I have to return to Isla Hermosa.*

Her stomach clenched. "You have a country to run."

Let me worry about that. You know I will be there for Peter if he needs me. Of course I could be there all the time if—

She knew where he was going and she didn't want to go there.

"How is the research coming?" she interrupted, changing the subject but feeling the awkward tension that was between them suddenly.

Good. I am glad to be working on it again. It was my one true passion. I never wanted to be a king. I just wanted medicine.

"I know—you've told me."

And what is your grand passion, besides our son?

"I don't know," she said. "I enjoyed my time in the military, and when I left Isla Hermosa I was excited to be working at this hospital in trauma. I guess I never really thought beyond those plans, because I found out I was pregnant and my focus shifted."

Come on, there must've been something?

"I once wanted to teach medicine," she admitted. "I wanted to teach at my alma mater."

Where was that?

"I went to medical school in London, Ontario. It's a small city, about two hours west of here. I just loved Lon-

don. Toronto is my hometown, but it's too big for me. The prices of the homes are astronomical here, but in London housing is a bit more affordable. I could actually buy a small house and Peter would have a yard to play in. Of course when Peter was born so ill I really had no choice. I had to stay here."

She laughed nervously.

"It's not as wild as your aspirations to win a Nobel prize for medicine or anything."

It's still a good aspiration. He smiled at her. *It's good to dream of something like that, because that sounds wonderful to me. I didn't have the luxury to go and play outside when I was a child.*

"Oh?" she asked.

Well, there were always threats when it came to the Young Princes. More so with Alek than me, but still... If I did get to go outside then I was followed by Security. There were a few times I managed to sneak away.

"And where did you sneak off to?" she asked with a smile.

To the ocean. I was fascinated by tidal pools and I liked to swim. My mother was terrified of the ocean. Her brother was carried away by a rip tide and died when she was a young girl, so when she found out that I was sneaking away from my bodyguards and heading to the ocean to swim I got in a lot of trouble. I was shipped off to boarding school in Switzerland. Just mountains—no ocean.

"I'm sorry you didn't have freedom. I didn't have a huge amount of freedom growing up in the city. There wasn't many safe places to play—and forget about learning to ride a bike. I grew up on the Danforth."

What's the Danforth? Kainan asked.

"A part of Toronto—a neighborhood. It was busy, so I played in a shoebox-sized yard. My parents didn't really

take me anywhere. We didn't travel. I think I was a bit of a burden to them."

He frowned. *Well, if it's any consolation I think I was a bit of a burden to my father too.*

"Not your mother, though?" she asked.

No, never my mother. Even though she died when I was ten. I was at boarding school when she got sick. I was brought back in time to say goodbye to her.

His expression softened and he had a faraway look in his eyes, like the one he'd had the day before he'd been sent up to the front lines, when he had been staring at the smoke rising from the gates of Helicia.

"I'm sorry to hear that. How did she die?"

Cancer. She did not suffer long. All she wanted was her freedom... He sighed.

"Freedom? Was she a prisoner?"

In a way. She wasn't locked up, but a member of the royal family has to follow certain protocols, certain rules, and my mother was a bit of free spirit. He smiled sadly. *She loved my father, though he never really loved her. Not in the same way.*

Reagan could understand that. She'd often wondered if her parents really loved each other because they seemed so cold and so indifferent. She had never been quite sure that they were capable of love. At least Kainan had had love. His mother had loved him, and from the way Kainan described his mother it sounded as if he'd loved her too.

"I understand," she whispered.

You do? he signed, looking confused.

"My parents were very emotionally closed off to me, and to each other. I didn't have the best childhood."

I'm sorry.

"I sometimes wonder if I can be the mother Peter needs." She blushed, annoyed with herself that she'd let that slip.

You're an excellent mother, Reagan.

Her pulse quickened as Kainan reached out and took her hand and they continued their walk to the pediatrician's office, moving in silence the rest of the way.

They stopped in front of Dr. Braccio's office and Reagan took a deep breath. She had a feeling about what Dan Braccio was going to tell her about Peter. She'd read his chart. Peter was dying. And time was running out for him to get a new heart.

Kainan, as if sensing her apprehension, gave her hand a squeeze and nodded with determination toward the door.

You can do this. You have to do this.

Reagan let go of Kainan's hand and knocked on the door.

Dan Braccio answered. "Reagan, come on in—and you must be Peter's father."

"Kainan," Kainan said carefully.

"Welcome—it's nice to meet you." Dan shook Kainan's hand, and as Reagan sat down on the edge of the chair Dan shut the door behind them, locking it so that no one would barge in.

Which was not a good sign.

Reagan's heart started to race and Kainan placed a hand on her shoulder to steady her, as if he knew that she was terrified.

"I'm glad you both could come, and I'm not going to mince words with you as you're doctors." Dan took a seat behind his desk. "Peter's cardiomyopathy is progressing rapidly."

"How long?" Reagan asked, her voice trembling slightly.

"A month, maybe, if we're lucky," Dan said sadly. "The pediatric cardiologist, Dr. Bruni, is very concerned."

Tears stung her eyes but she tried to keep it together. A month? That was it? That was all she'd have left with her son?

This couldn't be the end.

A year of life was all he got?

Her world was crumbling under her.

"He has been moved up the priority list on UNOS," Dan said. "He's right at the top now. But you both know that infant hearts are hard to come by. I wanted him to get a bit older."

"He's three months old now—that's surely got to give him a better chance?"

Reagan was grasping at straws, but she wasn't ready to accept defeat yet. Not when it came to Peter. He was her whole world. She didn't have a contingency plan for life without him.

"Yes, I am glad he's not newborn. That does give us a slight advantage. It's easier to find an older heart for an infant as opposed to a newborn heart, but it's still difficult." Dan opened up Peter's file. "We do have a better shot now."

Kainan tapped her shoulder and she saw he was signing. Dan was watching and waiting for her to translate.

"Kainan would like to know the specifics of what will happen. Will he go on a left ventricular assist device?" she asked.

Dan nodded and looked at Kainan when he addressed him. "I would like to hook him up to an LVAD as soon as possible." He slid the consent form toward Reagan. "He's no stranger to surgery, but I hate having to do this to him…"

"I know," Reagan said dully. "But it's his only hope."

Dan nodded. "I'm sorry, Reagan and Kainan. I truly am. This is not an easy situation. I don't like delivering this kind of news."

Reagan didn't respond. What doctor *did* like delivering this kind of news? None that she could think of. But it was a part of the job and being on this end of the conversation sucked. Big-time.

It was as if someone was trying to cut her heart out with a blunt instrument and hand it to her while it was still beating.

If only she could give her heart to Peter she would. She would give up her life for him. Anything to have him live.

Reagan clicked the pen she didn't even remember picking up and signed her name on the form, dating it before sliding the form back to Dan.

"When will the surgery take place?" Reagan asked stonily. She was numb.

"As soon as possible. He needs to go on the device. I'm having my team and the cardiothoracic team prep him for surgery and ready everything I need. I hope to have his surgery done within the next couple of hours."

Reagan nodded. "Can I be with him?"

"Yes, but you won't be able to handle him. I'm sorry. We have to take every precaution to prevent infection. This will be taxing for him."

"I understand." Reagan stood. "Thank you, Dan."

Kainan went ahead of her and unlocked the door, holding it open for her. There were so many emotions rushing through her she wasn't sure what to do. Instead she bottled everything up tight.

There was no time for her to feel.

Right now she had to be strong for Peter.

Kainan seemed to understand. He said nothing, just walked beside her. This time he did not reach out to touch her and she was glad, because if he touched her she would lose it, and she didn't want to fall apart right now.

They gowned, gloved, and put on surgical masks before entering the pediatric critical care unit.

There were a few nurses and a couple of young pediatric surgical residents hovering around Peter's crib, and Reagan let out a hiss of pain and turned away. She couldn't stand to look.

Kainan's arm came around her and she looked up into his eyes.

"Be strong. You are strong," he whispered, his voice hoarse.

He winced, and she knew that uttering those words had been hard for him, painful as well. His words, his voice—even broken—gave her strength.

"I don't know if I'm *this* strong," she said, her voice cracking with the emotion that she could barely contain.

Kainan removed his arm and signed, *You've been here before. Peter needs you. He will pull through. This is his best chance.*

"I know." She turned back around and stood on the periphery, watching as they readied Peter for surgery. Sophie glanced up once from her work to nod briefly, and then turned back to Peter. Kainan stood beside her.

"I have never heard him cry," Reagan whispered urgently. "Well, not since the day he was born."

Kainan's expression was pained, but he said nothing.

"I would love to hear him cry again." Tears were welling up in her eyes. "Just one more time. If I had a Christmas wish it would be that."

When he gets a new heart you will hear him cry all the time. It will probably drive you crazy.

Reagan smiled. "I would like that."

At least after the LVAD surgery you can hold him. In fact, it'll be encouraged. He'll need all your strength.

The surgical team came in and transferred her fragile son to a gurney, along with all his wires and tubes. He looked so small. She took a step forward, aching to reach out and touch him, but restrained herself.

"Touch him," Sophie whispered. "He needs you."

"I was told not to," Reagan said.

"Touch him. It's just a touch," Sophie encouraged.

Reagan nodded, tears rolling down her cheeks as she bent over her sick boy and touched his head through her

rubber glove, kissing the soft skin that she'd never got to touch through the surgical mask.

"I'll be waiting," Reagan whispered. "Right here."

Kainan stepped forward, but then he hesitated and turned away, shaking his head. He couldn't do it, and it hurt her that he wouldn't reach out to touch their son, but she saw the pained expression on his face and understood.

She knew that look of pain—she lived it every day.

The surgical team rolled him out of the pediatric critical care unit. Reagan followed them. She would follow the gurney until she could do so no longer. Until it entered the surgical floor, where she would not be able to follow because she was a parent in this moment, not a surgeon.

It was hard to stop at the double doors that closed off the surgical wing from the rest of the hospital, but she stopped and watched as they rolled Peter away.

She hated being in a patient's shoes. She hated being on this side of the door.

Kainan was beside her. "Come," he said.

Reagan shook her head. She wouldn't let him take her away. It was as if staring at those double doors would somehow protect Peter, somehow bring him back to her.

"Reagan," Kainan said more firmly.

"I'm not leaving."

Before she knew what was happening Kainan was scooping her up in his arms and carrying her away, in broad daylight.

"Are you crazy?" she screeched. "Put me down!"

Kainan didn't respond, and he wouldn't look at her as he carried her to a small exam room that was dark and unoccupied. He set her down and then shut the door, locking it, then pulling down the blinds.

"What do you think you're doing?" she yelled at him. "People could've seen—people probably *did* see, you maniac!"

Let it out, he signed.

"Let what out?"

Let it all out. You can't bottle up that emotion forever. Let it out. Stop locking your emotions away.

She just stared at him at first, because she was so stunned at what he was suggesting, and all she could hear was her mother's voice in her head.

"Honestly, Reagan. You're a big girl now. Stop crying. It's embarrassing. You can hold it together," her mother had hissed at her when she'd cried over the fact her dog had died. "Big girls don't cry."

"I don't have anything to let out." Her voice trembled.

Reagan, you don't have to hide with me.

The moment she saw what he'd signed it was like a floodgate opening up. She broke down weeping, covering her face with her hands, and let it all out—every piece of raw emotion that she had been bottling up inside her since Peter had been born.

Kainan took her in his arms and she clung to him. He ran his hand over her head, but it was hard for him to do that with the bun she had in her hair.

Still, it was what she needed.

She needed to be held. Her body trembled as he held her, the pain washing through her. The strength in his arms calmed her.

"There was nothing you could've done," Kainan had said back then, gripping her by the shoulders and shaking her. "You did everything you could."

"I didn't. I didn't save his life. That's what I could've done and I couldn't even do that!"

"His injuries were too severe. He stepped in the path of an IED. There was nothing anyone could've done, but you gave him comfort."

"Comfort?" She'd wiped away her tears.

"You held him and he passed away peacefully, know-

ing that he was safe and that he was without pain. You did all you could. In fact you did more. Not many surgeons in this military hospital would do the same."

He'd pulled her into his arms then, giving her a hug, holding her close so that she would calm down as she cried in his arms.

"He was so young," she'd whispered against his neck. "He didn't get a chance to live."

"Some never do." He'd tipped up her chin, those dark eyes so reassuring, so understanding, and she'd known that he also felt the pain she'd felt in that moment.

"You did everything you could. You were strong for him. You *are* strong."

Reagan looked up at Kainan now, longing to hear him say those same things.

He did say those words. You just didn't hear them.

She studied his face. There were a few more scars, some creases in his face from worry, and some grey in his dark curls. It suited him. But those dark eyes were the same. They were reflecting back the pain that she was feeling.

Acting on the need to be close to him, she kissed him. And it was as if she had come home. His arms wrapped around her, pulling her tight against him as they kissed. How long had she dreamed of this moment but been thrown back into reality, remembering that he had died?

Only he hadn't died.

He was here with her. He was here with Peter.

And for one brief moment, as she sank into the kiss that eased her sorrow, her pain and her worry, she forgot about it all. She forgot that he was King, that their son was dying and that she had been alone for so long.

She finally broke off the kiss and laid her head against his chest as he ran his hands over her back. He was still holding her as they stood in silence. The only sound was her own breath and the steady rhythm of his heart under her ear.

They stayed together in that stolen moment of peace, comforting each other as their son fought for his life.

Then Kainan's hand stilled and he moved away, knocking her out of the peaceful reverie.

I'm sorry for carrying you away like that, but it was the only way, he signed.

"I know. I'm sorry I called you a maniac."

He smiled, a dimple forming in his cheek. *I'm used to it. You've called me worse things before.*

She frowned. "When?"

Your Majesty. He made a sarcastic face, as if to drive home the point that she had said it in a spiteful way.

"I'm sorry about that too."

He shrugged. *I deserved it.*

"Still, thank you for being here with me. Thank you for bringing me here."

I thought you would've learned by now not to bottle up your emotions so much. You were about to burst.

She nodded. "I know. Thank you for coming to my rescue again."

He smiled, his expression softening. *You're welcome.*

Warmth crept up her neck into her cheeks. "I'm sorry for kissing you as well."

Never be sorry for that.

His dark eyes glinted with the promise of something more. Something she knew all too well. And as much as she wanted that, she couldn't do it. She couldn't divide herself between Peter's care and Kainan. It would be too much to bear. Peter and work—that was all she could handle.

Work was the only thing that kept her sane. It was structured and, though it was never predictable, she knew what she was doing. She could detach herself emotionally from it.

Starting something up with Kainan was not the answer, because she knew that she would never be able to detach herself emotionally from him.

He was definitely *not* predictable, and she wasn't sure she could handle losing both Peter *and* Kainan.

The thought of losing them both scared her beyond all reason. And she wasn't prepared to invest in that.

CHAPTER SEVEN

THE SURGERY SEEMED to take an eternity.

Kainan had stayed in the hospital until he was certain that Peter had pulled through and been hooked up to the left ventricular assist device. He'd done it with flying colors. Then he'd gone with Reagan to the pediatric critical care unit, where Peter had been moved to an isolation room.

There was only enough room for the nurses and the doctors to navigate and one chair, which was where Reagan had curled up in her street clothes with a hospital gown over her. She'd looked completely uncomfortable, but Kainan hadn't been able to get her to budge.

There had been no place for him. So he'd left.

He had to put some distance between himself and the hospital anyway. He felt so helpless.

Ever since he'd become King and been whisked away to Canada he'd felt this way, but it came into painful Technicolor how truly helpless he was when he gazed into the incubator at his son.

He was just like his father, who had been absent for most of his childhood. Kainan was following in his father's lead and he loathed himself.

You didn't even know Peter existed. That's why you weren't there, he told himself.

Only that didn't make him feel any better. Things had

to change. He refused to be like his father. His father who hadn't taken care of his illegitimate children...his father who had broken his mother's heart and been distant with his legitimate children.

Kainan refused to force Peter into an unhappy childhood like he'd had.

He'd already missed so much. Three months of Peter's life. And if he didn't get a new heart soon Kainan would never know him. Never speak to him.

Reagan said he didn't cry, that she'd barely heard Peter's voice.

Just like me.

Peter had no voice but he was still here, fighting to live.

Reagan was strong. She would be able to handle the burdens of royal life. He felt guilty for having to impose them upon her, but it was the only way to protect them if he died.

Remember how it broke your mother, though. How it hardened Alek and you.

He had almost lost it when he'd seen Reagan bend over Peter before they took him to surgery. She had bent down and whispered to him to be strong and she'd touched him, kissed him through the surgical mask.

It had alost been too much for him to take. It had taken all his strength to keep himself from breaking down.

Reagan had been so strong and he so weak in that moment. The thought of losing his son had too much for him to bear, but Reagan had needed him. He knew she liked to have walls up, not to show any weakness. But when she cracked he would swallow his worry, his sorrow, and step up to bear it for her.

He wanted to take Reagan and Peter's pain for them. To be better than his own father. If Kainan didn't survive his surgery, if Peter wasn't legitimized, then Kainan wouldn't be able to leave his fortune to them. It was the only thing he could think of doing to protect them.

It had made him think back to that night on Isla Hermosa, when the chaos had died down after the rebel attack on the front lines. When his foolish brother had demanded that the youngest and most untrained of the Hermosian Army should advance.

And that boy who had been no more than eighteen had taken the brunt of the explosion. All they'd been able to do was patch him together, but they had known it wouldn't stop him from dying. That boy had been alone and dying.

The boy had been from the coast. Most likely a fisherman's son, looking to supplement the family income from a dwindling industry by signing up to serve in the Hermosian Army. He'd probably been fresh out of training.

It had been apparent to Kainan that the boy hadn't been fully prepared for what awaited him, and it had broken his heart. It had broken his heart to see the youngest of his country dying in the name of his foolish brother.

In that moment Kainan had blamed himself for the boy's death, because he'd known that when Alek had begun to run amok he should have done more to rein in his brother. He'd tried. He'd tried hard. But then his brother had sought to end his life.

So Kainan had backed off and tried to help the people in another way. Serving as a surgeon on the front lines. But in moments like that, when that boy had lain there dying, afraid and alone, Kainan had questioned his choices.

And then Reagan had appeared, out of the darkness, in the quiet of the hospital where those on duty had been making their rounds on the patients who would live and trying to clean up the mess that the onslaught of injured soldiers from the front had caused.

She'd given the boy more medicine. More of the painkillers that had already been given to him. And then she'd sat next to him. Reagan could speak fluent Spanish, which

was the mother tongue of Isla Hermosa, and she'd spoken to the boy.

Javier had been his name.

She'd held him. She cradled him in his arms and sung to him, just as she had sung to Andreas, and Kainan had realized that she sang to many of those who were injured.

All he had been able to do was watch in awe as she'd administered the simplest form of healing: love, patience and human contact.

Reagan had held Javier as his tremors had ceased, as his breathing had become more shallow and as he'd breathed his last.

And she'd held him for a long time after. Singing to him…some sweet melody, something he had never heard before. But it hadn't mattered what she was singing. It had been her voice. It had been her kindness, her purity. So like his mother, who had helped the less fortunate, who had given everything to his father and got nothing in return.

It was in that moment that Kainan had melted for her. She might bottle up her emotions, but her compassion for others made her a brilliant, strong woman and he had desired her.

Only her.

He had seen her reaching out and comforting their son in the same way she had comforted Javier and all those other countless injured men and women from Isla Hermosa, Canada and the United States. It hadn't mattered to her what side they'd fought for. She had afforded each and every single one of them the simple gift of human compassion and caring. To her there had been no borders, no colors and no religions. No conflict had been too great to stop her from delivering what they had all needed and that was love.

Reagan had cared for them all. She had judged no one.

And at that moment, seeing her being separated from their child, Kainan had realized that their son might never

know what kind of strong woman his mother was and what a failure his father was.

It had broken his heart, and it had been too much for him to take in so he had turned away, missing that moment when they'd taken his son away.

He had turned back to find her trembling in front of the surgical wing, her eyes wide and her body looking as if it was about to bend and break under its burden. She'd been trying to stay strong, but her walls had come crashing down with the weight of it all. Of carrying the burden alone for too long.

That was why he'd picked her up and carried her away from it all. He hadn't cared who saw him in that moment. He'd wanted to afford her the same amount of care and compassion she'd shown to everyone else. To make up for not being there when she'd needed him.

He wasn't sure he could *ever* make that up to her, but he'd try.

She'd helped so many and yet there had been no one helping her. He had seen that. She'd been alone and she'd been standing there so lost. So broken.

And he'd taken her in his arms, as she'd taken Javier in hers, and he'd held her. Comforted her. And then she'd kissed him.

He'd thought about her kisses ever since they'd parted. As he'd been transported on his way to Canada, with an endotracheal tube breathing for him, with no voice to cry out, he'd thought of her.

He'd longed for her.

When she'd kissed him he'd forgotten about being King. About the conflicts in Isla Hermosa. About his late brother and the damage he'd wrought.

All he'd cared about was the fact that he was in her arms again.

It had taken every ounce of his strength to step back

from her when she'd broken the kiss, because he'd burned for her. He still did.

And that was not proper.

It was selfish of him.

Perhaps he was just as selfish as his brother was?

No. You're nothing like him.

Still, he'd needed to put some distance between them, and yet now that it was morning he realized that, no matter how much distance there was between them, he would still feel the same.

His blunder of picking her up and carrying her to that boardroom, where he could hold her, had cost Reagan and Peter something. Their privacy.

Word had got out to the press about his behavior with Reagan. The world knew about her and Peter. Peter was no longer safe.

There were pictures of him carrying Reagan. And although he'd thought they were alone in that boardroom someone had managed to get a picture of them kissing.

He loathed being King in moments like this. Private, precious moments were made into entertainment for the rest of the world. Something cherished became tawdry and debased. It was no longer a beautiful moment between Reagan and him. It belonged to the world.

He headed back to the pediatric critical care unit and watched Reagan sleeping. The guilt of subjecting her to this intrusion on her privacy was eating away at him.

I should've kept my distance from her in Isla Hermosa. I should've kept away.

He shouldn't have been so reckless, so selfish, but he could be *himself* around her. She gave him a sense of freedom that he'd never known. So he had been selfish, and had pursued her. When it came to Reagan he lost all sense.

Within a few hours the press and the rest of the world would know all about Reagan, and know that Kainan and

Reagan had worked together in Isla Hermosa. He felt guilty that Reagan's life was going to be exposed. The press would chew her up and spit her out. They would twist everything about her.

He was going to try hard to protect her.

Reagan stirred and then sat up, seeing that he was standing by her.

"What time is it?" she asked groggily.

Seven in the morning, Kainan signed, and handed her the coffee that he'd picked up in the hotel when he had been wandering. It was gourmet coffee, from his own country.

"Thank you." She took a sip. "Hermosian?"

He nodded. *You look like you didn't have a very comfortable sleep.*

"No, the chair was uncomfortable." She glanced back through the window. "But I'm used to cramming myself into hospital chairs and getting only a few hours of sleep while I'm waiting."

Was there anything to worry about last night?

"Nothing. Last time I talked to Sophie she said he was doing well." A wobbly smile spread across Reagan's face. "This will extend his life while we wait."

That's good.

Reagan stood and stretched. "I'm sorry, I'm a bit of a wreck. I can go change quickly, in the staff room, and then we can get to work."

No work today. I talked to Dr. McNeil. Christmas Eve is in two days and the medical students are already home for the holidays. I can work on my research and you can take some time to be with Peter.

"You spoke with Michael?"

Kainan held up his phone and grinned. *My robot voice did.*

Reagan laughed. "Well, if you need help with your re-

search I can do it. I really don't want to be idle. I need to keep busy."

He didn't want to talk about his research, because it was no longer something he could focus on. Once he returned to Isla Hermosa he would no longer be a surgeon or be able to practice medicine. All his years of research would be left unfinished, and it was hard for him to think about, but it was a sacrifice he had to make.

He changed the subject. *Reagan, you do realize that in a couple of days, if Peter stays on this upward trajectory, he's going to come out of his medicated coma and he'll be able to come home.*

Reagan's eyes widened and she sat down slowly. "What?"

I thought you knew? Kainan signed.

"I *do* know." She shook her head. "It's just that he's never been home. Never. I had the nursery sort of complete...but it's not ready. My home is not ready."

Well, let's go check out your place and get it ready, then.

"You have your research to do."

It can wait. It had waited this long. *My security detail can take us there in the town car and I will help you.*

"You're abusing your power now, Your Majesty," she teased.

How? It's their duty to help the King's son. He grinned.

Reagan sighed. "I suppose so. I don't think I'm ready for this..."

Ready or not, you have to do this. There will be no need for him to be here while he waits for a heart. They will move him to the pediatric ward, out of this critical care unit, get us used to the portable ventricular assist device, and then we can take him home.

"We?"

Kainan smiled and then knelt down in front of her. *You know that I can protect you, Reagan. Please let me take care of you.*

"Kainan, I'm *not* accepting your proposal of marriage. Besides, you said that keeping us secret was the best form of protection that you could give us. If I..." She trailed off when she saw his expression. "The press know, don't they?"

Kainan nodded sadly. *When I carried you into the boardroom. There was someone from the press watching and they got a picture of us kissing.*

Reagan groaned. She set down her coffee cup on the floor beside the chair and rubbed her eyes. "This is horrible."

I'm sorry.

"It's not your fault."

It sort of is. I am King, after all.

And nothing about his life was his.

She laughed at that. "You're not helping."

Marry me. I can protect you.

"No. I can't. I can't think about that now, and I can't consider entering into that life with Peter still so fragile."

Kainan's stomach knotted. He'd known it was a long shot, but he'd had to keep trying. It was the only way to protect her and Peter, to provide for them. He had to do better than his father ever had.

Will you at least let me assist you with your apartment? he asked. *If you're with me I can protect you from the press.*

"Okay. Do you want to go now, while they still have Peter sedated?"

Kainan nodded. *I will go tell the team to get ready and you gather your things.*

"It's going to be a short visit to my apartment," she warned. "I want to be here when he wakes up. It's important that I'm here."

Of course.

Reagan picked up her coffee cup and left the pediatric critical care unit. Kainan sighed and looked back at his son, who still needed a machine to survive.

He knelt down, and even though he couldn't touch Peter he stared into his son's face. Emotion overcame him. This was his child. His flesh, his blood. He couldn't lose him.

"I will do better by you," he whispered. "I swear."

He bowed his head. He would be better than his father ever had.

Even if he wasn't there to show him.

She was trying not stare at Kainan, who was looking out of the window, his chin resting on his hand. She wanted to tell him that she'd seen him, that she'd heard what he'd said to their son.

Any kind of reservation had melted away when she'd heard him whisper, "I will do better by you. I swear."

Reagan had had to leave the room or break down in front of him.

Kainan might be King, but he was good deep down. He was still that man she cared for.

He looked over and smiled. *Comfortable?*

"Very."

Reagan was thankful that Kainan had access to a town car, and that the car's windows were tinted, but the Hermosian flags that flew on the hood sort of gave them away.

"I thought you wanted to be the hidden King?" she said lightly.

Well, since word got out I thought it was time to use the embassy car that is kept here in Toronto. We can park anywhere. He grinned.

"That's good. There's not much parking near my place."

She didn't like it that they were in an embassy car, but if the world already knew about her then there was no sense in hiding. She could face whatever they threw at her. She was the one who'd got involved with Kainan.

Although it made her feel a bit nervous to be out with him. *How far away is your place?*

"I don't know. It's fairly new. I got it when I first came back to Toronto and was preparing for Peter's arrival. I just know the distance in subway stops."

"What's the address?" the driver asked from the front seat. "There's GPS."

"Three-sixteen Richmond Street West. It's not that far, I guess. Like I said, I only know by subway stops and how many blocks I have to walk."

"You're right, Dr. Cote. It's not far. We'll be there and back in no time."

The driver plugged in the route map and Reagan turned back to Kainan.

"Thank you for helping me. I'm sure my place is a disaster. I really didn't have a lot of time to settle in. I was trying to work as long as I could at the hospital, to save up and have a decent maternity leave, and then... Well, you know the rest."

Peter was born and was so ill. Sadly, I do know the rest. Kainan glanced out the window.

Perhaps he'll be on the regular pediatric floor by Christmas? I hear they do a lot of celebrations for the children in there over Christmas and New Year's.

"Maybe he'll be home in time for New Year," said Reagan. And that thought was scary indeed.

A strange look passed over Kainan's face. *Yes. Perhaps.*

It didn't take the driver long to navigate the streets to her condo complex. He parked in front—legally, not having to resort to the embassy park-wherever-you-want privileges.

Kainan slid out first and then helped Reagan.

"No press here," she said, relieved.

I am glad of that. Especially since they know what you look like. I am sorry they were snapping your picture so much as we came out of the hospital. And you were bombarded with questions.

"I ignored them." She took out her key and opened the main door.

Before she called the elevator she opened up her mail slot and pulled out the copious amount of mail that had been piling since she'd last been there. One of the things on top was a Christmas card from her parents.

A knot formed in her stomach as she thought about them. Thought how they didn't really care much for Peter—or her, for that matter. Still, what was socially acceptable was to send your offspring a Christmas card, and that was exactly what her mother had done. She was following protocol.

You haven't been back here in a while, I take it? Kainan signed, cocking an eyebrow as he glanced at her mail.

"No, I haven't."

What if you go into arrears on something?

"I do everything on my phone. There's an app for that," she teased.

She called the elevator and the doors opened up. She punched in her floor.

Her apartment was at the end of the hall. When she got to the door something seemed wrong. The door was splintered around the lock, and instead of having to put her key in she just turned the knob and it opened.

Kainan moved past her and into her apartment first. Reagan took a step inside and saw her place had been trashed.

The furniture was turned over and all her boxes had been opened up. Her things were everywhere, but her television and stereo were still there. Her computer was as well, but it was plugged in, and when she touched it, it woke up. It was on, and it looked as if her system had been hacked. All her personal files...

She began to tremble. She hated it that this had happened. Her life was strewn across the floor in a shambles...exposed.

Kainan came from the bedroom.

This doesn't seem like a robbery for valuables. It looks like they were looking for information.

"Information about *me*?" she asked, in shock still.

Or your ties to me.

Kainan began to text.

"Who are you texting?"

"My security team" he said hoarsely.

He finished the text.

"I can't believe this has happened." She wanted to sit down, but if the police were going to come she didn't want to disturb any of the evidence. "Is your team calling the police?"

Kainan nodded. *I'm sorry this has happened, but I can protect you.*

Reagan snorted. "You've said that before, and look what's happened."

I'm sorry.

Reagan ignored him and set her mail down on her kitchen table. She made her way to her bedroom. The contents of her nightstand drawer had been dumped out on her bed, and her dresser had been rummaged through.

The few pieces of jewelry she had were still there. Kainan was right. They had been looking for information.

She went over to the walk-in closet and opened it to look at where she had started setting up a small nursery for Peter. Nothing had been touched.

Tears stung her eyes when she saw the crib that was waiting for him and the fine layer of dust on the wood. She was the worst mother ever. She hadn't even made it up. The sheet and quilt, even the hanging mobile, were still in a box.

All she had managed to do was set up the crib and a change table. There weren't even diapers in there yet.

"Big girls don't cry, Reagan. This was your choice!"

Reagan cursed under her breath. Angry at herself. Angry for letting her mother's words back in.

How was she going to bring home a baby on a ventricular assist device and have him live here? This was no place for him. She was not ready for him to be out of the safe confines of the hospital. How was she going to be able to deal with this?

She picked up the small teddy bear that she'd bought for Peter three days before he was born. She held it close and tried not to cry again. She couldn't do this alone.

She didn't have to. Kainan had offered to help her. Kainan was *here*. But she wanted him to help her without having to make promises that she wasn't sure that she wanted to keep. She'd never wanted to get married. Not really.

Why couldn't they just work on raising Peter together?

Because Kainan will go back to Isla Hermosa after his surgery. He is King.

She had to do this on her own. Her parents were right in that she could only rely on herself. Peter was *her* responsibility. She had always been going to do this on her own anyway. Kainan's presence didn't change that. She had to protect her heart.

Kainan would do right by Peter, of that she was sure, but she wasn't so sure he would do the same for her, and she couldn't risk it.

He was King and he had a duty to his country. She understood that. She respected that.

Reagan set the bear back down. She would have to get used to doing things on her own. She couldn't leave Toronto. She had to stay close while they waited for Peter's new heart.

Kainan would return to Isla Hermosa to lead his country and Reagan would have to parent Peter on her own.

As she'd planned to do all along.

CHAPTER EIGHT

It DIDN'T TAKE long for the police to arrive, and all Reagan could do was stand to the side and watch them go through her things, dusting for fingerprints and looking for evidence. She felt so exposed, so vulnerable, and she hated every minute of it.

"You say it doesn't appear that anything has been taken, Dr. Cote?" the constable in charge asked.

"Everything seems to be here—my computer, my television, and even some money that I had hidden in my sock drawer. Until I clean I won't really know."

The constable nodded.

Kainan signed and the constable glanced at her in question.

"He says he thinks that my personal information was stolen. It appears my computer was hacked into," she said.

"Why does the think that?" the constable asked.

"Because he's the King of Isla Hermosa and…we have a child together."

The constable was shocked. "This may have to be taken up with the RCMP."

"I understand," Reagan said stonily. "I know you'll do what's best."

Only right now she wasn't sure what that was.

The constable nodded. "We'll take your laptop in and

have our forensic team go over it. There could be a digital trace."

"Thank you, Constable."

"No problem, Dr. Cote. Make sure you get your locks changed. As soon as we hear anything we'll give you a call."

The constable turned back to his team and they began to bag the evidence that they wanted to take a closer look at.

Reagan turned away. "What do you think they were after?" she asked Kainan.

They're were looking for information about you, me and our son. I have no doubts. Kainan shook his head. *I'm sorry this happened.*

"At least they didn't touch Peter's nursery. It's just as I left it."

Where is Peter's nursery? he asked.

"It's in the bedroom, in my walk-in closet."

Kainan frowned. *A closet?*

"It's a large closet, with a light. Lots of space. I was even able to fit a chair in there."

A closet seems highly inappropriate.

"Oh, yes? And what would you have me do? I'm alone and this is what I can afford."

His expression softened and she felt bad for snapping at him. It wasn't his fault that she'd thought he was dead.

You can't have a ventricular assist device in a walk-in closet.

"I'm aware of that now, but when I was pregnant I didn't think that my baby would be *on* a ventricular device."

Kainan sighed. "I'm sorry."

"It's okay. It's not your fault. I just feel…" She trailed off. *Violated. Afraid. Insecure.*

Only she didn't say those words out loud. She had been taught never to say things like that out loud. Never to show weakness.

"I'm tired."

Are you sure that's all? Kainan asked.

Reagan scrubbed a hand over her face. "I really should get back to the hospital. We've been gone for ages. What if Peter wakes up?"

It will take a while before they wake him up. He has been sedated for so long. You won't miss it. Besides, you have to get these locks changed and we have to clean up this apartment.

Reagan nodded. "You're right. I'm just feeling a bit anxious right now."

And you have every right to be.

"We've got everything, Dr. Cote," the head constable said. "We'll keep you updated."

"Thank you, Constable. Have a merry Christmas."

"You too, Dr. Cote."

Reagan opened the door for the retreating police officers and shut it behind them. "I suppose I'd better call a locksmith to come and change the locks."

I'll start cleaning in the bedroom.

"I don't know where to start…" Reagan muttered.

One room at a time.

Kainan wandered away to her bedroom. She had no doubt that he was going to check out the nursery she'd set up and tell her that it was unsuitable. And he wasn't wrong. It was unsuitable.

What am I going to do?

She felt lost at the moment. Everything was overwhelming her.

Step one: call the locksmith, and then you can think about step two.

Reagan looked up a local number on her phone and dialed, hoping someone would be able to come out on short notice right before Christmas.

* * *

Kainan wandered around the bedroom. It was small, but it was cozy. It was Reagan's room. Or it had been until a stranger had come in and violated her privacy.

Kainan clenched his fists, biting back the rage he was feeling thinking because someone had been in here. Someone who wanted information about him and Reagan.

This is all my fault.

If he hadn't got involved with Reagan this would never have happened.

He picked up a drawer that had been pulled out and tossed on the bed, slid it back into the dresser, remembering...

"Hey, can I get a picture of you?" the stranger had asked.

Kainan had looked up. "What?"

"You're a prince of Isla Hermosa, right?" There had been a blinding flash. "Come here."

"Who *are* you?" his mother had screamed as she'd thrown herself in front of him. "Get off my property!"

"Easy, Your Majesty. The public just wants pictures."

His mother had stood, her fists clenched. "Get off my property!"

The guards had soon been there, dragging the man away. When the photographer had been out of sight his mother had collapsed, trembling as she'd turned to him.

"He didn't hurt you, did he, Kainan?"

"No, Mama..."

He needed to protect Reagan, he thought now. And he couldn't protect her here.

He began to pluck clothing off the floor and fold the items, placing them back in the drawer. His gaze fell on the closed closet door. Kainan's pulse quickened as he thought about Peter. And, though he knew he shouldn't look in the closet, he did.

He opened the closet door and flicked on the light.

Reagan had been right. It was a large closet, but it was

a closet nonetheless, and his throat tightened when he saw the crib, the bedding in a bag on the floor, and the teddy bear that was lying on its side on a change table.

She had made it homey and cozy for their son. She had done the best she could, but it wasn't enough. Not for him.

He closed his eyes and guilt ate away at him for not being there. For not providing for them. She'd been all alone. This was not good enough for Reagan. She deserved more.

How? This will continue to happen. People will always pry into her life.

Even if Kainan didn't survive his surgery Peter was his heir and the press would be curious about him.

His throat tightened and it was hard to breathe. He closed his eyes and tried not to think of the moment when he'd tried to speak and hadn't been able to. When he hadn't been able to breathe.

"Kainan?" Reagan called out, and then she appeared in the doorway of the room.

Kainan set the bear back down, sitting him upright, and stepped out of the closet, closing the door behind him.

"Checking up on my handiwork?" she asked.

He smiled. *Perhaps.*

"The locksmith is here and I've cleaned up the living room the best I can. Once the lock is changed and I've grabbed a few things I want to get back to the hospital."

Of course. And I will have Andreas pack up the baby's things.

"What're you talking about?" she asked.

You can't stay here. It's not safe.

"Kainan, this is my *home*. This will be Peter's home. Where else would we go?"

I will get you a new place. One that is more suitable.

"I don't think so."

I do think so, Kainan signed. *Peter needs a larger room*

and you need to be moved somewhere safe. My security team will handle it.

"No, I'm not uprooting my life, Kainan. That's too much to ask."

You won't marry me, and you won't let me protect you. Let me do this. I can't have you come back here and be pestered. Not when Peter needs to rest and heal.

Reagan bit her lip. She was clearly thinking about it, but she didn't answer.

It will be days before he's discharged, Kainan signed. *More than enough time to get you a new place, close to the hospital, and move you. You won't have to do anything. Let me do this, Reagan. Please.*

"Fine," she said. "But it has to be close to the hospital."

I will find something.

He was relieved he could do something for them. That he could take care of them this way.

Kainan texted his team to let them know what he required. The new place would be large enough to house Reagan and Peter, and Kainan would be in a suite next to him, with his security detail.

Though Reagan didn't need to know that bit of information yet.

The press knew that he was at the Royal York and were camped out there permanently, so moving to a new location with a secure entrance would be better. He would be closer to Peter and Reagan and maybe, just maybe, he would be able to convince Reagan to marry him. Then he could keep them safe behind the palace walls.

Really?

That was his father's thinking, and he hated himself for it, but he felt powerless and didn't know what to do.

He was broken.

But he wasn't going to let Reagan or Peter out of his sight.

* * *

Kainan dropped Reagan at the hospital, where she wanted to be, and then went with Andreas to see a new place.

The condo was located two blocks south of the hospital and on the lakeshore. It had two suites, side by side, and one of them would comfortably house his security staff and himself. The smaller suite was larger than Reagan's current home, and would be more than adequate for her and Peter.

The only downside was that it wasn't on the subway route, but it was only a block to Union Station and the hospital was right across the street from that.

Reagan could walk or Andreas could drive her. If he was still here. If Kainan's voice surgery was successful then Andreas would return to Isla Hermosa with him.

But you can come back.

He wasn't sure about that. Would Reagan forgive him if he left?

He wasn't sure.

"They're just waiting for your signature, Your Majesty. I have made sure that they have signed confidentiality agreements and I have paid in cash," Andreas said, interrupting his thoughts.

Thank you, Andreas. How soon can we move in?

"Today," Andreas said. "I can have movers go to Dr. Cote's apartment and pack it up, so we can get her into this new home by tomorrow morning."

Do that.

Andreas nodded and opened the door to the condo complex. Kainan went through all the paperwork and signed everything that was needed.

Tonight he would tell Reagan about the plan over dinner. Even if he had to bring it into the hospital again. He wasn't giving her a chance to say no this time. This was for their own protection. This was something he could do for them.

They would be in their new home in time for Christmas, and perhaps this way he could show Reagan he was in. That if he left he would still be there.

How can you be "in" as King?

And then there was his surgery coming up. With the amount of scar tissue in his throat it was risky. He might die, abandoning Reagan.

He shook that thought away as he took the keys from the realtor and followed Andreas to the top floor of the complex.

"The suites are at the end of the hallway," Andreas said as he led Kainan down. "Dr. Cote's is twenty-nine B and you're twenty-nine A."

Kainan nodded and turned the key to Reagan's new place. It was bright and large. There were windows which faced the icy grey waters of Lake Ontario. He could not see the CN Tower from this viewpoint, but that was okay. The view of the islands and the water was all he needed.

It reminded him of Isla Hermosa. Endless water and islands scattered all around the main island. The only difference was that Isla Hermosa was tropical and here there was snow. And the grey, ice-filled water was a bit unforgiving.

Kainan was not a fan of winter.

Still, this was a much better space than her current home. She was surrounded by tall buildings there. It was stifling, as if there was no room to breathe. Here at the top of this complex, with Lake Ontario stretching below him, he felt he could breathe.

"Do you like it, Your Majesty?" Andreas asked.

Kainan nodded. and then handed Andreas the key that Reagan had given him when the locksmith had changed her locks.

Please make sure that Reagan is moved in right away.

"And what of you, Your Majesty?"

*Get some furnishings. My room can be packed up later.
I want us to have a close-by option—especially since we
don't know how long Peter will still be in the hospital.*

Andreas nodded. "Very well, Your Majesty."

*Thank you for all your assistance, Andreas. I don't think
I express it enough.*

Andreas was a bit taken aback by that. "Thank you,
Your Majesty."

There was a buzz on Kainan's phone and he looked
down to see that it was Reagan texting him. There was
news about Peter.

I have to go back to the hospital. Kainan slipped his
phone in his pocket.

"I will take you back there right now."

Kainan followed Andreas out of the apartment. He was
glad things were moving forward with Reagan, because he
was running out of time.

Reagan's pulse was racing. They had just moved Peter from
the pediatric critical care unit to the regular pediatric ward.
He was doing so well on the ventricular assist device that
they were going to bring him out of sedation.

She would be able to hold him. She hadn't held him in
so long. Her arms were aching to hold him, but she was
terrified too.

Deep down she was scared of this whole thing. It was a
way to extend his life, but there was a set time-frame. Peter
needed a new heart. There was no other choice.

There was a new set of nurses on duty and she waited
with bated breath as they moved about the room. Peter was
moving, and there were more subtle movements as the se-
dation wore off.

She'd done a rotation on Pediatrics when she had been

an intern, but she had forgotten how resilient kids were. How they bounced back.

She'd texted Kainan to come, because he'd wanted to know when they were going to wake Peter up.

She knew he was out property-hunting, but she seriously doubted that he would find anything on short notice. And, even though he didn't want her going back to her apartment alone, she was going to head back there and get Peter's nursery ready.

Kainan came into the room.

"Glad you could make it," she said, and she *was* relieved that he was here.

How is he doing? Kainan signed.

"Good. He's strong."

Kainan nodded and picked up the chart to read the notes. A brief smile crossed his face as he shut the chart.

This is good!

"I'll be back in a few minutes, Reagan," the pediatric nurse said. "I have to check on my other patients."

"Thanks, Maria," Reagan said.

Maria nodded and left the room.

Reagan took a step forward and stared down at her baby, wrapped up in his crib. There was a cannula running from his chest to the machine that sat on the table next to the crib. The machine that was pumping blood instead of his heart now.

His poor, weak heart.

She reached out to touch him but then took her hand back because she wasn't wearing gloves. She looked up at Kainan, unsure.

What's wrong? he signed.

"I'm not wearing gloves—just a surgical gown."

Did they tell you that you needed to be gowned and gloved?

"No, they didn't. I just put this on out of habit."

Kainan smiled gently at her. *Go ahead.*

Reagan reached out and touched Peter's smooth, soft skin. Emotion overcame her as she ran her fingers over his tiny hand and then over the dark curls on his head.

"I've waited so long for this," she whispered.

The tears were threatening to spill, but she cleared her throat—because this wasn't the end of scares. This was just a way to keep him alive longer, until a heart became available.

She couldn't let her guard down yet.

Peter stirred under her hand and she gasped. His head moved and he opened his eyes, blinking. And then those dark eyes that were so like Kainan's looked toward her. His brow furrowed as he tried to make sense of what he could seen through a drug-induced fog.

"Peter…" she whispered, she knelt down to look at his little chubby face. "Mommy's here."

Her voice hitched in her throat and it took every ounce of her strength not to cry as she connected with her son in his crib.

Peter's eyes closed, but he smiled. So many stages of his life she'd missed. Babies grew so fast and she was missing it.

There will be more stages that you will get to see, she told herself.

And for the first time in a long time she confidently believed that.

Then Kainan knelt down and stared at his son, his eyes glistening, and he beamed as Peter opened his eyes again and looked at Kainan.

"He has my eyes," Kainan said, and Reagan could see the pride in his face.

"Did he open his eyes?" Maria asked as she returned.

"He did," Reagan said, standing up.

"That's wonderful. It will take a while for him to fully wake out of his sedation, but he's doing very well," Maria said.

"How long do you think it will be before he's discharged?" Reagan asked, nervous about the answer, because here in the hospital he was safe.

"It's hard to say. It depends how well he does and his pain management. But since you're both surgeons Dr. McNeil will probably discharge him as early as Christmas Eve. And that will be an excellent Christmas gift!" Maria continued, checking Peter's lines as Reagan stood there in shock.

"That soon?" Reagan murmured in disbelief. "I have a lot to do to get ready."

Maria grinned. "I'm sure. Why don't you go do that, Dr. Cote? He will likely be asleep for a while longer. Get some diapers and get his nursery ready."

Reagan was about to argue when Michael entered Peter's room. He looked a bit panicked.

"Reagan, I'm so glad I found you," Michael said breathlessly, and then he saw Kainan. "Dr. Laskaris, I'm glad you're here too."

Dread crept down her spine. "What's wrong, Michael?"

"A section of the roof has collapsed at the shopping center. A lot of people are injured and I'm short-staffed due to the snowstorm that just rolled in off the lake. It's dumped three inches of snow since it started two and half hours ago."

"What?"

Reagan opened the blinds in Peter's room and couldn't even see the courtyard of the hospital. Just a wall of white.

"They're bringing them in on foot and our emergency room is packed," Michael said. "I could use you both."

Kainan signed, and she knew what he was thinking.

"Kainan wants to know how he can help even when he can't communicate," Reagan said.

"He can work with you, Reagan. I'm sorry to pull you away from your son, but it's all hands on deck."

Kainan nodded with determination and picked up his jacket.

"We'll be right there, Michael," Reagan said.

Michael left at a sprint.

"Don't worry, Dr. Cote. Peter will be fine," Maria said.

Reagan nodded, but she was unsure about leaving him. Still, she was needed. She was a surgeon and there were lives to be saved.

Kainan held open the door for her and they walked together to the staff change room, where all the on-call doctors who'd been able to get in were getting ready for the onslaught of patients.

There was also a team of doctors who would be working on clearing the operating theaters of nonessential surgeries and keeping the flow to X-Ray and the CT scanner free and clear. As well as finding bed space in an already cramped hospital.

Reagan changed quickly, stuffing her clothing into her locker. Kainan stood beside her, unbuttoning the dress shirt that he'd been wearing.

"No locker," he said quickly as he stuffed his clothes into hers.

"Save your voice, Kainan," she said as she shimmied out of her dress pants and pulled on her scrubs. "You're going to need it."

He smiled sadly and nodded as he grabbed a pair of men's scrubs from the shelf behind him.

She thought about all those times in the tight quarters of the field hospital and how much carnage they had seen and worked together on.

This was going to be the same.

A section of the roof falling in a packed shopping center at Christmas... The thought made her sick to her stomach.

After they were dressed and ready to go, with disposable surgical gowns and gloves, they headed straight into the chaos of the emergency room.

Michael was in charge as he spoke to his surgeons and assigned stations, putting the residents outside to receive the patients as they came in from the ambulances.

Kainan went straight to work and began to set up other triage areas for the less critical. Reagan translated for him and helped him to divide a hallway that was rarely used into small pods for the less injured.

The waiting room was packed as well, with patients who had wandered in with things like colds, sprains and an assortment of other cases. They would have to be seen to. and Michael mobilized a group of residents to take care of them and prioritize.

Reagan and Kainan worked well together, just as they had always done. She knew what he was thinking before he had to ask her, and vice versa.

"Just like old times, eh?" she teased.

Kainan made a funny face. Before he could respond there was the wail of sirens. Ambulances were working their way through the snow. Orderlies were outside, working on shoveling a clear path as the first ambulance pulled up.

"Reagan and Kainan—you're up!" Michael called over the commotion.

Reagan went outside, the bitter cold biting at her cheeks as the ambulance came to a stop. The doors opened and the paramedics jumped into action.

"Male, age forty-five, multiple injuries to the torso and abdomen. Glasgow coma scale of two on arrival."

Reagan and Kainan helped the paramedic push the gurney through the snow and they took their patient to one of

the trauma bays that were being used for priority patients. A man with multiple crush injuries to the torso and abdomen and a GCS of two was a priority.

Kainan signed off on the paramedics' charts while Reagan began to go over the man's ABCs. One pupil was blown. and she was worried that when he fell he'd hit his head hard and there might be a hematoma.

Kainan worked on the other side of her. He snapped his fingers to get her attention and signed, *Free fluid in the lungs. I'm going to do a chest tube.*

Reagan nodded. "Left pupil is blown. I want to get him down for a CT."

"Chest tray," Kainan said gruffly to the intern who was in the room with them, and he rolled his shoulders, wincing from the pain of exerting his voice. But he didn't hesitate as he cut away the man's shirt and examined his chest.

"Any lacerations from the debris that landed on him? I see blood," Reagan said as she started a large-bore IV and hung painkillers and fluids.

Kainan held up two fingers.

Reagan counted at least four wounds to the man's abdomen. There was also dark bruising under his skin. "He needs a CT scan as soon as you get that chest tube in."

She cursed inwardly as she tried to picture how the debris had fallen on the patient and what organs it might have damaged. Because there was fluid in the man's lungs she had no doubt that he was suffering a hemothorax, but what other damage had the debris caused?

"Here you are, Dr. Laskaris," the intern said, handing the chest tube tray to Kainan.

Kainan nodded and went about listening and finding the best place to insert the chest tube. He quickly wiped the skin and then made his move.

The patient flexed in a decerebrate motion, arching his

chest and his head, arms straight out, everything stiff in response to the chest tube being inserted.

As it did its job the patient's vitals steadied. Kainan smiled and secured the tube and they readied the patient to go down for the CT scan. Reagan needed to see what she was dealing with before she went in there and tried to fix the damage that had been done.

Kainan moved beside her silently, anticipating her every move. Just like in Isla Hermosa.

They were as one.

And, though she'd always prided herself on being a lone wolf, she was glad he was here in this moment. That he was here with her now and that she didn't have to explain her every move. He just *knew*.

And that thought scared her.

It scared her to think that she needed him when she had never needed anyone before.

CHAPTER NINE

"CAN YOU MOVE the retractor, please?" Reagan asked, and Kainan adjusted his hold on it.

Their patient had some head trauma, but nothing as serious as what was going on in his abdomen, because there were crush injuries and he was bleeding internally. The CT scan had shown her what damage had been done.

The spleen had been lacerated and was bleeding heavily. A kidney had been pierced, as well as his bowel, and the diaphragm, which was why his lungs had filled with blood. The heart was fine for now, as was the liver. Still, the bleeding needed to be controlled so he didn't die before they had a chance to repair his injuries.

She was hours into surgery. They were still hanging blood, but she was getting ahead of the damage. Even though Kainan could not speak he knew what to do, and she didn't often have to ask for his assistance. It was if he knew what her next step would be before she did.

They worked so well together. She'd forgotten how much she enjoyed working with him. Working with him to save lives.

The King of Isla Hermosa.

She shook her head, trying not to think about that fact. He was a surgeon too. He hadn't been a king when they'd worked together, when he'd taken her in his arms.

He had just been Kainan.

Now he was King, and yet here he was helping save lives. How many world leaders would do the same? It was at this moment that she saw the man he'd been before—the man she'd known and cared for.

She watched him briefly as a resident worked on stitching, studying him over her surgical mask. Those kind eyes were looking down at the work the resident was doing with keen interest, and she couldn't help but smile as she thought of him by her side, working with her as if nothing had changed.

It was nice, even though the situation was not. And her pulse quickened as she thought back to that kiss they'd shared, when Peter was in surgery for the ventricular device. His strong arms had comforted her, as had his kiss, and their connection had grounded her.

Kainan was her rock.

The realization shocked her, and she wasn't sure how she felt about it. She had been taught not to rely on anyone. So when had she begun to rely on Kainan so much?

It made her stomach twist in a knot, because she *had* to be self-sufficient. She couldn't rely on him, no matter how much she wanted to.

He was King of a foreign country and would eventually have to return to it. She couldn't leave Canada—not until Peter had a new heart. She had to be careful not to let *her* heart do all her thinking, which was what was happening when she was around Kainan.

She had to start thinking logically. She had to be careful. Peter's heart wasn't the only one that was fragile—hers was too.

They had been working on this man for hours, but he was going to make it and that was the most important thing. After they'd finished up here they would have to scrub out

and head back down to the emergency room and continue to work, to take the pressure off a bombarded trauma room.

On a tray across the operating room she could see her phone sitting there, silent, as a nurse monitored it.

Peter's fine. And after this is all done you can hold him.

Just that simple thought sustained her. It kept her focused.

She finished the surgery and gave instructions to the scrub nurse and the intern for the patient's postoperative care. Kainan followed her out of the operating room and they scrubbed out.

"Where to?" Kainan asked, and then winced, his throat paining him.

"Have you had your throat looked at by your otolaryngologist lately?"

Kainan sent her an exasperated expression. *Of course.*

"It's just that I know if you use your voice more than you should it can cause problems. I would hate for you to risk your surgery."

It's already a risky surgery and there is a lot of scar tissue.

"Why have they waited so long?"

The surgeon wanted to wait until I was strong.

"And…?" Reagan asked, drying off her hands. "You're stronger now."

Kainan pursed his lips together. *The surgery is coming, but there's no guarantee it will work.*

"I think it will," she said.

Why do you think so?

"A king needs a voice," she said.

I have you.

It was like a punch in her gut. "I won't always be there to be your voice, Kainan."

Why not? You could be my Queen. It's a solution that

would work for us both. We'd give Peter stability and you could assist me in my rule.

"I'm a surgeon, Kainan. Could I still practice medicine as Queen of Isla Hermosa?"

Kainan's shoulders slumped and she had her answer. She felt bad for Kainan, because soon his surgical career would be over. He was a king, and when he returned to Isla Hermosa he wouldn't be able to practice medicine any longer.

"You need to stop proposing to me, Kainan. You know my answer. It's no."

But the more time she spent with him the harder it was to say no. The dream of a happy family she'd always craved was tempting, but nothing worked out the way it was supposed to and she didn't want to risk it.

He didn't say anything, and didn't look her in the eye. It was hard to disappoint him, but she couldn't let her heart make this decision.

If her heart had had its way then she would have said yes the first time he'd asked her. The moment he'd walked back in her life.

You're a fool, her heart told her, but she knew that it would never work. The only person she could rely on was herself.

They headed back down to the emergency room and it was still chaotic. As she surveyed the scene her gaze landed on a tall man with dark hair in one of the beds. Alone and clearly in pain.

"Isn't that Andreas?" she asked.

Kainan spun around, pained as he rushed to his security guard's side with Reagan at his heels. He had been hurt, but it looked like just a flesh wound.

"Andreas," Reagan said sadly. "You were at the shopping center?"

"Dr. Cote…" He grimaced, and then his gaze fell on Kainan. "Your Majesty. I'm sorry."

For what? Kainan signed.

Andreas leaned back against the pillows, his face with the grey tint of pain and blood loss.

Reagan pulled his chart. "Your leg was caught under a cement beam, but it's not broken, and the laceration missed your femoral artery. That's good."

Andreas nodded. "It's just a flesh wound. I was trying to protect a child from the falling debris."

Kainan winced and bowed his head, gripping Andreas's shoulder.

"You have lost a lot of blood," she said, then bit her lip and stopped the resident who was dealing with Andreas. "Has blood been ordered? His platelet count is low."

"Yes, but the blood bank doesn't have any universal blood. There's another blood bank across the city, and they're trying to get through with the type of blood he needs, but the storm and this accident has depleted our reserves," the resident said.

Dammit.

I will donate blood, Kainan signed. *I'm Hermosian and I can donate for him.*

The resident looked confused.

"He can donate," Reagan said. "He's a universal blood type and both of them are Hermosian. Ready a transfusion kit and get this man on plasma while I handle the donation."

"Yes, Dr. Cote." The resident ran away.

"We'll be back, Andreas. Do you need anything for the pain?" Reagan asked.

Andreas shook his head. "No, Dr. Cote. I am fine. The child I helped lives, and that's the main thing, but I cannot accept blood from my King."

Reagan frowned and Kainan's brow furrowed.

You will, Kainan said.

"Your Majesty, I can't take your blood."

It's just blood, Kainan signed furiously. *You will take it and that is a royal decree.*

Andreas sighed and closed his eyes. "Yes, Your Majesty."

Kainan pulled the drapes around Andreas's bed. His face was like thunder. Andreas's injury was obviously bothering him. It bothered Reagan too. She hated to see Andreas hurt again. When he'd been injured during the Hermosian uprising it had been because he'd pulled a younger soldier out of the line of fire.

It seemed bizarre that on the front lines of battle in a foreign country they had more blood than here in a vast city, and all because of a snowstorm which was hampering their ability to get to it. It was silly.

Kainan took a seat in an exam room just outside the emergency department. He pulled off his white lab coat and stuck out his arm.

The resident brought Reagan the kit she would need to get the blood donation from Kainan. Reagan began to ready everything while Kainan stared at the wall, still fuming.

"Are you all right?"

Kainan nodded, but he wouldn't look at her.

"What's wrong? Are you mad at Andreas?"

No, he signed. *I'm angry at myself.*

"Why? You had nothing to do with his injury."

I sent him out to furnish my new apartment.

She raised her eyebrows as she wiped his arm with rubbing alcohol. "*Your* new apartment. I thought you were looking for a place for me and Peter?"

We found that too. They're next to each other.

She raised an eyebrow. "How convenient."

A small smile tugged at his lips. *Peter is my son too, and I want to be close to him for as long as I can.*

Right, because he would have to leave. There was an expiry date on his time in Canada.

"Sorry, of course you do." Then she realized what he was saying. "You got apartments that are available now?"

Kainan nodded. *With the right amount of money.*

"Kainan, how *much* money?" She'd agreed to a new place, but she didn't want him spending great sums of money on her.

There is no mortgage to worry about, Reagan. You can raise Peter there comfortably. And when I'm in Toronto I can be close to him.

Reagan cursed under her breath. "You shouldn't have done that."

He's my son too. I just want him to be comfortable. And I want to take care of you.

"Kainan, I have to be self-sufficient. I *can't* rely on you. When you leave it will just be me and Peter."

Kainan didn't respond. He set his jaw firmly in that stubborn way of his and looked away from her.

"So, when are the movers coming for my stuff—or have you arranged that too?" she asked sarcastically.

He grinned and she groaned.

"I'm probably already moved in, aren't I?"

In the process.

She shook her head and then tied the tourniquet around his arm. "Make a fist—and no more signing."

Kainan rolled his eyes, but that smug grin was still on his face.

She got the blood transfusion started and then removed the tourniquet. Kainan was a pro at this.

"It's not your fault for sending him to that shopping center, Kainan. A roof collapsed. No one is at fault. Things happen."

Kainan didn't say anything. He just closed his eyes and looked at the ceiling. She couldn't blame him. One of the things that bothered her about medicine was blood dona-

tion. It was good to do it, but she'd got a bit queasy the couple of times she had donated over the years.

"What you're doing for Andreas is good," she said. "You're a good king to your people. You may think you need a voice, but you don't. Your actions speak louder than your words ever will."

He raised his head and looked at her then, those dark eyes twinkling, and he mouthed the words *thank you* before closing his eyes and staring back up at the ceiling.

Kainan stood and watched as Andreas received his blood transfusion. After he'd donated he'd felt a bit dizzy, and Reagan had got him some orange juice and let him rest before she'd been called away by a resident.

When Kainan had felt better he'd headed back to the emergency room and gone to check on Andreas, who had already been hooked up to an intravenous and receiving Kainan's donation.

The color was returning to his friend's cheeks now.

Kainan still felt incredible guilty that Andreas had been put in harm's way. Twice.

He didn't like putting people's lives at risk. He was a surgeon. He *saved* lives.

You're no longer a surgeon, though.

And that thought sobered him. He was King, and a country full of lives depended on him. His life was no longer his.

Still, there was a part of him that didn't want to be King. Being back in the operating room and working with Reagan had been amazing. He'd forgotten what it was like to save a life. He hadn't practiced surgery since the day Reagan had left Isla Hermosa.

He missed it.

Missed the thrill of it all.

Still, if he died on the operating table with a surgeon trying to save his voice then there would be no monarchy

for Isla Hermosa. Peter was too young to be King and he was the last of his line.

Unless you appoint a regent to take Peter's place. An illegitimate king can still rule when he comes of age, as long as he's claimed, in writing, by the current King.

Reagan came in and glanced at Kainan in the seat next to Andreas's bedside. Andreas was still sleeping.

"You okay?" she asked.

Tired, but I will live.

"So will Andreas. Don't worry—your blood helped."

I know. Even if he didn't want it.

"I don't get that."

Because I'm King and...

"And?" she asked.

"It's not right," Andreas repeated, still in delirium.

Kainan chuckled softly as he looked at Andreas. *He's my half brother.*

Reagan's eyes widened. "Your half brother?"

Yes, though not legitimate. Andreas thinks of his adoptive father as his real father, not the late King. His adoptive father claimed him as his own, which is why Andreas could never be in the line of succession. He was luckier than me.

"Luckier? Why?"

He was loved and doted on. He had freedom. I did not. Kainan scrubbed a hand over his face. *I envied him for so many years.*

"Do you still?"

He looked up at her. If he'd had Andreas's life he probably wouldn't be a surgeon, and he wouldn't have met Reagan. For the first time he didn't envy Andreas's different upbringing.

No.

Pink bloomed in her cheeks. She cleared her throat. "How is your voice?"

He spoke aloud. "My throat is tight…sore. I should go see Dr. Shaw. Can you keep an eye on Andreas?"

She nodded, her gaze soft. "Yes."

Andreas opened his eyes. "Your Majesty?"

Kainan stood up and squeezed Andreas's shoulder. *Rest,* he signed.

Kainan left Andreas to sleep. He made his way out of the emergency room and to Dr. Shaw's office. Dr. Shaw had been the surgeon who'd looked at his throat when he'd first arrived in Toronto, and he had the information from the Ottawa surgeon about the surgical procedures that Kainan had endured in the field.

Dr. Shaw was packing up for the evening when Kainan knocked on his door. Dr. Shaw also knew American Sign Language, because of all the hearing-impaired patients he worked with. Which was fortuitous.

"Dr. Laskaris—or should I refer to you as Your Majesty?"

Kainan smiled. *Kainan will suffice.*

"It's some crazy storm out there, eh? I think I'm going to leave my car in the employee garage and take the subway home—although the tracks at Rosehill are covered."

I'm worried about scar tissue. I've been using my voice, Kainan signed.

Dr. Shaw's eyebrows rose. "Have you? How much? I told you not to overdo it."

Kainan ignored that. This was his chance to be strong for his son, for Reagan. He needed his voice.

Could you please check?

"I can." Dr. Shaw set his bag down and took a seat, firing up his computer as Kainan shut the door. "Hopefully you haven't overtaxed yourself too much."

I hope not. I need my voice by the New Year.

Dr. Shaw nodded and examined his throat, frowning. "The surgery may not work. Although during your last scan there were not as many adhesions. I would like to get

another scan, but I can still do your surgery on December twenty-sixth."

Kainan nodded. *Of course. When would you like the scan done?*

"Tomorrow morning, if that's okay? I know your boy just had surgery…"

Tomorrow is fine. My son is stable and I need to get this taken care of.

Dr. Shaw nodded. "Dr. McNeil told me that when you asked for the surgery I was to make it happen as if you were a head of state."

I appreciate it, and I'm sorry for inconveniencing you, but I was told you were the best.

"You're not inconveniencing me, Kainan." Dr. Shaw stood and Kainan did as well. "It's my pleasure. Come by my office tomorrow at seven in the morning and we'll get you down to the MRI and get it done. We'll see what we're working with. And stop using your voice!"

I will.

"I'm serious—no more talking. No more exercising it. I will see you tomorrow, Kainan."

Kainan shook Dr. Shaw's hand before heading back to the emergency room. He texted Andreas's second in command to see how the move was going and to let them know what had happened to Andreas.

He had to step up and do what was right.

He was terrified that he wouldn't survive surgery, which meant he would lose Reagan forever, leaving her and Peter alone.

Never know his son.

Never have happiness.

CHAPTER TEN

REAGAN HAD BEEN separated from Kainan since just after he'd donated blood for Andreas. She'd got pulled into another surgery. An injured person had been brought in and could only communicate in Spanish.

She'd planned to take Kainan into surgery with her, but then she had been informed that this man was a Hermosian refugee and, given Andreas's reaction to Kainan donating blood, she'd thought it was best to keep the King out of the operating room.

Her patient was sedated, so Reagan went about repairing the injuries that he had sustained when the roof had collapsed on top of him.

Thankfully, no one had died in the accident.

Not even her first patient, Mr. Lucas, with the multiple crush injuries and the head injury. Reagan had saved his life.

When she came out of surgery the chaos in the emergency room had died down, as had the snow.

It was after midnight, which meant that it was Christmas Eve now. Officially.

She was exhausted, but she had to find Kainan.

When she went down to the emergency room, where the staff were now cycling through the non-emergent cases that

had come in, she saw that Andreas was being moved to a room for overnight observation.

"Dr. Cote," Andreas said, smiling.

"How are you feeling?" she asked.

"Better. I would like to leave, but they want to keep me."

"You just had a major laceration and a blood transfusion. You need to rest here. Have you seen Kainan? I'm afraid I had to go into surgery and I lost track of him."

"Yes, I saw him a few hours ago. He was going to speak to another doctor before he checked on Peter, and then I believe he was headed back to the hotel to pack up his things because his new residence will be ready soon."

"I heard about that," Reagan said, crossing her arms.

Andreas grinned. "He will have the key to your new place, and I know that my team has got everything in your old place moved out. Do you want me to put your old place on the market?"

"I can handle that, Andreas. You need your rest."

"If you want to speak to Kainan you'll need this," Andreas reached in his pocket and pulled out a gold elevator keycard. "It's my extra copy and it will allow you to access his room."

"Thanks. I think I will go see him after I check on Peter."

Andreas nodded and the orderly wheeled him away.

Reagan turned the keycard over in her hand. She really needed to talk to Kainan, especially since they were planning on discharging Peter soon. They had to talk about the arrangements and what would happen when Kainan returned to Isla Hermosa.

How much longer could he stay here? He had duties to do.

Reagan pocketed the card and went to the staff change room. She got out of her scrubs and put them in the laundry hamper, changing back into her street clothes.

She went to check on Peter and found he was still asleep,

but he stirred when she touched him gently. Things were looking up. Even though Peter relied on a machine to keep him alive, he was here and responding. He was no longer in a medicated coma.

Even if Kainan left she would have Peter.

Except Peter wouldn't have Kainan.

That made her sad, but the timing was off. Kainan was King and his country needed him, and Peter needed a new heart. He had to stay in Toronto while he waited.

Reagan kissed her son's head and then left the hotel. She needed to have something to eat and a nap, and Kainan was the one who had the key to her new place where supposedly her bed and all her belongings were.

She didn't even know the address!

Reagan slipped down through the abandoned PATH walkway, which was devoid of commuters now, with the underground shops closed for the night. Then she went up the spiral staircase that connected The Royal York to the underground.

She was heading toward the gold elevators when she saw that Kainan was hanging out in a deserted piano lounge. He was playing the grand piano. The music was sad and haunting.

She headed toward him. Such strong hands, but gentle in the way he handled patients…and her. He was an imposing king, but he was so kind and sweet with their son.

It had completely knocked down her barriers to see him with Peter.

All her fears about Kainan being distant and not caring about Peter had evaporated away.

Kainan *cared.*

And she was lost to him. She was weak when it came to him and in this moment she didn't care.

Kainan glanced up as she approached him and smiled halfheartedly, scooting over so she could sit next to him.

"I didn't know you played," she said.

He didn't respond, but finished his piece and then turned to her.

I don't play often, but it helps clear my head. Where were you?

"I got pulled into surgery on another injured patient. He was a Hermosian refugee."

Kainan grimaced. "A Hermosian refugee?"

"Yes," she said carefully.

"Did he live?"

"Yes."

"That's good." Kainan rubbed his eyes. "I feel responsible for him—for all my people. As King, I feel it was my duty to keep my country together. My people shouldn't be here as refugees."

"It wasn't your fault that war broke out in your country. You weren't King then."

"I know, but I'm King *now* and it's my responsibility."

"He's safe here in Canada. As are you."

Kainan nodded, but didn't smile. He was sad, and it was apparent that the burden of his people weighed heavily on him.

That's good.

"I came to ask you where I live now," she said with a small smile.

Yes, I suppose that's important. Kainan reached into his pocket and pulled out a key. He handed it to her. *Your new condo is Golden Centre condos on Queens Quay. Your apartment twenty-nine B.*

"Thanks." Reagan pocketed the key. "They're going to send Peter home later today, and it's Christmas Eve."

Kainan nodded. *I know. It will be good. What should we do?*

"I need to go to my new place and make sure that Pe-

ter's room is ready." She was puzzled. "What do you mean, what should *we* do?"

To celebrate?

"I don't know." She laughed. "I never thought that I'd have anything to celebrate. I think I just need to ready Peter's room and make a home for him. I think that's all I can handle now."

Would you like to go there now? We can take a cab. Most of my security detail is over at my new place anyway.

"They left you alone here?"

They don't know that I'm here, actually. They think that I'm still at the hospital.

"I suspect that they wouldn't be too happy to learn that you were here."

Kainan shrugged. *Do you want to go?*

"Yes. I wouldn't mind having a short nap in my own bed for a change."

Kainan nodded. *That can be arranged. Let's go, then, it's late.*

They walked out of the empty piano lounge and headed out onto Front Street. The snow had stopped falling and the streets had been freshly plowed. Even though it was long after midnight there were still taxis waiting outside the prestigious hotel.

Kainan opened the door and Reagan slid in, telling the cabdriver the address. It didn't take the cabdriver long, on the deserted streets of Toronto, to get to the new condo building.

Reagan's mouth hung open when she saw it. She knew exactly how much these suites were. When she'd first moved back to Toronto, just pregnant, this building had been half-complete. She'd looked at purchasing a suite, but hadn't been able to swing it.

It was the perfect location. Even better than her apartment on Richmond Street West.

Do you like it? Kainan signed.

"It's too much," she whispered.

She paid the cabdriver and they got out of the cab. Kainan opened up the main door with his key and waved to the doorman. Reagan decided she would introduce herself later.

They rode the elevator, almost to the top, and down at the end of the hallway were two apartments. One was his and the other was hers.

She opened the door and saw the contents of her apartment were now in her new place. Her apartment on Richmond Street had been sparsely furnished, but because her old place had been smaller it had looked all right. Now she could see how sparse her belongings really were in this large new condo.

Kainan gestured and she followed him into a smaller room. He flicked on the lights and there was the crib, the chair and everything. All made up. Emotion overwhelmed her, and she covered her mouth to keep herself from crying.

It was too much. All of it. No one had ever shown her this kind of kindness or generosity before—not even her parents. Michael was like a father figure, but he had his own family. The only time she'd felt somewhat complete was when she was in Isla Hermosa with Kainan.

And then she'd thought he'd died.

Now this.

It was too much, and she wondered why she was fighting him. They could be a family.

She shook her head, because how *could* they be a family. How could she fall in love with a man who was King?

Are you okay? Kainan signed.

She nodded, overcome by his generosity. "It's wonderful. Thank you."

Kainan touched her face and then took her hand and placed it on his chest. Those dark eyes that had always been her downfall were tender and she couldn't help it.

She wanted to be with him.

Even if it was just one more time. She wanted to feel safe in his arms, to forget the world around them for just one moment. To forget all the horrors of this life and know that they had this. They shared so much.

She stepped closer and touched his face, running her fingers over the scars on his face and neck. He closed his eyes and under her other hand she could feel his heart beat faster. He wrapped his arms around her, pulling her against him.

Reagan closed her eyes and kissed him, melting into him as she had done so long ago. As she'd done a couple of days ago when he'd taken her to that room to calm down when she'd been so terrified of Peter having the surgery to attach the ventricular assist device.

Even without words he knew what she was thinking. He knew what she needed. Who needed words when all that was needed was action? And in this moment, that was all she wanted.

She wanted to feel his arms around her again. Even if it was only one more time. She wanted him.

She didn't want to think. All she wanted to be was lost—in his arms, in his kisses. All she wanted to do was *feel*. She'd been numb for so long.

Kainan's kiss deepened and he pressed her against the door, their bodies flush together.

The kiss ended and those dark eyes glittered with desire.

"Yes," she whispered.

And that was all he needed.

He picked her up and carried her to the bedroom, where her bed was made up in the center of the very large room. There were no window coverings, and all she could see was the darkness of the lake outside her window. There were no other buildings, no one to look in and see them, just the darkness of the frigid water and the sound of another squall blowing in off the lake.

* * *

Kainan couldn't believe this was happening. It was what he wanted. All he'd ever wanted. There had been no other woman who'd made him feel this way.

He cupped her face as she undid his belt, watching her eyes, those beautiful brown eyes which made him weak in the knees, and those full pink lips he loved to kiss.

"All I want is you, Kainan. Right here. Right now."

And that was all he needed to hear. Like the snow squall that was raging outside the windows, there was a storm in his soul. He needed to possess her again and never let her go. There was no turning back for them.

Even though he wasn't supposed to use his voice, because of the scar tissue forming in his throat, he whispered against her lips. "No protection."

This seduction, making love to her, was a part of him that he'd thought long gone. He'd thought the Kainan he'd been before his brother had died and he'd became King was long gone. He'd been so focused on duty versus desire he had never prepared for this moment when desire would win over. She made him forget his duty.

"It's okay," she said, kneeling in front of him and un-buttoning his shirt. "I'm on the pill. I won't get pregnant."

And what about last time? he signed, teasing her.

"I wasn't on the pill then. That was an entirely different situation."

He chuckled and leaned his head against hers. "You're... sure?"

"Yes. Very sure. I want you, Kainan."

She opened his shirt and ran her hands over his chest. Her simple touch made him burn with need for her. He wanted to possess her again and again. He'd lost all sense of reason.

There was no way he could turn back. She made him

feel—made him feel as if he could breathe and love. Things that he'd thought he would never feel again.

And although he wasn't sure what was going to happen in his future, he knew one thing to be true—and that was he never wanted to let her go in this moment.

He kissed her again, running his hand down her back, cupping her bottom to pull her tight against him. He didn't want any space between them and he didn't want to let her go.

All these thoughts ran through his mind. The things he wanted to tell her. How he'd thought only of her since they'd parted. How the memory of her had got him through so much.

How there was only her.

"I've missed you," she whispered, and then she let out a little moan of pleasure as he kissed her throat down to her collarbone, feeling her pulse quicken under his lips.

Kainan had nearly lost his mind with his want for her. *This* was what he'd been dreaming about for so long.

If he wasn't careful he would just take her—right here and now, half dressed—and he didn't want that. Not in this moment.

Kainan wanted to take his time with her.

He wanted to do right by her.

He'd been waiting so long for a chance. A chance to be with her again.

"Kainan…" she whispered, running her hands down his back, her touch leaving goose bumps across his skin.

He couldn't wait, and they made quick work of the rest of their clothes. He undid her rich mahogany brown hair from its confining bun and ran his fingers through the silken softness. Nothing was between them now. It was just the two of them…bared to each other and vulnerable.

I love your hands on my body, he thought as her hands moved over his skin.

"I can tell you like that," she whispered.

And then she continued teasing with her fingertips, running a finger down his neck, over his chest and lower. Her hand splayed against his abdomen before slipping lower and gripping his erection in the palm of her hand.

He groaned.

She chuckled, and then nibbled his neck. Every nerve-ending in his body was alive as she stroked him. His blood was on fire, and he tried to hold back another moan but couldn't keep it in. Reagan's touching him was driving him wild, and he was afraid that if she kept it up he would come. Only he didn't want her to stop.

Her mouth was on him now, and his hands slipped into her hair. His throat tightened but he couldn't stop. The pleasure was making his body wild with need.

He pulled her away and pushed her against the mattress, pinning her there below him. Reagan bit her lower lip and tried to wrap herself around him, but he let go of her wrists to push open her legs.

"Kainan…" she begged.

He grinned, and wouldn't give in to her pleas.

"Kainan, what're you…? Oh, my God," she gasped as he did what she had done to him. Tortured her the way she had him, driving her wild with need.

"Please," she begged.

He didn't respond, just ran his tongue around the most sensitive part of her, making her cry out. He wanted her to come, but he wanted to be inside her too. He was greedy and he wanted all of her.

Reagan arched her hips up and he moved over her, staring down into her eyes, then bent down to kiss her as he entered her slowly.

He groaned. She was so tight, so hot. It took every ounce of his control not to take her fast. It had been so long since

he'd been with her. There hadn't been another since her, he'd never had a desire for any other.

It was only her.

Just Reagan.

He sank deeper into her and quickened his pace. He couldn't hold back. He slipped a hand under her bottom, bringing her closer and angling his thrusts as he took all of her. It was hard to hold back, but he wanted Reagan to come first, and it didn't take long before she was crying out his name, tightening around him.

And that was when he sought his own release.

When it was over he rolled away, trying to catch his breath, but it was only a moment before he pulled her close against him. He didn't want her far from him. He needed her.

"Kainan..." she whispered in the darkness, her breath fast and heavy like his.

He ran his hands over her soft body and kissed her gently.

"Sleep," he said hoarsely. "I'm here."

Reagan smiled up at him and sighed.

Soon she was asleep, the even sound of her breathing letting him know she'd drifted off. The wind was howling outside, a high-pitched wail which usually set him on edge and made him shiver, but there was no shivering with her warm body pressed against his.

Tonight he had her.

Tonight she was his Queen. Even if it was only for one night.

CHAPTER ELEVEN

THE ALARM WENT off at six o'clock in the morning. At first Kainan forgot for a moment why he'd set the alarm so early, because all he wanted to do was lie in Reagan's arms all day long. Then he remembered that it was Christmas Eve and Dr. Shaw wanted him at the hospital so he could do another MRI and check the extent of new damage and scar tissue in preparation for the surgery coming up soon.

Try as he might, Kainan hadn't been able to keep silent when he'd made love to Reagan. He'd lost all sense of logic and reason, and now he was paying for it.

His throat was hoarse, sore and very tight. It was hard to breathe, but last night had been worth it.

Kainan disentangled himself from Reagan's arms and slowly got out of bed.

"Where are you going?" she whispered, and flicked on a light which blinded them both. "It's dark still."

I'm not trying to sneak away.

"Where are you off to then?" she asked, sitting up.

To the hospital.

"Is it Peter?" she asked, panicked.

No, it's me. He ran his hand through his hair. *I just need another MRI scan. There's more adhesions in my throat.*

"Oh," she said quietly, worried. "That will complicate the surgery."

Yes, and it also complicates my breathing, not just my voice.

She cocked an eyebrow. "I'm worried about you. Worried about this surgery."

He grinned and touched her face, whispering, "I am not."

It was a lie. He was, but there was no choice.

"What happens if you…? What happens to your country?"

Peter could be King.

Reagan frowned. "Peter is not legitimate."

You can change that.

She rolled her eyes and shook her head. "Are you crazy?"

Reagan, please. We belong together as a family.

She looked unsure, and for some reason he got an inkling that he was getting through to her. Maybe she would agree to be his Queen. Then he could take care of them.

That's if you survive the surgery.

He didn't want to think of that. He didn't want to think of putting Peter in a position of having no childhood. Perhaps he was being selfish, like his father. Still, he wanted both of them. He needed them both.

"I'm worried about this surgery, I really am," she said.

It touched him that she cared so much.

I don't know when or if I can have the surgery, he signed, and then started to pull on his discarded clothes.

"I'll go with you to the MRI."

He shook his head. *No, you need to go to Peter. They could be discharging him today. I will have a security detail available for you and a town car to bring you back here with him. Do you have a car seat?*

"I did…it's probably in the closet in his nursery."

He nodded. *I will be fine. I promise to keep you posted, and tonight we'll celebrate as a family.*

"Just don't do anything rash. You can be a voiceless king, Kainan. There is no shame in it."

I am not ashamed. I just want answers. If it can be resolved, then I would like to speak again—I would like to address my people. It was maddening not being able to work on my own during that trauma. I had to follow you like a shadow. I couldn't go into the operating room as lead surgeon because how can I sign with my hands inside a person? I have to return to my throne strong.

Kainan finished dressing.

Do not worry, Reagan. Everything will be okay. We'll order in food for tonight and celebrate our first Christmas, the three of us together.

She smiled. "You can invite Andreas and the other members of your security team. Andreas is family. He's Peter's uncle, whether he wants to admit it or not. And he cares for you."

I will try to convince him, but Andreas takes decorum very seriously. He didn't even want my blood. Kainan straightened his tie. *When the MRI is done I will come see you—or, if they decide to discharge Peter before I'm done, I will meet you here.*

"Okay…" she said, but he could tell that there was uncertainty in her voice and he wished he could tell her more. Tell her how much he cared, but that he was scared. Scare of ruining it all. Scared of breaking her heart if he died.

The pressure he felt was keen.

As he left Reagan's apartment he ran into Andreas, who was limping to the apartment next door with a cane.

"Your Majesty," Andreas said, wincing as he tried to bow.

Don't. Kainan stopped him. *Rest. Diego, another one of my security guards, is taking me to the hospital for a test.*

"The MRI?" Andreas asked hopefully.

Yes.

Andreas looked worried. "I should be with you, Your Majesty."

It is fine. Reagan is next door. Keep an eye on her, if you must.

"You spent the night with her? Has she agreed to be Queen?"

Not yet. Rest, Andreas. That's an order.

"Thank you, Your Majesty."

Kainan nodded and went downstairs, where Diego was waiting for him. He didn't say much and opened the door to the tinted-windowed town car. Diego knew where Kainan needed to go.

First the MRI, then the embassy. Time was running out. Kainan had to put his affairs in order before he had surgery, and he was angry with himself for letting it go this long. But he'd been too afraid before.

Now, with Peter and Reagan, Kainan was experiencing something he had not felt in a long time, and that was hope. He was always going to make sure everyone was protected if he died on the operating table, but that hope gave him courage. He wasn't going to die during surgery. He was going to fight. He was going to live to know his son and to return to Isla Hermosa and take his place as King.

Reagan was torn.

Last night in Kainan's arms had been so amazing and it had felt right. She had felt as if she belonged with him. And then he'd shattered her by telling her that he was still contemplating going through a risky procedure to restore his voice.

It wasn't so much the surgery itself that was terrible, but Kainan's injury…the scar tissue.

The idea was too much for her to bear, and she was torn between what she'd been taught her whole life and becoming a family with Kainan.

She found a towel in one of the boxes in her bedroom and had a quick shower in her brand-new walk-in shower.

When she walked out of the bathroom, she glanced out of the window toward the icy waters of Lake Ontario.

Right now it was full of foreboding. A stormy, gloomy body of water that had always freaked her out. But then she thought about the spring thaw and the summer, when she would be able to watch the ferry head from Queen's Quay to the islands, and that brought a smile to her face.

There was Centerville, out on one of those islands, and she thought about taking Peter there one day—taking all the rides with him and walking on the beaches there. She thought about all the things they could do. But now, instead of seeing only her and Peter in the picture, she saw Kainan.

Would it really be so bad to be his wife?

Once Peter had his new heart she could move to Isla Hermosa. Despite the war, she had enjoyed her time there—the ocean, the tropical weather and the lush jungle.

There was really nothing to keep her in Toronto after Peter got his heart. She could practice medicine in Isla Hermosa. Perhaps she could do even more, like teach the future physicians of Isla Hermosa. She'd always wanted to teach.

Maybe she *could* have it all?

Be careful. You can only rely on yourself.

She shook that thought away, because right now she was feeling something she had never felt before and that was love. The picture she had in her mind of her future didn't have to be Toronto or London, Ontario...it could be Isla Hermosa and Europe.

And Kainan.

She couldn't lose him again. She'd thought that she had lost him once and that had nearly destroyed her. This was her second chance, and she would be a fool not to take it, but she was terrified beyond all reason.

Reagan got dressed as quickly as she could and then dug the car seat out of Peter's closet. Starting tonight, with

Peter home for Christmas and Kainan here, she was going to make her life right.

She couldn't be scared anymore.

She wasn't going to ruin this second chance that she had been given.

As she locked her door, the door to Kainan's apartment opened and Andreas hobbled out.

"Andreas! They let you out?" she asked.

Andreas turned and smiled at her. "Yes, Dr. Cote. I am fine now."

"You need to rest," she said. "Where are you going?"

"Out. There is no food."

"You should order in."

Andreas sighed. "I was going to go to the hospital and check on Kainan."

"I thought someone else was with him? You really should rest."

"I should be the one to go to the hospital with him," Andreas said grimly.

"You really need to rest. But tonight come over and have dinner. You are family."

"I beg your pardon?" said Andreas.

"He told me that you're his illegitimate half brother."

Andreas frowned. "I wish he hadn't."

"Kainan cares about you."

Andreas sighed. "And I him."

"So come over and celebrate"

"No, it is not proper. There's nothing to celebrate. The surgery is too risky, and if he dies he will be leaving the country without an heir."

"It's a risky surgery, for sure, but—"

"The odds of his death are high."

Reagan's heart skipped a beat. "What are you talking about?"

"He has extensive scar tissue…"

"Kainan could *die*?" Her world spun out of control.

Andreas nodded. "Although your son could still be King if you marry him."

Reagan's heart sank. So that was why Kainan wanted to marry her. Why he constantly pestered her to marry him. It wasn't because he cared for her—it was all about the crown. It was all about saving his kingdom because he expected to die. He was going to abandon her and Peter after all, and abandon them to a life she didn't want.

If she hadn't had Peter then he probably wouldn't have bothered with her.

You've opened your heart to the wrong man, Reagan. You always do. This heartache is all your fault.

Reagan couldn't even respond to Andreas. She just turned on her heel and carried on her way. She didn't know what to think.

She was hurt that Kainan had used her. Played her for a fool. He didn't really care for her *or* Peter. He saw them as a means to save his country. To save its monarchy.

And it hurt.

Had their night of passion been a part of his game?

She slammed the "down" button at the elevator as hard as she could and it felt good to hit it—but it didn't quell the feelings of betrayal she was experiencing right now. The pain...

The fact he'd lied to her and hadn't even been able to tell her the truth.

Why had she thought she could trust him? She knew better than to listen to her heart. Her heart was thing that always got her into trouble. She was a fool.

She hailed a cab and climbed in, directing the taxi driver to take her to the hospital. She didn't know what she was going to do when she saw Kainan, but she knew one thing was for certain now. She was never going to marry.

Never.

CHAPTER TWELVE

AFTER KAINAN'S MRI he was scheduled for surgery with Dr. Shaw on December twenty-sixth in the morning. There were risks that the scar tissue was now threatening his ability to breathe, and that was not good. Dr. Shaw had put him on oxygen just now, and he was feeling light-headed because breathing was getting harder.

He had to get it done sooner rather than later.

When the surgery had bee booked he went straight to the embassy to talk to his delegates about his possible death.

Kainan had decided that it was time that the monarchy did not have absolute control over the people. Time for him to take a step back, so that if he died Peter would not be trapped as he had been.

He could be a figurehead, and he could help his people, but Kainan had to give them the tools to help themselves, and soon his delegates would be in the process of dealing with the Canadian officials in order to make that happen.

Which meant the deadline for him to be crowned was a moot point. He had it struck out in one of his last acts of power.

The burden that had been lifted from his shoulders was great.

He felt free.

He was still King, but it was different.

This was now a monarchy on his own terms—a monarchy that would serve its people. They could vote in a prime minister. There would be a democracy.

And Kainan would oversee these things to make sure corrupt people didn't get into power as long as he was their figurehead.

When he got to the hospital he went straight to Peter's room to talk to Reagan, but when he got there the room was empty.

Peter was gone and so was Reagan.

His heart lurched and he began to panic, thinking that something had happened to their son.

A pediatric nurse came into the room. "Dr. Laskaris, they've been discharged. They were discharged about twenty minutes ago, so they're probably at home."

Kainan breathed a sigh of relief and mouthed his thanks to the nurse before rushing out of the hospital. He was texting Diego when he saw Andreas limping in.

Dammit.

"Your Majesty," Andreas said. He looked concerned.

What's wrong? Kainan asked.

"It's Dr. Cote. She knows. She knows about the risks of your surgery."

His stomach sank like a rock. *How does she know? Did the press find out?*

Andreas shook his head. "I told her."

Kainan saw red, felt his blood boiling, and it took every ounce of his strength not to hit Andreas.

You did what?

"Your Majesty, I had to tell her. I am also the one who broke into her apartment."

Why would you do that?

"I wanted to push her into your arms. I wanted to protect my country and your birthright. Your son's birthright."

Kainan mouthed a few choice curse words and scrubbed

a hand over his face. *I can't believe you did this, Andreas. You've ruined everything!*

"How? She knows the truth now."

I was going to tell her, but I was also going to tell her that the monarchy no longer exists.

Andreas was confused. "I don't understand…"

I'm forming a democracy, Andreas. I will still be King, but I will just be a figurehead. I will help the people rebuild Isla Hermosa and they will vote in a prime minster and elect officials. The people will run Isla Hermosa. I will not.

Andreas blinked and then bowed his head, ashamed. "Your Majesty, I'm sorry that I doubted your abilities."

Kainan sighed and gripped his half brother's shoulders. *It's all right. I just pray that it's not too late to turn this around with Reagan. I still want her as my Queen, but only when she wants to become my Queen. And Peter can inherit one day, but he doesn't have to. There will be a government.*

"I'm glad to hear that, Your Majesty."

Andreas turned and they walked out of the hospital together.

Have the police come for you yet? Kainan asked.

"No, I know how to get away with murder, Your Majesty," Andreas teased. "I can fake an apartment break-in without being caught."

Kainan smiled. *I will still need a head of security, but I think that you should run for prime minister when we go back to Isla Hermosa. You would be a fine elected leader. You're a war hero, as was your father before you.*

Andreas nodded. "Perhaps—but right now I want to make sure you and your family are taken care of."

Kainan hugged Andreas. *I'm still ticked off at you for sticking your nose in where it doesn't belong.*

"I know, but if I hadn't then everything would've been lost."

Diego pulled up in front of the hospital and Kainan

helped Andreas in first and then climbed in himself. He had to make things right with Reagan before it was too late.

When they got to the apartment Diego helped Andreas out and Kainan ran inside. At least he knew that she would be there. Everything of hers was still there, and he had a key so she couldn't lock him out.

When he got to their floor he passed a locksmith and saw Reagan standing in the doorway, her arms crossed and her face like thunder.

He started to sign. *Let me explain—*

"Save it," she said. "Andreas told me everything."

Not everything.

"He told me that you needed me to marry you so you can legitimize Peter and that when you die he'll be King? Is that correct, or is there more to that story?" she asked.

That was true, but now there is more.

She raised an eyebrow. "I'm listening."

That was true up until this afternoon. Now I have changed everything. I don't need to marry you for Peter to be King.

Reagan reeled as if she had been slapped. "How nice for you."

Reagan, I'm creating a democracy. I will just be a figurehead now.

She didn't say anything, but he saw he was getting through to her. She hadn't shut him out yet.

Peter will become King whether we are married or not, he signed. *And he too will only be a figurehead. Isla Hermosa is to become a democracy. And with that the old monarchy was replaced. My officials at the embassy and back home are working with the prime ministers of Canada and Britain to make this happen. There will be peace now because of this.*

"I'm very happy to hear there will be peace," she said softly.

But...?

"You lied to me. You constantly asked me to marry you because you said you wanted to protect me."

I did.

"You *did*?" she asked, her eyes shining with tears. "And that's the trouble. Now that I'm not needed anymore, you're free. You don't need me."

Reagan, I still want to protect you.

"I wish I could believe that, Kainan. I really wish I could. But first you lie to me and then you don't tell me that you're King of a country. You don't contact me and tell me that you're still alive."

I couldn't tell you I was alive. I was in hiding. Besides, I didn't know where in Canada you were.

Reagan ignored him. "You told me your surgery was risky, but not how risky. Why did you feel the need to lie to me?"

To protect you!

She nodded. "I don't believe it. I can't. You've broken my trust, Kainan. You've hurt me too much. You're welcome to be a part of Peter's life, but I will fight you if you try and take him out of Canada and away from me. He's too fragile to live a life like yours."

Reagan, please don't turn me away.

Although he wouldn't blame her for doing so. And he couldn't sign the words he needed to say because he wanted to *say* them. To use his own words to tell her he loved her.

I need you, Reagan. I want you in my life.

Reagan sighed and a tear slipped down her cheek. "I wish I could believe that, Kainan. I wish that I could."

She turned back into her apartment and shut the door. Shutting him out of her life.

He sighed sadly, but he wasn't giving up.

He'd come too far to give up on her now.

Even if she didn't want to marry him, he was going to

have Reagan in his life and he would do anything to win her back.

He would not be the man his father had been.

It was heartbreaking to spend Peter's first Christmas alone with him, especially when she'd thought Kainan would be there.

She'd thought for a brief moment that they were becoming a family—and then she'd found out the real reason why he wanted a family.

To protect the crown when he died.

He needed them, but not in the way she'd hoped he would. Did he even really *want* them?

Still, this was the way she'd *thought* she was going to spend Peter's first Christmas, when she'd been pregnant with him and had thought Kainan was dead.

It was scary how dependent she'd become on Kainan without really realizing. She'd got used to having him around.

They had even planned to spend Peter's first Christmas together, but since she'd turned him away on Christmas Eve she hadn't seen him.

It was now Boxing Day, and she was considering going next door and talking to him. Perhaps she'd been too harsh on him. She wanted him involved in Peter's life, but that was it. They could work together for as long as he was at the hospital, and they could work together to raise Peter, but that was where she had to draw the line.

She couldn't risk her heart again.

But you love him. Love is always worth the risk.

Her phone started ringing and she answered it.

"Reagan, it's Michael."

He sounded completely stressed out.

"Michael? Is everything okay?"

"UNOS called. There's a match, and I've sent a recov-

ery team to Ottawa to get it. There's a heart for your son. You need to bring Peter in right away."

Her heart skipped a beat.

So soon.

She'd only just got him home. She had been enjoying her time with him and now she had to take him back and put him in the hands of the surgeons.

"I'll be right there. Thank you, Michael."

Reagan hung up the phone. She could hear Peter stirring through the baby monitor.

She grabbed the baby monitor and left her apartment, heading straight to Kainan's. She knocked on the door. She could feel panic rising.

Diego answered the door. "Dr. Cote?"

"Is Kainan here?"

"No," Diego said. "Andreas took His Majesty over to the hospital early this morning to have his surgery."

"His surgery? Right…that's today too."

The world began to spin out of control. Peter and Kainan were both having surgery on the same day. She could potentially lose them both.

"Is everything okay, Dr. Cote?"

"Can I get a ride to the hospital? It's Peter—they've found him a heart."

"Yes, of course. I will meet you downstairs in ten minutes."

Reagan nodded and went back to her apartment as Diego closed the door. She went straight to Peter, who smiled when she entered the room.

Her body shook and she smiled back at him. "My little love," she whispered as she carefully picked him up and held him tight.

What if this was the last time she got to hold him? What if he didn't survive?

Right now she wasn't in the mind-set of a surgeon. She

was in the mind-set of a mother who was terrified about what she might lose.

And Kainan was going to have surgery too.

She could lose it all in one fell swoop.

She had to make things right.

Reagan kissed Peter's head. "I'm going to make it right for you. I swear."

She would do better for her son than her parents ever had for her.

She packed up Peter's ventricular device and got him into his car seat, covering him with a blanket. She grabbed everything Peter needed and hurried out of the apartment.

Kainan was in pre-op with Andreas. He wanted to see Reagan. He'd gotten word that a heart for Peter had been found.

Screw this.

He got out of the bed where he'd been waiting for Dr. Shaw.

"Your Majesty?" Andreas said in alarm.

Tell Dr. Shaw I will be back in time for my surgery. I have to see Reagan and Peter.

Andreas nodded. "Yes, Your Majesty."

Kainan pulled on his street clothes and left the room. His throat was tight and his pulse was racing. He cleared his throat and rolled his shoulders. It was hard to breathe. It had been getting harder to breathe since Reagan had locked him out of her life.

She was his air. His freedom. And he needed her.

It was stress that was making him feel this way, and he knew he wouldn't relax until he saw Peter and Reagan.

He made his way to the pediatric floor, where they were prepping Peter. He could hear him crying. He'd never heard him cry before. Reagan hadn't let him see him since he'd been discharged two days ago. Not that he blamed her. He'd ruined everything by not telling her the truth.

Hearing Peter cry was an amazing thing.

It was strong.

Reagan turned around and her expression softened, making his heart skip a beat. He wanted to comfort her, but didn't want her to push him away.

"What're you doing here?" Reagan asked.

I'm his father, Kainan signed.

"I know, but I thought you would be in pre-op yourself."

Who told you?

"Diego. You're going through with it?"

Of course.

"You could die," she said, biting her lip as if she was holding something back. "If you're just to be a figurehead then you don't need to go through with this surgery. There are less riskier surgeries to remove adhesions."

I do.

"Kainan, it's too risky."

He nodded. *So is this.*

They both turned to Peter as the gurney came in and the pediatric cardiologist, Dr. Bruni, entered the room.

"Reagan and Kainan." He nodded at them both. "The heart is on its way from the airport. We're now going to take Peter into surgery and remove the ventricular device and put him on bypass. You both know the procedure. He will be in the pediatric critical care unit for some time and will be on anti-rejection drugs for the rest of his life."

Reagan nodded and Kainan felt numb.

She stepped forward and kissed Peter goodbye.

Kainan took a step toward his son. The last time he'd gone off to surgery Kainan hadn't even been able to look at him. It had been too painful—as was this.

What if something happened and he didn't ever get to know his son?

What if he died in the operating room himself?

Better me than Peter.

He touched his son's head and then kissed him. He couldn't say that he loved him. He had no voice with which to say it. But he hoped Peter knew that he did.

He couldn't lose Peter. Kainan wanted time with him. Parents were never supposed to outlast their own children, though he'd seen it every day when he was a surgeon.

Life was complicated and messy. And he wanted Peter to experience it all.

He stepped back and they wheeled Peter away.

Reagan broke down in tears, sobbing into her hands, her shoulders shaking. Kainan took her in his arms and she clung to him.

"I'm sorry," she whispered against his neck. "I'm so sorry."

When she looked up he signed, *What for?*

"For pushing you away. I never gave you a chance to explain anything. You were carrying around this tremendous burden and I should've been more sympathetic. I know what it's like to carry around a burden as big as that, and I'm sorry I didn't give you the chance. I was afraid."

Of what?

"Of relying on you and losing you. I've never had anyone before. Never had love…or a family. Not really."

Me neither.

"Only you have ever cared for me."

I understand. I had people to rely on, people to protect me, and I was never alone—but I really was. I was scared of relying on you too, Reagan. I was scared of…

Kainan felt his throat tighten and he touched her face. The room began to spin and he shook his head, trying to focus.

He was finding it hard to breathe.

And he couldn't call for help.

He couldn't tell her what was happening.

"Kainan?" she said, panic in her voice.

I love you. That was the last thought he had before everything went black.

Reagan screamed out as Kainan's knees buckled under him and she helped him to the floor. As she laid him out she couldn't hear any breath sounds. She hit the panic button on the wall to call a code and then she tried to breathe for him, compressing his chest to keep his heart beating.

He'd stopped breathing.

She couldn't lose him for real this time.

She hadn't even had a chance to tell him that she loved him. That she forgave him and that she wanted to try and make it work. That she was tired of carrying her burden alone and that she now knew it was okay not to handle everything on your own.

It was okay to lean on someone else—especially someone you loved.

The code team came for him. They got a tube down his throat and started manually ventilating him.

She had to take a step back.

She couldn't work on him.

They whisked him off to surgery.

"I can't lose him," Reagan said out loud to herself. "I thought I'd lost him once. I can't go through that again."

And she made a vow then and there that if Kainan came out of surgery she was going to make things right—just as she'd promised Peter.

She needed Kainan. She loved him.

As much as she had been taught that she didn't need anyone, she knew she needed Kainan and he needed her. She wasn't going to squander her second chance.

Not this time.

* * *

Pain was the first thing that Kainan felt. His throat was raw, as if it had been shredded with a thousand razor blades. His mouth was dry.

It took him a moment to realize what was happening and then he remembered. He had been with Reagan and they had just taken Peter away when he'd collapsed.

He tried to sit up, but it hurt.

"Don't try and sit up," Reagan said gently.

Kainan opened his eyes and smiled at her. He signed to ask her what had happened.

"Scar tissue blocked your airway. Dr. Shaw was able to get at it all, and repair your vocal cords, though it may be a few days before you will be able to speak. If you can't speak don't worry—it will come. You're in the ICU, still."

Peter? he asked, signing.

Reagan grinned, her smile bright. "He made it through. He did beautifully and is in the pediatric critical care unit."

Kainan let out a sigh of relief. *I want to go see him.*

"We will. You're still coming out of the sedation. Dr. Shaw wanted to make sure that you had some extra rest after your surgery yesterday, so he kept you in a medicated coma for a night."

What day is it?

"The twenty-ninth. The New Year is coming and your move to a democracy went through. Your coronation will wait and your people are voting for their first prime minister."

I am sorry about all that.

Reagan touched his face. "I know, and I'm sorry that I didn't give you a proper chance. I was so scared of relying on anyone. I've been used to doing things on my own for so long."

You have no reason to apologize.

"I do. I was devastated when I thought you were dead,

Kainan. It crushed me. It felt like I'd lost my best friend, my partner, and then you came back and you were so distant. It killed me. I just didn't want to risk my heart. I wasn't even sure that I was feeling anything, what with Peter."

I am the one who needs to apologize. I left you alone and I didn't try and reach out to you. You carried our son alone, dealt with his devastating diagnosis alone. I should've been there. I felt like I was failing you the way I failed my brother.

"You didn't fail your brother—he failed you *and* your country," she said.

He shook his head. *I should have tried harder to stop him. I could've done more to control him. And then maybe, just maybe, there wouldn't have been a war. Lives could've been spared.*

"Everything happens for a reason, Kainan. You weren't your brother's keeper. You did the best you could."

I'm sorry, Reagan. I'm sorry for deceiving you, for abandoning you. I love you more than anything.

Reagan leaned over and kissed him. "I love you too. And, if the offer still stands, I would like to be your wife."

Kainan grinned. *It will always stand, but are you sure? I have to return to Isla Hermosa at some point. Your home is here in Toronto.*

"My home is with you and our son. That's all the home I need." They kissed again. "I love you so much, Kainan."

"I love you too," he whispered.

Kainan developed a slight postoperative fever, which was not uncommon after the amount of blood that he'd lost. So he wasn't allowed to see Peter until New Year's Eve.

As he walked to the pediatric critical care unit, with Andreas following closely behind with a wheelchair, he couldn't help but think about how this should have been the night he'd prepared for this coronation. Now, instead of a

coronation, a parliament was being formed. It was an exciting time for Isla Hermosa and he couldn't wait to go back.

As soon as Kainan and Peter had healed, they would go back to Isla Hermosa and begin to heal the country—from the ground up.

Kainan had decided that the palace would be repaired, but would no longer be his home. It would instead house the new government that was being formed right now.

He much preferred his original home outside the city gates of Helicia—if it still stood. From there he could see the ocean and the beach. It reminded him of his mother and her longing to be free.

And, though he was still King, he would have more freedom now that Isla Hermosa was a democracy.

He wanted a safe place for Peter to play—not a prison for him to grow up in, like Kainan had had.

Reagan had been by his side. She'd moved between the rooms, taking care of him *and* Peter. Now that they were getting closer to the pediatric critical care unit, where Peter was, Kainan became nervous. Peter was no longer sedated and Kainan had never yet got to look into his eyes. Not really.

They put on gowns and were buzzed in.

Kainan walked toward his son's crib.

Peter was cooing and kicking, despite the incision in his chest.

As soon as Reagan came into view Peter responded happily to her presence and Kainan's heart melted.

He moved closer to the crib and Peter's eyes locked on his. Peter stared at him and Kainan could see eyes so similar to his studying him. Emotion overcame him as he reached out and touched his son. Peter grasped his finger, squeezing it before smiling up at him.

Kainan's heart swelled, and instead of signing he opened

his mouth, to hear his voice—not a whisper, but his *voice*—respond to his son.

"I love you."

He was no longer voiceless. He had a voice, his son had a new heart, and the three of them together were one. They were whole and healed.

EPILOGUE

Two years later, New Year's Eve, Isla Hermosa

"IT'S ALMOST TIME, Your Majesties," Andreas said, bowing as he came into the room.

Kainan's pulse was racing as he smoothed his hand over the traditional red military dress jacket that had once been worn by his father. His pulse was racing.

"You can do this."

Kainan smiled down at Reagan, who was dressed in white and wearing his mother's tiara, as well as some other jewels that had been hidden and saved during the war.

He sighed and nodded.

This was to be his first speech in Isla Hermosa since he'd returned, married Reagan and introduced the world to his son Peter, who was taking to his new heart so well. He'd spoken to his people briefly, but hadn't given his first address in the new parliament that had been built in the restored palace.

Which was where he was now standing.

He was dressing in his mother's old room.

He, Reagan and Peter lived in his mother's seaside villa, outside the capital city of Helicia.

For the first year after his return Kainan had kept to himself as he and Peter had healed.

His surgery had been a success, but it had taken some time for him to speak properly again. There were times he was still unsure of his voice.

Reagan took his hand and squeezed it. "Your voice is strong. You can do this."

"Did I tell you...?" He took a pause. "How beautiful you look?"

She blushed. "Don't even *try* to get out of this by complimenting me. I'm not letting you off the hook."

Kainan chuckled and held out his arm. "Are you ready for this moment? Standing by my side as I address parliament?"

"No!" She laughed nervously as she slipped her arm over his. "I'm afraid I'm going to mess something up. I'd rather be at the free clinic in town."

Kainan beamed at her. "You're giving my security team a hard time, you know. Andreas is finding it difficult to calm Diego down when you work at the clinic."

"Why?" she asked. "It's perfectly safe. I'm a *surgeon*, Kainan. You promised me I could continue as a surgeon. I don't want the crown jewels or the palace. I just want to work."

"You just want to work?" he teased. "What about the beach house and our son?"

"Well, of course. And there's also one more thing," Reagan said.

"What's that?"

"You."

She kissed him—just a light feather kiss, but it made his blood fire and he suddenly didn't want to be there any longer.

"Diego is very concerned about you working in the clinic."

"Why?" she asked.

"Diego can't stand the sight of blood."

"He should leave the room, then."

Kainan shook his head. "He's devoted to his Queen. He cannot."

Reagan's arm trembled. "I'm not used to that."

"You're doing fine."

Then Andreas opened the door.

Kainan held Peter's hand. Peter laughed and smiled at his parents. And Kainan's tension melted away.

In his son he saw himself, but he also saw Reagan. Peter had Reagan's spirit—the spirit that reminded him of his mother.

Every day Peter grew stronger, and their life in Isla Hermosa grew more idyllic. The beach house was the perfect hideaway for them to live in peace.

"Your Majesty," Andreas said with a hint of pride. "Prime Minister Monterro is ready for you."

"I am ready," Kainan said, but inside he was nervous.

This was the first time he would be addressing his people since the successful election of Alejandro Monterro as their first prime minster. Judging by the way Isla Hermosa had bloomed in the last couple of years, Alejandro was the perfect choice. And Kainan respected him.

Reagan squeezed his arm.

As Kainan escorted Reagan through the door he reached down with the hand that had been resting on his ceremonial sword and took his son's chubby hand in his.

"You're breaking protocol," Reagan whispered.

"I think that it does not matter anymore," Kainan whispered back.

They smiled at each other.

The three of them walked side by side towards the double doors. One the other side was Isla Hermosa's parliament and a handful of reporters. Not only were his people watching, the whole world was watching.

Before the double doors opened Kainan turned to Rea-

gan and she let go his hand and took Peter, because he had to walk in alone first.

"I couldn't have done this without you," he said, touching her cheek.

"You were always going to have the surgery—your voice would've been restored."

"I know, but you're the reason I'm alive. You and Peter have given me a reason to live. I love you."

Reagan's eyes glistened with tears. "And I love you."

"Me too," Peter chirped.

Kainan laughed and tousled his son's hair. He turned to Andreas and nodded. "I'm ready now."

Andreas beamed and opened the doors.

Kainan was blinded by bright lights, flashing bulbs.

"His Majesty, King Kainan the First!"

It was shouted over the din of scraping chairs as everyone stood.

Kainan gripped the hilt of his sword tightly, taking a step through the double doors into what had once been his father's throne room, but now held Isla Hermosa's democracy—

It was a step towards his destiny.

A destiny not only as a king, but as a father and husband.

As a man who had once again found his voice. A voice he never would have found if it hadn't been for Reagan.

This was all for her and Peter.

There was no turning back—and, thanks to Reagan, he never wanted to.

With her by his side he could do anything.

* * * * *

CROWN PRINCE, PREGNANT BRIDE

KATE HARDY

With special thanks to Mike Scogings for
sharing his expertise on stained glass, and to
C. C. Coburn for the lightbulb about the mermaid.

CHAPTER ONE

SHE WASN'T SUPPOSED to be there.

OK, Lorenzo knew that tourists were important. Without the income they brought when they visited the house and gardens of Edensfield Hall, his old school friend Gus would never have been able to keep his family's ancient estate going. Even keeping the roof of the house in good repair ate up huge chunks of the annual budget, let alone anything else.

But there were set times when the estate was open to the public. Right now wasn't one of them; the house and gardens were supposed to be completely private. Yet the woman in the shapeless black trousers and tunic top was brazenly walking through the grounds with a camera slung round her neck, stopping every so often to take a picture of something that had caught her eye. At that precise moment she was photographing the lake.

Strictly speaking, this was none of his business and he should just let it go.

But then the woman turned round, saw him staring at her, and snapped his photograph.

Enough was enough. He'd insist that she delete the file—or, if the camera was an old-fashioned one, hand over the film. He was damned if he was going to let a complete stranger make money out of photographing him in the

grounds of Edensfield, on what was supposed to be private time. A couple of weeks to get his head together and prepare himself for the coronation.

Lorenzo walked straight over to her. 'Excuse me. You just took my photograph,' he said, not smiling.

'Yes.'

At least she wasn't denying it. That would make things easier. 'Would you mind deleting the file from your camera?'

She looked surprised. 'What's the problem?'

As *if* she didn't know. Lorenzo Torelli—strictly speaking, His Royal Highness Prince Lorenzo Torelli of the principality of Melvante, on the border between Italy and France—was about to inherit the throne and start governing the kingdom next month, when his grandfather planned to abdicate. There had been plenty of stories about it in all the big European papers, all illustrated with his photograph, so no way could she claim she didn't know who he was. 'Your camera, please,' he said, holding his hand out.

'Afraid not,' she said coolly. 'I don't let people touch the tools of my trade.'

That surprised him. 'You're actually admitting you're a paparazzo?'

She scoffed. 'Of course I'm not. Why would the paparazzi want to take pictures of you?'

She had to be kidding. Did she *really* not know who he was? Did she live in some kind of bubble and avoid the news?

'I don't like my photograph being taken,' he said carefully. 'Besides, the estate isn't open to the public until this afternoon. If you'll kindly delete the file—and show me that you've deleted it—then I'll be happy to help you find your way safely out of the grounds until the staff are ready to welcome visitors.'

She looked at him and rolled her eyes. 'I'm not doing any harm.'

Lorenzo was used to people doing what he asked. The fact that she was being so stubborn about this when she was so clearly in the wrong annoyed him, and it was an effort for him to remain polite. Though he let his tone cool by twenty degrees. 'Madam, I'm afraid the house and grounds simply aren't open to visitors until this afternoon. Which means that right now you're trespassing.'

'Am I, now?' Those sharp blue eyes were filled with insolence.

'The file, please?' he prompted.

She rolled her eyes, took the camera strap from round her neck, changed the camera settings and showed the screen to him so that he could first of all see the photograph she'd taken, and then see her press the button to delete the file from her camera's storage card. 'OK. One deleted picture. Happy, now?'

'Yes. Thank you.'

'Right.' She inclined her head. 'Little tip from me: try smiling in future, sweetie. Because you catch an awful lot more flies with honey than you do with vinegar.'

And then she simply walked away.

Leaving Lorenzo feeling as if he was the one in the wrong.

The man was probably one of Gus's friends; he looked as if he was about the same age as Lottie's elder brother. And maybe he'd meant to be helpful; he'd clearly been trying to protect the family's privacy. Indigo knew she should probably have explained to him that she was a family friend who happened to be working on the house's restoration, not a trespassing tourist. Then again, it was none of his business what she was doing there, and his stick-in-the-

mud attitude had annoyed her—especially when he'd ac-
cused her of being a paparazzo.

She'd only taken his photograph because she'd seen him
striding around the grounds, scowling, and he'd looked like
a dark angel. Something she could've used for work. It had
been a moment's impulse. An expression on his face that
had interested her. Attracted her. Made her wonder what
he'd look like if he smiled.

But the way he'd reacted to her taking that photograph,
snarling about people taking his photo without permis-
sion... Anyone would think he was an A-list celeb on va-
cation instead of some dull City banker.

What an idiot.

Indigo rolled her eyes again and headed for the house.
Right now, work was more important. They were taking
the window out of the library today and setting it in the
workroom Gus had put aside for her in Edensfield Hall.
Indigo had already made a short video for the hall's web-
site to explain what was happening with the window, and
she'd promised to write a daily blog with shots of the work
in progress so the tourists could feel that they were part of
the restoration process. And she didn't mind people com-
ing over and asking her questions while she was working.
She loved sharing her passion for stained glass.

And the stranger with the face of a fallen angel—well,
he could do whatever he liked.

Lorenzo was still slightly out of sorts from his encounter
with the paparazzo-who-claimed-she-wasn't by the time
he went downstairs for dinner. When he walked into the
drawing room, he was shocked to see her there among the
guests. Except this time she wasn't wearing a shapeless
black top and trousers: she was wearing a bright scarlet
shift dress, shorter than anyone else's in the room. And

they were teamed with red shoes that were glossier, strappier and had a higher heel than anyone else's in the room.

Look at me, her outfit screamed.

As if anyone would be able to draw their eyes away from her.

Especially as her hair was no longer pulled back in the severe hairdo of this afternoon; now, it was loose and cascaded over her shoulders in a mass of ebony ringlets. All she needed was a floor-length green velvet and silk dress, and she would've been the perfect model for a Rossetti painting.

Lorenzo was cross with himself for being so shallow; but at the same time the photographer was also one of the most beautiful women he'd ever met. He couldn't help acting on the need to know who she was and what she was doing here.

He just about managed a few polite words with Gus before drawling, 'So who's the girl in the red dress?' and inclining his head over towards the trespasser, as if he wasn't really that interested in the answer.

'Who?' Gus followed his glance and smiled. 'Oh, that's Indigo.'

How could Gus be so cool and calm around her? Lorenzo wondered. The woman made him feel hot under the collar, and he hadn't even spoken to her yet this evening.

'A friend of the family?' Lorenzo guessed.

'She's one of Lottie's best friends from school.'

Which was surprising; Indigo didn't look as if she came from the same kind of titled background that Gus and his sister did.

'Actually, she's here on business, too; she's restoring the stained glass in the library for us,' Gus explained. 'My mother's asked her to work up some ideas for a new stained-glass window, so she's been taking photographs of bits of the estate.'

Which explained why she saw her camera as one of the tools of her trade. Lorenzo felt the colour wash into his face. 'I see.'

'What did you do, Lorenzo?' Gus asked, looking amused.

'I saw her taking photos this afternoon and I thought she was a trespasser. I, um, offered to help her find her way out of the grounds,' Lorenzo admitted.

Gus laughed. 'I bet she gave you a flea in your ear. Our Indi's pretty much a free spirit. And she really doesn't like being ordered about.'

He grimaced. 'I think I'd better go and apologise.'

'Good idea. Otherwise you might be in danger of getting an Indi Special.'

'An Indi Special?' Lorenzo asked, mystified.

'Indi. Short for Indigo, not for independent. Though she's that, too.' Gus raised an eyebrow. 'Let's just say she's an original. I'll let Lottie introduce you.' He caught his sister's eye and beckoned her over. 'Lottie, be a darling and introduce Lorenzo to Indi, will you?'

'Sure. Have you two not met, yet?' Lottie tucked her arm into Lorenzo's and led him over to Indigo to introduce them. 'Indi, this is Lorenzo Torelli, a very old friend of the family.' She smiled. 'Lorenzo, this is Indigo Moran, who's just about the coolest person I know.'

Indigo laughed. 'That's only because you live in a world full of stuffed shirts, Lottie. I'm perfectly normal.'

Lorenzo looked at her and thought, no, you're not in the slightest bit normal—there's something different about you. Something *special*. 'Gus said you were at school with Lottie,' he said.

'Until she escaped at fourteen, lucky thing.' Lottie patted Indigo's arm. 'Indi was brilliant. She drew caricatures of the girls who bullied me and plastered them over

the school. It's a bit hard to be mean when everyone's pointing at you and laughing at your picture.'

Indigo shrugged. 'Well, they say the pen is mightier than the sword.'

'Your pen was sharper as well as mightier,' Lottie said feelingly.

Now Lorenzo understood what an 'Indi Special' was. A personal, public and very pointed cartoon. And he had a nasty feeling what she'd make of him, given what she'd said to Lottie about coming from a world full of stuffed shirts.

'Can I be terribly rude and leave you two to introduce yourselves to each other properly?' Lottie asked.

'Of course,' Indigo said.

Her smile took his breath away. And Lorenzo was surprised to find himself feeling like a nervous schoolboy. 'I, um, need to apologise,' he said.

She raised an eyebrow. 'For what?'

'The way I behaved towards you earlier today.'

She shrugged. 'Don't worry about it.'

But he did worry about it. Good manners had been instilled into him virtually from when he was in the pram. He was always polite. And he'd been rude to her. 'I didn't realise you were a friend of the family, too.' He looked at her. 'Though you could have explained.'

'Why? For all I knew, you could've been a trespasser, too.'

'Touché.' He enjoyed the fact that she was back-chatting him. After all the people who agreed with everything he said and metaphorically tugged their forelocks at him, he found her free-spirited attitude refreshing. 'Gus says you're restoring the glass in the library.'

'Yes.'

'Forgive me for saying so, but you don't look like...' He

stopped. 'Actually, no. Just ignore me. I'm digging myself a huge hole here.'

She grinned, and the sparkle in her eyes made his pulse speed up a notch. 'I don't look like a glass restorer, you mean? Or I don't look the type to have been at school with Lottie?'

Both. Ouch. He grimaced. 'Um. Do I have to answer that?'

She looked delighted. 'So, let me see. Which shall we do first? School, I think.' Her voice dropped into the same kind of posh drawl as Lottie's. 'I met her when we were eleven. We were in the same dorm. And unfortunately we shared it with Lolly and Livvy. I suppose we could've been the four musketeers—except obviously I don't have an L in my name.'

'And it sounds as if you wouldn't have wanted to fight on the same side as Lolly and Livvy.'

'Absolutely not.' Her eyes glittered and her accent reverted back to what he guessed was normal for her. 'I don't have any time for spitefulness and bullying.'

'Good.' He paused. 'And I hope you didn't think I was bullying you, this morning.'

'If you'll kindly delete the file,' she mimicked.

He grimaced. How prissy she'd made him sound. 'I did apologise for that.'

'So are you a film star, or something?'

'No.'

'Well, you were acting pretty much like a D-list celeb, trying to be important,' she pointed out.

Should he tell her?

No. Because he didn't want her to lose that irreverence when she talked to him. He didn't think that Indigo Moran would bow and scrape to him; but he didn't want to take that risk. 'Guilty, m'lady,' he said lightly. 'Are you quite sure you're a glass restorer and not a barrister?'

She laughed. And, oh, her mouth was beautiful. He had the maddest urge to pull her into his arms and find out for himself whether her mouth tasted as good as it looked. Which was so not how he usually reacted to women. Lorenzo Torelli was always cool, calm and measured. He acted with his head rather than his heart, as he'd always been brought up to do. If you stuck to rigid formality, you always knew exactly where you were.

What was it about Indigo Moran that made him itch to break all his rules? And it was even crazier, because now absolutely wasn't the time to rebel against his upbringing. Not when he was about to become King of Melvante.

'I'm quite sure I'm a glass restorer. So were you expecting me to be about forty years older than I am, with a beard, John Lennon glasses, a bad haircut and sandals?'

Lorenzo couldn't help laughing. And then he realised that everyone in the room was staring at them.

'Sorry. I'm in the middle of making a fool of myself,' he said. 'Not to mention insulting Ms Moran here at least twice.'

'Call me Indigo,' she corrected quietly, and patted his shoulder. 'And he's making a great job of it,' she cooed.

'I, for one,' Gus's mother said with a chuckle, 'will look forward to seeing the drawing pinned up in the breakfast room.'

Indigo grinned. 'He hasn't earned one. Yet.'

'I'm working on it,' he said, enjoying the banter. How long had it been since he'd been treated with such irreverence?

Though a nasty thought whispered in his head: once he'd been crowned, would anyone ever treat him like this again, as if he was just an ordinary man? Would this be the last time?

'Indigo, may I sit with you at dinner?' he asked.

She spread her hands. 'Do what you like.'

Ironic. That was precisely what he couldn't do, from next month. He had expectations to fulfil. Schedules to meet. A country to run. Doing what he liked simply wasn't on the agenda. He would do what was expected of him. His duty.

CHAPTER TWO

WHEN THEY WERE called to dinner, Lorenzo switched the place settings so he was seated next to Indigo.

'Nicely finessed, Mr Torelli,' she said as he held her chair out for her.

Actually, he wasn't a Mr, but he had no intention of correcting her. 'Thank you,' he said. 'Your name's very appropriate for a stained-glass restorer.' Not to mention pretty. And memorable.

'Thank you.' She accepted the compliment gracefully.

'So how long have you been working with glass?'

'Since I was sixteen. I took some evening classes along with my A levels, and then I went to art college,' she explained.

Very focused for someone in her mid-teens. And hadn't Lottie said something about Indigo leaving their school at the age of fourteen? 'So you always knew what you wanted to do?'

She wrinkled her nose. 'It's a dreadfully pathetic story.'

'Tell me anyway,' he invited. 'It'll make me feel better when you savage me in one of your cartoons.'

'I was sent away to boarding school at the age of six.'

Lorenzo had been five years older than that when he'd been sent away, but he remembered the feeling. Leaving home, the place where you'd grown up and every centi-

metre was familiar, to live among strangers. In his case, it had been in a different country, too. With a child's perception, at the time he'd thought maybe he was being sent away as a punishment—that somehow he'd been to blame for his parents' fatal accident. Now he knew the whole truth, and realised it had been his grandparents' way of giving him some stability and protecting him from the potential fallout if the press had found out what had really happened. But it had still hurt back then to be torn away from his home.

'I hated it,' she said softly.

So had he.

'I cried myself to sleep every night.'

He would've done that, except boys weren't allowed to cry. They were supposed to keep a stiff upper lip. Even if they weren't English.

'The only thing that made school bearable was the chapel,' she said. 'It had these amazing stained-glass windows, and I loved the patterns that the light made on the floor when it shone through. I could just lose myself in that.'

For him, it had been music. The piano in one of the practice rooms in the music department. Where he could close his eyes and pretend he was playing Bach at home in the library. 'It helps if you can find something to get you through the hard times,' he said softly.

'I, um, tended to disappear a bit. One of my teachers found me in the chapel—they'd been looking for me for almost an hour. I thought she'd be angry with me, but she seemed to understand. She bought me some colouring pencils and a pad, and I found that I liked drawing. It made things better.'

He found himself wanting to give Indigo a hug. Not out of pity, but out of empathy. He'd been there, too. 'Why did

you decide to work with glass instead of being a satirical cartoonist?' he asked.

'Drawings are *flat*.' She wrinkled her nose. 'But glass… It's the way the colour works with the light. The way it can make you feel.'

Passion sparkled in her dark blue eyes; and Lorenzo suddenly wanted to see her eyes sparkle with passion for something else.

Which was crazy.

He wasn't in the market for a relationship. He had more than enough going on in his life, right now. And, even if he had been thinking about starting a relationship, a glass artist with a penchant for skewering people in satirical cartoons would be very far from the most sensible person he could choose to date.

Besides, for all he knew, she could already be involved with someone. A woman as beautiful as Indigo Moran would have men queuing up to date her.

'You really love your job, don't you?' he asked.

'Of course. Don't you?'

'I guess so,' he prevaricated. He'd never known anything else. He'd always grown up knowing that one day he'd become king. There wasn't an option not to love it. It was his duty. His destiny. No arguments.

'So what do you do?' she asked.

She really wasn't teasing him, then; she actually didn't know who he was. And he wasn't going to make things awkward or embarrass her by telling her. 'Family business,' he said. 'My grandfather's retiring, next month, so I'm taking over running things.' It was true. Just not the whole truth.

'Workaholic, hmm?'

He would be. But that was fine. He'd accepted that a long time ago. 'Yes.' Not wanting her to get too close to the subject, he switched the topic back to her work with glass.

* * *

When he smiled, Lorenzo Torelli was completely different. He wasn't the pompous idiot he'd been in the garden; he was beautiful, Indigo thought.

And she was seriously tempted to ask him to sit for her. He would be the perfect model for the window she was planning.

'If you're really interested in the glass,' she said, 'come and have a look at my temporary workshop after dinner.'

'I'd like that,' he said.

They continued chatting over dinner, and Indigo found her awareness of Lorenzo growing by the second. It wasn't just that she wanted to sketch him and paint him into glass; she also wanted to touch him.

Which was crazy.

Lorenzo Torelli was a total stranger. Although he seemed to be here on his own, for all she knew he could be married. And her radar to warn her that a man was married or totally wrong for her hadn't exactly worked in the past, had it? She'd made the biggest mistake of her life where Nigel was concerned.

Though at the same time she knew it wasn't fair to think that all men were liars and cheats who just abandoned people, like her ex and her father. Her grandfather hadn't been. Gus wasn't. And, from what Lottie had told her, their father had been a total sweetheart and had never even as much as looked at another woman. Though Indigo still found it hard to trust. Which was why she hadn't even flirted since Nigel, much less dated.

'Penny for them?' Lorenzo asked.

No way. She fell back on an old standby. 'When I'm about to start work on a new piece, I tend to be pretty much in another world.'

'There's nothing wrong with being focused on your work.'

Good. She was glad he understood that.

After coffee, he asked, 'Did you mean it about showing me your work?'

'Sure.' She took him through to the library. 'I guess it starts here. We took the window out this afternoon.'

'There's a facsimile of the window on the boards,' he said, sounding surprised.

'People come especially to Edensfield to see the mermaid window. I don't want to disappoint them by hiding everything behind scaffolding,' she explained. 'I went to Venice when they were doing some work on the Bridge of Sighs, and they'd put a facsimile of the bridge on the advertising hoardings. I thought that was a brilliant idea and I've tried to do something like that with my own work, ever since.'

'Good idea,' he said.

'Come and see the mermaid up close. She's gorgeous. Victorian—very much in the style of Burne-Jones, though she isn't actually one of his.'

He smiled. 'I was thinking earlier, if you'd been wearing a green velvet dress, you would look like a PRB model.'

'Thank you for the compliment.' She blushed, looking pleased. 'That's my favourite art movement.'

'Mine, too.' He almost told her that his family had a collection and that Burne-Jones had sketched his great-great-grandmother. But then he'd have to explain who he was, and he wasn't ready to do that yet.

'I'd love the chance to work on some PRB glass.' She gave a wistful smile. 'Maybe one day.' She led him into a room further down the corridor. 'Gus set up this room as my workshop. Obviously we've had to rope off my table

for health and safety purposes—I work with dangerous substances—but people can still talk to me and see what I'm doing. I have a camera on my desk and the picture feeds through to that screen over there, so they can see the close-up work in total safety.'

She was so matter-of-fact about it. 'Don't you mind working with an audience?' he asked. 'Doesn't it get in your way?'

'The house is only open for a few hours, four days a week,' she said with a shrug. 'The visitors won't be that much of a distraction.'

The window from the library had already been dismantled into frames; the one containing the mermaid was in the centre of her table.

'I took close-ups of the panel this afternoon so I have a complete photographic record,' she said. 'Next I'm going to take it apart, clean it all and start the repairs.'

'Which is why the camera's one of the tools of your trade.' He understood that now. 'I'm sorry I accused you of being a pap.'

'You've apologised—and nicely—so consider it forgotten.' She looked at him. 'Though if you really want to make it up to me, there is something you could do.'

Quid pro quo. It was a standard part of diplomacy. Though part of Lorenzo was disappointed that she'd asked. He'd thought that Indigo might be different. But maybe everyone had their price, after all. 'Which is?'

'Would you sit for me?'

He blinked. 'Sit for you?'

'So I can draw you.'

He'd already worked that out. 'Why?'

She spread her hands. 'Because you look like an angel.'

Heat spread through him. Was this her way of telling him that she was attracted to him? Did she feel the same

weird pull that he did? 'An angel?' He knew he was parroting what she said, but he didn't care if he sounded dim. He needed to find out where this was going.

'Or a medieval prince.'

That was rather closer to home. Though he thought her ignorance about his identity was totally genuine. 'And what would sitting for you involve?' he asked.

'Literally just sitting still while I sketch you. Though modelling is a bit hard on the muscles—having to sit perfectly still and keep the same expression for a minimum of ten minutes is a lot more difficult than most people think. So I'd be happy to compromise with taking photographs and working from them, if that makes it easier for you.'

Which was where this had all started. 'Is that why you took my photograph?'

She nodded. 'You were scowling like a dark angel. You were going to be perfect for Lucifer.'

'Why, thank you, Ms Moran,' he said dryly.

She grinned. 'It's meant as a compliment. Or you could be Gabriel, if you'd rather.'

'Didn't Gabriel have blond hair?'

'In the carol,' she said thoughtfully, 'his wings were drifts of snow, his eyes of flame.'

On impulse, he sang a snatch of the carol.

Her eyes widened. 'I wasn't expecting that. You have a lovely voice, Mr Torelli.'

'Thank you.' He bowed slightly in acknowledgement of the compliment.

'So will you sit for me?'

He was tempted. Seriously tempted. But it was all too complicated. 'Ask me another time,' he said softly. When he'd worked out how to say no while letting her down gently. 'Tell me about your work here. The mermaid's face is

damaged, so are you going to replace that bit of the glass with a copy?'

'I could do, but that would be a last resort. I want to keep as much of the original glass as possible.' She grimaced. 'I'd better shut up. I can bore for England on this subject.'

'No, I'm interested. Really.'

'Trust me, you don't want to hear me drone on about the merits of epoxy, silicon and copper foil,' she said dryly.

He smiled. 'OK. Tell me something else. What's the story behind the mermaid?'

She raised an eyebrow. 'Gus hasn't told you?'

'It's not exactly the kind of thing that comes up when you're a schoolboy,' he said, 'and since we left school I guess we've had other things to talk about.'

'Rebuke acknowledged,' she said.

He wrinkled his nose. 'That wasn't a rebuke.'

Maybe not. It hadn't been quite like the way he'd spoken to her in the garden, when he'd been all stuffy and pompous.

'Tell me about the mermaid,' he invited.

He really meant it, she realised in wonder. He actually wanted to hear what she had to say. 'So the story goes, many years ago the Earl was a keen card-player. He won against almost everyone—except one night, when he played against a tall, dark stranger. It turned out that the stranger was the devil, and his price for letting the earl keep the house and the money he'd wagered and lost was marriage to the earl's daughter. The earl agreed, but his daughter wasn't too happy about it and threw herself into the lake. She was transformed into a mermaid and lived happily ever after.'

'I thought mermaids were supposed to live in the sea,' Lorenzo said.

She grinned. 'Tut, Mr Torelli. Hasn't anyone told you that mermaids don't actually exist? Lottie says there's a version of the story that has the mermaid rescued by a handsome prince, but that might be a bit of a mix-up with the Hans Christian Andersen story.'

'I hope not, because if I remember rightly that doesn't have a very happy ending.'

Lorenzo's eyes were very dark. Beautiful. She itched to paint him, to capture that expression. If only he hadn't said no. Or maybe she could paint him from memory.

He reached over and wound one of her curls round the end of his finger. 'I can see you as a mermaid, with this amazing hair floating out behind you,' he said softly.

Oh, help. That sensual awareness of him over dinner had just gone up several notches. It would be so easy to tip her head back and invite him to kiss her...but that would be such a stupid thing to do.

Indigo was about to take a step backwards. Just to be safe. But then Lorenzo leaned closer and brushed his mouth against hers.

His kiss was sweet and almost shy at first, a gentle brush of his mouth against hers that made every single one of her nerve-ends tingle. And then he did it again. And again, teasing her and coaxing her into sliding her hands into his hair and letting him deepen the kiss.

Indigo had had her fair share of kisses in the past, but nothing like this. Even Nigel, the man she'd once believed was the love of her life, hadn't been able to make her feel like this—drowsy and sensual, and as if her knees were going to give way at any second.

When Lorenzo stopped kissing her, she held on to him, not trusting her knees to hold her up. The last thing she wanted to do was fall at his feet and make an idiot of herself.

Though she had a nasty feeling that she'd already done that.

'We really ought to get back to the others,' she said.

'Are you worried that they'll think you lured me here for other reasons than to talk about glass?'

'No.' She could feel the colour seeping into her face. 'Don't be ridiculous. They all know how I am about my work. They probably think I'm boring the pants off you right now.'

He gave her a slow and very insolent smile. 'Interesting choice of phrase, Ms Moran.'

Her face heated even more. Because now she could see herself taking his clothes off. Very, very slowly. And not because she wanted to paint him naked: because she wanted to touch him. Skin to skin. Very, very slowly. Until he was begging her for more.

Oh, for pity's sake. She'd only just been introduced to him. Insta-lust wasn't the way she did things. Why was she reacting to him like this? 'Let's go back,' she said, hoping she didn't sound as flustered as she felt.

'Has Indi been showing you what she's doing with the mermaid?' Gus asked Lorenzo when they rejoined the others in the drawing room.

'Yes.'

'She's brilliant. Maybe you ought to commission her to do you a portrait for the coronation. Glass instead of oils,' Gus suggested.

Indigo frowned. 'Coronation? Whose coronation?'

Gus looked embarrassed. 'Whoops. I think I might have just put my foot in it.'

'It's fine,' Lorenzo said.

Oh, no, it wasn't, Indigo thought. There was a lot more to this than met the eye. Especially as Lorenzo looked shifty, all of a sudden.

They chatted for a few moments more; when they were alone again, Indigo narrowed her eyes at him. 'What's this about a coronation?'

'The King of Melvante is abdicating next month and handing over to his grandson,' Lorenzo said.

She still didn't get it. Why had Gus suggested that Indigo should do Lorenzo's portrait in glass? 'And?' she prompted.

He wrinkled his nose. 'That would be, um, me.'

'You're going to be the King of Melvante?'

He nodded. 'Nonno's already passed on a lot of his duties to me. And he's going to be eighty, next month. I want him to enjoy his old age, not have the burden of the crown.'

'So that's what you meant about the family business. Being king.'

He shrugged. 'Running a country isn't so different from running a business.'

Even so, she was hurt that nobody had told her. Lottie was her closest friend, and she'd known the family for years. Lorenzo obviously thought that she'd tell tales to the media, but surely Lottie's family knew otherwise?

A king-to-be.

No wonder he'd been sensitive about having his photo taken, and no wonder he hadn't wanted to sit for her.

This changed everything.

When he'd kissed her, only minutes before, she'd thought this just might be the start of something. How stupid of her. No way could a king-to-be have a fling with someone like her. OK, so strictly speaking Indigo's father was an earl, so it wasn't so much the noble and commoner thing; but he'd been married to his countess when Indigo was born and not to Indigo's mother. The press would drag that up if they found out she was even vaguely involved with Lorenzo. Plus there was the whole mess of her rela-

tionship with Nigel and the way he'd let her down. That would look bad, too. A king couldn't afford to be touched by scandal.

So her common sense needed to kick back in, and fast. Absolutely nothing was going to happen between them now.

It *couldn't*.

'I'll make sure I address you properly in future, Your Highness,' she said coolly. 'It's a pity you didn't bother to tell me before.'

'It wasn't relevant. You're a friend of the family and so am I. Who we are outside Edensfield isn't important.'

'You still could've told me.'

'How? Was I supposed to correct you and tell you that, actually, no I'm not *Mr* Torelli, and it should be "Your Royal Highness Prince Lorenzo" to you?' He grimaced. 'Talk about an arrogant show-off.'

She blew out a breath. 'I guess you have a point. I understand now why you were annoyed with me for taking your photograph.'

'Because I try to protect my privacy—not because I think I'm a celeb or a special snowflake who deserves red carpet treatment,' he said.

Her frown deepened. 'What about your bodyguards? I assume you have them, and they're so discreet that I haven't noticed them yet.'

'I get a little bit more liberty than usual from my security team because I'm staying in the house of a family friend,' he said.

'But you still can't do anything spontaneous or even go for a walk without telling half a dozen people where you're going. Your life must be scheduled out down to the millisecond.'

'Most of the time, yes,' he admitted. 'But I'm officially

on leave at the moment. Taking a bit of time to get my head in the right place, so to speak.'

'Before you're crowned king.'

'Yes. Obviously I'm not entirely neglecting my duties while I'm here—I can do a lot of things through the internet and the phone—but Nonno thought I needed a bit of time out to prepare myself.'

'Your grandfather,' she said, 'sounds very sensible.' Like hers had been. 'But forgive me for being dim. I don't tend to read the society pages, so I really had absolutely no idea who you were.'

'You,' he said, 'are the last person I'd accuse of being dim.'

'You only met me today. I could be an airhead.'

He raised an eyebrow. 'Give me some credit for being able to judge someone's character quickly and accurately.'

'I guess in your position you have to do that all the time.' She paused. 'So how come you're taking over, and not your father?'

'He died in a car crash when I was ten,' Lorenzo said. 'Along with my mother.'

She could see the pain in his eyes, and then he was all urbane and charming again. Behind a mask. Clearly it hurt too much to talk about. She could understand that; there were certain bits of her own past that she didn't talk about.

'I'm sorry,' she said softly. 'That must've been hard for you. And for your grandparents.'

'It was a long time ago, now,' he said. 'You get used to it.'

'Yes, you do.'

'That sounds like experience talking,' he said.

She nodded. 'My grandparents brought me up.' She couldn't quite bring herself to tell him of the circumstances, not wanting him to pity her.

'Something we have in common,' he said.

Not quite. She didn't think that Lorenzo's parents were

like hers, choosing to abandon their child. In his case, his parents had been taken from him in an accident. In hers, her father had chosen to distance himself before she was born—his only contribution to her life had been to pay for part of her education—and her mother had been more focused on her own love-life than family life. 'Just about the only thing.'

He smiled. 'Sometimes that makes life more interesting.'

And more complicated, she thought. Lorenzo Torelli was gorgeous. The way he'd kissed her earlier had made her bones melt. Which meant she needed to keep a safe distance between them until he left Edensfield for his kingdom. 'I guess I ought to stop monopolising you and let you chat to everyone else. And I have a few things I need to do for work, so I'd better get a move on. Nice to have met you. Good evening,' she said.

He gave her a tiny little smile that very clearly called her a chicken. Guilty as charged, she thought—because he scared her as much as he drew her. She couldn't afford to let him matter to her.

Besides, a man destined to be king would've been taught how to be charming from when he was in the cradle. The attention he'd paid her had been flattery. And she already knew the dark side of flattery—the last time she'd let herself fall for a spiel, it had ended in tears. She'd learned the hard way that relationships let her down, but her work never did.

'Good evening, Indigo,' he said softly, and she fled.

CHAPTER THREE

INDIGO WASN'T IN the breakfast room when Lorenzo came downstairs, the next morning. And when he casually mentioned her name, Gus just smiled. 'She's even more of a workaholic than you are. She'll have been in her workroom since the crack of dawn.'

Lorenzo knew that he ought to be sensible and avoid Indigo. But the attraction from last night hadn't gone away. So he couldn't resist taking a detour to the kitchen, making her a mug of coffee and wandering casually into her workroom. Just to say hello, he told himself. There couldn't be any harm in that. Could there?

Today Indigo was back to wearing shapeless clothes and having her hair pinned back, and she was also wearing a pair of safety goggles. This had to be the most unsexy outfit in the world. And yet Lorenzo was aware of every drop of blood thrumming through his veins when she glanced up from her work and saw him.

'I thought you might like this,' he said, and handed her the mug. 'Milk, no sugar.'

'Thank you.' She pushed the goggles up on top of her head. 'How do you know how I like my coffee?'

'I noticed yesterday at dinner,' he said. He'd been taught from an early age to notice the details. 'Do you need a hand

with anything?' It was a stupid question, and he knew it even as the words came out.

'Thank you,' she said, 'but, apart from the fact that my work needs specialist training, I work with acids, flux, a hot soldering iron, sharp blades and glass—all things that could do serious damage to you.'

'I guess so.'

'Even if I didn't have bad intentions towards you—and, just for the record if you happen to be wired and your security team's listening, I don't—there's still the risk of an accident. My insurance company would have a hissy fit at the idea.'

He liked the fact that she'd clearly thought this through. Though it also surprised him that Indigo Moran had such a deeply conventional side, given the dress she'd worn last night. 'And that bothers you? I thought you had a reputation for being a free spirit.'

'Which isn't the same as being reckless and stupid,' she said. 'What do you expect me to do—jump into a lake and pull you in with me?'

He laughed. 'Point taken. No, I don't think you're stupid.' He paused. 'So can I watch you work, today?' he asked.

She looked surprised. 'Are you really interested in glass, are you being polite, or are you just bored and at a bit of a loose end?'

He liked her plain speaking. But either they could spend all day fencing, or he could come clean. Given how little time he had left here, he chose the latter option. 'It's an excuse to spend time with you. And I have a feeling it might be the same for you, too.'

She looked wary. 'I'm not so sure that it's a good idea.'

At least she hadn't denied that she wanted to spend time with him. So he could be just as honest with her. 'I *know* it isn't a good idea,' he said softly.

She said nothing, just looked even warier.

'If I wasn't who I am, would your answer be different?'

'Probably,' she admitted.

'Do you have any idea how refreshing it was yesterday,' he said, 'to have someone backchat me and treat me like a normal person, for once?'

'Poor little rich boy,' she said, folding her arms and giving him a pointed look.

He grinned. 'And you're still doing it. I like you, Indigo. I think you like me. What's the harm in two people getting to know each other?'

'As you pointed out yesterday, you're used to the paparazzi following you. You have a security team looking after you. You're not just a normal person. If anyone wants to get to know you, or you want to get to know someone, then the whole world will know about it.'

'This is a private house,' he said.

'Which is open to the public,' she reminded him.

'Who won't be expecting to see me—they might think, oh, that man sitting by the table over there looks a bit like that Prince Lorenzo guy, but they'll think no more than that.'

'What if they do recognise you?'

'They won't,' he said confidently. 'It's like when that famous violin player busked on the metro in Washington DC a few years ago, playing a Stradivarius. People weren't expecting a famous musician to be busking on the metro with one of the most expensive instruments in the world, so they didn't recognise him and hardly anyone stopped to listen to what he was playing. It's all about context.'

'You,' she said, 'are just used to getting your own way all the time.'

'Not *all* the time.'

'Did you get an A star in persistence lessons at prince school?' she asked.

He laughed. 'There isn't such a thing as prince school. Besides, you know very well I went to the same school as Gus.'

'In a different country, and when you were still very young,' she said thoughtfully.

'Not as young as you were when you went to boarding school—I was eleven.' And how he'd missed his family. Thought it had been good practice for his stiff upper lip. 'I know this is crazy,' he said. 'I just want to spend a bit of time with you. I have a free day, but I know you're working, so maybe I could make myself useful. Kind of multi-tasking.'

She scoffed. 'You're telling me that a man can multi-task?'

'Don't be sexist.' He grinned at her. 'I learned how to multi-task at prince school.'

She laughed, then. 'Says the man who claims that prince school doesn't exist.'

'They're not formal lessons, exactly, but over the years I've been taught about the importance of diplomacy and how to…' He wrinkled his nose. 'I was going to say, how to handle people, but I think you might take that the wrong way.'

Her blush was gratifying. 'Yes. I would.'

'I don't mean manhandle,' he said softly. 'That's not who I am. I'm not expecting you to fall into my arms because I'm about to become the King of Melvante. But I can't stop thinking about you. And I think it's the same for you, too. That kiss, last night…' He paused. 'I don't behave like that. I don't usually act on impulse and I definitely don't do insta-lust. I'm pretty sure you don't, either.'

'No.' Again, she blushed. Telling him that maybe, just maybe, it was different with him.

'It would be sensible if we just stayed out of each other's way. But I can't do that. Something about you...' He blew out a breath. 'OK. I'll shut up and stop distracting you now.'

'Maybe,' she said quietly, 'if you wear goggles, that'll be enough to disguise you. And you need to wear goggles anyway if you're going to be on this side of the rope. I don't want you to get a glass splinter or dust in your eye. And you need gloves, too, if you're going to work with me.' She reached under her table and rummaged around in a box. 'Try these.'

They fitted perfectly. Which was a sign, of sorts, he thought. 'They're fine.'

'OK.' She handed him a pair of protective glasses, and he put them on.

'What do you need me to do?' he asked.

'Help me clean the lead cames. That'd be easy to teach you.'

'I'd like that,' he said. It was so far away from his normal life that it really was like having a rest.

He watched her work, fascinated by how neatly and quickly she worked to remove the stained glass from the leads without damaging the fragile glass or the soft metal. And he noticed how she labelled everything before putting it in a specific place and then photographing it.

'I assume that's to be sure everything goes back in the right place?' he asked.

She nodded. 'Plus I'm documenting everything that I do, so the next time the glass needs work the restorer will know exactly what I've done and how.'

Her work was methodical, neat and efficient. She was good at giving instructions, too; when she showed him how to clean the leads, she gave him an old piece of lead from her box of tricks under her desk so he could practise first,

and corrected his technique without making him feel stupid. Lorenzo liked the fact that she was so direct and clear.

And when the house opened to the public, he discovered that Indigo was far from being the socially inept nerd she'd claimed to be. She was seriously good with people; she was patient, charming, and he noticed that she assessed them swiftly so she could work out whether they wanted a quick and simple answer, or if they'd prefer a longer and more detailed explanation.

Lorenzo noticed how patient Indigo was, never once making her questioners feel stupid or a nuisance. If anything, she went out of her way to make them feel appreciated.

Funny, all the formal training he'd had in diplomacy didn't even begin to approach this. Indigo was a natural with people, warm and open, and the rigidity of boarding school clearly hadn't left its mark on her. Lorenzo knew that she could teach him a lot, just by letting him shadow her. And maybe if he could focus on that, on the way that Indigo could help him prepare for his new role, it would stop him thinking of her in a different context. One that would cause too many problems for both of them.

Once the crowds had left, Lorenzo fetched them both some more coffee.

She looked up at him and smiled. 'Thank you—that's really kind of you. Sorry, I'm afraid I've rather ignored you this afternoon.'

'You were busy working and talking to visitors,' he said. 'And I have to say, I'm impressed by how at ease you are with people.'

She looked surprised. 'But you're a prince. You have to talk to people all the time. Aren't you at ease with them?'

'Not in the same way that you are,' he admitted. 'You

have this natural empathy.' And, because he was so used to formality, he had to work at being at ease with people. Which pretty much negated the point.

'I'm surprised they didn't teach you that sort of thing at prince school.'

He rolled his eyes. 'Very funny.'

'I still think you'd make an awesome model for a stained-glass angel,' she said. 'Though I can understand why you don't want to sit for me.'

'It's not that I don't want to. I *can't*. In another life,' he said softly, 'I'd sit for you with pleasure.' And he'd enjoy watching her sketch him, seeing the way she caught the tip of her tongue between her teeth when she was concentrating. And then maybe afterwards...

'But in this life it'd be a PR nightmare,' she said, going straight to the root of the matter. 'The new King of Melvante has to be squeaky clean.'

'Yes.' Until he'd met Indigo, that hadn't been a problem. But Indigo Moran made him want to break every single one of his rules and then some. To stop himself thinking about it, and to distract her from probing his thoughts too deeply, he made an exaggerated squeaking noise. 'Like this.'

She laughed. And, to his relief, everything felt smooth and light and sparkly again.

'I'd better let you get on. You've had enough distractions for today.'

She smiled at him again. 'You can stay if you want to.'

Tempting. So very, very tempting. And he wanted to spend more time with Indigo. He liked this side of her, the fun and the carefree feeling he didn't normally have time for.

But he really needed to let his common sense get back in charge. Preferably right now. He was supposed to be

preparing for his new role, not acting on impulse and indulging himself. 'Thanks, but I'll see you later, OK?' And then, hopefully, the next time he saw her he'd be back in sensible mode and he'd be able to treat her as just another acquaintance. He could be charming and witty, but he could keep his emotions totally in check.

And what he needed more than anything else, right now, was a little time at the ancient grand piano in the library.

Now the visitors had gone and the house was back to being fully private, the family dogs had the free run of the place again, so a couple of minutes after Lorenzo had settled at the piano he discovered that Toto, an elderly golden Labrador he'd known since puppyhood, was leaning against his leg. Just like home, except with a bigger dog, he thought with a smile, and reached down to ruffle the dog's fur. And then he lost himself in the music.

Indigo could hear piano music. Which was odd, because she had a very quiet cello concerto playing on her iPod. She reached over and paused the track, and listened again. Definitely a piano, but not something she recognised.

The piece stopped, and there was silence for a moment, before a snatch of something, and then a pause and a few bars of something else, as if someone was trying to decide what to play next.

Curious, Indigo made sure that all her electrical equipment was turned off and her pots of acid all had lids on, and went in search of the music. As she neared the library, the music got louder. She paused in the doorway of the library. Lorenzo was sitting at the piano; from her vantage point, she could see that his eyes were closed as he was playing.

In another life, she thought, this could've been his career. Though he didn't have the luxury of choice.

When he'd finished, she clapped softly, and Lorenzo opened his eyes and stared at her in surprise.

'What are you doing here?' he asked.

'I heard the music,' she said simply.

He grimaced. 'Sorry. I didn't mean to disturb you.'

'I was going to have a break anyway.' She paused. 'You're very good.'

'Thank you.'

Lorenzo accepted the compliment gracefully, even a little bit shyly. Indigo had the strongest feeling that this was a part of himself that he normally kept hidden. She couldn't resist asking, 'Would you play some more for me?'

'I...' He gave her another of those shy smiles that made her heart contract. 'Sure, if you want. Take a seat.'

She heeled off her shoes and curled up on a corner of the battered leather chesterfield sofa. The Labrador came over and put a paw on one of the cushions, clearly intending to lever himself up next to her.

'Toto, you bad hound, you know you're not allowed on the furniture,' she scolded him.

The dog gave her a mournful look and she sighed and slid off the chesterfield onto the floor. 'All right, then, I'll come down and sit with you.'

He wagged his tail, licked her face and then sprawled over her.

'And you're much too big to be a lapdog,' she said, but she rubbed the dog's tummy anyway and he gave her a look of absolute bliss.

'You like dogs?' Lorenzo asked. Then he rolled his eyes. 'That was a stupid question, because the answer's obvious.'

'I love them. But my work takes me all over the place and not everyone's comfortable with dogs, so I can't have one of my own. I come and borrow Lottie and Gus's every so often.' She paused. 'I see you didn't mind Toto lean-

ing against your leg while you were playing. I take it you like dogs, too?'

He nodded. 'I have dogs at home, but mine are a little smaller than Toto.'

She grinned. 'Prince Lorenzo, please don't tell me you have a Chihuahua.'

'And carry it around with me in a basket?' He laughed. 'No. We have various spaniels. And although they're nearly as old as Toto, they're not quite as well behaved. They sneak up onto the furniture as soon as you've looked away. Especially Caesar. He's my shadow when I'm at home.'

And she could tell that he didn't really mind. Which made him seem so much more human. A king who didn't necessarily expect all his subjects to obey him and would indulge an elderly and much-loved dog.

'What do you want me to play?' he asked.

'Anything you like,' she said, and listened intently as he ran through several pieces.

'That was fabulous,' she said when he'd finished. 'When you said last night that it helped to get through tough times if you had something... It was music for you, wasn't it?'

He nodded, and she had to stop herself from walking over to the piano and hugging him. She didn't want him to think she was pitying him; but she could understand how a lonely little boy, far from his home and his family, needed to take refuge in something. She'd been there herself. 'Did you ever think about being a musician?'

He shrugged. 'It wasn't exactly an option. My job's been mapped out for me pretty much since I was born.'

She frowned. 'Doesn't that make you feel trapped?'

'It's my duty and I'm not going to let anyone down.'

She noticed that he hadn't actually answered the question. Which told her far more than if he'd tried to bluff his way out of it. She knew she'd feel trapped, in his shoes.

Stuck in a formal, rigid culture where you were expected to know every single rule off by heart and abide by them all. Stifling. She'd hate it even more than she'd hated the rigidity of boarding school.

'If you could do whatever you wanted, what would you do?' she asked softly.

'Anything I wanted?' His eyes were very, very dark.

'Uh-huh.'

'Right here and right now?'

She nodded.

'I'd do this.' He got up from the piano stool, walked over to her, drew her to her feet, wrapped her in his arms and kissed her.

Just like last night. Except it was more intense because, this time, she knew how perfectly his mouth fitted against hers. How his touch made her pulse beat faster. How *right* it felt.

Oh, help.

She really didn't want Lorenzo to know how much he affected her. After the way Nigel had betrayed her trust and abandoned her, she didn't want to be that vulnerable ever again. Hopefully being a little sarcastic with him would defuse the situation and make her feel more in control again.

She fanned herself with one hand. 'You're not too shabby at this, Your Royal Highness,' she drawled. 'Did they teach you this at prince school, too?'

He narrowed his eyes at her. 'Indigo, will you please shut up about prince school?'

But her idea of a defence mechanism turned out to be a total failure, because then he kissed her again, tiny nibbling kisses that inflamed her senses and left her breathless. And she ended up kissing him right back.

This had to stop. Now. 'Had a lot of practice, have we?'

It didn't seem to faze him in the slightest. 'That'd be

telling, and a prince should never kiss and tell,' he shot back. 'You talk way too much, Indigo Moran.' He caught her lower lip between his, sending her pulse skyrocketing again. 'But, since you clearly want to talk—let's talk about last night,' he said. 'At dinner. That dress.'

She frowned. 'What was wrong with my dress?'

'Nothing.' He sighed. 'Apart from the fact that it made me want to pick you up, haul you over my shoulder in a fireman's lift, and carry you to my bed.'

Which put another set of pictures in her head.

If he carried on like this, she was going to do something seriously stupid.

'Droit de seigneur?' she asked.

'No.' He kissed her again. 'For the record, I don't believe in forcing anyone to do anything they don't want to do. Being a troglodyte and carrying you off to my bed is—' he licked his lower lip '—well, a fantasy. Which I would only do if you liked the idea, too.'

Now he'd said it like that, she could really picture it. And what would come after, too...

She shivered.

'What's the matter, Indigo?' he asked softly.

'You've just made it hard for me to breathe,' she admitted.

'Good. Now you know how that dress made me feel last night. And your shoes. I noticed just how long your legs are. And if you'd had any idea how much I wanted to touch you...' He traced the outline of her mouth with the tip of his forefinger. It made her tingle all over and she couldn't help parting her lips in response.

And then he actually grinned.

Oh, *really*? she thought. He honestly believed he had more self-control than she did? Well, two could play at that. She held his gaze, then sucked the tip of his finger into her mouth.

Instantly his pupils dilated and there was a slash of colour in his cheeks.

'Touché,' he whispered. 'Indigo, we need to stop this. Now.' He dragged in a breath. 'It wouldn't be fair or honourable of me to lead you on. I'm going back to Melvante soon. My life's going to change out of all recognition.'

Of course it was.

He looked tortured. 'I can't offer you a future.'

'I know. And even if you could, I'd be the worst person you could ask,' she said. What with the scandal surrounding her birth, and the fact that she'd been naive enough to trust Nigel and not work out for herself that he was already married, she was totally unsuitable even to be a king's mistress. 'I take it you need to find yourself a princess.' Which would put her totally out of the running. Not that she wanted the formal, rigid life of a royal family.

He rolled his eyes. 'I probably do have to choose a bride within the next six months, yes. And she probably has to be from a noble family. Though, just for the record, I don't care if your parents aren't aristocrats. It's how you treat other people that matters to me, not how many coronets are in your family tree.'

'Actually, my father's an earl.' He looked surprised, and honesty made Indigo add, 'The problem is, though, he was still married to his countess when he had a fling with my mother and she fell pregnant with me.'

'So that's why you ended up at the same school as Lottie?' he asked.

'It was my father's idea of providing for me,' she said dryly.

'Money instead of attention?'

He'd hit the nail right on the head. 'My father and I are never quite sure if we ought to acknowledge each other or not,' she said. 'I don't want to hurt his family by claiming

him as kin—I mean, I'm the child of an affair, and it'd be horrible to rub their noses in that. It wasn't their fault that he behaved badly. So it's easier...' She sighed. 'Well, for me not to acknowledge him and for him to pretend that I don't really exist.'

'But that hurts you.'

Did it still show? Or was Lorenzo just particularly perceptive? She shrugged. 'I'm lucky: my grandparents loved me. I was never deprived of love, if that's what you're thinking.'

'But your grandparents let you go to boarding school at such a young age?'

'They didn't exactly have a lot of choice. My grandmother wasn't very well at the time—they had enough on their plates without having to look after a small child.'

He frowned. 'What about your mother? Why didn't she look after you?'

She blew out a breath. 'You might as well know the worst. When it was obvious that the earl wasn't going to leave his wife for my mother, she left me with her parents and bolted.' She looked away. 'With someone else's husband.'

Lorenzo knew first-hand what kind of damage affairs could cause. Collateral damage, too. His own mother's affair had blown his whole world apart. If she'd been able to cope with life in the royal family, then she wouldn't have had the affair—and his father wouldn't have reacted by driving their car into a wall. And just maybe he would've grown up with both his parents, in a happy family, and it would've been another thirty years before he'd had to think about becoming king.

Or maybe it would've been a different kind of unhappy childhood, with his parents always arguing in private and

pretending everything was just fine and dandy where the public was concerned.

Not that he was going to tell Indigo about that. He didn't talk about the scars on his heart to anyone. Ever. 'That's tough on you.'

She shrugged. 'As I said, my grandparents loved me.'

The implication was clear: her mother hadn't. 'Do you see your mother now?'

Indigo shook her head. 'She ended up in a yachting accident with Married Man Number Four. She drowned. All I have of my mother are photographs and some very fleeting memories.'

It was the same for Lorenzo. Photographs and fleeting memories. Except nobody knew the true circumstances of his parents' accident. Nobody except his grandfather and their legal adviser. They wouldn't have told him the truth, except some papers had been misfiled and he'd come across them when he was eighteen and discovered the truth for himself. He'd gone off the rails for a week, shocked to the core that his father could've done something so terrible. The paparazzi had taken a picture of him looking haggard and with the worst hangover in the history of the universe; and then his grandfather had hauled him back to the palace, had a very honest and frank discussion with him, and Lorenzo had reassumed his stiff upper lip.

'That's tough on you,' he said again.

'It was tougher,' she said, 'proving to everyone that I wasn't like my mother.'

Yeah. He knew all about that, too—having to convince his grandfather that he wasn't like his father.

'Especially when I wanted to leave boarding school. But I hated the rigidity of the place, and the sense of entitlement that so many of the girls had.'

'What did you do?' he asked.

'Gave my father a business plan,' she said. 'If I went to a normal state school at the age of fourteen, he'd save four years of fees—which would be enough to buy my grandparents' cottage. If he let them live there rent-free for the rest of their lives, then he'd get his investment back when he sold the cottage. Win-win. He got money, and I got freedom.'

Lorenzo's heart bled for her. How could her father have been so cold-blooded that she had to offer him a business plan as a way out of a school that she hated? 'And he agreed to it?'

'Yes.'

For a second, he saw pain in her eyes.

And then she grinned. 'I told him the alternative was that I'd behave so badly, I'd get thrown out of every boarding school in England. But he knew I was right. And I proved to my grandparents that I wasn't like my mother. I wasn't running away, I was making the right choice. I got a weekend job in the local supermarket as soon as I was old enough, and a bar job to keep me going through art college until I graduated.'

'And you got a First?' he asked.

She inclined her head. 'I made my grandparents proud of me before they died.'

Though her father had obviously not acknowledged her achievements. 'Indi. I'm not pitying you, but right now I want to hug you,' he said.

'It's OK. I'm a big girl. I learned to deal with it years ago.' She shrugged. 'It's the earl's loss, not mine.'

And what an idiot the man was, not realising what a treasure he had in Indigo.

Lorenzo stole another kiss. 'Indigo. Will you please tell me to stop this?'

She kissed him back. 'Colour me bad, Your Royal Highness, but what's the alternative to stopping?'

His breath hitched. 'I think you've just spiked my blood pressure. Are you suggesting…?'

'We both know where we stand. You're about to take over from your grandfather and become king. You don't have time for a relationship. I have an empire to build with my business—I don't have time for a relationship, either.' She paused. This was crazy. But, at the same time, it was safe, because what she was proposing involved a time limit. Which meant she wouldn't get involved with him. 'I'm here until the end of the month. You said you don't have to go back to Melvante for a little while. Are you staying here until you go back?'

'Yes.'

'So we're in a private house. Among friends who would never rat us out to the press. Lottie's my oldest friend, and I'm guessing that Gus is one of your oldest friends, too.'

'He is. And I trust him totally.' He lifted her hand to his face and pressed his lips against her wrist, feeling the way her pulse beat hard against his mouth. Indigo Moran was everything he couldn't have. A breath of fresh air. Vibrant and lively. Totally unsuitable. And he knew without having to ask that she'd hate his world just as much as his mother had. This was never going to work.

Yet, at the same time, neither of them could deny the attraction between them.

'So you're suggesting we have a fling,' he said slowly.

'A *mad* fling,' she corrected. 'Because we both know that, although we're attracted to each other, in the real world we're not remotely suitable for each other. So we go into this with our eyes open. And we both walk away at the end of it. Intact.'

Which told him someone had walked away from her before, and left her very far from intact. 'It feels a bit— well, dishonourable. To offer you just a fling.' Especially

now he knew about her background. She was the child of a fling, and she'd paid the price by losing a whole generation of her family.

'Lorenzo, I'm not suitable marriage material for you, so you're not in a position to offer me anything else,' she pointed out. 'Which means either we have to spend the next couple of weeks having a lot of cold showers and trying to avoid each other, or…' Her breath caught. 'Just for the record, I don't normally proposition men.'

He stole another kiss. 'I already know that. Despite that dress you were wearing last night, you're not the type. And I'm very flattered that you should proposition me.'

Her eyes narrowed. 'But you're going to say no.'

'My head's telling me that this is a bad idea,' he said. 'But…' He blew out a breath. 'I don't do this sort of thing, either. I'm just a boring businessman.'

'You're a king in waiting,' she corrected.

'Same difference. Running a country's the same as running a business. It's just a slightly different scale.' He shrugged. 'Indigo, I always act with my head. I think things through and I look at all the options. I never do anything on impulse.' Not since that week of getting seriously drunk—and he hadn't touched brandy ever again after that. 'Yet I can't stop thinking about you. And kissing you just now was more impulsive than I've been in years.' He leaned his forehead against hers. 'Have you ever wanted something so much, you feel as if you're going to implode?'

She didn't answer; and he was pretty sure it had something to do with the man who'd walked away from her.

Which was precisely what he was going to have to do.

And he didn't want to hurt her. Though he had a feeling that it might already be too late for that. She'd been rejected by her father, dumped at boarding school, and left

in pieces when someone she loved had walked away from her. The fact that she'd been brave enough to suggest a fling also meant she'd made herself vulnerable.

He pulled back just enough to drop a kiss on her forehead. 'Cold showers and avoidance it is.'

'I'm not so sure that's going to work. I have pictures in my head. And I think you do, too.' She moistened her lower lip with the tip of her tongue, and he was near to hyperventilating. He really wanted to kiss her again.

'Indigo, I'm trying really hard to maintain control, here.'

'What if you didn't have to?' She stroked his face, and he turned his head to press a kiss into her palm. 'What if you could be whoever you wanted to be, just for, say, one night?'

'What scares me,' he admitted, 'is that I don't think one night with you would be enough.'

'A week, then. A fortnight. Maybe until you go back to Melvante. Look, you can still do whatever it is you planned to do here—spending time with Gus, thinking things through, sorting out kingly strategies. And I have work to do on the window. I'm not going to back out of my business commitments.' She paused. 'But, in between the business stuff, there are spaces.'

He could see what she meant. 'Spaces where we can just be.'

'Together,' she confirmed softly.

He sat down on the chesterfield and pulled her onto his lap. 'Your arguments are very persuasive, Ms Moran.'

She inclined her head. 'Why, thank you, Your Royal Highness.'

'Though I still feel dishonourable, offering you nothing but a fling.'

'They're the only kind of terms that either of us is in a position to offer,' she pointed out. 'So it's your choice,

Lorenzo. Cold showers—or this.' She cupped his face in her hands and skimmed her mouth against his.

His lips tingled where her skin touched his, and he couldn't help tightening his arms round her and responding to her kiss in kind.

'This,' he said when he could finally drag his mouth away from hers. *'This.'*

CHAPTER FOUR

ALTHOUGH INDIGO WENT back to her work when she left the library, she found herself stopping often to think about Lorenzo. She still couldn't quite believe what they'd agreed to. Since when did she do anything crazy like this? After Nigel's betrayal and the way her life had collapsed, two years ago, she'd kept all her relationships strictly platonic.

And now she was about to have a mad fling with a man who was about to become king.

Mad being the operative word, she thought wryly.

It took her ages to choose what to wear for dinner. At home, Indigo didn't bother changing for dinner—there wasn't much point when her meal was a hastily grabbed snack and she was going straight back to work for the rest of the evening. But she knew that Lottie's family always dressed for dinner, and when she stayed at Edensfield she always tried to fit in, so as not to embarrass her friend.

Last night's dress had made Lorenzo want to be a troglodyte and carry her off to his room.

Tonight, then, she'd wear something more demure. Something that would give him the chance to change his mind, maybe. Because she was pretty sure that one of them needed a dose of common sense, and right at that moment she didn't think she was the one who'd get it. So she picked a dress that one of her friends from art college had made

as a prototype Edwardian costume and then presented to her because it practically had her name written over it: a midnight-blue velvet creation with a high scooped neck and cap sleeves, which came down to her ankles and was teamed with a silk sash in the same colour, a chunky faux-pearl necklace and a matching bracelet.

And hopefully seeing Lorenzo in a dinner jacket—looking a bit too much like the actor who played James Bond for her comfort—wouldn't make her do anything rash...

Lorenzo knew the second that Indigo walked into the room, but he forced himself not to turn round and stare at her.

They hadn't yet discussed whether they were keeping their mad fling just between themselves, but for now he was going to err on the side of caution. Besides, what if she'd come to her senses during the afternoon and had changed her mind?

He played it as cool as he could when Gus beckoned her over to join them. He couldn't read her expression at all. But then, just for a second, she dropped the guard on her gaze and he could see the heat in her eyes. He returned the glance, hoping that she could read exactly the same thing in his eyes, and then they went back to polite, neutral conversation.

Except inside he was far from feeling polite and neutral.

Last night's dress had been the equivalent of a cheeky come-hither whistle.

Tonight's was clearly meant to be demure. Except it wasn't. The velvet dress skimmed her curves and just made him want to see more. And he wanted to undo every single one of the tiny buttons on the back of her dress and kiss each millimetre of skin as he bared it.

Not to mention seeing that glorious hair spread all over his skin.

Right now, he could really do with a cold shower to shock some common sense back into him.

For all he knew, he was speaking utter gibberish and he could barely concentrate on the people he was speaking to. This was insane. He never lost it like this. What was it about Indigo Moran that made him react like this?

It made it worse that he was seated opposite her at the dining table. So near, and so out of reach. He knew it was appallingly rude of him, but he just wanted dinner and all the social chit-chat to be over, so he could be on his own with Indigo and kiss her until they were both dizzy.

'And she drags me off to the most obscure little churches,' Lottie was saying, but her tone was so indulgent that Lorenzo could tell she wasn't really complaining.

'And you love it, because it always means finding a nice little tea-shop nearby afterwards,' Indigo teased back.

'Exactly. It's so civilised. Where would we be without afternoon tea?' Lottie asked. She ruffled Indigo's hair. 'Actually, it's lovely to know someone who can find beauty so easily and help others see it. I'm so going to get you that "vitrearum inconcinna" T-shirt we saw at the stained glass museum that time.'

'Glass geek,' Lorenzo translated with a smile. That would be just about perfect for Indigo.

Indigo gave him a sassy look. 'I'm glad to see that prince school didn't skimp on your education in Latin, Your Royal Highness.'

He coughed. 'Given my native language, it'd be pretty embarrassing if I didn't know any Latin.'

'Though I guess you'd call it *il vetro antico*.'

He inclined his head. 'Or maybe *il vetro artistico*, depending on how old it was.'

Gus topped up their glasses. 'We really should've introduced you two *years* ago. You could've had so much fun out-geeking each other.'

Indigo laughed. 'I'm not that competitive.'

'Yeah, right,' Lorenzo drawled, and she just laughed again.

From the chatter over the dinner table, Lorenzo could see how well Indigo fitted in at Edensfield; she was clearly loved by all the family, not just Lottie, and it sounded as if she was a regular visitor to the estate. He wondered why they'd never met before, given how long they'd both been friends with the family. Maybe they'd just visited the house at different times. But surely she'd been invited to Gus's wedding to Maisie two years ago, when he'd been Gus's best man? Though he didn't remember meeting her then, and he was pretty sure that he would've remembered.

And then he looked up to discover that she was watching him. He raised his glass casually, as if to take a sip of wine, then held her gaze and gave her the tiniest, most discreet toast.

She smiled, and copied his actions.

So she hadn't had second thoughts about their mad fling, then. Good. And funny how it made him feel so warm inside. To the point that, after dinner, Lorenzo let Gus coax him into playing the piano for them. They all crowded into the library round the baby grand, and Lorenzo played the slow bit of Beethoven he'd played for Indigo that afternoon. He hoped she'd work out that he was playing it for her. Would it make her think of the way he'd kissed her afterwards in this very same room? He sneaked a discreet glance in her direction, and the slight wash of colour in her face was gratifying in the extreme. Yup. She was thinking about that kiss, too.

And then he switched to pop, choosing songs that he

knew would get everyone singing. Then he discovered something else about Indigo. Her singing was *terrible*.

But he liked the fact that nobody called her on it. She was just—well, part of the family and accepted as one of them. Something he had a feeling she hadn't experienced that much.

He saw her expression change from pleasure to utter horror, the moment she realised that she was singing aloud, and he had to fight back a smile. Did she really have no idea how cute she was?

'I'm afraid I'm going to be a bit of a party pooper,' she said, when he stopped playing. 'I need to load the photographs I took this afternoon and finish off the restoration blog post for tomorrow morning.'

In other words, she was embarrassed about her singing and was desperate to escape, he thought. How could he tell her that it didn't matter, without bringing up the very subject she wanted to avoid? And if he asked her to stay, he might as well be wearing a T-shirt emblazoned with 'Hey, everyone, I'm interested in Indigo'. Or worse.

Lottie gave her a hug. 'Don't work too hard, Indi. You're not here as our slave, you know. You're here as our friend.'

'I know,' Indigo said. 'But I'm also here to do a job.'

'And you love your job more than anything else.' Lottie ruffled her hair. 'Go be a glass geek, then. See you later.'

According to Lottie, Indigo loved her job more than anything else. Which made Lorenzo wonder again about the man who'd clearly hurt her in the past. Was she using work to block it out? Then again, he didn't have much room to talk. He'd always had workaholic tendencies, too, trying to make up for the way his father had disappointed his grandfather. Which was stupid, because you couldn't make up for someone else. He knew that. But he still couldn't seem to stop himself trying. And Indi had already admit-

ted that she did the same. She was the first person he'd met who really understood what made him tick. Was it the same for her, too?

He stayed at the piano for just long enough to be polite and make it seem that he wasn't following Indigo, and then he headed over to her workroom and leaned against the doorway. To his surprise, she really was typing away on her laptop; so maybe her swift exit hadn't just been an excuse because she'd been embarrassed by her voice.

She looked up and saw him, then gave him a sheepish smile. 'Sorry. I'm an awful singer.'

'Don't apologise,' he said. 'Actually, it was nice that the music carried you away. And you don't have to be perfect at everything, every second of the day.'

'Uh-huh.' But she didn't sound convinced.

Why was she so hard on herself? Was it something to do with the strained relationship with her father? But he had a feeling that Indigo's flaw was the same as his own: she tried to be perfect. When she wasn't, she covered it up by being boho and arty. When he wasn't...well, that didn't happen. He always did the right thing.

Except for this mad fling with her. Which he wasn't going to let himself think about.

'You're busy,' he said. 'I'll leave you be.' He paused. 'Unless you want some coffee.'

'Coffee would be very nice,' she said softly. Then she looked him straight in the eye. 'But you would be better.'

His common sense vanished entirely. 'I'm giving you fair warning that I'm about to switch to troglodyte mode,' he said.

She blushed, just a tiny bit. 'Good. Though you should have noticed that I dressed demurely tonight.'

'I beg to differ.'

'High neckline, low hem.' She gestured to her dress.

'An indigo dress for Indigo.'

'That's what Sally said when she gave it to me. My friend from art school—she was studying textiles. We shared a flat and I sometimes used to model for her.' She smiled. 'It's a copy of an Edwardian design. What's not demure about it?'

'The buttons,' he said succinctly.

'The buttons?'

'The ones down the back of your dress. They make me want to undo them.'

'Oh, really?' She gave him a slow, insolent smile. 'Give me ten minutes to check this and upload it. My room?' Then she paused and looked awkward. 'Wait. Your security team.' She bit her lip.

'Bruno and Sergio? They're discreet. Totally and utterly.'

'It still feels a bit…' She grimaced. 'Well. As if we have an audience.'

'We don't,' he reassured her. 'This afternoon, when I was playing the piano, they knew I was in the library and they left me to it because they knew I needed some space. They didn't see me kiss you then, or the evening before.' He paused. 'I take it you want to keep this just between us?'

She nodded. 'It's a temporary thing,' she said softly, 'and we both know nothing can ever come of it, plus we're both staying at a friend's home. We're not in our own space.'

'If you're worrying about what people might think of you,' he said equally softly, 'I'd say the corridors of this house have seen plenty of people quietly slipping through them in the dead of night to a different bedroom, over the years.'

'I know.' She sighed. 'Sorry, I'm being silly. Not to mention very unsophisticated.'

'No, I know what you mean.' He smiled at her. 'I did wonder if you'd changed your mind.'

'I thought you might've changed yours.'

He shook his head. 'Every time I remember that I'm this sober, sensible and ever so slightly *boring* man, I look at you. And then all I can think is how much I want to kiss you.'

'In that case, it would be terribly rude of me not to let you,' she said.

'I'll see you in ten minutes,' he said. He checked which room was hers and was pleased to find that they were at least on the same corridor. There would be nothing more embarrassing for both of them than for him to be found wandering around on the wrong side of the house—because then Gus and his family would guess exactly what was going on.

Ten minutes later, Indigo was in her room. Adrenalin was fizzing through her veins, and she couldn't sit still; she couldn't even concentrate on browsing through the latest textbook on glass she'd bought before coming to Edensfield, planning to study it in her free time. Instead, she found herself pacing the room and looking at her watch every two seconds.

All she could think about was Lorenzo. The fact that he'd be coming to her room. The fact that they'd be starting their mad fling. And it made her feel like a teenager after her first kiss, light-headed and giddy with desire.

Well, the giddiness had to stop. She was going to enjoy every second of this, but she was also going to keep remembering that this was temporary. No promises on either side. And then they'd both be able to walk away with their hearts intact. She wouldn't be broken and helpless and hurting, the way she'd been after Nigel. She'd be strong and happy and absolutely fine.

There was a soft rap on the door.

Lorenzo.

She could barely get the words out. 'Come in.'

He walked in looking even more like James Bond, still wearing his dinner jacket but with his shirt collar open and his bow tie untied. And he had both hands behind his back, just as you always saw royal men walking. It brought it home to her that she was having a mad fling *with a king-to-be.* How crazy was that?

But then he lifted her up and swung her round before setting her back on her feet. 'Indigo Moran, I've wanted to kiss you all evening.'

'I've wanted that, too,' she admitted. 'A lot.'

'Good.' He traced the edge of her face with a finger-tip. The feel of his skin gliding against hers made every nerve-ending fizz.

'Kiss me, Lorenzo,' she whispered.

He did.

Slowly. Taking his own sweet time about it and heating her blood to fever pitch until she forgot everything else except him.

He removed the sash, spun her round so her back was to him, scooped her hair over her shoulder to bare her nape to him, and then traced the edge of her dress with one fingertip. 'I like this, Indi,' he said. 'The softest velvet. Except your skin's even softer. Though I need to prove that theory. Empirical evidence is very important.' He undid the first button, then the next, and stroked every centimetre of skin as he uncovered it.

And then she felt his lips brushing her skin very lightly. She shivered. 'Lorenzo.'

'You're beautiful,' he said softly. 'And you smell of roses.'

She smiled. 'It's my favourite scent. I love the garden here in summer because it's like drinking roses when you breathe.'

'I'm going to think of you every time I smell roses,' he said, and traced a path with his mouth all the way down her spine.

Then he turned her to face him again, slid the dress off her shoulders, and scooped it up from the floor when she'd stepped out of it. To her amusement, he hung her dress neatly over the back of the rococo chair next to the matching dressing table. 'Details?' she asked. 'Or are you just a buttoned-up neat freak?'

'Details,' he said. 'Attention to them is…' His gaze heated. 'Essential.'

Meaning that he intended to pay very close attention to her? Her knees went weak at the thought.

'You're wearing too much,' she said, aware that she was only wearing skimpy, lacy underwear and the only thing out of place for him was his bow tie. 'I think we need to even this up slightly.'

'What do you suggest?' he asked.

The choice was too delicious. 'I'm not sure whether I want you to strip for me, or whether I want to undress you myself,' she confessed.

'I have a practical solution. Pick one,' he said, 'and you can do the other next time.'

There was definitely going to be a next time?

'Then right now I get to undress you,' she whispered. And she did it very slowly, helping him shrug out of his jacket and then enjoying discovering the texture of his skin as she unbuttoned his shirt. 'I've changed my mind about you being James Bond. I think you're Mr Darcy.'

'Are you suggesting skinny-dipping in the lake, Ms Moran?'

'No. It's like the director said—it's better when something's left to the imagination.' She smiled. 'But you in a

white shirt, rising out of the lake and looking all sexy—yes, that would be very nice. Very nice indeed.'

'I'll see what I can do,' he promised. 'You'd make a rubbish valet, by the way.'

'How?'

'You're much too slow. I've lost patience.'

'Pulling rank, are we?' she teased. The king-to-be and the commoner.

'Totally.' He kissed her, and swiftly finished stripping. Then he placed his hands on her shoulders, holding her at a distance so he could look his fill. 'Indigo Moran,' he said huskily, 'you are totally luscious.' With that, he picked her up and carried her over to the bed.

And after that neither of them spoke for a long, long time.

CHAPTER FIVE

THE NEXT MORNING, Indigo woke, her head pillowed on Lorenzo's shoulder and his arms wrapped round her.

For a moment, she felt cherished and safe.

And then she shook herself. That wasn't the deal.

Even so, she couldn't help wondering: how long had it been since she'd woken like this, wrapped in a man's arms?

She really couldn't remember.

She'd dated men before Nigel, but she'd been more focused on her work than on relationships in art college. She'd wanted to prove to her grandparents that she'd done the right thing in rebelling against the education her father had planned, and that she wasn't flighty like her mother. She'd always put her studies first. And it had paid off, because she'd ended up with a first-class degree and a job working for a very prestigious glass studio.

Though Indigo hadn't been one for all work and no play. She'd attended plenty of parties, dated whoever she wanted to see, and when it had suited her she'd let things go further than a chaste kiss good-night at the door of her flat. But committing to a relationship, putting herself in a position where her heart could be broken—she'd avoided that as much as possible, keeping her relationships light and fun through college and most of her working life.

Until Nigel.

And that had been the biggest mistake of her life. She'd fallen in love with him and got her heart well and truly stomped on in the process. And, with Nigel, she'd never actually woken in his arms. He'd never stayed overnight in the six months they'd been together and he'd never invited her back to his place, saying that he lived and worked on the other side of London from her and the extra commute would be a nuisance for both of them.

Why had she never questioned that? Why had she just accepted it?

But there was no point in beating herself up about the past. Indigo knew she wasn't going to make the same mistake again. This time, she was protected against heartbreak. Right from the start she and Lorenzo had agreed that this was just a mad fling. One with a time limit. She wasn't going to fall in love with His Royal Highness Prince Lorenzo Torelli. This was going to be light and sweet and fun, a kind of respite for both of them. And she was going to enjoy every second of their fling.

It was still very early in the morning, and the summer sunlight was just seeping around the edges of the curtains. She shifted slightly so she could lie on her side and watch him sleeping.

In repose, Lorenzo was truly beautiful. He had a perfect bone structure and long, long lashes that made her itch to sketch him. And the way his mouth turned up at the corners naturally made it look as if he was smiling in his sleep. Or maybe he *was* smiling in his sleep. Dreaming of her, perhaps, and the way they'd made love in the ancient four-poster bed?

She smiled. Lorenzo had proved himself a spectacular lover, too. He'd paid attention to detail, noticed where she liked being touched and how she liked being kissed. The first time they'd made love should've been awkward and

ever so slightly embarrassing, but it hadn't been that way. It had felt so natural, so right: unexpectedly and wonderfully perfect.

She couldn't resist leaning over and kissing his mouth, very lightly.

His eyes opened. She saw the second that he focused and realised where he was. And then he smiled. The kind of smile that could melt the most frozen heart.

'Good morning, Indi,' he said softly.

Her heart did a backflip. 'Good morning, Lorenzo.'

He moved slightly closer. 'Was that my imagination, or did you just kiss me awake?'

She wrinkled her nose. 'Sorry. I didn't mean to wake you. But you looked like Sleeping Beauty, and I'm afraid it was a bit too much to resist.'

He coughed. 'I hate to tell you this, Indi, but Sleeping Beauty was a girl. And I'm not a girl.'

No. He was all man. And the thought of how they'd made love last night, how his body had felt inside hers, sent a warm glow through her. 'Hey, there's no reason why a man can't be beautiful.' She spread her hands. 'I mean, "Sleeping Handsome" doesn't sound right, does it?'

'Is that how you see me?' he asked.

'Kind of yes and kind of no.' She thought about it. 'I like the idea of playing around with fairy tales, seeing what happens if you change an element.'

He looked at her and sighed. 'I have a nasty feeling I know where this is going. Please tell me you're not planning to do a series of stained-glass windows with all the fairy tale roles reversed—and with me as the model.'

'If things were different,' she said, 'I'd talk you into that, because it's a *brilliant* idea. But it's not going to happen,' she reassured him, stroking his hair back from his forehead. 'That's why I said yes, that's kind of how I see

you—because you're from a different world. And being here with me is almost like a temporary enchantment. Except in this case it doesn't involve spinning wheels and pricking your finger, you're not going to sleep for a hundred years—oh, and a kiss isn't supposed to break the spell,' she added hastily.

'I'm glad to hear it.' He shifted so that he could pull her back into his arms. 'Well, now you've woken the sleeping prince, I think there's only one thing to do.'

And he kissed her until they were both dizzy.

'Now that's a way to start a morning,' she said with a smile.

He smiled back. 'My thoughts exactly. But I'd better go back to my own room before everyone else in the house wakes up. Do you always wake at the crack of dawn, Indi?'

'Not always, but I'm not actually that used to sharing my sleeping space,' she admitted.

He stroked her face. 'Good. Just for the record, neither am I.'

'Good.' She kissed him. 'Now disappear before you bump into Gus's mum, still wearing last night's clothes, and embarrass everyone.'

'Yes, ma'am,' he teased, and climbed out of bed. He gave her a sidelong glance. 'Shouldn't you be looking away while I get dressed?'

'My degree's in art. I've taken enough life drawing classes that I'm very comfortable with people being naked in front of me.' She raised an eyebrow. 'Has anyone told you that your posterior view is nicer than that of Michelangelo's David?'

To her delight, he actually blushed. 'No. But thank you for the compliment.' He finished dressing—though he left his shirt collar open and didn't bother with the bow tie—

then came to sit beside her on the bed. 'When will you be free today?'

'After the house and garden are closed, late this afternoon.' Much as she wanted to spend time with him, enjoy every precious second, she had commitments and it wouldn't be fair to back out. Though she knew he understood; he was busy, too, and they'd agreed to see each other in the spaces between each other's work.

'Maybe we could take a walk in the grounds when you're free.'

'I'd like that,' she said. 'Maybe I could text you when my workroom's clear, and you can text me back to let me know where and when to meet you.'

'Good idea.' He fished his mobile phone from his pocket. 'What's your number?'

She told him. A couple of moments later, her mobile beeped. She opened the text. 'A smile and a kiss. Works for me,' she said, smiling and kissing him. 'See you later, Lorenzo.'

She didn't see him at breakfast, because she ate a hasty bowl of granola, yoghurt and fruit in the kitchen rather than the breakfast room and she took her coffee through to her workroom. Lorenzo didn't come to see her while she was working on the glass in the morning; no doubt he had king-in-waiting stuff to do, she thought. And then the house opened for visitors, and she was busy talking to people and showing them what she was doing.

Once the last visitor had left, she sent a quick text to Lorenzo, letting him know that she was free.

See you in the rose garden in half an hour, was his reply.

When she walked into the rose garden, he was sitting on one of the wrought iron benches beneath a bower of roses. Again, she thought of the Sleeping Beauty story and how she'd love to paint Lorenzo in a stained-glass

window. And she smiled when she realised that Toto, the elderly golden Labrador, was sitting patiently next to him, his chin on Lorenzo's knee.

'I hope you don't mind us having a companion. Toto rather insisted on coming along,' Lorenzo said wryly.

She laughed and made a fuss of the dog. 'No, it's nice having a dog around. Especially in a garden as gorgeous as this one.'

'Did you have a good day?' he asked.

She nodded. 'I made quite a lot of progress on the mermaid and had some interesting chats with the visitors. You?'

'I worked through some files for my grandfather.'

'And you need some downtime?' she guessed.

'Just a little,' he admitted.

She heeled off her shoes, and sighed in bliss as her feet sank into the soft lawn. 'Ah, that's better. The only thing I don't like about my job is that you need to wear shoes all the time.'

'In case of splinters?' he asked.

She nodded. 'And this is bliss. The softest grass in the world.'

The way she'd just pushed off her shoes and was walking barefoot on the lawn... Lorenzo envied the way that Indigo could just act on impulse. It was something he never did; he was always aware of the consequences of his actions. Which was a good thing, but it also meant that he missed out on the joy that Indigo seemed to find so easily in things. 'Don't you worry about getting a thorn in your feet?'

'Hardly. Roses drop petals rather than thorns,' she pointed out.

'Even so. Sometimes they drop branches.'

'Which I can see and avoid.' She laughed. 'Though I admit I wouldn't walk barefoot by the lake. The ducks are a bit indiscriminate about where they have a toilet break and it's annoying having to watch where you put your feet instead of being able to watch the water and the sky.' She looked at him. 'Why don't you take your shoes off?'

'What, now?'

'Yes, now. Feel the grass under your feet. It's cool and springy and lovely.'

When was the last time he'd walked barefoot on the grass? Probably not since he was a small child. But, not wanting to appear a total stick-in-the-mud, he complied. He tucked his socks into his shoes and let his shoes dangle from one hand, just as she was doing.

'You're right,' he said, when he'd taken a couple of steps on the cool, soft grass. 'It's wonderful.'

'When was the last time you walked barefoot on a beach?' she asked.

He shrugged. 'I really can't remember.'

'Is there some rule at prince school that you should always be fully, impeccably dressed unless you're in the shower?'

He knew she was teasing him, but at the same time she had a point. As a prince, he always had to look the part. Not that he was going to let himself dwell on that side of things. 'Or swimming,' he said lightly. 'Unless of course you're dressed in Regency costume and want to turn some heads. Then you're allowed to be partially undressed. Especially in a lake,' he added, knowing that it would amuse her.

She laughed, and he loved the way she tipped her head back, her face up towards the sunlight and her face full of smiles. 'You half promised me that before, Lorenzo. I am *so* holding you to that Mr Darcy moment.'

'Talking about holding…' He brushed his free hand against hers.

'Would that be a hint, Your Royal Highness?' she teased.

He rolled his eyes. 'Are you saying that I have to give you an official royal order?'

'No. I probably wouldn't obey an order. But I can take a hint.' She smiled again and twined her fingers through his.

Walking through the rose garden with her, hand in hand, with the dog pattering along beside them, felt like being in another world. An enchanted bubble. Maybe she was right when she said he reminded her of Sleeping Beauty, Lorenzo thought, because this was like a dream. It wasn't real. They couldn't have a future. He needed to find a future queen for Melvante, someone his grandfather and his political advisers would approve of—and they definitely wouldn't approve of Indigo, despite her charm and her work ethic. And he already knew that Indigo hated his world; she'd escaped it before and wouldn't want to go back.

So he was going to enjoy every second of their fling together and take it for what it was: a beautiful interlude, a few moments out of time.

'So why do you have a thing about roses?' he asked.

'They're beautiful, they smell nice, and they look stunning in a stained-glass window. They're probably the perfect flower,' she said.

He smiled. 'My grandfather would agree with you. He has a rose garden.'

'One he tends himself?'

'When he gets the chance, yes. I'll know exactly where to find him when he's retired.' Lorenzo was surprised by her perception. She'd clearly worked out that what music did for him, roses did for his grandfather. 'So do roses figure much in stained glass?'

'Quite a bit,' she said. 'I'm trying to talk Syb into letting me do a window of roses for the library. Well, I know technically Gus should make the final decision, but he wants it done as a birthday present for his mum and he says it's her choice.' She looked wistful. 'I'd love to make a window full of roses. I'd have one myself if I had the right house.'

'And your house isn't right?'

'It's a modern bijou flat. Rented.' She gave a half-shrug. 'I'm not there very much, so it doesn't make sense to have a large place. I'm either at my studio, or working on location somewhere.'

'I guess,' he said. But still he wondered, if what Indigo really wanted was to have roots? She'd grown up with her grandparents; deep down, did she want a space of her own?

'So what about you? I assume as the prince you have to live in the castle?'

'I have an apartment in the castle,' he said. 'I can be independent if I choose and cook my own meals.'

She smiled at him. 'As *if* a prince is going to cook for himself. I bet you have a team of chefs who pamper you to within a millimetre of your life.'

That was a little too close to home. When was the last time he'd cooked for himself? Normally, he was so busy that it was easier to eat something prepared by the castle chefs when he was in Melvante, and to get takeout if he was in London. 'I make an excellent chilli, I'll have you know,' he protested. 'I learned to cook when I was a student—and, actually, I like cooking.' He just didn't do it that often, any more.

She raised her eyebrows at him. 'Is that a cue for a challenge, Your Royal Highness?'

'Maybe.' He knew he'd enjoy cooking for her; he could imagine her sitting at his kitchen table in bare feet, chatting and maybe sketching as he cooked. Then he shook

himself. Such domestic scenes weren't going to happen, however much he might like them to. She wasn't going to be in his apartment at the castle and he was hardly ever going to get the time to cook or play the piano. He definitely wasn't going to have much time to do ordinary things like this—walking hand in hand with a pretty girl in a rose garden.

He pushed the thought away.

As if she noticed that he'd gone quiet and brooding, and she wanted to change the subject to something that would be less painful for him, she asked, 'So what's your castle like?'

That was an easier topic to talk about. 'It's pretty much your standard picture-postcard European castle. White stone, lots of turrets with pointed tiled roofs, a drawbridge and a moat.'

'That sounds nice. What about inside?'

'Red carpets, oak panelling and suits of armour—and there's a gallery with pictures of every King of Melvante since Carlo the First.'

'Will you be the first Lorenzo?' she asked.

'The third—my grandfather's the second.' His father had been supposed to be the third, with himself as the fourth. How different his life would've been, had his father lived.

'So you were named after your grandfather?'

He nodded. 'How about you?'

She looked rueful. 'I think my mum just picked the most unusual name she could think of. And possibly something that would annoy my father, because it's not very traditional.'

He thought of the traditional royal English names. 'I can't see you as an Elizabeth, a Mary or an Anne.'

'Maybe if I'd been Elizabeth, I would've fitted in at

school. I could've been Lizzie in the four musketeers of our dorm,' she mused.

He shook his head. 'Even if you'd had an L in your name, you wouldn't have been part of those girls. Besides, if you'd really hated your name, you could've used your middle name. Or any other name you liked, for that matter.'

'I hated my name when I was really small—in the days when I needed to feel I fitted in,' she admitted, 'and back then some of the girls weren't very nice, saying it wasn't a proper name for a girl because it was a colour.'

'There are plenty of colours used as names. Ruby, Jade and Amber,' he said, taking the first three that came into his head.

'They're gemstones,' she corrected.

'How about Violet and Rose?'

She shook her head. 'Flowers.'

'Scarlet,' he said. 'Even you can't argue against *that* one.'

'I guess not.' She grinned. 'Nowadays, I like my name.'

'So,' he said, 'do I. It suits you and it suits your job.'

She gave him a half-bow. 'Why, thank you, Your Royal Highness. Anyway, before I sidetracked you, you were telling me about your art collection. Lots of portraits of kings.'

'My great-grandfather collected art. You'd like what he bought.' He smiled at her. 'And there's a picture of my great-great-grandmother you'd really love. She sat for Burne-Jones when she was a child.'

'How fantastic. I hope you know I'm horribly envious.'

'Maybe you can come and see it.' The offer was out before he could stop it.

'Maybe.' She gave him the sweetest, sweetest smile.

And he knew without having to ask that it was a polite way of saying no.

She paused. 'OK. You like the building and you like the art. But is it home?'

He thought about it. 'Yes, it is. I have a lot of happy memories there.' Despite his parents' early deaths, the lies he'd been told to spare him from the truth and the shock of discovering that his father had had such a dark side.

'I'm glad.' Her fingers tightened briefly round his. 'So what are you going to do when you're king?'

'Build on the work of my grandfather and make my people proud of me,' he said promptly.

'Good goals,' she said approvingly. 'How do you plan to get there?'

Lorenzo found himself talking seriously to Indigo about Melvante, about his people and what he wanted to do for his country. Whenever he stopped, thinking that maybe he was being too boring and ought to change the subject, she drew him out a little more, asking questions that showed she'd been paying attention to what he'd said and coming up with ideas that really made him think. And he was oddly pleased that she was showing as much of an interest in his job as he had in hers.

Toto flopped down with a grunt; she stopped, and made a fuss of the old dog. 'I think we've tired him out, poor old boy.' She glanced back at the house. 'Look how far we've walked. I don't think he's going to find the return walk very easy.'

'Then I'll carry him back.' Lorenzo put his shoes back on, preparing to pick up the dog. Toto was slightly overweight and a bit on the heavy side, but no way was Lorenzo going to abandon the old dog. He'd allowed Toto to join them for a walk and he hadn't thought enough of the fact that the dog was elderly now and couldn't walk as far as he'd been able to run alongside them when Lorenzo and Gus had been students and Toto had been a boisterous pup.

'Lorenzo, you ca–'

Her protest died as he picked up the dog.

'You're an elephant, Toto. You need to go on a doggy diet,' he informed the dog, who licked his nose gratefully.

When he glanced at Indigo, he was surprised to see a film of tears in her eyes. 'What's wrong, Indi?' he asked gently.

'You're going to be a king next month. And there you are, carrying an old dog home.'

'Toto and I go back a long way. And you always look after your own, don't you?' He smiled at her. 'Strictly speaking, he's Gus's dog. But I spent enough time here as a student to think of him as at least partly mine.'

'Even so. A lot of people would...' She swallowed hard. 'Well, just leave him.'

'Until he'd had a rest and could find his own way back to the house? No way.' He grimaced. 'I suppose we could've gone to find a wheelbarrow and a blanket for him, but I wouldn't abandon him just because he's old and tired and needs a break.'

'I guess.'

She was quiet until they got to the house, where he gently set Toto back on to his feet.

'You're a good man, Lorenzo Torelli,' she said softly. 'And you're going to make an awesome king.'

'I hope so,' he said, equally softly. 'I really hope so.'

CHAPTER SIX

OVER THE NEXT WEEK, Lorenzo and Indigo spent as much time together as they could, while trying to be discreet and not flaunt their affair in everyone's faces. Every sneaked moment was precious.

'I'm still thinking about how you carried Toto back to the house. He weighs a ton, and you carried him for ages. Do you do weight training or something?' Indigo asked when they were curled up on Lorenzo's bed together.

'Or something.'

'Which is?'

'Come and train with me in Gus's fitness room, and I'll show you,' Lorenzo said.

The fitness room? It was one of the rooms at Edensfield Indigo had never set foot in; she'd never been remotely interested in running on a treadmill or picking up weights. 'But I'm not sporty. I was always the last one picked for the team at lacrosse. And even when I moved to the local secondary school, I was never any good at netball, hockey or rounders. I used to get an A for effort and a D for achievement.'

'The trick is to find something that you enjoy doing.'

'I didn't enjoy team sports. At all,' she said with a grimace. 'I don't mind going for a long walk—I'm not a total couch potato—but I'm really not sporty.' She stroked his

pectorals and his abs. 'You have muscles—a proper six-pack. So I guess that means you're really sporty.'

'Mens sana in corpore sano,' he intoned.

'A healthy mind in a healthy body,' she translated. 'More prince school stuff?'

He laughed. 'You translated it, so I thought you'd know where it comes from.'

'I only studied Latin to help me with the glass—sometimes you get wills or what have you to help you with the provenance of the glass. People donating particular windows to a church, that kind of thing.'

'It's Juvenal, from the *Satires*. And it doesn't just apply to princes—it's a list of what he thinks you should ask for in life. I can't remember the whole lot, but it includes a stout heart, one that's not scared of hard work and isn't angry or lustful...' He leaned over to kiss her. 'Most of that works for me. Except the lustful bit. Because you're incredibly desirable, Indigo Moran, and you make me feel lustful. Very lustful indeed.'

'Why, thank you, Your Royal Highness. I would curt-sey in gratitude—'

'Would you, hell.' He stole another kiss.

'Let me finish. I would curtsey in gratitude for the compliment, but...' She laughed. 'Well, I'm comfortable and I don't want to move.'

'I don't want you to move, either.' He tightened his arms round her.

'So what sport do you do?' She thought for a moment. 'You promised me a Mr Darcy moment, so I'm guessing swimming.'

'I can swim, but it's not my favourite.'

'Rowing, then?' She looked at him. 'And I bet you got a Blue for it at Oxford.'

'Well, yes,' he admitted. 'But rowing isn't my favourite, either.'

She was intrigued. 'Tennis? Cricket? Rugby?'

'That's three more guesses—and all wrong. Forfeits are due,' he said, claiming a kiss for each.

'OK. I give up. Tell me.'

'Sparring.'

'*Boxing?* No way.' She shook her head. 'They'd never let a king-to-be take a risk like that. Boxing's dangerous. People get seriously hurt.'

'Sparring just means padwork. So I get all the fun of boxing but without the risk of being hurt,' he said. 'Come and spar with me.'

'I hate to point this out, Your Royal Highness, but you're six inches taller than I am and I'm not exactly muscle-bound. I'm not going to be a very good sparring partner, am I?'

'Sure you are. You'll work with the gloves, not the pads.'

'And I don't have any workout gear.'

'Borrow some from Lottie or Maisie. They're both about your size, so one of them is bound to have something she can lend you.'

He clearly wasn't going to let this go. 'So when are we doing this training, then?'

'Tomorrow morning. I was thinking the crack of dawn, given that you always seem to wake so early.'

It really wasn't her idea of fun, but she'd indulge him. 'OK.'

'Good.' He nuzzled the hollows of her collarbones. 'So, where were we?'

Later that day, Indigo borrowed a T-shirt and a pair of shorts from Lottie—at least she had a pair of training shoes with her—and the next morning she followed Lorenzo to the fitness room.

He handed her a skipping rope. 'This is a speed rope. It's weighted so you can skip properly.'

'Skipping?' She looked at him, mystified. 'I thought we were doing boxing stuff?'

'We are. This is to warm up your muscles.'

She managed five skips before she tripped over the rope.

'You need to jump over the rope with both feet together,' he explained, 'not one foot at a time as if you're a rocking horse.'

She spread her hands. 'That's the way I learned to skip at school.'

'This is boxing skipping. It's much more effective at getting your heart rate up and warming up your muscles.'

'What's the difference?'

'Watch.' He skipped slowly, jumping over the rope; then he quickened his pace and it was as if he were floating on air. His feet didn't even seem to touch the ground—he just seemed to be hovering mid-air.

'Now that's just showing off,' she grumbled, wanting to hide just how impressed she was.

He laughed. 'No, that's practice. Do a little bit every day and eventually you'll be able to do this.'

She didn't think so. 'Show me again.'

He coughed. 'You're trying to wriggle out of doing it.'

'All right.' She rolled her eyes. 'I admit that was seriously impressive, Your Royal Highness, and I'd like to see you do it again.'

He laughed. 'OK. I'll skip for you again. But you have to earn it.'

'That's mean,' she said.

'It's a carrot for a reward,' he corrected. 'If you want to see me skip, you have to do some skipping yourself, first. OK. Let's work on your technique.' He walked her over towards the mirror. 'Now, watch yourself in the mirror.'

'Haven't we just proved that I can't skip?'

'We've just proved that you panicked and you need to change your technique,' he corrected. 'Remember what I said: jump over the rope with both feet together, and watch your feet in the mirror. Focus on lifting your feet.'

She tried again, and this time managed a few more skips before she tripped over the rope and had to stop.

'See? You're getting better. Now do it again. Watch your feet in the mirror and focus on the rhythm. Jump, jump, jump.'

She was hot and breathless by the time he finally let her stop. 'This is vile. I'm all sweaty and disgusting.'

He just grinned and kissed the tip of her nose. 'Tut, Ms Moran. Didn't your teachers tell you that horses sweat, men perspire and ladies glow?'

She glowered at him. 'I'm not a lady.'

He brushed his mouth against hers. 'I beg to differ. You're all woman, Indigo Moran, and right now you look as sexy as hell.'

And how was she supposed to concentrate, when he was looking at her like *that*?

He took the skipping rope from her and put the gloves on her. 'Right—now you need to keep your knees soft, crouch slightly, and keep your hands up to guard your face.'

He talked her through doing a jab and a cross, then put his hands into two pads and held them up. 'OK, now jab the pad to your right, then punch the one on your left. Remember to keep the hand you're not using up by your face.'

She hit the pads as he directed. This was surreal: *she was throwing punches at a king-to-be*. Surely there had to be laws against this.

'Harder,' he said.

She shook her head. 'But I might hurt you, Lorenzo.'

He smiled. 'Indi, my sweet, you're not going to hurt me. I wouldn't get you to hold the pads for me because I'm used to this and I'd hit too hard for you, but this is new to you and I assure you that you won't hurt me, however hard you hit. Now punch.'

By the time he called a halt, Indigo was breathing hard—and she was full of exhilaration. 'That was amazing! I get why you love it.'

'It's a great cardio workout, plus it's good for your arms and your abs. We're going to stop now or you'll be really sore tomorrow—actually, you might be sore anyway.' He looked faintly guilty. 'Sorry. I was enjoying that and I probably should've stopped earlier.'

'It's fine. I enjoyed it, too, even though I thought I'd hate it,' she said. 'And if anyone told me that a king-to-be would love putting on a pair of boxing gloves...'

He kissed her lightly. 'I'm a man first, Indi. Remember that.'

And the heat in his gaze sent a shiver of pure lust all the way from the top of her spine down to her toes.

'So now what?' she asked, her voice ever so slightly shaky.

'Now,' he said, 'we go and shower.' He bent down so he could whisper in her ear, 'And my vote is for us to do that together.'

'No arguments from me,' she said, feeling breathless.

He took off the gloves, and kissed the back of her hand. 'You did really well.'

'Because you're a good teacher.' She smiled at him.

'So were you, when you talked me through cleaning the lead cames.'

'It's just a matter of being clear with your instructions, paying attention and adapting things to suit the person you're teaching.'

'It's the same with this,' he said, and kissed her again. 'Right. Shower. Now.'

'Yes, Your Royal Highness,' she said, and kissed him back.

The following morning, Lorenzo walked in to Indigo's workroom at half past eleven. 'Time for lunch.'

'Lunch?' She glanced at her watch. 'Isn't it a bit early?'

'No. It means we'll be finished before the house and grounds open at one.'

'Fair enough.' She made sure that all her electrical equipment was switched off and all the liquids were safely in sealed containers, and followed him out of the house.

He was carrying a wicker basket, she noticed. They found a nice spot on the lawn outside the hothouses with a view of the lake. Lorenzo produced a rug for them to sit on and shook it out. Then he spread out a red and white checked tablecloth next to the rug and set out plates, cutlery and two champagne flutes.

So much more stylish than the plastic box of food and slightly scuffed plastic cups she was used to on a picnic.

'So you talked someone in the kitchen into making all this for you?' she asked.

'Actually, no. I sent one of my team into the local town with a very specific list. And I put this together with my own fair hands.'

'Resourceful and able to delegate. Good combination,' she said. Though part of her wondered, did he ever yearn to be just an ordinary man who could nip out to the shops himself on the spur of the moment without it having to be planned like a military operation, complete with security detail, or having to send someone else out with his list?

The first box contained watercress, baby plum tomatoes, strips of yellow pepper and slices of mango. Then

there was a box of sliced chicken, which he arranged on top. He added a pot of dressing. 'Creamy chilli and coconut. I forgot to ask if you liked spicy food,' he said.

'I do.'

He brought out some rich seeded bread, which he carved into chunks, and his next foray into the picnic hamper was for a pot containing a red purée. She sniffed as he took the lid off. 'It smells like strawberries.'

'Puréed,' he said, and deftly put some in each champagne flute, which he topped off from a tiny bottle of champagne. 'I thought we'd have just enough for one glass each, so it won't make you drowsy or affect your work,' he said.

She took a sip. 'This is fabulous—what is it, a kind of strawberry Bellini?'

'Yes. It's called a Rossini.'

'Where did you discover these?'

He laughed. 'Elementary class at prince school?'

'Yeah, yeah.' She raised her glass in a toast to him. 'To you. And thank you so much for spoiling me so delightfully.'

'My pleasure.' He leaned over and kissed her lightly.

Indigo enjoyed the food and the sunshine; and she especially enjoyed the company.

When they'd finished the salad, Lorenzo fed her more strawberries and miniature macaroons the colour of pistachio that tasted of coconut.

'They're perfect,' she said blissfully.

He smiled. 'We aim to please.' He reached over and kissed the corner of her mouth. 'Crumb,' he said.

Two could play at that game, she thought, amused. She kissed the corner of his mouth. 'Smear of sugar.'

He just laughed, and kissed her until she was dizzy.

Finally, he settled back with his head in her lap, look-

ing pensive. She stroked his hair away from his forehead. 'What are you thinking?'

'Sometimes I wish I could keep a moment in time,' he said.

'You can. In here.' She rested one hand over his heart. 'And in here.' She stroked his forehead.

'I'd keep this moment,' he said softly. 'A perfect English summer afternoon.'

She knew exactly what he meant. Sunshine glinting on the lake, birds singing, the scent of roses, strawberries and champagne... There was really only one thing missing. She reached over to pick some daisies.

'What are you doing?' he asked.

'Nothing. Just close your eyes and chill out,' she said, and proceeded to make a daisy chain. When she'd finished, she made it into a crown. 'For you,' she said, and he opened his eyes to see the crown just before she draped it over his head.

He looked unutterably sad for a moment, as if she'd just reminded him that he'd be wearing a much heavier crown in a few short weeks.

'Actually, I was thinking Oberon,' she said softly.

'"Ill met by moonlight, proud Titania"?'

'I hope we're not ill met.' She smiled at him. 'Trust you to know Shakespeare—or was your degree in English?'

'Economics. But I had friends who read English.'

'Did you not think about studying music?' she asked. Surely that had been the subject of his heart?

He shrugged. 'Economics was more practical.'

'But if you'd had a choice?'

'Then, yes, I probably would've studied music,' he admitted.

'I was lucky,' she said softly. 'I got to do what I love.'

'I love what I'm going to do,' he said, though his words

sounded a little hollow to her, and just for a second he looked so very, very lonely.

The only way she could think of to make it better was to kiss him.

His arms tightened around her as if he really needed her. When he broke the kiss, he said, 'I guess we'd better get back.'

She helped him clear away the picnic. 'Thank you for spoiling me, Lorenzo. I really enjoyed this.'

'My pleasure.' He stroked her face. 'I'm glad I could share it with you.'

And she was glad, too.

Later in the week, Indigo woke to find herself alone.

Lorenzo hadn't said anything to her about needing an early start or going up to London.

Or had he changed his mind about their fling?

Hurt, she got up and slipped her dressing gown on. Then she saw a note next to the bed. A 'Dear Jane' letter? she wondered.

Well, they'd agreed it was a fling. The fact that she was falling for him—more fool her.

Steeling herself, she picked up the note and read it.

Meet you at the lake, by the boathouse.

Not a 'Dear Jane' letter, then. He'd clearly left the note on his pillow and it had fallen off. And they'd had those conversations about Mr Darcy. Was he really going to do that? Or was he doing something crazy and spontaneous, like planning to row her across the lake to watch the sunrise?

She smiled, dressed swiftly and headed out to the lake.

Lorenzo was sitting there on the steps of the boathouse, wearing full Regency dress—including knee-length leather boots. He looked utterly fantastic and her heart did a backflip.

He sketched a salute to her as she neared him, then took off his boots.

She stopped. Was he really going to do what she thought he was about to do?

She watched as he shed his dark jacket, his cravat and finally his silk waistcoat, leaving them on the steps of the boathouse. And then he gave her the most sensual smile ever and dived into the lake, still wearing the cream-coloured breeches and loose white shirt.

'Oh, my God,' she said softly. 'Mr Darcy in the flesh.'

She watched him swim, his arms moving powerfully through the water. And then he emerged from the lake, the white cotton of his shirt plastered to his skin.

It was the sexiest thing she'd ever seen.

'Did I get it right?' he asked as she walked over to join him.

'Oh, yeah, you got it right.' And how embarrassing was it that her voice had practically dropped an octave, going all husky? 'And your hair goes slightly curly when it's wet. I never really noticed that before—and you've got those lovely huge dark eyes, just like Colin Firth...'

Lorenzo gave her a pained look. 'Oh, please. Don't go all fan-girly on me.'

'Hey, you ask Lottie—she'll say the same,' she protested. 'Mind you, I'm sure I read somewhere that Jane Austen based Mr Darcy on Byron.'

'I'm not sure about that. But even so I'm not mad, bad or dangerous to know,' he said.

She laughed and thought, actually, you are dangerous to know, because I could so easily fall in love with you, and that would be the most stupid thing ever—because I wouldn't fit into your world and you couldn't leave yours and join mine. Instead, she said more prosaically, 'I hope you brought some dry clothes.'

'Of course. Just as well, actually, because the lake was a bit colder than I thought it was going to be.' He took her hand and led her into the boating house, then stripped off and towelled himself dry.

'I'm pretty sure Mr Darcy didn't have a spare set of clothes nearby,' she commented, hoping that he couldn't hear how hard her heart was beating.

'But I didn't want to meet you in the garden and make small talk. Or drip water all over the carpets at Edensfield. Besides, Darcy would've needed a valet,' he pointed out.

She grinned. 'I would offer, but I've been told I'm a rubbish valet.'

He gave her a smouldering look. 'This could be your chance to prove me wrong.'

'I'd rather sketch you than dress you.'

He groaned. 'Don't tell me you've got pencils and a sketchpad with you.'

'No. But I do have this.' She tapped her head.

'You're wired with a hidden camera? Female James Bond, so there's a microphone in your lipstick and a camera in your contact lenses?'

'Very funny. You know what I meant.' Her memory.

And that was what they were doing, wasn't it? Making the most of their fling and making wonderful memories in their brief time together. Memories that were going a long, long way to wiping out some of the heartache Nigel had caused her.

He kissed her lingeringly. 'Come on. I need a hot shower. Preferably with you.'

'If that's a royal order,' she said with a grin, 'then it's one I'm quite happy to obey.'

'Good.'

This time, when he undressed her, he just let everything

drop to the floor in a crumpled heap—so different from the way he'd hung her velvet dress so neatly over the chair.

She laughed and kissed him. 'I'm glad you're losing your neat-freak ways.'

'You've taught me that spontaneous can be good,' he said.

She loved the fact that he was trying. For her. 'Planning can be good, too,' she said. It had definitely taken planning to sort out the picnic and that Mr Darcy moment, and she'd loved every second of them.

'Indi, you talk too much,' Lorenzo said, and proceeded to kiss her.

CHAPTER SEVEN

'ARE YOU BUSY tomorrow morning?' Indigo asked Lorenzo on the Friday morning.

He shrugged. 'I can move things if you want to do something.'

'Some of my favourite bits of glass in the country aren't very far from here. I thought I could take you to see them.'

He looked thoughtful. 'I'd like that. Bruno can drive us.'

'In your official car?' She hadn't really considered it before, but of course Lorenzo probably didn't drive himself very often. He couldn't go out without his security team being nearby, so everything he did had to be planned. 'But if people see a big black car in the car park, they'll immediately think there's a celeb in the church and rush in to see who it is. If they see my slightly battered van with "I Moran, Glass Restoration" on the side, they'll guess we're there to see the glass, so we won't be interrupted.'

'Is there room for my security team to sit in your van?' he asked.

She shook her head. 'There aren't any seats in the back—it's where I keep my tools or transport frames.'

'Much as I'd like to go—and I know your intentions are good,' he said softly, 'it wouldn't be fair on you or on my grandfather to leave here without my security team.'

'Sorry. I didn't think it through.' Whereas Lorenzo was

used to having to plan everything with military precision. And how awful it must be for him, she thought, never being able to do things on impulse and always having people watching his back. When did he ever get space just to *be*?

He leaned forward and kissed her lightly. 'We could compromise. There's always a way.'

Was there? She wasn't so sure.

'Your van isn't suitable and neither's my car. But maybe we can borrow a car from Gus that's a little more subtle. Bruno can drive us, and he and Sergio will give us space in the church to look around.'

'I'd like that,' she said.

'Good.' He kissed her lightly. 'I'll go and see Gus.'

'She's talked you into doing glass geek stuff with her?' Gus laughed. 'Lottie's going to be most put out at missing coffee and pastries.'

'I'll grovel and I'll promise to bring back some pastries for her,' Lorenzo said, laughing back.

'Of course you can borrow a car, idiot. Indi's right— if you take that huge black monster of yours, everyone's going to know there's a celeb about.'

'I'm not a *celeb*,' Lorenzo said, his voice pained.

'You are, where the papers are concerned.' Gus paused. 'This thing between you and Indi—are you sure it's a good idea?'

Lorenzo felt the colour seep into his face. 'We know what we're doing. It's temporary.'

'You've got the same look on your face as I'm sure there was on mine when I met Maisie,' Gus pointed out. 'And I've never seen you like this before.'

'It's temporary,' Lorenzo repeated. 'We'll both walk away when I go back to Melvante. And we'll part as friends.'

Gus raised an eyebrow. 'She's a lot more vulnerable

than she makes out, you know. If you hurt her, Lottie will fillet you.' He paused. 'Actually, no, I'll be first in line to call you out and I'll fillet you myself.'

'I'm not going to hurt her.' Lorenzo placed his hand briefly on Gus's shoulder. 'Though I'm glad she has someone to look out for her.'

'She's had a rough deal where her family's concerned.'

'I know. She told me.'

'She told you?' Gus looked surprised. 'Then it's worse than I thought. She never talks about her family.'

'I'm not going to hurt her,' Lorenzo repeated.

'This is going to end in tears,' Gus warned, shaking his head.

'No, it's not. I'll make sure of that,' Lorenzo said.

Though he thought about Gus's words all afternoon. His best friend had fallen for Maisie and married her within six months. Two years later, they were still deliriously happy.

But the difference was, Gus and Maisie came from the same world. He and Indigo didn't. Well, they'd both been born to noble fathers, but that was as far as it went. Indigo had escaped from that world as soon as she possibly could, and no way would she ever go back to it. And she loved her job; she wouldn't be prepared to give that up for what she'd see as life in a goldfish bowl.

He shook himself. He wasn't in love with Indigo Moran, and she wasn't in love with him. They weren't planning a happy-ever-after. They were having fun and enjoying each other's company—taking a moment out of their usual lives. Gus was just seeing things through the rosy-tinted glasses of a happy marriage and impending fatherhood. Everything was going to be just fine.

On Saturday morning, Lorenzo breakfasted quickly with Indigo in the kitchen, then met his security team as ar-

ranged next to the car Gus was lending them. Bruno tapped the details of the church into the satnav system and drove them through narrow country lanes into a pretty little village. The flint-built church was set high on a mound at the edge of the village and, as Indigo had predicted, when Lorenzo twisted the huge iron ring in the heavy oak door the latch clicked up and allowed him to push the door open and follow her inside.

The church was beautiful; with two storeys of windows, it was full of light.

'Come and see my centaur. He's my favourite piece of glass in the world,' she said, and drew him over to one of the windows.

There was a circle of glass set into the diamond-paned window. The outside of the circle had a thick border of purple glass, and in the middle was a black and white picture highlighted with bright yellow, of a centaur playing a violin with a little dog running round his feet.

'And then there's this.' She turned him round and pointed at an angel.

He smiled. 'Trust you.'

'OK, so I have a thing for angels.' She smiled back. 'I just love Gabriel's feathery trousers. Did you know that when they did the medieval Mystery Plays, this is the sort of costume the angels wore?'

Her love for her subject was infectious as well as endearing. He loved her enthusiasm, and the fact that she had the scholarly information to back it up.

Just then, a woman walked in carrying an armful of flowers. She smiled at them. 'Oh, sorry, don't mind me. I'm just sorting out the flowers. We have a wedding here this afternoon,' she confided.

Lorenzo and Indigo exchanged a glance.

Weddings.

For one crazy moment, Lorenzo could imagine standing there in front of the altar, the church filled with roses and crammed with people wanting to share the moment, waiting for Indigo to walk down the aisle towards him.

Oh, help. Maybe Gus had had a point, because Lorenzo had never, ever visualised something like that before. He hadn't even thought about his future wedding, knowing that it would be more or less an arranged marriage for diplomatic purposes because the needs of his country had to come before his personal desires.

But, now the idea was in his head, he couldn't shift it: Indigo in a wedding dress and a veil, carrying a simple bouquet, walking down the carpeted aisle towards him.

'This would be the perfect place to get married,' Indigo said softly.

Was she thinking it, too? Imagining herself walking down the aisle...towards him?

As they moved away from the woman arranging the flowers, he couldn't help asking, 'Is this where you want to get married?'

'I'm never getting married.' She lifted her chin. 'Marriage is just a piece of paper, and it doesn't stop people lying or cheating.'

The hurt was obvious in her voice. Was she thinking about her parents' situation, he wondered, or had she been married before and been hurt by someone who'd cheated on her?

Her face twisted. 'Besides, marriage is an institution and I'm not very good at institutions.'

How he wanted to hold her. Tell her that everything would be OK and he'd never let anything hurt her again.

But it was a promise he knew he wouldn't be able to keep. Short of keeping Indigo wrapped in cotton wool, he couldn't guarantee to protect her from everything. And if

she was wrapped in cotton wool, she'd lose her freedom. She'd suffocate. Just as his mother had.

How could he turn this round?

'If you ever did change your mind and get married, I bet it would be in a church with amazing glass,' he said. 'And I bet you'd have a really untraditional wedding dress and outrageous shoes.'

She smiled. 'I'd get my friend Sally to design it for me—the one who made the indigo dress. But I'm not getting married.' She took a deep breath. 'And you'll get married to someone wearing a specially made, hugely elegant and very traditional dress with lots of handmade lace. In a cathedral.'

'I guess.' Let it go, he told himself. *Let it go.* But his mouth had other ideas. 'You'd like the cathedral in Melvante. It's very gothic.'

'Good glass?'

'You'd be a better judge of that than I would.' He paused. 'Come and see for yourself.'

She shook her head, looking sad. 'We both know that when you go back, we won't see each other again. So let's not talk about this. We were talking about cathedrals.' She smiled. 'I love the cathedral in Norwich. There's a Burne-Jones window there and it's absolutely beautiful. I remember going Christmas shopping with Lottie one year, and we went to the carol service at the cathedral. There was a huge Christmas tree and lots of candles. It was totally magical, with the scent of the tree, the singing of the choir and the glass. We went to a patisserie afterwards, and it was just starting to snow, making it feel even more Christmassy. We had hot chocolate and the nicest coffee cake I've ever tasted.'

'Maybe we could go there now,' he suggested.

She shook her head. 'We're taking enough of a risk vis-

iting a tiny country church. Bruno and Sergio would definitely not be happy with an unscheduled visit to the city.'

'I guess,' he said.

She looked at him and thought, there were so many things he couldn't do. She was so lucky to have her freedom and not be in his world.

She put some money in the church collection box; then they said goodbye to the flower-arranger and headed back outside into the bright sunlight.

'We need to go to the patisserie on the way back,' he said.

'Why?'

'Because I owe Lottie nice pastries. For coming out here with you in her place,' he explained.

She looked at Sergio. 'Are we allowed to visit a patisserie? Or maybe if I go in while His Royal Highness waits here in the car with you and Bruno?'

Lorenzo coughed. 'My life's not *that* restricted.'

Oh, yes, it was, she thought.

'We can all go to the patisserie, if His Royal Highness wishes,' Sergio said.

Indigo smiled. 'So I get to have morning coffee with three handsome men? Cool. That works for me.' She nudged Lorenzo. 'And would I be right in thinking that, being royal, you're like the Queen and you don't carry money, so this will be my treat?'

'No, you would not.' He looked offended. 'I can pay for coffee.'

She smiled. 'I was teasing. And offering. I'd like to buy you a coffee. Especially as you spoiled me with that picnic.'

'I'll pay,' Lorenzo said.

'You're not listening. I'm independent, Lorenzo. I've paid my own way since I got my first Saturday job at the age of fourteen. And I want to buy you coffee. I'd like to do something nice for you. So just shut up and let me do it, OK?'

* * *

For a moment, Lorenzo wondered if her ex had tried to take away her independence. Was that why she guarded it so very fiercely now?

He took her hand and squeezed it. 'Then thank you. Coffee would be very nice.'

The patisserie was crowded, but nobody seemed to pay much attention to the four newcomers. They were just part of the crowd. How long had it been since he'd managed that? he wondered.

Indigo ordered coffee and pastries for four, and Lorenzo was surprised to discover that the coffee was every bit as good as what he was used to in Melvante, and the pastries were delicate and delicious. And all the time, she chatted easily to Bruno and Sergio. He'd never known them so talkative, ever, even if one of them was training with him or sparring in the gym. Indigo had a gift for drawing people out. She could teach him so much. But what could he offer her, in return?

Indigo bought a box of treats for Gus, Lottie, Syb and Maisie before they left. And then she noticed a box of home-baked dog treats on the counter, so she bought some for all the dogs, too.

Lorenzo went quiet on the way back to Edensfield, but he held her hand all the way. And Indigo was aware that she was getting way too close to him. If this carried on, she'd get hurt. She really had to keep her heart protected and remember who he was. He could be her Mr Right Now, but not her Prince Happy-Ever-After. Much as she'd like him to be.

CHAPTER EIGHT

LORENZO'S LAST WEEK at Edensfield was idyllic. By day, he worked on official court business; his nights were spent making love with Indigo and sleeping with her wrapped in his arms; and in the spaces between they found time to go for long walks, hand in hand, or he'd play the piano for her, or she'd read to him with his head resting in her lap. Sometimes they watched the sun set over the lake; sometimes they lay on the damp grass and watched the stars. All the sweet, simple things that lovers did.

And he actually found himself writing music again—something he hadn't done in a long, long time. He knew he'd been inspired by Indigo and the way she acted on impulse and saw joy in everything.

Each day grew more bittersweet, because each day was nearer to the moment when he'd have to leave her.

And then it hit him.

He didn't want to leave her. He liked having Indigo in his life, and he was pretty sure she liked having him in her life. OK, so they'd agreed this would be a fling and it would end when he left for Melvante. But there was no reason why they couldn't renegotiate that agreement.

'Indi—I've been thinking,' he said, when they were lying on a blanket by the summer house, looking up at the stars.

'Should I be worried?' she teased.

'I leave in three days.'

'I know.' She stroked his face. 'I'll miss you.'

'I'll miss you, too.' He shifted so that he was facing her and could look into her eyes. 'That's why I've been thinking. It doesn't have to be like this.'

'Yes, it does. You're going off to be King of Melvante, and I'm staying here at Edensfield to finish my work on the library windows.'

'You've made a business commitment, and of course you want to honour that. But when you've finished here, there's nothing to stop you coming to Melvante and being with me.' He stole a kiss. 'Between-times, we're going to have to be pretty much long-distance, but we're only a couple of hours apart by plane. We can work something out.'

'Hang on. Are you saying you want to make this thing between us…?' She looked at him, wide-eyed.

'Official and no longer temporary. Yes.'

He wanted to be with her. In public as well as in private. And she wouldn't be Indigo Moran, stained-glass restorer, any more. She'd be the equivalent of a royal WAG, living her life on a public stage, hobbled by rules and regulations.

Yes, she'd be with Lorenzo. She wouldn't have to give him up.

But the misery of his lifestyle would eat into their relationship, sucking up all the love and leaving nothing but emptiness and hurt.

And she really, really didn't want that. She wanted to keep these memories intact. Perfect.

'Indi?' he asked.

Telling him the truth would hurt him. But going along with what he wanted would hurt him more, in the end. 'No, we couldn't,' she said softly. 'I wouldn't fit into your world, Lorenzo.'

'How do you know?'

'I just do.'

Which gave him nothing to argue against. He needed to know why she was so set against it. So he asked her straight out. 'Indi, what's so bad about my world?'

'It's full of rules and regulations. You're stuck in a box and you're expected to stay there. And you have to watch what you do, the whole time. Especially now there's social media—it means you can never switch off. You're being watched every second of the day. One accidental slip, and suddenly you've told the whole world something that maybe you would rather have kept private. It's like talking with a megaphone in the middle of a plinth on Trafalgar Square. And it gets passed on within seconds—juicy gossip.' She shuddered.

'And then someone else does something, and what you said or did is forgotten about.'

'Until the next time. Then it's dragged up again. Every little mistake is catalogued and held against you.'

'You'd be in a different position, as my partner,' he said. 'Nobody would try to put you down.'

She could see in his expression that he really believed it. For someone so clever, she thought, sometimes he just didn't have a clue what it was like in the real world. 'Maybe not to my face, but behind my back they would. Everyone expects you to marry a princess. And the press would be merciless. They'd want to know what you see in me. They'd dig up all the stuff about my parents.' And about Nigel—and she really didn't want to tell Lorenzo about that. She was too ashamed of how naive and stupid she'd been, having a relationship with a man who'd turned out to be married. And it still hurt to think about the miscarriage; talking about it was next to impossible.

'You can't be held to ransom by the choices your parents made,' he said.

'I can't fit into your world, Lorenzo. Don't ask me. I don't want to be the stick that the press uses to beat you. And we only have a few days left together. Please don't spoil it.'

What could he say to that?

All he could do was hold her.

And, that night, his lovemaking was much more intense. Yearning. If only she'd give them a chance, he was sure they could make it work.

But stubborn was definitely her middle name, and he didn't have a clue where to start convincing her that life with him wouldn't be anywhere near as scary as she feared.

On Lorenzo's last night, he fell asleep in Indigo's arms. She lay there, unable to sleep and wishing that she could somehow freeze time.

He'd asked her to make their relationship permanent. But how could she? She'd expose him to the kind of scandal he really didn't need, especially as he was just going to start ruling Melvante. She didn't want that tarnished.

'You're going to be a brilliant king,' she whispered, holding him close. 'Go with my love, always, and I wish things could've been different.'

Now, she knew she was always going to be on her own, because Lorenzo had spoiled her for other men. Nobody would ever match up to him, and it wouldn't be fair to get involved with someone else, knowing that he'd always be second best to Lorenzo. But being single was fine. She had good friends and her job. They'd see her through.

Though, when Lorenzo did marry his suitable princess, Indigo definitely wasn't going to tune in to the televised

broadcast. She'd wish him luck, but she couldn't watch him marry someone else.

'I wish we'd met in another life,' she said softly. 'When things could have worked. But it wasn't to be, and we're going to be grown up about it. We're going to shake hands, say goodbye, and walk away from each other with our hearts intact.'

Even though she knew she was lying to herself.

When Lorenzo woke, the next morning, Indigo was still asleep. Her mermaid hair was spread all over the pillow, and her eyelashes were so long. So cute.

'If only you weren't so stubborn,' he said softly. Why couldn't she see that they could make it work? This was the twenty-first century, and a lot of the old social taboos had been broken. It didn't matter that she wasn't a princess. It didn't matter that her parents hadn't been married and that she was the child of an affair—it wasn't her fault. And he knew that Indigo was strong enough to hold her own in any social situation; she had a genuine warmth and enthusiasm that would draw people to her. Even those who maybe wouldn't want to accept her at first would come round, once they'd met her.

But the main stumbling block was Indigo herself.

If she didn't believe in herself—in their relationship— then it couldn't work.

How could he get her to believe?

He held her until she woke, then made love to her one last time. And he knew his own eyelashes were as wet as hers.

'We don't have to say goodbye,' he said, holding her close. 'We can make this work.'

She simply shook her head, as if not trusting herself to speak.

He sighed, and reached for his wallet. 'Here.'

She looked at the storage card. 'What's this?'

'For you. I wrote a song. Well, there aren't any words. But it's called "Indigo".'

'You wrote a song for me?'

'About how you make me feel.'

'Nobody's ever written a song for me before.' She stared at him in wonder. 'Thank you.'

'You might hate it.'

'I won't.'

Funny how she could be so sure of that, and yet she didn't have that same belief in *them*.

'Actually, I have something for you.' She slid out of bed and rummaged in a drawer, then handed him a cardboard tube. 'Don't look at it now. Later.'

She'd drawn something for him?

'Thank you,' he said softly.

She swallowed hard. 'I guess this is goodbye. I don't... not in front of everyone else.'

She'd be working when he left, he guessed. So she could hide behind her glass.

'I know,' he said softly. 'I'm not going to say the words.'

'Be happy,' she said. 'And you're going to be an awesome king.'

There was a lump in his throat and it was hard to get the words out. 'You be happy, too. And I hope you find someone who can give you what I can't.' Freedom. But he was pretty sure that she wouldn't find someone who loved her the way he'd grown to love her.

Later, on the plane back to Melvante, he opened the cardboard tube and took out the piece of cartridge paper. She'd drawn an angel in a rose bower—and the angel had his face.

Indigo and her angels. He smiled fondly, remembering

the church they'd visited together and the joy in her face as she'd shown him the glass.

Then he looked closer. Was it his imagination, or were those roses covering the bars of a cage?

That was how she saw his life. Trapped in a cage.

But it didn't have to be that way. It could be just roses. Somehow, he was going to have to convince her. And not just her: he also had to convince his grandfather that he'd found the woman who would be right for him and right for Melvante.

And maybe a little space between them—space where she had time to think and time to miss him—would help him do that.

CHAPTER NINE

THE BED WAS too wide, the days were too long and everything felt muted.

So much for being able to walk away intact at the end of their affair, Indigo thought. She'd really been deluding herself.

Still. Lorenzo had gone back to Melvante, where he belonged, and that was that. She still had the job she loved, and some good friends who were every bit as good as family. So she'd be just fine, she told herself sternly. Crying herself to sleep was pointless and ridiculous.

But she found it really hard to face breakfast in the mornings.

And she kept waking up at night. Which was ridiculous. At her age, she shouldn't need to get up in the middle of the night to go to the loo.

And maybe it was time she started watching what she ate, because her bra was feeling too tight.

A nasty, insidious thought wormed its way into her brain. Wonky appetite, tight bra, needing the loo in the middle of the night...She'd been there before, a couple of years ago. When her life had imploded.

No. Of course not. She was being paranoid. She and Lorenzo had always been careful about contraception. The last thing a king-to-be needed was an accidental baby,

particularly when there was no way he could marry the baby's mother. And she had seriously unhappy memories from her miscarriage, two years ago.

But, now she thought about it, her period *was* a few days late. And she was usually regular down to the hour.

Maybe her period was late because she was stressed and upset about Lorenzo leaving. She hoped so. Because the alternative—that somehow their contraception had failed—would make life way, way too complicated.

Toto had taken to following Indigo about since Lorenzo had left, and tended to stay by her side in the workroom. The Labrador thumped his tail against the floor and nuzzled her knee, as if to say that he could tell she was upset and he was there.

'Lovely boy.' Indigo bent to make a fuss of him. 'I'm being stupid. Of course I'm not pregnant. I can't be.'

Though being pregnant would also explain why she kept crying. The tears could be due to her hormones running amok, not just because she missed the man she loved but knew she couldn't have.

'I can't be pregnant,' she said again.

Though she knew she wouldn't be able to settle until she knew the truth.

After the visitors had left Edensfield and her workroom was silent again, she drove to the nearest large town where she knew she'd be anonymous and bought a pregnancy test from the supermarket.

'Indigo Moran, you're being totally ridiculous. Of course you're not pregnant, and this is going to prove it once and for all,' she told herself sternly.

Back in her bathroom at Edensfield, she did the test, and watched the windows. One to show that she'd performed the test properly, and one that could turn her life upside down.

The last time she'd done a pregnancy test, she'd cried with joy, thinking that although the baby wasn't planned it would give Nigel the excuse he needed to commit properly to her. That she'd have their baby. That once again in her life she'd have someone who was related to her by blood, someone she could love and who'd love her back.

Nigel's reaction to the news had shocked her to the core. But she'd decided to keep the baby; after all, it wasn't the baby's fault that its father had turned out to be a cheat and a liar.

And then, six weeks later, she'd felt the drag low in her belly as she'd miscarried.

She sucked in a breath. This wasn't going to be like that. At all. Because she wasn't pregnant. She wasn't. She couldn't be.

Shaking herself mentally, she glanced at the test stick again.

And then she saw the result.
Positive.

Melvante might be his home, but it wasn't where his heart was, Lorenzo thought.

Being without Indigo for the last few days had crystallised for him exactly what he wanted in a life partner—someone who was bright and sparkly in her own right, who would support him and help him think straight by asking awkward questions, and who would keep her own interests in life, too. He loved her free-spiritedness.

Except he knew she was right about the sticking point. She'd hate what his lifestyle would become, once he was crowned king.

But there had to be a middle way. There had to be space for compromise. And hopefully, if she missed him as much

as he missed her, she'd help him work out a compromise to suit them both.

He lasted two more days before he tackled his grandfather at the breakfast table.

'Nonno, you know you said I should think about marriage?'

'Yes.' His grandfather poured them both more coffee. 'So you're ready to discuss it? Good. I've drawn up a list of suitable brides.' He smiled at Lorenzo. 'Just as my father did for me.'

'That's the point, Nonno. I've already met the woman I want to marry,' Lorenzo said. 'Her name's Indigo Moran, she's a stained-glass restoration specialist, and she's—well, she makes me a better man. And I know I'll be a better king if I marry for love rather than duty.'

'I've had this conversation before.' His grandfather grimaced. 'With your father. He married for love, and look what happened.'

He'd ended up driving his car into a brick wall, with Lorenzo's mother by his side, killing them both. The rest of the world thought it was a tragic accident, but Lorenzo and his grandfather knew the truth: it had been a deliberate act, because Lorenzo's father couldn't bear the idea of his wife leaving him.

Lorenzo looked his grandfather straight in the eye. 'Nonno, I've spent most of my life trying to show you that I'm not my father. Indigo is nothing like my mother.'

'Your father married for love and it went wrong,' his grandfather pointed out. 'I married for duty, and your grandmother and I were happy together. We both knew what was expected of us.'

'I want to marry someone who understands my work and supports me,' Lorenzo said.

'Which your grandmother did for me.'

'Did you love Nonna?' Lorenzo asked.

'I respected her and I admired her,' his grandfather said. 'So, yes, I loved her.'

'Whenever you saw her, did your heart beat faster and the world seem a little brighter?'

His grandfather smiled ruefully. 'Lorenzo, you're confusing passion with love. Love is something that grows out of respect and mutual understanding. Something solid. Passion...that never lasts. It's like a firework—it burns brightly, it feels spectacular, and it's over almost immediately. Take my advice, and marry for sense—don't marry for passion. Your father married for passion, and he regretted it.'

'I'm not my father,' Lorenzo said again. 'I was thinking—you wanted to do something to mark the coronation. We could commission a rose window for the castle.'

'And you just *happen* to know a glass specialist,' his grandfather said wryly.

Lorenzo smiled. 'OK, so that was a little unsubtle. But it's a good way for you to meet Indi without raising any expectations on either side.'

'How does she feel about you?' his grandfather asked.

'That's tricky,' Lorenzo said. 'She has doubts about the world we live in. She thinks it's like a goldfish bowl.'

'It is, and she's right to have doubts. Our world isn't an easy one.' His grandfather sighed. 'You need to understand that you and I have responsibilities that other people don't. We have to put the needs of our country before our own needs. Which is why you need to marry someone who can cope with our world. Someone who's been brought up in it. Someone who doesn't have doubts.'

'Just meet her,' Lorenzo said. 'Give her a chance. And maybe she can give our world a chance.'

'And then?'

'We'll play it by ear,' Lorenzo said decisively.

'You've changed,' his grandfather said. 'The Lorenzo I know plans everything a long way in advance.'

Which was how he'd been brought up. Formal and rigid and disconnected from people. 'I still do,' Lorenzo said. 'But I've learned a lot from Indi. Sometimes, to really connect with people and make a difference, you have to be a bit more flexible.'

'She taught you that?' His grandfather looked thoughtful. 'She sounds an intriguing young woman.'

'She is.' Lorenzo smiled. 'I'll call her and arrange it.'

There was a gentle but insistent rap on the door. 'Indi? Indi, are you all right? Can I come in?'

Lottie.

Should she lie and pretend that she had a crashing headache?

But Lottie was perceptive. Even if Indigo could stall her for now, Lottie would notice that something was up. And she was a close enough and old enough friend to ask what was wrong.

'Come in,' she croaked.

'Indi, you've been crying,' Lottie said as she walked in and closed the door behind her.

Indigo felt the tears well up and forced them back.

'Sweetie, what's wrong?' Lottie asked. 'Is this to do with Lorenzo?'

'Sort of,' she hedged.

Lottie hugged her. 'I know you're missing him. Look, do you want Gus to have a word with him?'

'No, I'll be fine.' Indigo shook her head. 'I'll pull myself together.'

'Why don't you go to Melvante and see him?'

She blew out a breath. 'I can't do that. He's busy preparing to be king.'

'But you're missing him, and I bet he's missing you just as much.'

'We agreed it was just a fling and we were both going to walk away at the end.'

Lottie raised her eyebrows. 'I think it was more than just a fling. You fell for him, didn't you?'

Indigo bit her lip. 'Is it that obvious?'

'Sweetie, you two might have thought you were being discreet, but it was obvious to everyone,' Lottie said, squeezing her hand. 'You both always seemed to disappear at the same time, so we knew you were together—and the way you looked at each other across a room was, well…' She fanned herself. 'Scorching.'

'Oh.' Indigo felt the colour flood into her face. 'Sorry. We didn't mean to—' Then, to her horror, she burst into tears.

Lottie held her close and let her cry.

'Sorry. I'm being really wet,' she apologised.

'No, you've been alone for a long time and you just fell in love with Lorenzo.'

'He's the worst person I could fall in love with.'

'I can think of worse,' Lottie said darkly. 'Besides, Lorenzo's one of the good guys. Actually, Gus has already had the big-brother talk with him about you.'

Indigo scrubbed away the tears. 'That's so sweet of him.'

'Gus thinks of you as his other little sister. Actually, you're the sister I would've chosen, if I'd been able to.'

Indigo sniffed. 'Don't, Lottie, you'll make me cry even more.'

'What is it, Indi?'

She dragged in a breath. 'I don't know where to start.'

'Try the beginning—or the middle, if it's easier. Or just cut to the difficult bit and come straight out with it,' Lottie suggested.

'The difficult bit.' Indigo raked a hand through her hair. Well, she'd been here before. And Lottie had listened before. She was a safe person to tell. 'I'm pregnant.'

Lottie placed a hand on her shoulder. 'Indi, are you sure? You're not just late because you're stressed about Lorenzo going back to Melvante?'

'I'm sure.' Her breath hitched. 'I did a test. Three days ago.'

'You've known about this for *three days* and you didn't tell me?' Lottie looked hurt.

'I didn't want to dump it on you like I did last time, and I'm—I'm—oh, God, I'm so sorry.' She felt her face crumple again.

'Stop apologising. You're not dumping it on me. That's what friends are for, and I know you'd be there for me if it was the other way round.' Lottie hugged her again. 'So what do you want to do?'

'I don't know what to do for the best.' Three sleepless nights hadn't helped her decide a single thing. 'I mean, I have to tell Lorenzo—of course I do, it wouldn't be fair to keep the news to myself—but I'm not expecting anything from him.'

'He's not Nigel the Scumbag. He's an honourable man.'

'That's the point, Lottie. He's about to become the King of Melvante. Having an illegitimate child just isn't going to work for him.'

Lottie spread her hands. 'So make the child legitimate and marry the man. You and Lorenzo are crazy about each other.'

'But I won't fit into his world.' Indigo sighed. 'And it'll be like living in a goldfish bowl, with everyone watching what I do all the time. I can't just decide to go to the park

or the beach because it's a glorious day. His schedules are mapped out months in advance and there are security people everywhere. I don't want that kind of life for me or for my baby.'

'What about what Lorenzo wants?' Lottie asked.

'He's got enough on his plate without having to deal with a baby.'

'Indi...you're not thinking...?' Lottie looked horrified.

Indigo shook her head. 'I haven't exactly slept well for the last three nights. I've had time to think about it. And I'm going to make the same decision as I made last time.' She dragged in a breath. '*Last time.* And we both know what happened then. Who's to say this won't resolve itself in the same way?'

'You lost the baby then, but it doesn't mean to say you're going to lose this baby. Right now, what you need,' Lottie said, 'is to see a doctor and get checked over. Get all the blood tests done and what have you. And I'll come with you to hold your hand.'

'I can't ask you to do that.'

'You're not asking—I'm telling you,' Lottie said. 'And, for once, that independent streak of yours is going to have to shut up and listen. Right?'

Indigo gave her a watery smile. 'Right.'

When Indigo came out of the doctor's surgery—with her pregnancy confirmed and a dating scan booked in at the hospital—she switched on her phone.

The message flashed up onto the screen: two missed calls. Both from Lorenzo. And there was a voicemail from him asking if she could give him a call.

She swallowed hard. How stupid to find herself almost in tears just at hearing his voice. That had to be the hor-

mones whizzing round her system. She really wasn't that pathetic and needy.

Why did he want her to call him? Surely he didn't...?

She shook herself. No. Of *course* he didn't have any idea about the situation she was in right now. He couldn't read her mind, and she knew that Lottie wouldn't have betrayed her confidence.

Returning his call would at least give her the chance to talk to him. Maybe she'd get an opening to broach the subject of the baby. Not that telling him on the phone was ideal, but talking to him would be a start. She could see how he sounded and play it by ear.

Once back in the privacy of her car, she rang Lorenzo. Although she'd half expected to end up leaving a message on his voicemail, he answered immediately. 'Indi. Hello. Thanks for calling back.'

'You're welcome.' And she was *not* going to burst into tears. She played it as cool as she could. 'What can I do for you?'

'I have a commission for you. In Melvante. I was thinking maybe a rose window.'

Her dream job. She'd talked to him about what she'd love to create, given the chance. And he was offering her that chance—albeit in his home, rather than her own.

'Would this be in the palace?' she asked tentatively.

'Yes. It's for the coronation. I know it's ridiculously short notice, but do you think you could fit it in?'

So he wanted her to work for him?

How naive she'd been, thinking that he might've wanted just to talk to her. After all, he'd asked her to make their fling permanent and she'd turned him down. He had no reason to think she might have changed her mind or regretted the decision. Their affair was over and life had moved on; he was about to become king. And he even sounded

different—slightly more formal and a little distant. Which made what she needed to tell him even more difficult. Just how was she going to bring up something so emotional, when all he wanted to talk to her about was work?

'I could look at where you want to site it and come up with some designs, yes,' she said carefully. She had some more projects scheduled in for when she'd finished at Edensfield, but she was pretty sure that her clients would be flexible about the timescales if she asked them nicely. 'When were you thinking?'

'Tomorrow?' he suggested.

'Sorry, I really can't. I'm fitting the mermaid window back into place at Edensfield tomorrow.'

'How about the day after?'

'The day after is fine,' she said. Though he'd forgotten one crucial little detail. 'Provided I can book a flight. If there isn't one available, it might have to be later.'

'You don't need to book a flight.'

'As a mere mortal,' she said crisply, 'I don't actually have wings to get me to Melvante under my own steam.'

'I didn't mean that. I meant, I'll get it arranged for you.' He laughed. 'Oh, Indi. I've missed your straight talking.'

Maybe. But he clearly didn't miss *her*.

As if he could read her thoughts, he said softly, 'But not as much as I've missed you.'

She had to swallow really, really hard. Because right then she really, really missed him. Talking to him and knowing that he was hundreds of miles away was sheer torture.

'Come to Melvante,' he said, his voice as warm and tempting as melted chocolate.

'Because you want me to design some glass for you?'

She regretted the words as soon as they were out, know-

ing how needy they made her sound. And she didn't want Lorenzo to think she was pathetic.

'The commission's genuine,' he said, 'and I'll pay the going rate—I'm not expecting you to give me some ridiculously huge discount. But I guess it's also an excuse to see you.'

And she really needed to see him. Oh, God. The idea of Lorenzo wrapping his arms round her and holding her close, telling her not to worry and that everything would be OK because he loved her...

But how could he possibly do that? He was about to become the King of Melvante. She knew Lorenzo was attracted to her, and she knew he liked her. Maybe the two together made up love. Though Indigo had learned not to trust love, because in her experience it just ended in heartache. Nigel had dumped her as soon as he'd discovered that she was pregnant, and then she'd found out how deep his betrayal had been. OK, so Lorenzo wasn't a cheat and a liar—but, even so, how could he possibly support her and the baby, with all that he had going on in his life right now? Plus the press would have a field day if they found out that the new King of Melvante was going to have a love-child with a woman who was the illegitimate daughter of an earl...

She couldn't see any way out of it. Lorenzo had to follow his duty, and that would mean dumping her because she was totally unsuitable to be a queen. And, even if her life hadn't been so tarnished in the past, there was the fact that he'd live the rest of his life in the glare of the public eye—which wasn't what she wanted for herself or for the baby.

'Indi? Are you still there?' he asked.

'It's a bad connection,' she lied.

'OK. I'll get Salvatore to call you with the flight details and an agenda.'

'Who's Salvatore?'

'My assistant. I'll see you the day after tomorrow. *Ciao.*'

He hung up, and Indi stared at her phone. This didn't seem real. She'd just agreed to go to Melvante and see him. And the way he'd dropped so easily into speaking Italian at the end of their conversation... Well, it wasn't surprising. He was right where he belonged, in his European kingdom. While she belonged here in England. And she had a nasty feeling that the distance between them now wasn't just geographical.

CHAPTER TEN

LATER THAT AFTERNOON, Indigo's phone rang. She didn't recognise the number on the screen and almost didn't answer it, assuming it was some cold-caller; then again, Lorenzo had said that his assistant would contact her about the flights. Maybe it was him.

She answered the phone warily. 'Hello?'

'Signorina Moran?' The stranger's voice had a very slight accent, something which sounded as if it came from the southern Mediterranean.

'Yes,' she said. 'Who's calling?'

'My name is Salvatore Pozzi. I'm the personal assistant to His Royal Highness Prince Lorenzo of Melvante. He asked me to get in touch with you with the details of your flight.'

'Thank you.' Oh, and how formal was this guy? No wonder Lorenzo was so buttoned up if this was the way things were in Melvante. The chances were that she wouldn't fit into his private world, either, she thought with a sinking heart.

'Do you have an email address so I can send you the information and the agenda for meeting His Royal Highness?' Salvatore asked.

Agenda? Meeting?

It all felt very cool, very brisk—and it was the total opposite to what she'd shared with Lorenzo here in England.

Well, it was her own fault for blurring the lines between business and personal stuff. Here at Edensfield, they'd been in a bubble, protected from the rest of the world. In Melvante, Lorenzo was in the full glare of the public eye. A business meeting with him was the best she could hope for. And what he'd said about missing her—maybe he did, but things were different now and she knew he couldn't afford to act on those feelings.

'Yes, I have an email address.' She dictated it coolly and professionally. Because, after all, this was a job. She was planning to meet her client, not her lover. And she'd better keep that in mind if she wanted to keep what was left of her heart intact.

'*Bene*. Good. I'll email you now. If there are any problems or you have any questions when you've read through the details, please call me.'

'I will. And thank you for your help,' she said.

'My pleasure, Signorina Moran.' Though there wasn't really any warmth in his voice. It was just politeness.

By the time she'd powered up her laptop, the email from Salvatore was waiting in her in-box. Her flight was at ten a.m. the day after tomorrow—from the local airport rather than one of the larger London airports, so she guessed there would probably be a connecting flight somewhere in Europe. And there was an agenda giving her times when the prince would be meeting her over the next few days. A briefing meeting. A tour of the castle. A tour of the cathedral. A status update. A meeting with His Majesty King Lorenzo II and His Royal Highness Prince Lorenzo to discuss final details—oh, help. Not just Lorenzo, then. His grandfather as well. And his grandfather definitely wouldn't approve of her.

Everything was tightly scheduled, she noticed, down to the minute. Well, obviously Lorenzo had a thousand and

one demands on his time right now. She was lucky he was giving her this much time.

But just when was she going to get the chance to tell him about the baby?

She blew out a breath. She'd definitely have to play that one by ear. But at least she had enough time in between those meetings to work on the designs and come up with something she hoped would do him justice.

She finished scanning the list. Charity ball? What? Why on earth did he want her to go to that? Oh, for pity's sake. He must know she wasn't the kind of person who went to glamorous events like charity balls. She was a glass geek who was more likely to go to an exhibition or find the nearest art gallery or medieval church.

Apart from the fact that Lorenzo had made it very clear he was busy—otherwise he would've called her himself with the flight details and he wouldn't have asked his assistant to send her an agenda—Indigo didn't trust her voice not to wobble when she spoke to him. Salvatore had said to call him with any queries, but this one was a little bit too personal. So she sent Salvatore a brief, polite email thanking him for the information, then texted Lorenzo. Why is there a charity ball on the agenda?

t took him a while to respond. Probably, she thought, because he was in a meeting and there would be tons of other messages on his phone. Assuming he didn't just forward everything to his assistant to deal with; and then the fact that she'd texted the prince instead of contacting his assistant wouldn't go down too well.

Too late, now. She couldn't recall the message.

She was just finishing up a last piece of work on the mermaid window when her phone beeped to signal a text. She made herself wait to read it and not rush straight to

it. So you can meet some of the people of my country, get more of a feel for the background. Are you worried about it?

Trust him to pick up on that. Of course not. she lied.

Of course she was worried about attending a charity ball in Melvante. Even though she'd be there as a business associate, there was still a chance that people might guess that her relationship with Lorenzo hadn't been strictly business in England.

Just checking the dress code, she typed.even though she was pretty sure she knew what it was already.

Black tie, he responded.

Which meant a ball gown. Something she didn't own. Luckily, she knew two people who did and who'd be prepared to lend her one—and they were both here in this house, which would save her a rushed journey. OK. Thanks.

He didn't text her back, this time. Super-busy, she guessed. Still. At least she was going to see him. And she would have plenty of time in Melvante to think, to work out how to tell him about the baby.

Funny how just talking to Indigo had made him antsy, Lorenzo thought. It brought home to him how much he'd missed her. How much he wanted to see her.

But she'd sounded very cool, calm and businesslike on the phone. So was she going to treat this as just another commission, or was she using it as an excuse to see him—the way he was using it as an excuse to see her?

He really couldn't tell.

So he'd just have to compartmentalise things and

keep his feelings separate. Maybe he'd be able to tell more when he saw her.

Work kept Indigo occupied for the rest of the day; she spent the evening looking up everything she could about Melvante and making notes. The next day was spent putting the mermaid window in place; and then it was time to pack. Just as well, she thought, that she had her passport with her; she and Lottie had spent a girly weekend in Paris just before she'd started work on the window, and she'd gone to Edensfield from Paris rather than via her flat in London.

'I'll drive you to the airport—I've got stuff to do in town anyway, so it's not very far out of my way. And you can leave all your stuff here while you're in Melvante. You need to be back here for the official unveiling of the window, in any case,' Lottie told her.

'Thanks.' She paused. 'Lottie, I meant to ask you last night—can I borrow a ball gown, please?'

'A ball gown?' Lottie looked surprised.

'Lorenzo wants me to attend a charity ball. He says it's good background for designing his window.'

Lottie raised an eyebrow. 'He must live on a different planet.'

One where Indigo knew she wouldn't fit in. 'I guess.'

'Of course you can borrow a ball gown. Come and raid my wardrobe.'

Doing something girly helped to occupy Indigo's mind for a little while, but once she'd chosen a plain black ball gown—one she intended to wear with her red strappy shoes, to give her a bit of courage—and packed some business suits, her mind went back to Lorenzo. How was he going to react to her? And how would he react to the news about the baby?

Worry kept her awake for most of the night, having end-less conversations in her head with him. And she couldn't even drink coffee to keep her awake, the next morning—apart from the fact that it wouldn't be good for the baby, the smell of it made her feel queasy. Maybe she could have a nap on the plane or something.

She didn't say much on the way to the airport; her stom-ach felt as if it was tied in knots and panic rather than blood was flowing through her veins. But she made an effort when Lottie dropped her off.

'Thanks, Lottie.' Indigo hugged her. 'I'll text you when I get there.'

'Good. And remember, Indi, Lorenzo's not Nigel. He's not going to abandon you.'

'I know.' Though he might not actually have a choice in the matter, Indigo thought. He might *have* to abandon her.

Why couldn't she have fallen for a man who didn't come with complications?

At the customer services desk, she said to the assistant, 'I think I have a ticket to pick up?' She gave her name and the flight number.

'Of course, Madam. This way.'

To Indigo's surprise, she was waved straight through Customs. There were none of the usual checks she was used to—not even her passport, much less having her bag X-rayed and walking through a scanner. What was going on?

When she was escorted out to the runway, she saw a small private jet.

What?

'Is there—well—some mistake?' she asked. 'I was ex-pecting a connecting flight to Melvante.'

'There's no connection needed, Madam,' the attendant told her. 'This is the Melvante royal plane.'

Lorenzo had sent the royal plane for her? But…

'I—um—thank you,' she said, flustered. No wonder he'd said that she wouldn't need to sort out a flight. This one was just for her. Which was crazy. She barely even travelled first class, let alone in super-luxury. This wasn't the kind of life she was used to.

Clutching her suitcase, she walked up the steps to the door of the plane, where a woman in a smart navy suit greeted her.

'Good morning, *signorina*. My name is Maria, and I'm your flight attendant today. Let me take your luggage.'

Indigo had to blink twice as she stepped into the aisle. This was nothing like the kind of planes she'd flown in before, with slightly cramped seats and a narrow aisle. This was more like a hotel business suite than a plane. There were cream leather sofas at one end, and a table at the other end which looked as if it belonged in a board room together with the deeply padded chairs. There was even an arrangement of fresh flowers on a coffee table.

'His Royal Highness asked us to make sure you were comfortable on your journey, *signorina*,' Maria said, ushering her over to one of the sofas. 'May I get you something to eat or drink?'

'A glass of water would be lovely, please, Maria,' Indigo said, summoning a smile. Right at that moment she felt very much out of her depth. Lorenzo hadn't sent her a plane ticket—he'd sent her a *plane*. How unreal was that?

'Can I offer you a magazine?'

Indigo shook her head. 'That's very kind of you, but I was actually planning to do some work.'

'Of course. You're very welcome to use the table, if you prefer it to the sofas. There are plugs if you need them to charge a laptop.'

'Thank you, Maria,' she said, and settled herself at the table.

When Maria returned with a glass of water, Indigo noticed that it had ice and a slice of lime too. And the glass was lead crystal rather than the disposable plastic cups she was used to seeing on a plane.

'If you wish for anything, please ring the bell and I'll come straight away,' Maria said.

'Thank you, Maria.' Indigo tried out some of the Italian she'd learned over the last day or so. *'Mille grazie.'*

Maria's smile showed her how much the gesture was appreciated.

So this was what a royal lifestyle meant. The ultimate in comfort and convenience. And yet it wasn't super-flashy; the room had a businesslike air.

And she'd better remember that she was going to be in Melvante on business, first and foremost.

She read through the file she'd made on Melvante, the day before, and made some more notes for possible designs. The flight went incredibly quickly; at the airport in Melvante, she was also waved straight through Customs with no passport check. Then again, she supposed, if you were travelling on the king's private plane, that kind of guaranteed you were expected and welcome in the country.

There was a car waiting for her; she recognised the chauffeur standing outside. 'Bruno! How lovely to see you.'

'And you, too, Signorina Moran,' he said with a formal little bow.

'It's Indi to you, as you know very well,' she said with a smile, and gave him a hug that made him blush.

When Bruno opened the rear door for her, she asked, 'Can I be cheeky and ask if I can sit in the front with you,

please, Bruno? All this…' She grimaced. 'It's a little bit overwhelming.'

'Of course, *signo*—' he began, then with a smile corrected himself. 'Indi.' He opened the door for her and waited for her to settle before closing it again and going round to the driver's side.

Indigo had seen a similar large black diplomatic car with tinted windows at Edensfield, but Bruno hadn't been in livery there. Here, he wore a smart uniform with gold braid and a cap, and he looked every inch a royal chauffeur. This was feeling more and more unreal with every second.

In a different life, Lorenzo might have met her at the airport himself. He might have run towards her, lifted her off her feet, swung her round, and kissed her until they were both dizzy.

But Lorenzo in England wasn't the same as Lorenzo in Melvante. Here, he was about to become the king. And it most definitely wasn't suitable for a king to meet a contractor at the airport, much less greet her with such warmth.

How would he greet her when the schedule said he'd meet her? Would he be cool, calm, collected and distant? Or would he still be the man he'd been in England, passionate once his defences were down?

She damped down the panic. 'I assume His Royal Highness is in a meeting?'

'He's always in meetings,' Bruno said. 'He works harder than anyone I know.'

That didn't surprise her. She knew that Lorenzo had a strong sense of duty, and she respected that. 'Uh-huh,' she said.

Although Indigo could normally chat to anyone, and she'd chatted quite happily to Bruno at Edensfield, right now she was feeling ever so slightly intimidated. As they

drove through the city towards the castle, she could see that it was just as Lorenzo had said: a picture-postcard style white stone castle with turrets and pointy tiled roofs. Had she been visiting the place on holiday, she would have thought it pretty. But, at that moment, it felt as if it towered over her disapprovingly.

Bruno parked the car on the gravel outside the castle, opened the door for her and took her bag, then ushered her in to the castle through what she guessed was the equivalent of the tradesman's entrance.

He took her through to an office; as she stepped onto the carpet, her feet sank into it. Everywhere was polished wood and gilt—like the office of a CEO in a major company. Which, Indigo supposed, was effectively Lorenzo's position. Only his 'company' happened to be a country.

A middle-aged man in a three-piece suit looked up from behind his mahogany desk as the door opened, and stood up. He said something swiftly in Italian to Bruno—too fast for Indigo to translate, with her meagre stock of tourist vocabulary—and inclined his head at her. 'Good afternoon, Signorina Moran. I am Salvatore Pozzi.'

'Good afternoon, Signor Pozzi.' She stepped forward and offered her hand; and when he took it she made sure that her handshake was firm and businesslike. 'Thank you for arranging my flight and the car here.'

'No problem.' Though he still wasn't smiling.

'Bye, Bruno,' she said as the chauffeur left, sketching her a salute. It felt as if her only friend in the place had gone. Salvatore was perfectly polite, but his expression was inscrutable. Indigo had no idea what Lorenzo had told him about her, or if he knew about their fling back in England.

The only thing she could think to talk about was business. 'The agenda says that I am to meet—' Hmm, so

how did she refer to the prince in front of his assistant? She could hardly call him by his first name—not in such formal surroundings. 'His Royal Highness,' she finished, 'at three.'

'I am afraid His Royal Highness's meeting is running a little late. But if you would care to wait in the sitting room, *signorina*, I can arrange for some tea to be brought to you.'

'Thank you, but I'm fine. Please don't feel you have to order tea.'

'As you wish, *signorina*.' Salvatore led her through to another room. There was still the same deep carpet, exquisite furnishings and silk drapes at the window. It really brought it home to Indigo that she was in a palace, not just a normal office or home.

'Please sit down.' Salvatore indicated the sofa.

Just then a dog burst through the doorway, trotted over to them with his tail a wagging blur, and sniffed at her.

'Caesar!' Salvatore scolded. 'Bad dog—you shouldn't be in here.'

'Lorenzo's favourite spaniel. The one who sneaks onto sofas.' Indigo smiled, remembering what he'd told her about the palace dogs.

Salvatore looked surprised, and she realised what she'd just said. 'I mean, um, His Royal Highness's spaniel,' she corrected herself swiftly.

He looked slightly less disapproving now she'd remembered her place and resumed formal protocol. 'Yes.'

'I like dogs,' she offered. And at least having a dog to make a fuss of would give her something else to think about instead of worrying how it would be when Lorenzo finally came out of his meeting to see her again. 'I don't mind if he stays.'

Again, that cool inscrutable expression. 'If you're sure, *signorina*.'

'I'm sure.' She sat down. 'Come and sit with me, Caesar.'

The dog gave a happy wriggle at the sound of his name and trotted over to the sofa.

Salvatore gave a brief nod. 'I will call you as soon as His Royal Highness Prince Lorenzo is ready to see you.'

'*Mille grazie,*' she said, but Salvatore didn't seem as impressed as Maria had been by her effort to speak Italian. He just gave another of those curt little nods and left.

'So it's just you and me, Caesar,' she said.

The dog wagged his tail and put his paws on her knee.

'I'm really glad you're here,' she said. 'Because I have no idea how your master's going to react to me. Whether he meant it about missing me, or whether he just wants me to design a window for him—I haven't a clue.' Lottie had said that Lorenzo wasn't like Nigel, and Indigo knew that was true; at least his first words when she told him about the baby wouldn't be to demand that she had a termination.

But as to how he'd really feel, what he'd say…

She swallowed hard. 'And how he's going to react to my news—that scares me even more. I don't fit in here. I might be the daughter of an earl, but I didn't grow up in his world and I'm no Cinderella. I'd be much happier in the kitchen, chatting to the cooks and swapping recipes for cake.'

Caesar licked her hand.

'I guess it's a matter of wait and see,' she said, and leaned back against the back of the sofa.

Twenty minutes later, Lorenzo walked into the sitting room to discover Indigo fast asleep on the sofa, with Caesar curled up on the sofa in the space behind her knees. She looked exhausted, with dark hollows under her eyes.

Clearly she'd been pushing herself as hard as he'd been pushing himself.

Part of him really wanted to wake her with a kiss, to see those gorgeous blue eyes open and see her smile at him. But part of him thought it would be kinder just to let her rest. He found a blanket and tucked it round her.

'Keep an eye on her, Caesar,' he said softly, and the dog wagged his tail ever so gently, as if trying not to wake her.

'Your Royal Highness, would you like me to—?' Salvatore began.

'No, let her sleep for a bit longer,' Lorenzo said quietly. 'I'll work on my laptop in here for a while.'

CHAPTER ELEVEN

INDIGO WOKE WITH a start, and realised that there was a blanket tucked round her and Lorenzo's spaniel was curled into the crook of her knees. The dog stretched and yawned as she struggled to a sitting position, trying to get her head straight. There definitely hadn't been a blanket anywhere near her. Who had tucked her in like that? She didn't think it would've been Salvatore, who had been cool with her to the point of disapproval. And she was probably late for her meeting with Lorenzo now.

Oh, great. Her first day at the palace, and it had been a total disaster so far.

She glanced at her watch. Not just late—she'd missed the entire meeting.

'Oh, you *idiot*,' she groaned.

'Why am I an idiot?'

She looked over to where the voice had come from.

Lorenzo was sitting in the chair opposite, working on his laptop.

For a second, the world spun. Was this the man who'd been so passionate in England, or was this the king-to-be? She erred on the side of caution. 'Your Royal Highness. I'm so sorry.'

He smiled. 'Don't be. You clearly needed that nap. Been working stupid hours, have we?'

'Pots and kettles. You have bags under your—' She stopped abruptly. This wasn't Edensfield, where they'd both been friends of the family and on an equal footing—where he'd been her lover and she could tease him with impunity. This was Melvante, where he was her client and he was also about to become the head of the country. Which meant she had to deal with him in a completely different way. 'Sorry, Your Royal Highness,' she muttered.

'You really are different, out of England.' His eyes crinkled at the corners. 'Do you think I'm going to have you thrown into the palace dungeons for insubordination, or something?'

'Are there palace dungeons?'

He laughed. 'Yes, but they're not used. We have a progressive judicial system. Lighten up, Indi. I was teasing you.' He smiled. 'Besides, it was cute when you snored in tandem with Caesar.'

He was still teasing her. Which ought to be a good sign. But Indigo was still feeling groggy from her nap, and the secret she had to tell him felt as if it was gripping her in a vice. She had to tell him the truth—but not until she'd worked out the right words to use and the right time to say them.

'I'm sorry,' she said again. 'It was totally unprofessional of me to fall asleep like that.'

'You'd been travelling, and I'd guess you've been working nonstop over the last few days.'

'I have,' she admitted. And she'd missed him, so much. Part of her really wanted to walk over to him, wrap her arms round him, kiss him and tell him how glad she was to see him. Yet, despite the fact that they were in the same room, there was still a huge gulf between them. She couldn't even call him by his given name, because she was too aware of who he was: the future King of Melvante.

What a mess.

'Have I made you late for your next appointment?' she asked.

'No. Salvatore has rearranged my diary slightly.'

Which made her feel even more guilty. And it was another reason for Lorenzo's assistant to disapprove of her. 'Why didn't you just wake me up?'

'Because you looked comfortable.'

'Did you tuck me in?'

He nodded. 'And Caesar was happy to keep you company.'

'He's a nice dog.'

'He's horribly spoiled,' Lorenzo said, but his tone was indulgent.

If only he'd just come over to her and hold her close. How could they be in the same room and yet the gap between them feel wider than the geographical distance when they'd been in different countries?

'I, um, forgot to ask Salvatore which hotel he'd booked me into,' she said. And she really hoped it was one with a reasonable tariff, rather than a super-luxury one with an astronomical room rate. Her finances wouldn't run to the kind of places that Lorenzo would stay.

'You're not. You're staying at the palace.'

Staying with him?

For one mad moment, she thought he was telling her that this was going to be just like Edensfield, and they'd spend their nights curled up together and wake in each other's arms. Then common sense kicked in as he began speaking.

'We have several apartments for guests.'

'I'm not really a guest,' she said. 'I'm here to work.'

'Maybe a bit of both,' he said. 'Come on, I'll take you to your suite.'

And maybe there, in private, he'd be different with her.

She damped down the flicker of hope before she got too carried away. Of course he wouldn't. He was about to be the king. He didn't have time for this.

'Where's your suitcase?'

A prince most definitely couldn't wait on her. 'It's light. I'll carry it myself.' And she gave him a look just to make quite sure he knew she meant it; she was used to relying on herself, and that was the way it would continue to be.

'As you wish,' he said coolly, and she wished she hadn't been quite so quick to knock back his offer. He came from such a formal, restricted world. How would he know how to be anything else?

She still felt faintly groggy, but she followed him through the corridors with the little dog trotting along beside them. Lorenzo stopped by a door and opened it. 'Your suite. I'll let you freshen up.'

So he wasn't planning to spend too much time in private with her, then. She was really in danger of misreading everything. Best to keep it cool, calm and super-professional. 'Thank you very much. Perhaps we can reschedule our briefing meeting.'

'Of course. You still have my mobile phone number, yes?' At her nod, he said, 'Call me when you're ready and I'll come and collect you. Not because you're a prisoner, but because the castle's a bit of a maze and until you know your way around it can be a bit daunting.'

'Thank you.' Not that she was ever going to get to know her way around this castle.

He kissed her lightly on the cheek. 'Come on, Caesar. We need to let Indi settle in,' he told the spaniel, who gave Indigo a mournful look, but followed him down the corridor.

When he'd left, Indigo explored the suite. The sitting room was huge, with a sofa, coffee table and a couple of

armchairs. There was a shelf of books in a variety of languages, a television and a state of the art music system. The bathroom was just acres of marble, with the most enormous walk-in shower, a deep bath and thick fluffy towels. The bedroom held a huge oak four-poster bed, with a wardrobe running the length of the room, a cheval mirror and a chest of drawers. She opened the wardrobe doors and hung up her clothes neatly. A couple of business suits, a couple of pairs of jeans, and Lottie's ball gown; and how meagre her outfits looked in that enormous space. Even if she'd had her entire wardrobe with her, her clothes wouldn't have made much impression.

The pillows looked deep and soft and inviting; she glanced longingly at them, then shook herself. She'd already made enough of a fool of herself, falling asleep on Lorenzo's sofa while she was waiting for his meeting to finish. If she let herself give in to the demands of her pregnancy now and slept again… Well. Lorenzo was sharp. He noticed little details. And she wasn't ready for him to put them all together and work it out for himself. She wanted to tell him the news herself.

Just not quite yet.

She showered and freshened up, then called Lorenzo's mobile.

It went straight to voicemail. Which wasn't so surprising.

'It's Indi. The time's four-thirty in the afternoon. I'm ready whenever you are,' she said, then hung up. She had no idea how long he'd be. But, given that she'd slept straight through their meeting, she was hardly in a position to demand anything.

She worked on her laptop for a while, until there was a knock at the door.

'Come in,' she called.

Lorenzo walked in, with Caesar at his heels. 'Sorry to keep you waiting.'

'No problem. I know you're busy.'

He inclined his head in acknowledgement. 'I meant to ask you, is there anything you'd like for dinner tonight so I can tell chef?'

'Anything, really,' she said, not wanting to be difficult. As long as it didn't have a strong smell. Not that she could explain to him why she wanted bland food without opening up a conversation at totally the wrong time. 'I wasn't expecting you to feed me.'

He smiled at her. 'We're not going to starve you, Indi. I wish I had time to have dinner with you tonight myself, but something's cropped up.'

'It's fine,' she said. Of course he wouldn't have dinner with any of his contractors. Not unless it was scheduled in and rubber-stamped by Salvatore.

'I would have asked you to come with me this evening, but it's state business and it'll be horribly dull.'

At least she would still have been with him, but never mind. She damped down the hurt. 'I know you're up to your eyes,' she said softly. 'It's OK.'

Just for a second, the formality in his face vanished and he looked lonely and lost, as if she was the first person who'd actually noticed that he was struggling to deal with everything. And, after all, it was a huge weight he was about to shoulder, becoming the state leader of his country.

Then the moment passed and Lorenzo was back to being His Royal Highness, ever so slightly remote and aloof. 'Is there anything else you need?'

Only for you to hold me and tell me that everything's going to be all right, she thought. But she knew she couldn't ask for that. Better to stick to business. 'It'd be useful to see the room where the window will be sited.'

'Of course. I can take you there now.'

'That would be good. I'll bring my equipment so I can measure up and take photographs.' Then she grimaced, remembering how he'd been about photographs at Edensfield. 'That is allowed, yes?'

'I'm not going to make you hand over your camera or delete the files,' he said with a smile, clearly remembering their first meeting too.

'And they won't go anywhere but my computer—I won't download them anywhere,' she said.

'I know. But thank you for the reassurance.'

Once she'd gathered her camera, notepad and laptop together, Lorenzo ushered her down the corridor.

Everywhere there were thick carpets and wood panelling; and all the surfaces were so shiny that it was clear there must be a huge number of staff all dusting and polishing the castle to perfection.

'State dining room,' he said, opening one door and letting her peek inside.

Solid gold cutlery, was Indigo's first thought. Followed by *solid gold candelabra.*

She was used to opulence, from her visits to Edensfield, but this was another world entirely. And she'd just bet the crystal glasses were antique, just as any meal served at that table would be presented on antique porcelain.

'Drawing room,' he said, showing her the next room. She glanced at the comfortable upholstered chairs, antique occasional tables and arrangements of fresh flowers—and then stopped dead. 'Is that a Burne-Jones over there on the wall?'

He nodded. 'It's the portrait of my great-great-grandmother I told you about.'

'May I?'

'Of course.'

She walked over to it and studied it for a while. 'It's beautiful—you're very lucky.'

'Salvatore knows a lot about our art collection. Talk to him tomorrow. He'll show you round when he has a moment.'

She didn't think that Salvatore would unbend enough with her to do that, but smiled politely. 'Thank you.'

Finally Lorenzo led her to a room at the very end of a corridor. 'This is where we thought the window could be sited—in the library.'

Like the mermaid window at Edensfield, she thought, and was filled with wistfulness. She would love to have the Lorenzo from Edensfield back rather than the formal, very polite and very guarded stranger walking next to her.

'This is one of my favourite rooms in the house,' he said as he ushered her into a long room.

The two longest walls were lined with books in dark wooden cases with glass fronts and a sliding wooden ladder, so anyone who wanted a book from the upper shelves could reach them. But there were also a couple of leather chesterfields and a low coffee table with a chessboard on it. There was a desk sited in front of a large window with a number of gold-framed photographs—and she'd bet it was solid gold, not gilt framing—and a grand piano in the centre of the room.

And that, she thought, was why it was Lorenzo's favourite room. No doubt he spent as much time at that piano as he could. Which wouldn't be very much, now.

The spaniel pattered over to the fireplace and stretched out on the rug, clearly used to being there.

There were some stained-glass windows at the far end of the room. 'Is that where you want the new window?' she asked.

'Yes.'

As they passed the desk, she glanced out of the window and saw the rose garden. 'Oh, that's gorgeous,' she said, noting the way the colours of the roses blended. 'It's like a rainbow of roses.'

He looked out. 'I've never really noticed that before, but you're right.' He smiled at her. 'Funny, I thought I knew everything about the castle, but you're making me see it with new eyes.'

There wasn't much she could say to that. She distracted herself by taking a couple of photographs and making a couple of sketches. And, unsurprisingly, he had half a dozen messages on his phone that he needed to answer.

He'd just finished with them when she took out her tape measure. 'Need a hand measuring?' he asked.

'If you don't mind,' she said. 'That would be helpful.'

But, as she finished the last section, his hand touched hers briefly, and it felt like electricity coursing through her veins.

'Indi,' he whispered.

She looked up at him and he dipped his head, brushing his mouth against hers. She closed her eyes as he deepened the kiss.

God, she'd missed this so much. Missed *him* so much that she felt the tears stinging her eyelids.

And then she dropped the tape measure.

On his foot.

He broke the kiss and retrieved her tape measure. 'I'm sorry,' he said. 'I probably shouldn't have done that.'

She knew what he meant. The attraction was still there. The same feelings they'd had for each other back at Edensfield. But this was a different world and he just wasn't free to give in to those feelings.

Which made it even harder for her to tell him about the baby; she knew he had such a strong sense of duty and

he'd want to marry her for the baby's sake. But she most definitely wasn't a suitable royal bride, so marriage was out of the question.

Time to back off—and to change the subject, before she said something stupid.

Be professional, she reminded herself. This is about your job.

'Would you mind sitting for a couple of portraits?' she asked. 'Photographs, I mean. I'm not going to make you sit for hours while I sketch you.'

He raised an eyebrow, as if remembering their conversation about the fairy tales with a twist. 'You really need to do that?'

'If I'm putting you in a stained-glass window, then the portrait needs to look like you,' she pointed out.

'I guess so.'

'And it would be useful to see your robes of state, or whatever it is that kings wear.' Not just because she could use them in a pose, but because it would remind her of who he was. That he was out of reach.

'Ceremonial robes,' he said.

'And a crown.' Just to hammer it home.

'We can do a crown,' he said, looking thoughtful.

'And where does all this happen? The cathedral?' She forced herself not to think about the fact that the cathedral would also be where he would eventually get married. To a suitable princess.

'Yes—and there's a special coronation chair. I'm scheduled to show you round tomorrow.' He met her gaze. 'Or Salvatore can, if you'd rather.'

It would probably be easier if Salvatore showed her round, she thought. Then she wouldn't slip up and say something inappropriate, because she'd remember who she was talk-

ing to and why she was here in Melvante. She'd have it at the front of her mind that this was strictly business and not because Lorenzo wanted her there.

But, to do her job fully, she needed to understand what was in his head. How did he feel about becoming king? And she'd slept through the briefing meeting, so she still had a dozen or more questions. She needed to know if they wanted him to look serene, statesmanlike, or what.

'I'd rather you showed me round, if you don't mind— that means we can catch up with the briefing meeting I missed, too. If you're sure you can spare the time,' she added quickly.

'I'll make sure I do.' His phone shrilled; he glanced at the screen and sighed. 'I'm sorry. I need to take this.'

'Don't worry, I'll find my own way back to my quarters.'

'Are you sure?'

She smiled, giving him her bravest face. 'If I get lost, I can always ask someone for directions.'

'OK. We'll talk later,' he said.

It was weird to be wandering through the palace on her own, Indigo thought as she left the library. She felt like a trespasser; she really didn't belong here. Lorenzo had said that the castle was home and he had happy memories of the place, but to her he looked tired and slightly strained. He'd retreated behind formality, apart from that brief kiss—and he'd apologised for that straight away, telling her outright that it had been a mistake.

Right at that moment, she couldn't see any common ground between them. It underlined how sensible she'd been to say no when he'd suggested continuing their affair. Lorenzo as a man—yes, she could trust him enough to fall in love with him. She already had. But His Royal Highness Lorenzo had so many walls up that it could never work.

She still had to tell him about the baby. It wouldn't be fair either to him or to the baby to keep that quiet. But no way was her baby growing up inside the walls of this quiet, formal, over-restrained palace. She wanted a home where a child could laugh and shout with joy—not an old-fashioned place where children were shut away in a nursery and should be seen and not heard.

CHAPTER TWELVE

THIS REALLY WASN'T going how Lorenzo had expected. Indigo was completely different, out here; she seemed nervous and quiet, not like the independent, sparky woman he'd fallen for in England.

He wanted to hold her and tell her how much he'd missed her. He wanted to kiss her again and feel her warmth seeping through him. But he also knew how his mother had felt so trapped at the palace, and he didn't want that for Indigo. No way would he push her into something that would make her unhappy.

And that was the final proof that he wasn't his father—because, if he had to, he was prepared to let Indi leave.

But first he was going to do his utmost to persuade her that sharing his life here wouldn't be so bad.

He raided the palace gardens before his meeting; afterwards, he grabbed a quick sandwich, then dropped in on Indigo. 'Sorry,' he said, handing her the flowers. 'I've been a rubbish host so far.'

She looked surprised. 'You didn't need to do that, but they're lovely. Thank you.' She breathed in their scent. 'And I understand that you're busy. The coronation's very soon and you have tons to do.'

'Yes, and Nonno's away for a few days—that's why I haven't introduced you to him yet.'

'I'm kind of nervous about meeting your grandfather,' she admitted.

'There's no need.' He spread his hands. 'Nonno's a pussycat.'

'He's a king,' she corrected.

'He's a man first,' Lorenzo said softly. Just as he was. But could Indigo learn to see that?

Indigo didn't want to fight with Lorenzo, so she said nothing, but she disagreed with him completely. If you were in that position, no matter how much you wanted to be seen as a person first, you'd always be seen as what you were rather than who you were. 'I'd better put these in water.'

He followed her into the kitchen and helped her find a couple of glasses to contain the flowers. 'Sorry. I didn't think this through properly. I should've brought you a vase as well.'

'No, I like that you were spontaneous. It's sweet,' she said.

'Just so you know, I wanted to meet you at the airport,' he said softly.

'It's fine. Bruno was there.' Though it warmed her that he *had* wanted to be with her. 'Besides, I'm here as a consultant, so people would think it strange if you met me at the airport.'

He shrugged. 'I guess.'

'Come and sit down—can I make you a drink or something?' She'd checked out the kitchenette and seen that there was a selection of tea and coffee, plus a supply of fresh milk in the small fridge.

He smiled. 'How come you manage to be a good hostess when you've only been here a few hours?'

She shrugged. 'It's just how I was brought up. You always offer someone a hot drink the second they walk

through your door. Well, strictly speaking this is your door, not mine,' she amended, 'but you know what I mean.'

'Do you know what I want more than coffee, right now?' he asked.

'Mind-reading isn't one of my special skills,' she said.

'I know.' He laughed. 'OK. I'll tell you. I just want to hold you.'

'That isn't such a good idea,' she said. 'I'm here on business.'

'You're here because I wanted to see you, and right now I can't come to England, so bringing you here seemed like the best solution.'

'You sent a plane for me, Lorenzo. Don't you think that's a little bit flashy?' she asked.

'Probably,' he admitted, 'and it's bad for the environment as well. But, given that you're a mere mortal and don't possess wings...'

When he was like this, it would be so easy to give in and just be with him. He was adorable—sweet and funny, Lorenzo the man and not Lorenzo the Crown Prince.

'Hello, Indi,' he said softly, and kissed her.

She managed to stand her ground. Just. 'We can't do this, Lorenzo. We're not in England any more. You're about to become king.'

'And you're putting obstacles in the way. Why are you so scared?'

'Because,' she said, 'you're not going to be allowed to be with me. No matter what our personal views on the matter might be, you have to think as a king first and a man second. You can't just do what you want.'

'You,' he said with a sigh, 'sound like my grandfather.'

'And he won't think I'm remotely suitable for you. So it's better not to start something we can't finish.'

'What if the barriers were all taken away?' he asked.

If only, she thought. 'And how are you going to do that? There isn't anyone else who can take over from you, is there?'

'No,' he admitted. 'But I think you could be suitable, Indi, if you give yourself a chance.'

'If I change, you mean?'

He shook his head. 'Don't ever change. You're warm and honest and a breath of fresh air. You make things sparkle.'

She stroked his face. 'Lorenzo, don't make this any more difficult than it already is.'

He moved his head so he could press a kiss into her palm. 'You're so stubborn.'

'If the press drag up my past...'

'Then it'll be a two-day wonder, they'll find someone else to gossip about pretty soon after, and nobody's going to judge you on your parents' mistakes.'

'Not just my parents,' she said softly. 'I made a really bad mistake myself.'

Maybe telling him would go some way to making him understand why this couldn't ever work. And it would make him agree with her decision when she found the right words to tell him about the baby.

'Three years ago, my grandfather died.'

'Meaning you were on your own in the world?' Lorenzo asked. 'Well, except your father, and he doesn't count.'

She gave him a wry smile. 'Pretty much, on both counts. Anyway, not long after that I was dragged off to some party. I didn't really want to be there.' She sighed. 'And I met Nigel. He asked me out. I said no, but he was persistent, and I guess... It's weak of me, but...' She stopped, unable to frame the words.

'You were still grieving for someone you loved very much,' Lorenzo said softly. 'It's only natural that you

wanted to try and fill some of the hole your grandfather's death had left in your life.'

'I guess.' She stared miserably at the table. 'So I started seeing him. And I was busy sorting out my grandfather's estate and finding a new studio and somewhere else to live, so that kind of distracted me from the things I should've noticed.'

'Why did you have to move?' he asked.

'Because my deal with the earl was that the cottage was my grandparents' for life. After they died, it reverted to him.'

'And he didn't offer to let you stay, at least until you'd found your feet?' Lorenzo looked shocked. 'How mean can you get?'

'That's possibly a bit unfair. I didn't actually give him the chance to offer,' she admitted. 'I moved straight out.'

'Stubborn.'

'Too much so for my own good, sometimes.' She gave him a wry smile. 'So I guess I had enough going on in my life not to notice that Nigel was sometimes a bit cagey when he answered his mobile phone. Or that he only ever visited me—he never invited me back to his place. When we went out, it was always to obscure places—the kind of places I like, because I'd prefer to go somewhere for dinner because the food is amazing rather than because it's trendy. I thought that was why he chose the restaurants.' She shook her head in frustration. 'But I guess he picked them because he wouldn't know anyone there. I never met any of his friends, and he didn't seem interested in meeting mine. It never *occurred* to me that he might be married. I mean, when I look at it now, the signs were all there and it's blindingly obvious, but I was too stupid and naive to read them at the time.'

'It's easy to see things in hindsight. No, you were busy

and you were grieving and you put your trust in the wrong person,' Lorenzo said.

'Yeah.' She couldn't quite bring herself to tell him about the miscarriage. 'Anyway, then I found out he was married. And that he had a baby. He cheated on his wife when she was pregnant, Lorenzo. And he cheated on her with *me*. I can't forgive myself for that.'

He frowned. 'If you'd known he was married, you would've kept turning him down.'

She stared at him. 'Of course I would. I'd seen the damage my mother did. I didn't want to follow in her footsteps.'

'You don't have to tell me that, Indi,' he said softly. 'I already know that you're not your mother.'

'But don't you see? If the press find out...' She bit her lip.

'You met Nigel when you were vulnerable, and he took advantage of that. It isn't your fault.'

'I could have said no.'

'You were grieving and lonely. Anyone else would've done the same, in your shoes.'

'Lorenzo, I've just told you that I had an affair with a married man. Doesn't that...?' She shook her head, frustrated that she couldn't find the right words to make him see her point.

'No, it doesn't make any difference. And if the press does manage to drag it up, then my press team will make sure they're aware of your side of the story to balance things out. You're human, Indi.'

'And you need someone who's perfect.'

'No. Right now,' he said softly, 'I just need you.'

And she could see in his eyes that he meant it.

Even though her common sense knew that this was a huge mistake, how could she push him away when he'd let his barriers down with her like this?

She opened her arms; he held her close, then picked her up and carried her to the sofa in her living room. He settled down with her half lying across his lap. 'Right now,' he whispered, 'I just want to be with you. No talking, no nothing—I just want to *be*.'

That was just fine by her. Back in their bubble, where they had the chance to be together. Warm and comfortable and cosy and...

Indigo had no idea when she fell asleep—or when he did—but she woke when Lorenzo carried her into her bedroom and laid her on the bed, then tucked a duvet round her.

'Lorenzo?' she asked sleepily. 'What time is it?'

'Three in the morning. I'm sorry. I guess I relaxed with you so much that I dozed off,' he said softly. 'I'd better go.'

'You could stay,' she said.

He shook his head. 'I can't. But I'll see you in the morning.' He kissed her lightly. 'I'll take you round the cathedral.'

'And I promise not to be late. Or sleep through the meeting.'

The next morning, Indigo was in Salvatore's office ten minutes before she was due to meet Lorenzo.

'You look up to your eyes in work, Signor Pozzi,' she said.

He shrugged. 'It's a busy time, Signorina Moran. It's the same for everyone.'

'Can I fetch you a cup of coffee or something?' she asked.

He looked at her in surprise. 'Why would you do that?'

'Because you're very busy, and I have ten minutes before His Royal Highness is expecting me, so I have the time to make you some coffee,' she said. 'Do you take milk or sugar?'

'I...' And then he gave her the first real smile she'd seen

since she'd come to the castle. 'Thank you very much. That would be lovely. No milk or sugar, thank you.'

'Just very strong, the way His Royal Highness drinks it?' she asked dryly.

Salvatore spread his hands. 'What can I say?'

'You're from Melvante. Which isn't quite Italian, but pretty near it,' she said with a smile.

She made coffee in the small kitchen next to the office—just about managing not to gag at the scent—and took the mug through to Lorenzo's assistant along with a glass of water. He was on the phone when she got back, so she just placed the mug and glass on a coaster within his reach, and sat quietly in the corner of the office, sketching out some ideas for the window.

Dead on time, Lorenzo came through into his assistant's office. 'Good morning, Signorina Moran. Are you ready to go to the cathedral?'

She put her sketchbook away. 'Of course, Your Royal Highness.'

'You'll like the glass,' Salvatore said. 'Don't let the prince rush you past the rose window.'

'I won't,' she said with a smile.

'What did you do to Salvatore?' Lorenzo asked when they'd left the office.

She shrugged. 'Nothing. Why?'

'Because his job is to be a dragon and protect my time, and there he was telling you not to rush.'

'I made him a mug of coffee, that's all.'

Lorenzo raised an eyebrow. 'I don't think anyone due in a meeting with me has ever done that before.'

'The poor man's up to his eyes, fielding calls and organising things for you. It was the least I could do.'

'Typical you,' Lorenzo said, but his gaze was warm rather than full of censure.

Even from the outside, the cathedral was stunning, all white stone and Gothic arches. Inside, it was even more grand, with soaring arches everywhere and tall, narrow windows—and then a window that made Indigo stop and gasp in pleasure.

'It's beautiful. Like the rose window at York Minster. Why didn't you tell me it was this good?'

He smiled. 'I did tell you to come and see the glass for yourself.' He added softly, 'Remember when you took me to see your angel and the centaur?'

And they'd talked about weddings.

This was where Lorenzo would get married.

Not to her, because she wasn't suitable. But Indigo hoped that Lorenzo would find a royal bride who really loved him—a woman who felt the same way about him that she did.

And then it hit her that she really was in love with him. Bone deep in love with the father of her unborn child. The one man she knew had integrity and she could trust with her heart. Except…they came from different worlds, and she just couldn't see how they'd ever get past that.

'It's beautiful,' she said, forcing herself to focus on the glass.

She enjoyed the rest of the tour of the building, and seeing the ancient throne on which Lorenzo would be seated during the coronation; but all the time she was aware of the widening gulf between them. Just how was she going to be able to tell him about the baby?

They were walking back down the aisle when a small girl came running towards them, tripped on one of the flagstones and fell flat on her face. Indigo scanned the area quickly but couldn't immediately see anyone who looked like a concerned parent or nanny rushing to the child's aid.

The little girl was crying and holding her knee. Indigo went over to her. 'It's all right, we'll find your mummy for you.'

She was rewarded with a blank stare and more tears.

Of course—the little girl didn't speak English. And Indigo knew that her Italian was too scrappy to be useful right now. 'Lorenzo, can you translate for me?' she asked swiftly. 'Tell her that it's OK, and we'll find her mummy for her.'

The little girl was still crying, but she listened to Lorenzo and nodded.

'I've got something in my bag that will stop her knee feeling sore,' Indigo said, taking the small first aid kit out of her bag and finding the antiseptic wipes and a sticking plaster. 'Can you distract her—get her to find something in one of the windows?'

If Lorenzo had been faced with a crying child on his own, he wouldn't have been quite sure what to do or say. But, with Indigo by his side, it was surprisingly easy. 'It's all right, little one. We'll make your knee better and find your mummy,' he said. 'Can you see all the pretty colours in the windows?'

She nodded.

'What's your favourite colour?' he asked as Indigo wiped her knee clean.

'Pink,' she said, and he couldn't help smiling.

He kept her talking while Indigo ministered to her knee and put a sticking plaster over the cut. They'd just finished when a woman ran up to them.

'Melissa! What happened? Are you all right?' She scooped the little girl into her arms. 'I looked round, and you'd gone.' And then she looked at Lorenzo and did a double-take. 'Your Royal Highness! I'm—oh—um…'

'It's all right,' he said, smiling at her to put her at her

ease. 'Your little girl fell over and cut her knee. My friend's just cleaned the cut and put a sticking plaster on it. I hope that's OK.'

'I—oh, yes, thank you so much. But you're…you're… Your Royal Highness,' she blurted out, clearly still flustered.

'We just did what anyone else would've done,' he said.

'Thank you so much, Your Royal Highness. Melissa, you must always hold Mummy's hand when we're out and never, ever go off without Mummy,' the woman said to her little girl. 'Now, curtsey to the prince and say thank you.'

'*Mille grazie,*' the little girl said, her lower lip wobbling slightly as she tried to do a graceful curtsey.

'Very nice to meet you, Melissa,' Lorenzo said solemnly.

She looked almost as overawed as her mother.

'I'm afraid I'm expected elsewhere now, but do enjoy the rest of your time here,' Lorenzo said.

'Thank you, Your Royal Highness.'

The woman was about to curtsey, but he placed his hand lightly on her arm. 'You really don't need to curtsey to me.' He smiled. 'Have a nice day.'

'I think you just made a hit,' Indigo said as they left the cathedral.

'Only because you were with me. I wouldn't have had a clue what to say otherwise,' he said.

'You would've improvised,' she said, giving him a cheeky wink. 'And you would've been fine.'

Funny how her belief in him warmed him so much.

All he needed now was to get her to believe in *them*.

Ha. All.

Back at the castle, Lorenzo had a swift conversation with Salvatore, then checked his schedule. 'I'm doing a photo

shoot with Indigo for the window, so she can see the state robes,' he said. 'We'll be in my apartment if there's anything urgent, but I'm going to switch my mobile off during the shoot so we don't get constant interruptions.'

'Very good, Your Royal Highness,' Salvatore said. 'Did you enjoy the cathedral, Signorina Moran?'

'I did, Signor Pozzi—the rose window is stunning,' Indigo said. 'And please call me Indi. I prefer being on first-name terms with my clients and their colleagues.'

'Then you shall call me Sal,' he said with a smile.

Lorenzo led her off to his apartment. 'Salvatore has really taken a shine to you,' he said. 'I wish I could make people warm to me so quickly.'

'You can,' she said. 'Just be yourself, and don't put all the formal barriers up.' She wrinkled her nose. 'Though I guess that's easier said than done, when you have to deal with protocol all the time.'

'Protocol,' he said, 'maybe needs to learn to change with the times.'

'Dat's ma boy,' she said with a grin. 'You're learning.'

'Give me ten minutes to change. Be as nosey as you like,' he invited.

'Thank you. I will.'

Lorenzo's apartment was at the opposite end of the castle to hers. It had a view of what looked like a format knot garden; but the interior was lovely, with simple furnishings rather than the ornate Louis XIV tables and chairs she'd seen in the rest of the castle. And she loved the artwork on the walls.

There was a piano in his sitting room, along with a bed for the dog that looked as if it were rarely used—from what she'd seen of Caesar, the spaniel would head straight for the rug in front of the fire or a comfortable corner of the sofa. Bookshelves, containing a mixture of biographies,

historical tomes and some very geeky science fiction; no music, she noticed, but knowing Lorenzo his collection was probably digital and centrally organised in a system so that he could access it anywhere in his apartment. There was a television, so obviously he watched the occasional programme, but there were no films on the shelves; she assumed that again he used a digital cloud-based service.

The kitchen was all clean lines. His fridge wasn't that well stocked, so she guessed that most of the time he was served by the palace kitchens rather than cooking for himself. There was a table so he could eat in the kitchen if he wanted to, but this was very much a bachelor apartment, she thought, rather than a family one.

She didn't quite have the nerve to explore his bathroom—a bit too personal, she thought, and his bedroom was definitely out of bounds. He'd made it clear that he wanted to change into his robes without an audience.

The sitting room would be the best place to take the photographs, she decided, when he emerged from his room in a dress uniform with a dark blue floor-length cloak trimmed with gold and ermine.

'Very nice, Your Royal Highness,' she said.

'Hmm. Have a nice snoop, did we?'

'Pretty much. You don't have any cake in your kitchen,' she said, teasing him a little to cover the fact that she felt just a little bit out of her depth. 'And I couldn't find your music or films.'

'They're all cloud-based,' he explained. 'Except the cake. Which is an omission I clearly need to remedy.'

'Uh-huh. Well, let's get this shoot sorted.' It didn't take long for her to get the shots she needed. Or, rather, most of them. 'It won't kill you to smile, you know,' she said.

He gave her a formal smile—one that didn't reach his eyes and made him look totally unreachable.

How could she make him take those barriers down?

She knew it was crazy—totally crazy—but she went with the impulse. She walked over to him, slid her arms round his neck and kissed him.

And then she took a step back. 'Lorenzo,' she said softly.

And he smiled at her.

A real smile, full of warmth. The look she loved most on him, all soft and sweet and touchable.

She took the shot, and he grimaced. 'Do you use that strategy with all your models?'

'I don't usually have models,' she said. But she knew he knew the answer. Of course she didn't. She didn't react to anyone the same way she reacted to Lorenzo.

'You kissed me just to get a photograph.'

He looked thoroughly put out, and she couldn't help smiling. 'Not just to get the photo. I kissed you because right now you look like Prince Hottie. Sexy as hell.'

The light came back into his eyes. 'Put the camera down, Indi.'

'Can't.' She shook her head. 'I'm working.'

'That's a royal command, I'll have you know. Put the camera down.'

She lifted her chin. 'Or what, Your Royal Highness?'

'Or face the consequences.'

She smiled. 'Bring it on, Lorenzo.'

'You asked for it,' he said, and took the camera gently from her hand, placing it safely out of the way. And then he kissed her until her knees were on the point of buckling.

'That has consequences, too, you know,' she said, and undid the clasp of his robe before sliding it off his shoulders. She folded it neatly and placed it over the back of the chair.

'Interesting,' he commented, but his voice was full of warmth. 'You've turned into a neat freak, Indi.'

'No chance.' She spread her hands. 'But this is your coronation robe. I don't want you to get into trouble with your wardrobe people.'

He laughed. 'This is the twenty-first century. It's not how things were a hundred years ago, when people with titles still employed valets and ladies' maids.'

'Even so, I don't want to crumple your robes.' She stroked them, enjoying the softness under her fingertips. 'I have to say, Your Royal Highness, you look mighty fine in navy.' She looked at him. 'And even better without your robes.'

'Was that a hint?' He stripped out of his uniform, laying it neatly on top of his robes, and maintaining eye contact with her the entire time. By the time he'd stripped down to his underwear, Indigo felt as if she was about to spontaneously combust.

And then he simply picked her up and carried her into his bedroom. When he set her down on her feet again, he made sure that her body was in close contact to his, so she was left fully aware of how much he wanted her. And then he proceeded to make love to her until she felt as if her bones had melted.

Later, lying curled in his arms, Indigo thought how this was every bit as good as their time spent in England. The physical attraction between them was still strong.

But would it be enough to help them keep the world at bay?

And how would he cope when she told him her news?

'Penny for them?' he asked, stroking her hair away from his forehead.

No. Now wasn't the right time. 'Just worrying that I've made you late for something.'

He glanced at his watch. 'Um.'

'Sorry. You're going to be up to your eyes, now.'

'Yes,' he said regretfully, and switched on his phone. Immediately his phone started beeping with a barrage of incoming messages.

'Go and do whatever you need to do,' she said, 'and I'll sort things out here.'

'Are you sure?'

'I'm sure,' she confirmed. 'Go and do all your prince stuff.'

'You're wonderful.' He dressed swiftly, kissed her again, and vanished. She took her time, and made sure she hung up his uniform and his robes properly before putting his bed to rights, then took her work things back to her apartment and went back to sketching out designs.

Later that afternoon, Lorenzo came by her apartment. 'We forgot the crown.'

She raised an eyebrow. 'Aren't you supposed to be in a meeting?'

'I can afford to be spontaneous,' he said.

Hmm. She remembered just how spontaneous he'd been in his apartment, and warmth spread through her. 'So where do I get to see you model the crown?' she asked.

'In the vaults. Bring your camera.' He waved a key at her.

She laughed. 'You're telling me that, in this day and age, you're using old-fashioned technology?'

'A little more than that. There are layers.' He took her hand as they walked down the corridor. Even though Indigo was pretty sure that it was going to cause a mad rush of gossip once it was spotted on the palace CCTV, she couldn't quite bring herself to pull away. It felt good, having her fingers tangled with Lorenzo's. She'd loved walking hand in hand with him in the gardens at Edensfield, and this wasn't so very different.

To get to the vaults, they had to pass through a series of doors and use a series of different things to unlock them—codes, fingerprints and even iris recognition.

'I take it back. You're in full James Bond mode,' she teased.

'Which means I get to dally with the beautiful girl.' He stole a kiss, shocking her.

'Lorenzo—was that just caught on CCTV?'

'Probably.'

'But…'

'I don't care. And, for someone who's supposed to be a free spirit, you worry far too much,' Lorenzo said and kissed her again.

Inside the vaults, he took out a box and unlocked it.

'Oh, my.' Indigo had never seen so many jewels in one place—or such large ones.

He took the crown out of the box. 'I can remember my grandfather placing this on my head.'

'When you were little—like dressing up?' she asked.

He shook his head. 'When I was eighteen. I'd just spent a week going off the rails, and he wanted me to understand that I had a commitment. That I needed to—well, strengthen myself so I could carry the burden.' He handed her the crown.

'It's really heavy,' she said, shocked and also a little afraid of dropping it and denting it.

She handed it back to him. 'So why did you go off the rails?'

He was silent for a long, long time. And then he sighed. 'I'm going to tell you something now that maybe half a dozen people know, and they're all sworn to secrecy. Everyone thought my parents died in a car accident when I was ten. But it wasn't an accident.' He blew out a breath. 'My mother was having an affair. She was planning to

leave my father, and my father found out. He drove their car into a wall with her beside him, deliberately, because he couldn't bear to be without her and he couldn't bear the idea of her being with anyone else. My grandparents told everyone that it was a tragic accident—but then I found some papers when I was eighteen. Papers that my grandfather had thought were destroyed. And that's when I learned the truth.'

Indigo looked at him, shocked. 'Your father killed himself and your mother? But that meant he'd be leaving you on your own. How—' She shook her head, completely not understanding. 'How could he do that?'

'It's not a choice that I would make,' Lorenzo said. 'If I married someone who hated the world I lived in, I'd find a compromise.'

Was this his way of telling her that that was what he was trying to do, right now? Find a compromise so they could be together?

'I'd love my wife enough to let her go, if I had to. I'd want her to be happy. And if that meant not being with me—well, so be it. I wouldn't stop her,' Lorenzo said. 'But I'd try my hardest to find a way round it, so we could be together.'

She stroked his face. 'And the accident—' she couldn't bear to think of what it really was '—happened not long before you were sent away to school. That's so hard, Lorenzo.' And she could understand now why he'd been brought up in such a rigid, formal way. His grandparents had tried to protect him from the truth.

'I've had a long time to get used to it,' he said softly. 'Take the pictures, Indi. I wasn't intending to be maudlin. I just wanted you to understand.'

'I do. And I promise you it won't go any further than me. Ever.' She kissed him swiftly on the lips. 'And I get

now why you keep everyone at a distance. It stops you getting hurt. But if you let people close, Lorenzo—the whole world will love you.' Just as she loved him.

Perhaps, he thought. But there was only one person he wanted to love him.

And he thought that maybe, just maybe, she might feel the same way about him as he felt about her.

But would they be able to find a compromise so she could feel comfortable in his world?

He placed the crown on his head. 'OK. Do what you need to for the designs.'

She took several photographs. And then he placed the crown back in the box, locked it again, and returned it to its place in the vault.

CHAPTER THIRTEEN

THE NEXT DAY, there was a story in the newspapers about the Prince of Hearts, with a photograph of Lorenzo and another of the little girl they'd rescued in the cathedral, standing with her mother.

'I've never had anything like this before,' Lorenzo said, handing her a translated version of the story on a tablet. 'People have always seen me as—well, a bit remote.'

'Low-key's fine. But let them get to know you,' she said, 'and they'll see you're not in the slightest bit remote.'

She scanned through the text. 'Oh, no. They're talking about a mystery woman being with you.' She swallowed hard. 'That means they're going to dig up what they can about me.' Panic flooded through her.

'Stop worrying. For now, the press office will handle it. They'll explain that you're a glass specialist and I was briefing you in the cathedral.'

'But what if…?'

He kissed the tip of her nose. 'Then I'll deal with it. I promise you, there's nothing to worry about.' His voice was very calm. 'And I don't break my promises, Indi. I don't tell lies.'

Whereas she was telling him a lie, sort of. A lie of omission. She was going to have to tell him the truth, very soon. She just needed to work out how.

* * *

He took her through to the palace gardens, that morning. What she'd thought was a formal knot garden turned out to be a series of concentric circles made from stone slabs.

'What's this—some kind of sculpture?' she asked.

'A water maze. If you stand on the wrong slab, it tilts and you get sprayed.'

How come a stuffy, formal palace would have something as crazy and fun as this in the garden?

The question must have been written all over her face, because he said, 'It was my grandmother's idea. She grew up in a house with a hedge maze and she liked the idea of having something fun in the garden. I remember when I was small, I loved the mazes here. I used to spend all day playing here and in the hedge maze.' He looked slightly wistful. 'Life was a bit simpler, back then.'

Before his parents had died? Or before he'd realised what being king would mean?

'OK. So the idea is that you reach the middle without getting wet.' He spread his hands. 'Your challenge, should you wish to accept it…'

'But what,' she asked, 'is my reward, should I beat the challenge?'

He leaned forward. 'Spontaneous inventiveness on my part.'

And, oh, the picture that put in her head.

'You're on,' she said, and picked her way through the first ring.

'Four more to go,' he said.

One and a half rings later, she stepped on the wrong stone. It tilted, and a fountain of water sprayed over her.

She just laughed. 'When you were a kid, I bet you jumped on every stone to make sure you got soaked every single time.'

'I might've done,' he said with a grin.

'Which makes you the expert on how to do it without getting wet, because you know where the tilting slabs are. Show me how it's done,' she said.

He picked his way round the circles until he reached her, then took her hand and showed her which stones to leap over.

Until they were about to reach the centre of the maze, and she jumped on the slab that he was clearly about to avoid. Water sprayed up and over him. 'Gotcha,' she said, laughing.

He laughed back, and jumped onto the same stone, pulling her into his arms at the same time so that the water sprayed over both of them. And while the droplets were still falling, he kissed her stupid.

This was the Lorenzo she'd fallen in love with back at Edensfield. The Lorenzo who'd dressed up in Regency clothing and copied the Mr Darcy scene from the movie, just for her. The Lorenzo who'd carried a tired, elderly dog home through the gardens.

'Lorenzo,' she whispered.

Now was the right time to tell him. When they were laughing in his garden, enjoying some harmless fun. When he was reliving some of the fun of his own childhood. When he could see how it might be for his own child. He'd told her his deepest, darkest secret in the castle vault; and now it was time for her to tell him the truth about the baby.

'Indi.' He kissed her again, and she could see the passion in his eyes.

'There's something I—'

Her words were cut off by his phone shrilling.

He made a nose of frustration. 'Sorry. I'm expecting this.'

And he'd already taken time out to spend with her. Time

he couldn't really afford. 'Go,' she said. 'Is it OK for me to walk in the gardens for a bit longer?'

'Sure. Go where you like. I'll see you later.' He kissed her again, then took the call.

Indigo went back to her room for her camera and sketch-book, then headed out to find the rose garden. Up close, she might get the last ideas she needed for the window design.

And, up close, it was even better than she'd hoped. She closed her eyes and breathed in the scent. The essence of summer, she thought.

Then she became aware of someone speaking to her in rapid Italian. She opened her eyes to see an elderly man carrying secateurs. He was probably one of the palace gardeners, she thought, and he probably thought she was a trespasser.

She dredged up her limited Italian. 'Um, *mi scusi— parla inglese?*'

The man smiled. 'Yes, I speak English.'

And very well, too, she thought; he had only the slight-est trace of an accent.

'Can I help you? Are you lost?' he asked.

How ironic that she'd met Lorenzo at her best friend's house and he'd thought she was a trespasser—and now she was in Lorenzo's home and being mistaken for a tres-passer again.

'I'm not trespassing,' she said hastily, 'I'm working on some designs for a glass window for the palace, and I wanted a closer look at the roses—is that all right?'

'Of course, *signorina.*' He paused. 'May I ask, why the roses?'

'Because they're beautiful and they remind me of home,' she said wistfully. 'My grandparents had a rose garden—nothing on the scale of this, of course, but I love the scent of roses. And I saw the garden from the library

window the other day. It's like a rainbow of roses, with the way the colours shade from white to yellow to peach, pink and red. How could I resist coming to see them?'

He looked pleased. 'You like our roses here at the palace?'

She nodded. 'And I like that they're not all the same type—you have floribundas here, mixed with hybrid teas and Bourbons and ramblers.'

He inclined his head. 'So you know your roses.'

'I'm not an expert, by any means,' she said, 'but I know what I like.'

'You grow them yourself?'

She shook her head. 'I only have a windowsill in my flat, so I have a couple of pots of miniature roses. But if I ever move to a place with a garden, I'll have a bower of roses just like we used to have at home.' She smiled back at him and held her hand out for him to shake. 'Sorry, I've been very rude—I should have introduced myself. I'm Indigo Moran.'

'Enzo,' he returned. 'You have a very pretty name.'

'Thank you.'

'Would you like me to show you round?'

'If that's not going to interfere with your job or make you late for something, then yes, please, Enzo. That would be really kind of you.'

She spent the next half hour wandering through the garden with him, learning about the oldest roses in the garden and taking some photographs. 'I really love this one. It's so pretty,' she said, pointing out a crimson rose with pink and white stripes. She leaned over. 'Oh, and the scent's amazing.'

'*Rosa mundi*,' he said. 'It's one of the oldest striped roses known, nearly a thousand years old.'

'It's beautiful,' she said.

'It was the favourite rose of my wife,' he said quietly.

'Oh, I'm sorry—I didn't mean to bring up something that would hurt you.' In impulse, she took his hand and squeezed it.

'They're good memories,' he said. He glanced at her sketchbook. 'May I see?'

'They're just scraps of ideas,' she said.

He flicked through it until he came to a sketch of Lorenzo. 'The young prince.'

'Yes—it's one of the ideas I'm working on.'

'So you've met the prince?'

She nodded. 'Actually, his best friend is the brother of my best friend. He came to stay with them while I was restoring their mermaid window. He liked my work and asked if I would do some designs for a window.'

'For the coronation?' Enzo asked.

'Yes, so I want to make sure I get it right and come up with a design to do him justice. He's a good man and I think he'll make an excellent king.' She grimaced. 'Sorry, I'm not from Melvante and it isn't my place to comment. I don't mean to be rude.'

'But you say things how you see them.'

'Honesty,' Indigo said, 'is always the best policy. Then everyone knows where they are.' She smiled. 'Which isn't an excuse for being rude. You can still be tactful and kind.'

'True.'

They chatted for a bit longer, then Enzo cut half a dozen of the *rosa mundi* roses and gave them to her.

She gasped. 'Is this going to get you into trouble with the king?'

'No. I'm the head gardener, so I can cut any roses I choose,' he said. 'If anyone asks you, say Enzo gave them to you and you're using them to help design your window.'

'I will—and thank you for being so kind and spending so much time with me. *Mille, mille grazie,*' she added.

'My pleasure, child,' he said with a smile, seeming touched that she'd bothered thanking him in his own language.

That evening, it never seemed to be the right time for Indigo to tell Lorenzo what she'd tried to tell him at the water maze. And, the next morning, she had an email from Lottie telling her that she needed to look at the newspapers.

When she did, she discovered a buzz of media speculation. A paparazzo had managed to capture a photograph of her with Lorenzo in the water maze, her hand on his arm, with them looking at each other. And they both looked as if they'd just been thoroughly kissed.

Is our prince falling in love?

Oh, no. She tried to get hold of Lorenzo, but his phone was switched off. In the end, she went to the office to talk to Salvatore. 'When His Royal Highness is free, please can you apologise to him for me?'

'About the papers this morning, you mean?' Salvatore asked.

She nodded. 'That wasn't meant to happen.'

To her relief, he didn't look angry. 'There's nothing you can do about the media, Indi. And it wasn't just you in the photograph, remember. Don't worry. The press office will handle it.'

'They already have enough on their plates, with the coronation.' And she dreaded to think of the media reaction to the rest of the news. A baby, and definitely no wedding because she wasn't a suitable princess.

'You look out of sorts,' Salvatore said, 'and would I be right in thinking it's not just the press?'

She sighed. 'I can't get the design for the window right.

I need to do something with my hands. Normally I'd make something in glass so I can let my subconscious work on whatever's blocking me, but I don't have my tools with me. This visit was just to look at the site and present some designs to His Majesty and His Royal Highness.'

'My sister always makes cake when she wants to think,' he said.

'Making cake would work for me. Or cookies.' She wrinkled her nose. 'Except I don't have a proper kitchen in the apartment.'

'You know we have a little kitchen here in the office. You could use that. And I'll arrange that you can borrow whatever you need from the palace kitchen.'

'And in return you get cookies?' she asked with a smile. 'Sal, thank you, that would be wonderful.'

He made a swift call, then smiled at her. 'Go and see Tonia in the kitchen and she'll get you what you need.'

'You,' she said, 'are a wonderful man.' She kissed his cheek, making him blush; then she headed to the palace kitchen and spoke to Tonia to sort out what she needed, carried the lot back to the office kitchen, and lost herself making shortbread biscuits.

She'd just melted some chocolate ready to decorate the top of the shortbread when Lorenzo walked in. 'What's this, commandeering my office kitchen?'

'Yes.'

'I love the smell of vanilla.' He stole one of the warm biscuits and tasted it. 'Mmm. This is good.'

She tapped the back of his hand. 'I don't know about Prince of Hearts—I think you're the knave, stealing shortbread.'

'The knave of hearts,' he said, 'allegedly stole tarts, not shortbread.'

'Same difference.'

He laughed. 'I never get told off in the palace kitchen.'

'Really? Well, you're getting told off in mine.' On impulse, she dipped her finger into the melted chocolate and dabbed a stripe on each cheek.

He looked at her. 'That's war paint. Hmm. Now there's an idea.' He dipped his finger into the melted chocolate, too.

As soon as Indigo realised his intentions, she ran.

Too late. He caught her, and painted her lips with the melted chocolate. And then he kissed it off.

Very, *very* slowly.

'I give in,' she sighed.

'Good.' He paused. 'So why are you baking?'

'I needed time to think about my design—I'm stuck on something, and my subconscious needs to work through it,' she said. She grimaced. 'And then there's that bit in the paper. I'm so sorry.

'The photograph.' He didn't look in the slightest bit fazed. 'Yes, the press office has been fielding calls all morning.' He shrugged. 'Maybe it's better out in the open.'

'But you—we—we *can't*. You're supposed to marry a princess.'

'This is the twenty-first century. And, apart from the fact that I can marry someone not of royal blood if I choose, you're the daughter of an earl.'

'Illegitimate daughter,' she corrected. 'And my past is messy.' She still hadn't told him quite all of it. Or about their baby. But, the longer she left it, the harder it became, and she didn't want to just blurt it out.

'You're human,' he said. 'And people like you.' He tipped his head slightly to one side. 'People like the man I am, when I'm with you. *I* like the man I am, when I'm with you.'

'But it's not just you. There's your grandfather,' she said.

'I have a feeling he's going to like you.'

'But it's not enough,' she said. 'You have your position to think of.'

He grinned. 'Which is, right now, in my office kitchen, covered in crumbs and with chocolate all over my face. Very princely.'

'Lorenzo, why are you making it so hard?' she asked.

'I'm not,' he said softly. 'From where I'm standing, it's easy. You just have to believe. In *yourself*, as well as in us.'

That, she thought, was the rub. She couldn't believe in them until she believed in herself. And how could she possibly see herself as the wife of a king, having to live up to so many expectations when she'd been found so wanting in the past?

'I believe in you. And in us,' he said softly, and kissed her again. 'I'm stuck in official stuff all evening. But I'll see you tomorrow. We'll talk then.'

And she'd have to tell him then, she thought. She'd really, really have to tell him. She couldn't put it off any longer.

Predictably, Lorenzo was caught up in palace business until just before the time when he was due to introduce Indigo to his grandfather for the presentation of her designs, on the morning of the charity ball.

'Sorry,' he said, and kissed her on the cheek.

'It can't be helped. I know you're busy,' she said. Though inwardly she wondered: just supposing they did manage to make a go of things between them, would he be able to carve out enough time to spend with their baby?

Not that she could ask.

He ushered her in to one of the state rooms. And Indigo froze in horror when she saw the man sitting at the head of

the table: the man she chatted to in the garden. She nearly dropped her laptop.

'I—you're Lorenzo's grandfather?' she asked, staring at him.

Lorenzo frowned. 'What's going on? Nonno? Indi?'

'We met in the rose garden, the other day,' Enzo explained. 'I was a little...mendacious, perhaps.'

A little? He could say that again. 'I thought there was something familiar about you, but I told myself I was just being ridiculous,' Indigo said.

Enzo shrugged. 'And when you see an elderly man wearing sensible clothes for gardening, you don't expect him to be the king.'

Even though, she thought, Lorenzo had pretty much warned her back in England. Hadn't he said that he would know exactly where to find his grandfather after he retired—in the rose garden? She really should have thought a little harder.

'You told me you were the head gardener,' she said, forgetting all about protocol and the correct method of addressing the King of Melvante.

'Strictly speaking, I am,' Enzo said.

Indigo blew out a breath. 'Well, I apologise if I was rude or said anything out of line. Your Majesty,' she added belatedly.

'I think,' Lorenzo said, 'Nonno was just as much in the wrong as you were. More so, in fact, because he misled you. And you probably weren't rude.'

'She wasn't. Though she does believe in plain speaking,' Enzo said. 'Which is refreshing. Now, Signorina Moran— Indigo—would you like to show us your designs officially?'

'You saw the rough sketches,' Indigo said. 'These are the proper proposals, Your Majesty. I hope you'll allow me to talk you through my ideas.'

* * *

Lorenzo sat back and watched as Indigo went into professional mode. She had a presentation on her laptop which she'd clearly run through a few times because her words were flawless. Then she gave them both paper copies so they could take a closer look; and she'd also made a rough copy of some of her designs on tracing paper and held it up to the window so they could see the colours.

'So the roses aren't a prison, this time,' Enzo said.

Colour flared in Indigo's cheeks. 'You saw the drawing?'

'It was why I agreed to the commission,' Enzo said. 'I notice my grandson isn't an angel this time.'

'He can hardly be an angel at his coronation,' she pointed out.

He looked more closely at one of the designs. 'Is that Caesar at his feet?'

'Um, yes,' she said. 'I could make the window without the dog, if you prefer. But I thought it might be a nice touch to make Lorenzo seem more human.'

Lorenzo coughed. 'I am still here, you know.'

'I know.' She smiled at him, her expression all warm and soft and sweet. 'Lorenzo, having your dog with you is something your people will be able to relate to—a beloved pet. It'll make them feel closer to you.'

'Good point,' Enzo said, sounding approving. 'I vote to keep him. And I like this one, very much. You've captured something in my grandson, Indigo. Something I never expected to see.' This time, he met Lorenzo's gaze. 'But I'm glad it's there.'

Lorenzo knew exactly what his grandfather was saying, and relief flooded through him. Now all he had to do was convince Indigo.

Once they'd finished their discussion, she curtseyed and left the room.

'Thank you,' Lorenzo said quietly, and hugged his grandfather.

Enzo raised an eyebrow. 'She's changed you. And it's a good change.'

'I need to talk to her.'

'Go, child. With my blessing,' Enzo said softly.

Lorenzo caught up with Indigo just outside her apartment. 'Are you OK?'

'Yes.' She sucked in a breath. 'Just a bit shocked that the man I was chatting to in the garden turned out to be your grandfather. I must've broken all kinds of protocol.'

'Sometimes protocol needs to be broken—and, if you think about it, he broke it as much as you did.' He paused. 'He's on our side, Indi.' When she didn't look convinced, he leaned forward and brushed his mouth against hers. 'Trust me,' he said softly.

That was the rub, Indigo thought. She wanted to trust him. She knew he was an honourable man. But that made everything even more mixed up and harder to say. 'You must have a million and one things to do.'

'I can postpone them, if you need me to.'

No. She was never, ever going to stand in the way of what he had to do for his country. 'I'm fine. I need to work out the glass order for your window. Go and do princely stuff.'

He smiled. 'I'll see you at the ball tonight.'

And then—then, she would definitely tell him. After the ball. 'See you later,' she said, and forced herself to smile as sweetly as she could.

CHAPTER FOURTEEN

IT TOOK INDIGO the second half of the afternoon to get ready for the ball. Lottie's gown was gorgeous—plain black and strapless, with a frothy ankle-length skirt that reminded Indigo of a ballerina's dress. And Lottie had given her an early birthday present to go with the dress—an enamelled pendant in the shape of a butterfly, coloured iridescent green and blue. That was the only jewellery she wore.

She didn't look in the slightest bit like a princess, she thought as she looked in the mirror. She looked like a little girl playing dress-up. This wasn't who she was—but it was who she'd have to be in Lorenzo's world.

He'd said that he liked the man he was when she was with him.

Could she learn to like the woman she'd have to be, by his side?

She shook herself, and marched down to the ballroom—luckily Salvatore had given her directions earlier. Salvatore was at the door of the ballroom, and smiled when he saw her. 'You look enchanting, Indi.'

'*Grazie*, Sal.' Even if he was just being polite and flattering, she'd take it. Because right now she could feel every bit of adrenalin running through her veins and spiralling into panic.

'Let me introduce you to some people.' With relief, she noticed that he introduced her as a professional glass expert. And everyone spoke English, so her limited Italian wasn't stretched too far.

Even so, she was aware of people watching her and she knew they were speculating about the photographs and stories in the press. Who was Indigo Moran—Cinderella, or a gold-digger out for what she could get?

It was worse when Lorenzo walked in, because everyone was watching both of them. And either he wasn't aware of it or he was trying to make a point, because he came straight over to her. 'Come and dance with me?'

'I—haven't you got loads of meeting and greeting to do?' she asked, panicking.

'It's a ball. People are supposed to dance at balls, Indi,' he teased.

'Proper ballroom dancing. I've never done this sort of thing. I'm going to trip over and fall flat on my face.'

'Not if your partner knows how to lead you properly,' he reassured her.

For one horrified moment, she thought he was going to kiss her. *In public.* But, to her relief, he simply smiled. And then he swept her into his arms.

'All you have to do is remember to use alternate legs, and go where I steer you,' he said softly as the waltz began.

She discovered that he was absolutely right. In his arms, and with him guiding her, she couldn't fall and make an idiot of herself. And she found herself relaxing, enjoying being in his arms.

He danced with her twice more during the evening. So did Salvatore, as if he realised she was feeling just a bit unsure of herself and could do with some back-up.

But then she went to the Ladies'. She was adjusting her dress when she heard people talking.

'She's plainer than I thought she'd be,' someone said.

In English. Indigo's skin crawled. Did they know she was here and meant her to overhear every word? Or were they just gossiping and at least one person in the group didn't speak good Italian so they were speaking in English to keep her in the loop?

'Darling, she must have something—the prince seems besotted with her.' This voice was more heavily accented.

'But he can't marry her, surely? She's not blue-blooded,' someone else said.

'She's definitely got her eye on the crown. Lorenzo's easy on the eye, but he's so reserved. He'd be such hard work as a husband. But I guess if you want money, you don't care about that sort of thing.'

Indigo was livid that these women had got Lorenzo so wrong and were being so mean about him. But she also knew that if she stormed out of the cubicle and put them straight, they wouldn't believe her—because they'd already decided that she was a gold-digger and her word wouldn't be accepted

She wouldn't be acceptable as Lorenzo's partner, either.

And although she knew he'd be gallant and fight her corner for her, it would place their relationship under such a strain.

He'd said that he wouldn't be like his father; if the woman he loved was unhappy in his world, he'd let her go because he wanted her to be happy. So now she needed to do exactly the same for him—to let him go, so he could find someone that the world would deem a suitable bride for him and let him be happy.

She stayed in her cubicle until the gossiping women had gone—not because she was a coward and afraid to face them, but because she knew that nothing she said would make a difference so it would be a waste of time and ef-

fort to confront them—and then slipped back out into the ballroom and found Salvatore.

'I've got a bit of a headache,' she said. 'I think I'm going to have an early night.'

'Can I get you some painkillers?' he asked.

She shook her head. 'That's really sweet of you, Sal, but a bit of sleep's the best thing for me.' Not that she'd be able to sleep. It'd be another night of lying awake at two a.m., worrying and wondering just how she was going to fix things. 'Can you give my apologies to whoever needs them, please?'

'Of course. Would you like me to walk you back to your apartment?'

'Thanks, but you don't have to do that. Really. I'll be fine.' She kissed his cheek. 'I'll see you later.'

As she headed back to her apartment, her heart was breaking.

She was doing the right thing—she *knew* she was—but why did it have to hurt so much?

Tomorrow morning, she'd tell Lorenzo about the baby, and then she'd get a flight back to England. She could work on the window over there and ship it over to Melvante when it was finished. And maybe they could time it so Lorenzo was away from the palace when she came to put the window in place.

'Where's Indi?' Lorenzo asked Salvatore. 'I can't see her anywhere.'

'She had a headache. She's gone back to her apartment for an early night,' his assistant said.

'Hmm.' Lorenzo frowned. 'Something's wrong.'

'Maybe the ball's a little overwhelming.'

Lorenzo shook his head. 'There's more to it than that. I've got a funny feeling. Cover for me, will you?'

'Are you sure about this?' Salvatore asked.

'More sure than I've been about anything,' Lorenzo said, and left the ballroom.

When he knocked on Indigo's door, she took a while to answer. She'd changed out of the ball gown into jeans and a T-shirt; with no make-up on and her hair pulled back, she looked young and very vulnerable.

'How are you feeling?' he asked.

'I'm OK,' she said, and he knew she was lying. 'You shouldn't be here. You're supposed to be at the ball.'

'You disappeared,' he said.

'I have a headache. An early night will sort me out.'

But he could see through the open door to her bedroom—and to the suitcase on the bed, half packed. 'Indi, I think we need to talk.'

'I…' She sighed and stood aside to let him in.

'Are you planning to leave?' he asked when he'd closed the door behind him.

'Tomorrow. I've finished the design. I'll go back and make the window.'

'Can't you make it here?' he asked.

'Better not.'

He frowned. 'What about us?'

'There can't be an us,' she said softly. 'Lorenzo—sit down. I need to talk to you about something.'

He frowned, but did as she asked and sat on the sofa.

Instead of sitting next to him, she sat on the arm of the chair furthest from him. 'I've been trying to find the right words to tell you, but I can't, so I'm going to have to be blunt about it.' She swallowed hard. 'I'm pregnant.'

'You're…' He couldn't quite take this in. 'How long?'

'About nine weeks.'

'How long have you known?'

'A couple of weeks. I've had a dating scan at the hospital.'

'Why didn't you tell me before?'

'Because I couldn't find the right words—or the right time.'

That was fair comment. He'd been rushing around all over the place and hadn't spent much time with her. Though there had been moments when they'd been close. Why hadn't she trusted him with the news then?

He blew out a breath. 'OK. We'll get married.'

'We will *not*,' she corrected.

'Indi, you're expecting my baby. What do you think I'm going to do, abandon you?'

She flinched.

Which wasn't so surprising. She'd been abandoned by her parents, and then dumped by a man who'd cheated on his wife with her.

'It's kind of traditional in my family to get married before you have a baby,' he said, hoping that he sounded light and gentle enough to ease her worries.

Her face was set. 'That's not going to work, and you know it. We've already talked about why we can't be together. Marriage is *that*—' she gestured wildly '—multiplied by a hundred.'

'We need to talk about this, Indi.' He moved to take her hand, but she pulled away. Hurt, he stared at her. 'Indi?'

'Just—please don't touch me. I need to keep a clear head,' she whispered.

That had to be the most backhanded compliment ever: she didn't want him to touch her because she didn't trust herself to think straight if he held her hand. Or did she not trust him not to bully her? He damped down his feelings. 'OK. Let's cut to the chase. You're expecting my child. Of course I want to be there and support you. And the best way for me to do that is if you marry me.'

'Because a king-to-be can't possibly have an illegitimate child?' she asked.

'I don't want to marry you out of duty or to satisfy any social conventions, if that's what you're thinking.' He blew out a breath. 'Right now, you're upset and you're worried. I don't think you'll believe me if I tell you how I feel about you.' He looked her straight in the eye. 'But I'm going to tell you anyway. I fell in love with you, back in Edensfield. You're a breath of fresh air, Indi. My world's a much better place when you're in it. And I'd like you there permanently. You and our child.'

'That picture I drew for you—did you look at it?' she asked. '*Really* look at it?'

'The prince in a bower of roses. Except the roses don't quite hide the fact that he's actually in a cage. Yes, I noticed,' he said dryly.

'That's your life, Lorenzo. It was what you were born to and you're accustomed to it. But I don't want that kind of life for our child,' she said. 'I don't care how gilded the cage might be, it's still a cage. Our baby won't have the freedom to make mistakes and learn from them.'

'So what's the alternative? Freedom, but not having his or her parents together? Not being part of a family?'

She flinched. 'Plenty of people grow up in single-parent families, and they're just fine. They're still loved and the parent they live with gives their best.'

'You and I,' he said, 'were both brought up by our grandparents. Both of us were sent away to school. I think, if we're both honest about it, we were lonely and we felt pretty much a burden to our grandparents. And I don't want that for my child. I want to live with my child. I want to be there for the first smile and the first tooth and the first word and the first step. I want my child to be part of a family. With *me*.'

Her eyes widened. 'Are you saying you'll fight me for custody?'

'No.' He raked a hand through her hair. 'What kind of monster do you think I am? I'm saying I want to do all that with you *and* our baby. Yes, you're right, as my consort you won't have the kind of freedom you've been used to in your life so far. You'll have a security team and a schedule. But there's room for compromise.'

'Is there? Because it seems as if I'm the one giving up everything.'

'You don't have to give up your friends or your job,' he said. 'OK, I admit, you won't be able to do your work to quite the same extent that you do now, because sometimes I'll need you to support me in state affairs and that means attending functions with me. But you don't have to give it up completely. It's important that you have your own interests.'

She still didn't look convinced.

'I want you in my life, Indi,' he said softly. 'Not because you're carrying my child, and not because I think this is the quick way to get everything a king is supposed to have—a crown, a queen and an heir. I want you for *you.*' He paused. 'You've talked about what you have to give up, but have you thought about what you'd gain if you married me?'

'Marriage to a king, and an unlimited budget. Social status and money might be what some people would want—and it's what people think I want.'

'What people?'

She swallowed hard. 'In the Ladies'. I heard them talking about me. They think I'm after a crown.'

He snorted. 'Like hell you are. That's not what you're about, and if they're too narrow-minded to see that then it's their problem.' He shook his head. 'And, actually, it's not what I meant. I think we can give each other some-

thing that neither of us has ever really had. We'll both be the centre of our family, not a burden tagging round the edges. Not someone who's going to be sent away.'

For a second, he saw longing in her eyes. He was pretty sure she wanted this, deep down, just as much as he did. But he knew that if he pushed her too hard, too fast, he'd drive her away. She had to come to terms with her own demons, the things that stopped her from wanting to be with him. Maybe she'd come to trust him enough to help her, but at the end of the day the only person who could really fight her fears was Indigo herself.

'At Edensfield,' he said, 'I asked you to make our relationship permanent. I gave you a choice. I knew what I wanted—just as I know what I want now—but I'm not going to bully you into choosing that. I want you to be with me because you want to be here. I don't want you to stay because you think you ought to for our child's sake or because you feel pressured. I want you to stay because you love me and you want to be with me, the way I want to be with you.'

She bit her lip. 'But how can I ever be acceptable in your world? How, with my past?'

'Everyone makes mistakes. The trick is to learn from them and not repeat them.' He sighed. 'Indi, you're hiding behind an excuse.'

She glowered at him. 'No, I'm not.'

'If I wasn't the heir to Melvante and I asked you to marry me, would it be different?'

She was silent for a long time. Then she sighed. 'Yes.'

'And that's the rub,' he said. 'I can't be someone I'm not, Indi. I'm an only child and so was my father. There's nobody else to take over from me. If I abdicate, so I can be the ordinary man you want, then I'd be letting my family down and I'd be letting my country down. But if I don't

abdicate, I don't have you. Either way, I lose.' He looked at her. 'Unless you can be brave enough to believe in yourself and take me for who I am.'

'I'm not sure if I'm brave enough,' she said, biting her lip. 'I'm scared that it's all going to go wrong.'

'You're scared that I'll let you down, the way Nigel did? I'm not your ex, Indi.'

'No. You're an honourable man. You didn't even question whether the baby was yours.'

'Why on earth would I? Of course the baby's mine.' He frowned. 'Did *he* do that?'

She nodded. 'And he wanted me to have a termination.' She dragged in a breath. 'He said he already had one brat and he didn't want another.'

'That's despicable,' Lorenzo said. 'I want him in a boxing ring with me. Right now.'

She shook her head. 'Violence doesn't solve anything.'

'I know, but it'd be very satisfying to bring him to his knees and make him grovel to you.'

'I don't care about Nigel. I stopped loving him when I realised what a louse he was,' she said.

'Good. Because I'd hate to think he could hurt you again.' He stroked her face. 'Indi. I'm not him. I'm not going to abandon you—or our baby. And I'm certainly not going to ask you to have a termination.'

'I lost the baby. At thirteen weeks, I had a miscarriage. I'd already had a scan. I'd seen my baby's heart beating. And I...I...' She looked away.

Lorenzo stood up and went over to her, scooped her up in his arms and sat down, settling her in his lap with his arms wrapped tightly round her. 'I'm so sorry you had to go through all that. And on your own.'

'I wasn't on my own. Lottie held my hand all the way.'

'I'm glad.'

'She nearly missed Gus's wedding. I said she had to go because she was a bridesmaid, and I'd be fine on my own.'

'So that's why I didn't meet you at Gus's wedding. I was the best man,' he said. He kissed her hair. 'I'm sorry you lost the baby. That must've been hard for you. But, Indi, having a miscarriage in the past doesn't mean that you're going to lose our baby this time round.'

'I know. At least, the sensible bit of me knows,' she admitted. 'But there's a bit of me that can't help thinking, what if?'

'Which is only natural. But you'll have the best medical attention, I promise you. I'll look after you.'

'And that scares me, too. I'm used to being independent, Lorenzo. I don't want to be wrapped in cotton wool.'

'Noted,' he said gently, 'but at the same time I hope you'll understand that I want to keep you and the baby safe.'

'Because the baby might be your heir?'

'No. Because the baby's *ours*,' he corrected.

'Thank you. And thank you for believing me.' She hugged him back.

'Indi, you're not a liar and anybody who meets you would know that within about two seconds.' He stroked her hair. 'I can't believe we're going to be parents. It's...' He couldn't find the right words to explain how overwhelmed he felt.

'I'm sorry,' she said, sounding miserable.

'Don't be. It's not a bad thing. I'm terrified—but it's awesome, too, and I want to jump up and down and tell the whole world that I'm going to be a dad.'

She looked panicked. 'I'm not ready to tell the world.'

'Not until at least twelve weeks,' he reassured her. 'And definitely not until you're ready. This one's your call.'

'You're not angry?'

'Of course I'm not.' He smiled and held her closer. 'I'm thrilled. I don't care that our baby wasn't planned. We're going to have a *baby,* Indi. We've made a family. Do you have any idea how amazing that is?'

'Really?' For the first time since she'd told him, she started to look less scared and more like the sparky, independent woman he'd fallen in love with.

'Really,' he confirmed. 'I have no idea what kind of father I'll be, but I hope I'll be like my grandfather, and give love as well as boundaries.' He wrinkled his nose. 'Maybe slightly less rigid boundaries. And I'll have you to help me do that. You've already made a difference to the way people see me. I'm a better man with you by my side, and I want to be the best husband and father I can possibly be. Right by your side, Indi. No compromises.'

'But—those women in the Ladies'…'

'Were having an idle gossip. And, actually, they're totally wrong.' He took his phone out of his pocket and flicked into a social media site. 'Look. You're trending. There are a lot of influential people talking about you.'

'And how unsuitable I am for the King of Melvante,' she said gloomily.

'No. Look.' He showed her the screen. 'How you're warm and natural. How you're the perfect modern royal, low-key and approachable. How you've brought out a different side in me and they think I'm definitely ready to be king, now. How they hope the stories in the paper are true and that we really are having a secret romance.'

She stared at him, eyes wide, and a tear spilled over her eyelashes. He kissed it away. 'But the most important one for me was my grandfather. Yes, he had doubts. Especially when I told him that you had doubts about our lifestyle. He said that was sensible, but you were probably right. Today, he told me you're still sensible, but you're totally wrong

about us. He thinks you'll fit in just fine, and that you're exactly what I need. Someone who'll have my back, who'll tell me things straight, and who—most importantly—will love me as much as I love you.' He kissed the tip of her nose. 'Indi, I want to marry you. I brought you over here to introduce you to my country and because I hoped you'd see that, although I have duties, I'm not just a king-to-be. I'm a man. I love you, and I want to be with you. Not because of the baby, but because of *you*.' He shifted so that she was sitting on her own, and dropped to one knee in front of her. 'I don't have a ring, but that's probably a good thing because it means we get the fun of choosing one together. But I'm asking you first and foremost as a man, and only secondly as the future King of Melvante—will you marry me, Indi? Will you love me, and let me love you all the way back? Will you make a real family with me?'

She dropped to her knees next to him and wrapped her arms round him. 'Yes. Most definitely yes.'

EPILOGUE

TWO MONTHS LATER, the enormous cathedral at Melvante was standing room only.

The previous month, they'd celebrated the coronation of King Lorenzo the Third.

The PR team at the palace had outdone themselves and organised Lorenzo and Indigo's wedding in the shortest possible time. European royalty and heads of state had managed to switch things round in their diaries, and the streets were packed with people eager to catch a glimpse of the new bride and groom.

'You look amazing,' Lottie said, making a last adjustment to Indigo's veil.

'Thanks to Sally.' Her friend's clever dressmaking had managed to hide the bump of the eighteenth week of Indigo's pregnancy. 'And you look amazing, too.'

'Don't. I'll start crying, and then you will, and Lorenzo will throw me in the dungeons for making you cry on your wedding day.'

'I'm not crying,' Indigo said. 'I've never been happier.'

'I'm so glad.' Lottie hugged her, then made a noise of annoyance and fussed with her dress again. 'That's better.'

A carriage drawn by white horses—or, as King Geek had informed her, 'matched greys'—took Indigo to the cathedral.

'Ready?' Gus asked at the door.

'Ready.' She took his arm. 'This is the best day of my life.'

'Just as it should be.' He smiled at her and guided her through the front door of the cathedral, and the organist began to play the beautiful piece of music that Lorenzo had written for her.

The traditional red carpet led all the way to where Lorenzo was waiting for her at the aisle. And instead of cut flower arrangements on the ends of the pews, there were roses in pots, in a rainbow of colours. Half of them had been given by specialist rose-growers, and the other half had been given by ordinary people from their gardens; after the wedding, the roses were going to make a new garden at the palace. And right at the altar was one grown by Lorenzo's grandfather and named after Lorenzo's grandmother.

As Gus delivered her to the altar, Lorenzo looked at her and mouthed, 'You look amazing and I love you.'

'I love you, too,' she mouthed back.

The bishop smiled at them. 'Dearly beloved, we are gathered here...'

And Indigo knew that from now on, it was going to be just fine.

* * * * *

LET'S TALK
Romance

For exclusive extracts, competitions
and special offers, find us online: